Praise for SUE HARRISON and THE STORYTELLER TRILOGY

"A timeless tale of the best and worst of humankind in a land where the mundane mixes naturally with the mystical."
Minneapolis Star Tribune

"Exceptional power and lyricism . . . Under Harrison's hand, ancient Alaska comes beautifully alive."
Denver Post

"A considerably more elegant writer than Jean M. Auel."
Cleveland Plain Dealer

"Emotionally powerful . . . Sue Harrison will captivate readers . . . Her characters are distinct, her locales are colorful, and her plots, with their layers and surprises, can leave readers on the edge of their seats in suspense."
Flint Journal

"Stunning . . . Harrison displays her first-rate storytelling talents in a rousing tale of murder, revenge, and internecine warfare."
Kirkus Reviews

"An expertly told story of prehistoric life."
Topeka Capital-Journal

SUE HARRISON

CALL DOWN THE STARS

AVON BOOKS
An Imprint of HarperCollinsPublishers

AVON BOOKS
An Imprint of HarperCollins*Publishers*
10 East 53rd Street
New York, New York 10022-5299

Copyright © 2001 by Sue Harrison
ISBN: 0-380-72605-X
www.avonbooks.com

First Avon Books paperback printing: December 2002
First William Morrow hardcover printing: December 2001

Avon Trademark Reg. U.S. Pat. Off. and in Other Countries, Marca Registrada, Hecho en U.S.A.
HarperCollins ® is a registered trademark of HarperCollins Publishers Inc.

Printed in the U.S.A.

10 9 8 7 6 5 4 3 2 1

To my husband, Neil,

and

To those students who took my
creative writing classes at
Lake Superior State University

Encouragers and teachers all!

CHARACTER LIST

TRADERS' BEACH, 602 B.C.

Elders:
 Kuy'aa, (female) River
  People storyteller

Men:
 Sky Catcher, First Men
  storyteller
 Yikaas, River People
  storyteller

Women:
 Qumalix, First Men
  storyteller

TRADERS' BEACH, 6435 B.C.

Elders:
 Qung, (female) First Men
  storyteller

Men:
 Cen, River People trader, fa-
  ther of Ghaden
 Dog Feet, Walrus Hunter
  trader
 Ghaden, River People hunter,
  son of Cen
 He-points-the-way, Walrus
  Hunter trader
 Seal, First Men trader, adop-
  tive father of Uutuk, hus-
  band of K'os
 Trail-walker

Women:
 K'os, wife of Seal and adoptive mother of Uutuk
 Spotted Leaf, third wife of
  the village's chief hunter
 Uutuk, First Men, adopted
  daughter of K'os and Seal

CHAKLIUX'S VILLAGE

Elders:
  Sun Caller (male)
  Wolf Head, father of River
    Ice Dancer
  Gull Beak (female)
  Ligige', aunt of Sok and
    Chakliux
  Twisted Stalk, deceased
    aunt of Dii

Men:
  Black Stick, brother of
    Squirrel
  Chakliux, husband of
    Aqamdax, father to
    Angax, brother of Sok,
    adopted son of K'os
  Cries-loud, son of Sok,
    husband of Yaa, stepson
    of Dii, brother of Carries
    Much
  Ghaden, brother of
    Aqamdax and stepbrother
    of Yaa
  River Ice Dancer, deceased
    son of Wolf Head
  Sok, brother of Chakliux,
    husband of Dii, father of
    Cries-loud and Carries
    Much
  Squirrel, brother of Black
    Stick

Women:
  Aqamdax, wife of Chakliux,
  sister of Ghaden, stepsister
    of Yaa
  Dii, wife of Sok, stepmother
    of Cries-loud and Carries
    Much
  K'os, stepmother of
    Chakliux
  Yaa, stepsister of Ghaden
    and Aqamdax, wife of
    Cries-loud

Children:
  Angax, son of Chakliux and
    Aqamdax
  Carries Much, son of Sok,
    brother of Cries-loud

BOAT PEOPLE'S VILLAGE

Men:
  Carver (deceased)
  Fire Mountain Man, father of
    Day Soon (Daughter,
    Uutuk), husband of Cedar
    and First Wife
  Water Gourd (Tree Hawk,
    Taadzi)

Women:
  Cedar, mother of Day Soon
    (Daughter, Uutuk), second
    wife of Fire Mountain
    Man
  First Wife, first wife of Fire
    Mountain Man

Flower Root, niece of Water
Gourd (Tree Hawk,
Taadzi)

Children:
Day Soon (Daughter, Uutuk),
daughter of Fire Mountain
Man and Cedar

FIRST MEN'S VILLAGE, YUNASKA ISLAND

Elders:
Water Gourd (Taadzi),
adoptive grandfather to
Uutuk (Daughter)

Men:
Chiton
Seal, husband of K'os and
Eye-Taker, adoptive father
of Uutuk (Daughter)
White Salmon

Women:
Eye-Taker, sister-wife of
K'os, first wife of Seal
Green Twig
K'os, second wife of Seal,
adoptive mother of Uutuk
(Daughter)
Uutuk (Day Soon,
Daughter), adopted
granddaughter of Water
Gourd, adoptive daughter
of K'os and Seal

FOUR RIVERS VILLAGE

Elders:
Blue Lance, chief-hunter,
father of Bird Hand and
Moon Slayer
Ptarmigan (male)
Near Mouse (female)
Two-heeled Fish (female)

Men:
Bird Hand, son of Blue Lance,
brother of Moon Slayer
Cen, husband of Gheli, father
of Ghaden and Duckling,
stepfather of Daes
Long Wolf
Moon Slayer, son of Blue
Lance, brother of Bird
Hand

Women:
Crane
Daes, daughter of Gheli and
stepdaughter of Cen
Gheli (Red Leaf), wife of
Cen, mother of Daes and
Duckling
Lake Woman, deceased wife
of Bird Hand
Wing, third wife of Blue
Lance, mother of Bird
Hand

Children:
Duckling, daughter of Cen
and Gheli, sister of Daes

ACKNOWLEDGMENTS

As with each of my novels, I owe a tremendous debt of gratitude to the many people who helped me with the research and editing of *Call Down the Stars*.

First, many thanks to my husband, Neil, gifted with wisdom, always an encourager and willing to listen. I am also much indebted to my parents for fostering my love of books and stories, for reading the various versions of this novel, and for their support, which means the world to me. My gratitude to my daughter, Krystal, and son and daughter-in-law, Neil and Tonya, all experts at adding joy to my life, all astute readers who have come into wisdom young.

My heartfelt gratitude to Rhoda Weyr, the best agent anyone could hope for, and a miracle in my life. She always warms my heart with her positive attitude and *joie de vivre*. She also keeps me from a multitude of errors and saves me from my own poor judgment with her astute and gentle wisdom. My thanks also to Rhoda's assistant Alexa, an island of sanity and efficiency, always kind to a sometimes very inefficient author. To my editor at Avon Books/HarperCollins Publishers, Lucia Macro, and to her staff, also my sincerest gratitude. Their expertise makes me look like a much better author than I am!

To my readers, my former writing students, and those book critics who comment on my work, you have all taught me much about honing my craft, and I thank you. I could not have written *Call Down the Stars* without your input.

I have had the privilege of receiving much information from many people. In this short acknowledgment, I can mention only a few, but my gratitude goes to all who have sent articles, made comments or corrections, discussed ideas, and shared their knowledge and expertise. I owe an immeasurable debt to Dr. William Laughlin and his daughter Sarah for their continued support, to Mike and Rayna Livingston and Dr. Ragan and Dorthea Callaway for too many kindnesses to mention. My thanks to Jim Waybrant for his caribou journal and video, and to Paul Peck (recently deceased) for his expert outdoor writing and commentary and for books and materials he sent me. My gratitude, also, to Sally Rye, R.N., who is always available to answer my medical questions.

To Hashida Yoshinori, many thanks for his introduction to the ancient Jomon Culture of Japan. This book would never have been written without his generosity in sharing his knowledge and research materials.

To others who lent or gave me research materials used in this novel, my gratitude: Glenn and Edith Anderson; Bill Boerigter; Patricia Okalena Lekanoff-Gregory; Bonnie, Chris, and Samantha Mierzejek, Caroline Whittle; Dr. Mark McDonald; Forbes McDonald; Ray Hudson; Chris Lokanin; Keith Krahnke; Don Alan Hall, editor of *Mammoth Trumpet;* Mike, Sally, Crystal, and Mary Swetzof; Ethan Petticrew; Kaydee, Candee, Hollie, and Joe Caraway; and Mary Attu.

Much appreciation to my husband, Neil, and to Daniel Morrison for their work on my website. I love to hear from my readers. Please visit me at www.sueharrison.com and send your email to sue@sueharrison.com.

Last, but certainly far from least, my thanks to those who read my manuscript and offered thoughtful, wise advise: my parents; my friend and fellow writer Linda Hudson; my sister Tish and her husband, Tom Walker; and my friend Joe Claxton.

Any errors in presentation or interpretation are my own and not the fault of those so generous in giving time, sharing expertise, and lending research materials.

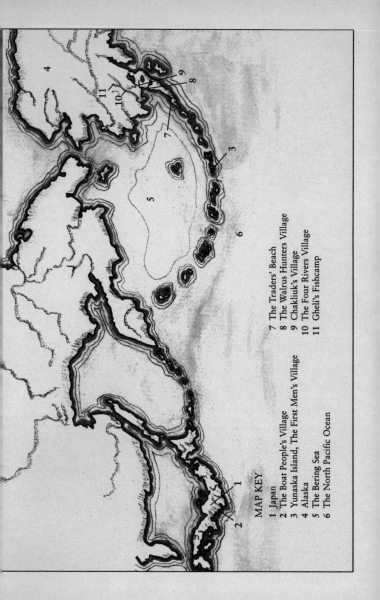

MAP KEY

1 Japan
2 The Boat People's Village
3 Yunaska Island, The First Men's Village
4 Alaska
5 The Bering Sea
6 The North Pacific Ocean

7 The Traders' Beach
8 The Walrus Hunters Village
9 Chakliuk's Village
10 The Four Rivers Village
11 Gheli's Fishcamp

CALL DOWN THE STARS

PROLOGUE

Herendeen Bay, Alaska Peninsula
602 B.C.

The old woman's bones protested against the tight space where she lay. She shivered and looked up at the oiled sea lion skins stretched taut little more than a handbreadth above her nose. She worked her way farther into the bow, shifting her hips, scooting with hands and heels.

The traders had not allowed her to use hare fur blankets as padding, but rather had given her fur seal. Fur seal was thicker and warmer, they had told her, and she knew they were right, but it was foreign to her nose, and she longed for the good earth smell of hare pelts.

You think you would be able to stand the cold if the traders had given in to your wishes, old woman? she asked herself. And she was disgusted at her own childishness, allowing her wants to blur her reason.

She wrapped her arms over her chest and braced herself as Yikaas climbed into the iqyax, thrusting strong legs on either side of her. She heard his paddle as he pushed it against the shore, the grating of gravel on the bottom of the iqyax, and the sudden sway of the craft as the land released them.

Her stomach twisted, and she held her eyes wide, as though by stretching her lids open, she could see the sky through the yellow wall of skin that covered the iqyax's red-dyed wooden frame. Though Yikaas's body gave off heat, the cold stole in from the sea, and her ankles began to ache, crossed as they were to fit at the point of the bow.

She thought back to the last time she had traveled in such a way, like ballast rock, dead weight in a man's iqyax. Then her husband had been alive, and she was young, though she had felt old, her womb empty for some seven winters, her oldest child grown and a hunter, her youngest certainly able to live a summer without her. Her husband had decided to take her to the Traders' Beach so she could visit with other storytellers, some from villages as far away as the Whale Hunter Islands.

She had been shy, saying little, listening much, but their stories had stretched her mind and sent her on journeys of words that made the world she had known seem small.

Over the past few winters, she had watched as Yikaas became a man. His shoulders grew wide, and even his otter foot took on strength. Young women honored him with coy glances, lured him with boldness, and he wore his pleasures as proudly as a warrior bears the scars of his battles.

He was Dzuuggi, already knew the secrets of the River People, but like many young men, he had become too full of himself. She had no choice but to show him how large were the boundaries of the earth, how small his understanding.

He had seen the journey as an adventure, come willingly, and now they had traveled for more days than she could count. Each morning they joined traders from the River villages, and these past few days even a few Sea Hunters had traveled with them. Each morning she berated herself for her foolishness in choosing to come with Yikaas. After all, he was young and strong. He could have made the journey alone.

She had been teaching the boy the few words of the Sea Hunter language that she knew, and now she brought those words into her mouth, held them there, thick in her throat, as an amulet against the power of the sea. Each day on this journey she had told herself Sea Hunter stories of Chagak and Shuganan, Kiin and Samiq, called those ancient people to dance above her, silhouetted against the sea lion skins like shadows cast in a caribou hide lodge by those who live within. Today, though, to help her forget her fear and discomfort, she would rely on the tales of Chakliux, that great storyteller, and his wife, Aqamdax.

The old woman, Kuy'aa, spoke softly, filled the inside of Yikaas's iqyax with whispered words, and by midday, the movement of the paddle, the comfort of the stories allowed her to sleep. She fell into dreams, and her mother's voice came to her. For a little while, she became an infant, new in the world to which she had been born, bound in a cradleboard, knowing the rhythm of her mother's body.

Suddenly the iqyax lurched, and her belly knotted in fear. She was old again, her hands reaching in reflex to scrabble at the iqyax's carved ribs. She felt the bump of something beneath them. Animal, she thought, and could not remember whether she had checked her feet for stray bits of grass before they started out that morning. Sea Hunters said that a bit of grass caught between the toes was all sea animals needed to take offense. Then they would come from the depths in anger to bite holes in iqyax walls.

Her toes were numb, cold and stiff as wood, but she thought she could feel long strands of grass between them, tickling the bottoms of her feet, prickling her ankles.

Another bump, this one so strong that the iqyax frame bent and groaned; the knotted joints moved and heaved like the bones of a skeleton. The old woman cried out, and when she did, the Sea Hunter words she had been holding as amulet in her throat escaped into the iqyax, and the air around her was suddenly so thick with them that she could scarcely breathe.

Then she heard Yikaas's voice, like a parent calming a child. "We are here, Aunt," he said. "At the Traders' Beach.

It's low tide, and we've found a few rocks. If it's too rough for you, I'll wait in the bay until the sea rises."

The old woman lifted her fingers to her lips, pushed a path through the Sea Hunter words, and said, "Go in now, if you are able."

She pulled the fur seal blanket like a caul over her face, wrapped her arms around herself, and tried to become small, so Yikaas could guide the iqyax, not only with his paddle but with the shifting of legs and buttocks.

Finally the hull ground into sand, and Yikaas untied his hatch skirting. A rush of cold air slid into the iqyax, released the stories, the words, her fear. Then his strong hands were under her arms, drawing her out, peeling away the layers of the fur seal blanket. He helped her stand, and she spread her feet wide on the earth to keep her balance.

"You have brought your grandmother?" someone asked. He spoke in the River language, but his voice carried the accent of a Sea Hunter.

"Her name is Kuy'aa," Yikaas said. "It was *she* who brought *me*. We are storytellers, and we have come to learn."

It was an answer he might have given when he was a child, and it pleased Kuy'aa to hear the humility in his words. What space is left for stories if a man fills his mind and heart with thoughts of his own importance? Soon those people he speaks about meld into himself, and he is no longer storyteller, but braggart.

"We are always in need of storytellers," the Sea Hunter said. "Tonight we will hear tales from a woman who has come to us from the Whale Hunter Islands."

Aaa, thought Kuy'aa, there are two of us then, foolish in our old age, grandmothers who would dare a death at sea to have one last chance to tell and hear stories at the Traders' Beach.

Lost in her thoughts, she did not realize that Yikaas was speaking until it was too late to stop him.

"I had hoped to tell my own stories tonight," he was saying, and the old woman flushed in embarrassment at his boldness.

The trader smiled and said, "We will be glad to hear you, but first you should rest. Tonight, you must listen."

Kuy'aa lifted her chin at the trader, gave a nod, and knew that the man understood her gratitude.

He clapped Yikaas on the shoulder and laughed loud and long, reminding the old woman of the joy with which Sea Hunters live their lives. "There is much to trade for here," the man said. "See that you trade well and wisely." He lifted his chin toward the rise of the beach, toward iqyax racks and the path that led to the Sea Hunter village.

The old woman helped unload the iqyax, then carried a heavy pack of food and trade goods up the slope of the beach. The promise of stories was a balm that soothed the horror of the days spent in the iqyax and held at bay the fear that Yikaas, her chosen Dzuuggi, was less than her hopes.

The Dzuuggi pushed his way into the circle of people nearest the center of the lodge. The Sea Hunters called a lodge an ulax, Kuy'aa had told him. Each ulax was like a mound, built partially underground, raftered with driftwood, roofed with woven mats, sod, and grass thatching. The thick earthen walls seemed to press down on him, and he had to fight the urge to hunch his shoulders against their darkness.

It was not difficult to tell the Sea Hunters from the River People. Those hunters of sea mammals squatted on their haunches, arms around upraised knees. Yikaas snorted in derision and sat down in the way of men. But as he waited for the stories to begin, moisture seeped from the packed earth floor into his caribou hide pants, and he suddenly understood one reason they sat as they did. With his left foot turned on edge as it was—an otter foot, Kuy'aa called it, with webbed toes—he decided he would be more comfortable as he was rather than trying to balance himself crouched on his feet. So he remained sitting, but he decided to bring the fur seal pad from his iqyax for the next story-telling so he could stay dry.

He was tired, but his excitement at being with the story-tellers was enough to keep him awake. When Yikaas's eyes adjusted to the dim light of the seal oil lamps, he turned his head to search for Kuy'aa and finally saw her sitting with several old women at the back of the lodge. He could tell that she struggled to hold her eyes open, her head bobbing now and again as she drifted toward sleep. She had told him that the storytelling might last the night, people going and coming, listening for a while, then leaving to return later.

Among the River People, when a group of storytellers gathered, one story seemed to spawn the next. A person would give one version, then another told the same story in a different way. The older the story, the more variations. Most people claimed the old stories were best, but Yikaas thought that new stories were better. They seemed to stay in his mind long after the storytelling was over, as clear to his eyes as if he had lived them.

Soon the lodge was full of people. Women passed seal bladders of water and heaps of sea urchins, a rare delicacy for River People. Yikaas took two handfuls of the prickly shells and heaped them between his crossed legs. He used the flat of his stone knife to crack one open, then with his thumbnail dug out an egg-filled orange ovary and sucked it into his mouth. He closed his eyes at the richness of the taste, fat and salty.

Finally there was a whispering among the storytellers, and Kuy'aa stood up and tottered over to sit beside him. She poked him with one crooked finger, pointed with her chin at a man standing in the center of the lodge. He was so bent and wrinkled, so thin, that Yikaas was surprised he could stand. The old one began to speak, and Yikaas realized that though the years had melted away the old man's flesh, they had not taken his voice. His language was Sea Hunter, but different in accent and rhythm, his words rising and falling like waves, loud and soft, harsh and calm.

"Whale Hunter," Kuy'aa leaned over to whisper.

The young Dzuuggi looked at her with wise eyes and nodded as though he had known. He listened carefully to the old man, caught the word *woman*, and some reference to the sea, then found himself wondering if all the stories would be told in Sea Hunter languages. If so, he had made a useless journey. What good would it do him to sit forever listening to stories he could not understand? But then a young woman also stood. Daughter to the old man? Granddaughter?

She was wearing Sea Hunter clothing, a loose hoodless parka, her dark hair tucked into its collar rim. The parka hung nearly to her ankles, and the sleeves were long enough to cover her hands. It was black, decorated with shell bangles and sewn in squares of what looked like cormorant feathers. Her hair was cut short over her forehead in a fringe that hung to her eyebrows, and a thin needle of ivory pierced the septum of her nose. Her face was delicate, her cheekbones high under slanted eyes, her mouth small. He found that in watching her, he was holding his breath. She would visit him in his dreams, without doubt, that one.

She helped the old man sit down, then leaned over to hand him a water bladder, and with her woman's knife cracked open an urchin shell. Wife, was she? Yikaas was disappointed. But if the old man were important enough—a Dzuuggi among Sea Hunters—then he had earned the right to a young and beautiful wife.

She began to talk to the people, first in the Sea Hunter language, then in the River tongue. Yikaas smiled. She was a translator, not wife, and best of all she spoke the River language well, with only the trace of an accent.

Perhaps when she translated his stories, she would decide she wanted to spend a night in his bed. His heart grew large with hope, and he sat very straight, lifted his head. He was wearing a fine parka, one of two his mother had made him especially for storytelling. It was caribou hide, scraped and smoothed until nearly white, then decorated at shoulders and sleeves with rows of wolf teeth and dyed caribou hair. His mother had left fringes across the chest, each knotted around a jade bead.

When the translator's eyes, resting for a moment on each storyteller, finally came to him, he smiled at her, but she gave no sign of recognition, skipped over him as though he were only a boy, slave to Kuy'aa.

He snorted his disgust. *She* was probably the slave. If so, he could have her in his bed for a bauble.

He waited, grew impatient as the old man continued to fumble with crooked and swollen fingers at the sea urchin the girl had given him. Would he never begin the stories? But suddenly the girl lifted her arms, spoke in a clear, strong voice. The old man looked up at her, smiled, then again fixed his attention on the sea urchin.

She was the storyteller? A girl barely old enough to be a wife? Was this how the Sea Hunters honored River People who had traveled so far? He started to get up, but Kuy'aa laid a hand on his arm.

"Be still and listen," she said. "I heard this woman tell stories when she was just a child, when you were still learning and not yet ready to attend this celebration."

Yikaas did as she bid, but anger filled him from navel to ears, making the girl's voice difficult to hear. She spoke first in the Sea Hunter language, then in the River tongue. She began with polite comments, and Yikaas, realizing he needed to learn the story traditions of the Sea Hunters, made himself listen. She gave her name: Qumalix, a difficult word for a River man to say, spoken so deeply in the throat, but the Dzuuggi wrapped his tongue around it, let it settle as a whisper in his mouth until he knew he could say it without faltering.

Qumalix explained that her name meant *to be like light, to brighten.*

Yikaas sat with his mouth open, and in his surprise the anger flowed out of his body, was caught in the thin smoke of the seal oil lamps and pushed up through the square hole cut in the top of the ulax.

Qumalix, so close in meaning to his own name—*Yikaas, light.*

He looked at Kuy'aa, saw the knowing in her eyes, as though she were able to read his thoughts.

Then Qumalix said, "Aa, children, this is a story of times long ago. Listen and hear me." She spoke boldly, like a woman who could rely on her own wisdom.

"The Bear-god People came like a tsunami from the sea. . . ." she said.

The Bear-god People? Yikaas thought. A story he had not heard before. Perhaps, then, he should listen, at least for a while. Kuy'aa wanted him to stay, and it was always good to please an elder, nae'? Besides, he would not forget that in spite of her powerful name, Qumalix was only a girl, much too young to be given the honor of telling the first story. . . .

PART
ONE

ONE

Outlet of the present-day Oi River, Suruga Bay,
Honshu Island, Japan 6447 B.C.

DAUGHTER'S STORY
The Bear-god warriors came like a tsunami from the sea,
their poorly made and misshapen outriggers sunk so deeply
in the water that at first the Boat People only stood on the
shore staring, sure that a wave would swamp the dugouts before the warriors could beach them. But the sea gods were
asleep, and no waves rose, the water smooth and gray as
alder bark.

Cedar, second wife of Fire Mountain Man, had been
grinding seeds with the stone pestle and mortar her father
had given her as one of her bride gifts. Her little daughter,
Day Soon, was tied to her back, the child content to play
with bright shells an aunt had pierced and sewn to the deer
hide sling that bound her to her mother.

As a child, Cedar had lived in another village far to the
north, closer to the string of small islands where the Bear-
god People lived. Though her own village was never attacked, she knew the stories of what they did, those hairy
ones, more animal than human. She had told the people of

this village about the Bear warriors, how their hair had gradually changed from straight black human hair to brown, wavy bear fur. How their arms, legs, and chests were also hairy like the bear they worshipped, and how their teeth were pointed like bear teeth. Even their language was only grunts and growls, like the bear language.

They had come long ago, the storytellers said, from the west and the north, bringing their strange customs with them, their savage worship. They kept bears captive, and when the animals died, the Bear-god People saved the skulls to bind on the doors of their homes so the bear spirits would protect their village.

They were a people of the land and did not know how to build good boats, how to hollow the straightest, strongest cedar tree using fire and adz to cut away the center so that many men could fit inside. They did not even have harpoons, except for those stolen from the villages they destroyed.

While the others stared, watching, wondering, Cedar raised her voice and called out a warning, to tell her husband's people that these were Bear-god warriors, that they would rape the women and do worse to the men, take boys captive to feed to their bears, and dash out babies' brains on rocks.

But they all looked at her in wonder. What men would do such hideous things? Surely if the Boat People welcomed them and offered food, these strangers would be content to establish a trading partnership. Did they not come from the north? Perhaps they would bring obsidian, like the traders from Hokkaido.

The Boat People flicked their fingers at Cedar, turning her words back so her foolish message would not taint their greeting. Then Fire Mountain Man came to her and, taking her arm, walked her to the edge of the beach, bid her stand in her place as second wife, seven steps behind him, two behind his first wife.

Cedar's heart beat like bird wings in her chest, battering her lungs and ribs until they ached. Day Soon began to fuss, and First Wife gestured with a quick snap of her hand that Cedar should leave, take the child away so these men in their boats would not be insulted by a little girl's cries. Cedar ran, her head lowered as if in shame, but she was grateful. She left the beach and hurried to her husband's *iori*.

All Fire Mountain Man's family lived in the *iori*—his uncles and brothers and their wives, one sister who was a widow and her children. It was a good, warm place, even in winter, with a huge central hearth and the floor dug into the ground, three or four handlengths down. The walls were framed with chestnut logs, sided with their bark, and the roof was thatched new every few years so rain could not make paths through the straw. Their *iori* was not as large as some of the others in the village, but the floor was well-packed, swept clean each day with the straw brooms Cedar made herself. She had brought the alder handles from her own village, and they were a comfort to her hands when she longed for the cooler winds of the north.

Each wife in Fire Mountain Man's *iori* had an area for herself and her children. Cedar's was the smallest of all, but good nonetheless, especially for a woman who had only one child, and that one a daughter.

She hurried inside and filled an earthenware pot with chestnut cakes and dried venison, a few smoked fish. She took three bottle gourds filled with water, a woman's knife, Day Soon's good luck charm, two deerskin blankets, and a pack made of rush matting. She shoved the knife, pot, blankets, and gourds, as well as some soft skins to swaddle Day Soon's bottom, into the pack and hefted the awkward bundle to her head. She handed Day Soon a stick of dried fish to chew on and left the *iori*, walking quickly toward the hills that cupped the village. She passed the builders' huts, saw that her husband's newest boat lay on the estuary beach, the outrigger already attached, the main body deep and hollow, in need of only a little more adz work to remove the last of the char.

He had made the boat for First Wife's oldest son, a man in

his own right and trying to earn the respect of the village elders so he could claim a wife. A great lump of sorrow wedged itself into Cedar's throat. What would happen to her husband and that boy-man? To all the good people of this village? Was it fair that their desire to live peacefully would mean their deaths? And what about the boat her husband had worked so hard to build? Made in honored ways, it would carry good luck for anyone who used it, perhaps even a Bear-god warrior who did not know enough to worship the sea gods.

In considering those sea gods, Cedar suddenly remembered the small carvings her husband honored above all things. He kept them near the hearth, hanging from the support rafters on braided strings of whale sinew. They had been blessed by priests, and carried great powers. She could not leave them to fall into the hands of the Bear-god warriors. What chance did the Boat People have if those Bear-god men stole more power for themselves, even the power of the sea?

A scream came from the beach, and a terrible cry that sounded like a bear roaring. Almost, Cedar turned to run, but again, she thought of the sea god carvings, and so she quickly set Day Soon into Fire Mountain Man's boat, placed the pack beside the child.

"Be quiet, Daughter. Stay in the boat until I come back to get you," she said, and knew that the girl—now three summers old—would do as she asked. Cedar pulled out the deerskin blankets and covered Day Soon and the pack, then she ran back into the village, crept on hands and knees to her husband's *iori*, and once inside cut down the sea god carvings.

When Water Gourd became old, his eyes grew too dim for him to aim his harpoon. Soon after, his hands knotted, and he could no longer work the adz to build boats, and his legs were too weak to chase the deer that roamed the mountains. Had the choice been his own, he would have claimed a place with the elders, giving out advice to those who had not lived long enough to become wise. But wisdom had never been one of his gifts, and now, in his old age, all he had to offer were his strong shoulders. Each day, tottering on wobbly legs, he made the journey to the spring that bubbled sweet water at the base of the second hill from the village. Each day he took empty bottle gourds, filled them, and brought them back—cool, wet bulbs sprouting from the ends of the nutmeg yoke he had carved especially to fit the curves and hollows of his ancient shoulders.

His name had once been Tree Hawk, but that had been long ago, and now they called him Water Gourd, so that only the oldest in the village knew who he truly was. Only the elders remembered when he was young and strong, the father of four sons, now all dead. Most people in the village knew him only as uncle to Flower Root, and she was lazy and not worth much.

He filled the last water gourd, plugged it with a cedar stopper, and tied it in place on his yoke, five gourds on each end, jostling and bumping together like fat yellow bees. Sometimes he brought a boy with him, to help lift the yoke to his shoulders, but this day the boy had been mending his father's fish nets, so Water Gourd had come alone. Like a woman, that boy was, Water Gourd thought, foolish and weak. He had told the boy stories of his own youth, how he had lifted stones, carried them up the hills to build the muscles in his arms and legs, how any young man, if he wasn't too lazy to look, could see the piles of stones Water Gourd had carried, still there, still stacked, grown over with grasses and moss, proof of Water Gourd's ambition and fortitude.

But the boy seemed to derive no inspiration from Water Gourd's stories, and Water Gourd had become disgusted with him. It was just as well he had stayed on the beach today, just as well that Water Gourd didn't have to put up with him.

He set the ends of his yoke on two piles of flat rocks he had stacked for that purpose and, crouching to the level of the yoke, backed himself underneath. He settled it against his neck, flexed his shoulders, then painfully straightened his aching knees.

If the sea gods allowed him to live through another year, he would most likely have to reduce his gourds to four on each end. It worried him to think about that. Four had never been a lucky number for him. The birth of his fourth son had killed his favorite wife, and the child had chosen to follow her spirit four days later.

He himself had had four wives, the fourth so vicious of tongue that he had celebrated rather than mourned her death. Four gourds were not good. Perhaps he could find smaller gourds and still carry five.

He walked slowly, and the sun heated the top of his head until sweat trickled from the edges of his hair, tracking a route through the gullies and furrows of his face. The gourds sweated as well, as if it were difficult work hanging from a yoke. Water Gourd kept his eyes away from them, for the drops of water on their sides always made his mouth pucker in longing.

Though it was not yet summer, grass already grew tall on each side of the path. Until he broke over the top of the first hill, he could see nothing except green, but he had taken some time to chop away the growth at the hill's crest, so that in his walking he could get a breath of wind from the sea.

He stopped, straightened as best as he could, and lifted his eyes to the blue of water and sky.

Ah ee, he had been a hunter once. Ah ee, how his muscles had bulged under his skin. Any woman, he could have taken as wife; any father would have been glad to call him marriage-son; every mother had longed for the grandchildren that would come from his loins. He had eaten well then, too. Whale and squid and sea urchin, meat of deer and any manner of bird. Chestnut cakes, the young women made for him, each hoping to win his favor. Ah ee, life had been good.

He sighed, and his memories brought a film of water to coat his eyes, clearing his vision long enough so he could see the separation between ocean and sky, long enough for him to place a flotilla of short, low-slung boats just offshore. He blinked, sure his old eyes were seeing foolishness. What man among the Boat People would claim such poor dugouts? He would be a laughingstock. Water Gourd pursed his lips in ridicule. Even he—his hands knotted and curled with age—even he could make a better boat than those he was seeing.

Then suddenly he knew who was in those boats, and the knowledge nearly dropped him to his knees. He gripped the yoke as if a tight hold could save him, and he spun on the path, intending to make his way past the spring to the caves hidden just under the crest of the third hill.

But although he was used to the weight of the yoke on the uphill climb, the filled gourds added more than he could bear. He lost his footing and tipped backwards, fell slowly, as if in a dream. He landed on his back, his arms still flung forward over the yoke, and, like a turtle, could not right himself. He slid on the grass until he was near the bottom of the first hill, within crawling distance of the village. He lay still for a moment to catch his breath, then extricated himself from gourds and yoke. One gourd had broken, and to preserve the precious water that still remained inside, the old man cupped the largest shard in his hands and drank.

The water, cold from the spring, renewed his strength, and, leaving his yoke on the ground, Water Gourd crept forward to the back wall of an *iori* and pressed himself tightly against the chestnut bark siding.

He heard a gasp from within, then a woman's voice as she babbled and begged. He knew the voice. It belonged to Fire Mountain Man's second wife, Cedar. She was young, that woman, and pretty, with smooth, fair skin and tiny teeth. He pried at the bark of the wall and tried to see inside.

A large hairy man stood over her, a short thrusting lance in one of his hands.

"Bear-god," Water Gourd whispered, and shuddered, remembering stories he had heard Cedar tell.

On hands and feet he began to sneak away, but then he remembered his yoke. If he left it there, the gourds still wet, they would know he was near. By following his path through the grasses, they would have no difficulty finding him. If he were young, he would welcome a chance to fight, to kill men who would attack a peaceful village, who would force women as the Bear-god man now forced Fire Mountain Man's wife.

Even with his old ears, Water Gourd could hear her groans of pain. He considered going back to help her, but what good would that do? The Bear-god man had a lance, and Water Gourd had no weapon save a small knife sheathed at his wrist. He would die, and probably could do nothing to help the woman. Perhaps the Bear-god man would only use her and let her go. Of course, most likely Cedar, so used, would take her own life in shame rather than return to her husband.

Ah ee, why try to help a woman who was already dead?

Water Gourd picked up his yoke, slung it over his shoulders, and crept away through the grasses, weaving his steps in stops and starts so any attacker who might decide to follow would think he was animal rather than man. At the top of the hill, he started down the worn path again, his breath wheezing in his throat until he had to stop. He would never make it to the caves if he tried to carry his yoke.

He decided to leave a false trail, abandon his yoke at the end of it, then return to the path. If he hurried, he might make it over the crest of the second hill before he was seen. He cut into the grasses, again made a wandering trail, like an animal who in hunting or fleeing finds wisdom in crooked ways.

Finally he dropped the yoke, started back toward the caves, but then he began to imagine himself there, safe, but slowly dying of thirst as he waited out the Bear-god warriors' stay in his village. He could envision his thoughts centered on the yoke and its burden of sweet water, cupped in the fat bellies of those gourds. He could see them mock him in his dreams, those gourds, water-rich and slick with moisture.

He returned to his yoke, cut away one of the clusters of bottle gourds, and, clutching it to his belly with both hands, scurried back toward the path. The gourds slowed him a little, but at least with the water, he could stay in the caves for a few days without venturing to the springs.

He crouched low amidst the grasses, and at the crest of the second hill he looked down toward the village, stifled the groans in his throat as he saw flames rising from many of the huts. He trembled in his helplessness and clutched his armful of gourds more closely, then again started toward the caves.

He had taken only a few steps when he stopped in horror. Bear-god warriors were ahead of him on the trail. His fear was so great that his bladder spilled out its load of water. He did not allow himself time to feel ashamed, but a thought sped through his mind: amazement that he, an old man who belonged to no one and had no one to claim, would want so desperately to live. He turned the other way, toward the burning village, stopped short of Fire Mountain Man's *iori*—it, too, now in flames—to run the overgrown path to the boatmakers' beach, where the River Oi emptied into the sea.

As he ran, a voice in his mind chided him. You are foolish. Why come this way? The Bear-gods will be here, too. Better to fight and win yourself some glory to take with you to your death.

But whether because the entrance to the path was overgrown with hemp or because the Bear-god warriors had already been there and left, when Water Gourd came to the first hut, he found it empty. He crept quietly among cedar and nutmeg trunks, some still whole, others scarred with flame where the craftsmen had begun their work of hollowing and shaping. Smoke blowing in from the houses burned his throat and pulled water from his eyes, and the screams of fear and fighting tore at him like claws.

He hid in the darkest corner of the hut, farthest from the

open side that faced the estuary. The builders had set the tree trunks they were shaping nearest the hut's entrance. They claimed it was good for those trees, as the fire chewed them hollow, to look out at cool water. Then as boats they would leave the land more willingly, go where their paddlers directed.

Water Gourd had heard stories about boats left onshore for a night that grew roots and bound themselves again to the land, stranding paddlers and hunters so far from their village that their families never saw them again. The best boatmakers not only burned out the land-heart of the tree, but gave it a vision of other possibilities. What hunter wanted to be trapped in some foreign land by the whim of a tree, not quite boat?

Water Gourd hunkered down on his knees, his arms still hugging the gourds. Their weight unbalanced him, but he did not want to set them down. They were one more wall between himself and the Bear-god People, perhaps even had some small power of protection. If water would protect anyone, why not him? He had always honored the spring with his gratitude, with clean hands and grass-wiped feet. But the gourds contained only a small amount of water. Enough to keep a man through four, perhaps five days, but not enough to douse the flames should the Bear-god People decide to burn this hut.

Suddenly, through the soles of his feet, Water Gourd felt the pounding of the earth, and he knew men were coming. He rolled himself into a ball and, taking his water with him, broke out through the thatching of the hut's back wall. Humped around the gourds like a beetle, he crept through the undergrowth away from the hut, toward the estuary that angled up from the sea like an arm bent at the elbow. Boats lay on the shore, new boats, those nearly finished, hauled for testing balance and buoyancy to this gentler, shallower water. Most had no outriggers and lay with backs up, oiled wood glistening. But one had its outrigger log attached with sturdy poles, and the bow close to the water as though its maker had been ready to launch it. Inside was a paddle, a worker's rush fiber shirt, and two deerskin blankets, humped as though they covered supplies.

The old man threw in his water gourds and, using all the strength in his ancient arms, he pushed the boat into the estuary, praying that the boatmaker had done his work well. Water Gourd could swim, but why pit himself against those sea gods who find sport in grabbing ankles, hauling people into the depths?

When the water reached the old man's knees, he climbed into the boat, grabbed the paddle, and quietly pushed away from the shallows. The boat was steady, the outrigger stable. He pushed again, this time almost losing his paddle as the land fell away, and the estuary grew deep. He crept forward a little ways in the boat, tucked his heels under his rump, his knees widespread for balance, but as he continued to paddle, the tree boat started to circle, so that he was gaining no real distance from the shore. He thought he might be safe if he could get the boat from the estuary into the river. The growth of trees, vines, and moss was so rich and thick that he could hide himself under the branches that arched to dip their new spring leaves into the water.

As a young man, he had been harpooner rather than paddler, but still he knew that to keep going straight, he must paddle with equal strength on both sides of the boat. He scooted himself to the other side, earning splinters in his knees. But he ignored the pain and thrust his paddle into the water two times, then lifted it to the other side, again paddled twice. He went back and forth, until blood from his knees dyed the raw wood crimson, but finally the boat was at the center of the estuary. He turned it, headed against the current, up toward the river, but each time he switched sides, he lost whatever distance he had gained.

He tried three strokes, then four, and found he made headway with that, though the course he took was no longer straight. Each time he lifted his paddle, he looked toward the shore, sure he would see Bear-god warriors watching him, perhaps even launching one of the other boats to follow him, but no one came, and finally, as the thick black smoke from the burning village billowed up through the trees and curled down to the estuary, Water Gourd's boat entered the river.

He closed his eyes in a moment of gratitude as the shadows of the trees welcomed him, then he found a snag, an upended cedar with roots and earth woven into a circle, the weight of it compressing the bank so that the tree had slid, roots first, into the water. The old man maneuvered the boat until it was upriver from the snag, then he turned it and used the paddle like a fish uses its tail, allowing the current to move the boat, the paddle to direct its path until the bow snugged itself into the interstices of the root mass.

Then Water Gourd, peering out through the tunnel of trees, could only wait while the smoke filled the estuary and blocked his vision of the sky.

TWO

Sometime during the night, Water Gourd fell asleep. It was a sleep visited by demons, and when he finally managed to awaken, it was still dark, still night. The smoke from the village had dissipated, and he could see stars in that circle of sky afforded him from his seat in the cedar log boat.

The tide had come in, and the river had risen so that the bow of his outrigger was not wedged as tightly in the roots of the fallen tree. The bumping of the boat—away from the root mass and again into it—had brought him back from his terror-filled dreams. The wind had gathered strength, and he could hear the rattle of leaves above him, spinning their tales to one another.

Did they tell stories of women raped, babies killed, old men tortured? Most likely not. Why should they care about that? Surely the trees hated his people. After all, what cedar, what nutmeg would choose to leave the close green forest to be gutted by the fire and knives of boat builders? Maybe the trees around him celebrated, as did the Bear-god warriors, rejoicing at the deaths of the Boat People.

Water Gourd wished he could close his ears to the noise. He shut his eyes and curled into a ball at the center of the boat, his gourds, still cold and damp from their bellies of water, cradled in his arms. Although the night air was warm, the mists rising from the river hovered over him until they had worked their way through his skin to his joints, until he ached with the damp as though winter had suddenly come upon the land, disrupting the gentle weather of spring, the cycle of the seasons suddenly and inexplicably forgotten.

The boat rocked up, then bumped ahead, rocked again and jerked back. The motion settled behind Water Gourd's ears in an ache that tensed his muscles into pain. The splinters in his knees throbbed, and new dreams invaded his eyes—monsters that were half demon, half bear. They laughed at his fear, his mourning, and blew with fetid breath to coax new life into the fires that had destroyed his village.

Then suddenly the boat tipped and swirled, and, as though a hand had gripped the stern, it pulled away from the circle of roots and was thrust violently upriver.

What giant had captured him? Water Gourd's panic propelled him to sit upright, hands clasping the outrigger poles. Then he saw the trees sway, though there was no storm. He felt the earth buckle, and suddenly the river spewed him out into the estuary, sending his boat ahead so quickly that Water Gourd nearly tumbled backward. He heard a thin wail, and at first thought it came from his own mouth. Again the sea shook, waves came from both shores, picked the boat up, and thrust it from the estuary into the sea. Again he heard the wail, but this time he knew it was not from him, for he had clamped his teeth tightly together to keep from biting his tongue.

It was the boat; it had to be. The tree part of it was not quite dead, and as they sped out toward the sea, it called to its brother trees in fear.

"It will save you some burning and scraping," Water Gourd shouted to the boat over the tumult of waves.

If he could convince the tree that it was better off in the sea, it might not dump him in its effort to return to the sanctuary of river and forest. He reached for the paddle. Perhaps if the boat saw that he, too, wanted to remain in the river, it would help him. He thrust the paddle into the water, thrust again and again until he had managed to turn the boat toward the estuary. A wave caught him and pushed him forward, and he dipped his paddle, working as hard and fast as he could. A second wave took him and a third, until finally he felt the contrary current of the river. Though it was dark, with the eyes of his memory, he saw the green river water mingling with the blue sea, swirling into a dance that would complete itself out past the estuary in a place where fish fed from the river's generosity.

Water Gourd paddled, blessing arms kept strong by carrying water, cursing muscles pulled long and stringy by old age. Two strokes to counter the river's flow, two to pull the boat forward, then the shift to the other side to wield his paddle between the outrigger shafts. Two strokes to straighten the bow and two to regain the ground he had lost in shifting his paddle. He counted his strokes, singing them under his breath like a chant, and he nearly wept with joy when he regained the entrance of the estuary.

Then, above the sounds of river and sea, of his chanting and the splash of his paddle, he heard voices. His heart clenched like a fist, and for a moment he did not have the strength to lift the paddle, but merely kept it in the water, the blade turned flat against the side of the boat.

Bear-god warriors. He saw their torches lining the banks of the estuary, saw one then another lift his fire until they cast light in long sheaths across the water to his outrigger. They lifted their spears, threw. The spears were thrusting lances, not so good for distance. One fell into the estuary, but another thwacked hard inside the boat, cutting a gouge into Water Gourd's thigh before the tip embedded itself in wood.

He knew then there was no hope. He raised his paddle and brought it into the boat, laid the blade over his belly. Better to take a spear in chest or throat and have his life end suddenly than to suffer a gut wound. He felt the river current thrust him toward the sea, but then the boat turned sideways and a wave brought him back. The Bear-god men threw more spears as sea and river played with his boat, like children throwing a pig bladder. A spear clattered against the outrigger and one landed in the bow. Water Gourd pinched his fingers over the oozing wound in his thigh. It was not a terrible cut, shallow and less than a handbreadth in length, but it hurt.

Suddenly the earth heaved again. Water Gourd saw it first in the flames from the Bear-god torches, the light moving in odd circles, one torch dipping down until it had extinguished itself in the water. As though the river were inhaling, the boat was suddenly sucked far into the estuary. He closed his eyes, tried to prepare for death, but then just as unexpectedly, the river exhaled and thrust the boat and Water Gourd out into the sea, past the waves that would return him, far beyond the reach of any spear.

The torches were only tiny needle pricks in the night, and in his relief Water Gourd began to laugh. Better to drown than face the tortures the Bear-gods would inflict. At least he could throw himself into the sea and have it done quickly.

Or better yet, he would wait until morning, rest a little, then turn his boat toward the next village, warn them that the Bear-god warriors were coming. They might see him as a hero and, if they were successful in fending off the attack, would welcome him in their village. Surely they would want him as one of their wise elders. Perhaps he would even find himself a wife and get himself sons in his old age. Hadn't his own grandfather once put a son into the belly of a young wife?

Water Gourd lay back in the boat, retrieved the woven rush shirt that the builder had left in the stern, and pulled it on over his head. He tried to sleep, but the dreams returned, and he blinked himself awake, sat up.

The moon had risen, lending light, bouncing it from wave to wave. The wind cut across the water, not strong, but cold enough to raise the flesh on Water Gourd's arms. His eyes fell on the bundle of supplies in the bow, and he remembered that it was covered with deerskin blankets. He crept forward, but suddenly the top blanket began to move, raising itself as though it were alive.

Water Gourd had once seen a deer that had been chased into a river, and he had not forgotten how hard it struggled to get back to the sure footing of land. Perhaps this blanket, too, wanted to find its way to shore. He thought for a moment of plucking it up and dropping it into the waves, but he was cold. How foolish to throw away a blanket just because it had a little life of the deer still in it! Better to wrap it around himself, subdue whatever weak power it claimed by sitting on it.

He clutched the blanket in one hand, and with a quick jerk flipped it up and swaddled it around his legs.

The blanket settled around him, warm and still. Water Gourd nodded his approval. Even an old man had more power than a deerskin blanket. But suddenly the boat again started to wail, more loudly this time, so that Water Gourd lost his temper.

"You want to go back and be captured by the Bear-god men?" he shouted. "They know nothing about boats. They wouldn't take care of you. They would let you rot."

The wails continued, louder now—surely not the sound a tree-boat would make. Then Water Gourd's old ears remembered the cries of his sons when they were babies. He leaned forward, groped under the other deerskin blanket until his hands came upon flesh—warm and soft and round. A child!

He felt until he found the head. The boy was well-haired, his mouth filled with small, hard teeth. Water Gourd pushed his hands under the baby's shoulders, lifted, prodded, and pulled until he managed to get it to his lap. Two years, perhaps three, he thought, for the number of teeth in the child's head. The baby rooted and thrust against Water Gourd's chest.

"I am not a woman," Water Gourd said. "I have no milk." The child's cries grew more frantic. Water Gourd twisted one corner of the blanket and thrust it into the boy's mouth. He began to suck, and his wailing stopped. Water Gourd patted the baby's back, mumbling his consternation. The boy's mother must have hidden him in the boat when the Bear-god People attacked. The baby jerked the blanket from his mouth and began to fuss again.

Water Gourd sighed and pulled the plug from one of his gourds, took a swallow of water. He sucked out another mouthful, then lowered his head to the baby's head, pressed his lips to the baby's lips and released a stream of water. The child choked at first, but then he drank, and Water Gourd chuckled to himself at his own cunning. After several mouthfuls, the baby seemed content, and Water Gourd leaned forward, opened the pack of supplies that had lain under the boy in the bottom of the boat.

There was a heavy pot, the kind women store food in, also a few of the small soft skins mothers use to pad their babies' bottoms. A woman's knife and three full bottle gourds. A packet that was probably a good luck charm for the baby. A small one, it was, smaller than most women carry for their sons.

Water Gourd's stomach suddenly lurched, and he fumbled at the skins that swaddled the child, worked his way through them until he could feel the baby's soft, damp rump. He thrust a finger between the baby's legs, then withdrew his hand, moaning softly.

What had he done to deserve all the curses that had befallen him? He thought back through his life, to the sons and wives he had outlived, to the lazy niece he depended on for food. And now this. The baby was a girl. A worthless girl.

Surely there was no hope. What sea animal coming upon them would allow them to live—an old man who could no longer throw a harpoon, and a baby who would curse the very wood of their boat with her urine?

Water Gourd set the child away from him, back into the

nest her mother had made her in the bottom of the boat. He turned his back and did not allow himself to think about her as he watched over the bow, looking east, waiting for morning.

THREE

Night clouds moved in, darkened the moon, and though Water Gourd was determined to stay awake, he fell asleep, slept long and hard until the girl's wailing broke into his dreams.

He comforted her as best he could, and when the sun rose, he gave her some venison, and much of the water in one of his precious gourds, but she still whined and cried, asking for her mother, her father, her aunt. He considered dumping her into the sea, but he had placed her by then, knew she was Fire Mountain Man's daughter. Fire Mountain Man had always been good to him, willing to share meat and fish, and for that reason, Water Gourd stayed his hand. He remembered the cries of the girl's mother as she was being attacked, and though in his mind he defended his choices, he also had to push away thoughts that accused him of cowardice.

Cowardice? No. Wisdom. If he had been killed, who would warn the next village about the Bear-god warriors? Surely the sea gods had saved him for that purpose. Of course it was possible that they had only meant to save the girl, though why she would be worth saving, he could not understand.

He finally decided that her discomfort was due to the

soiled rag she wore between her legs. He humbled himself to take on the duties of a nursemaid and cleaned her, dipping her to the waist in the sea until the filth was washed away, then wrapping a clean rag around her. He rinsed out the old and laid it across the boat to dry, apologizing to the wood for the indignity of such a thing. But the boat did not seem to mind, played no tricks on them, and so gave Water Gourd further proof that the girl, rather than he himself, was the reason he was now safe and beyond reach of the Bear-gods.

After he ate, Water Gourd purposely paddled farther out, until only by squinting could he see the convoluted line of land, hovering like distant clouds at the edge of the horizon.

Then he paddled south until he was sure he was parallel with the next Boat People's village. That village was not as strong as his own had been, but with warning, they might prevail against the Bear-gods. Water Gourd knew many of the fishermen of that village, had celebrated with them during their summer festivals, and they traded back and forth— fish and deerskins, shell beads and harpoons for the big earthenware pots those fishermen's wives made so well.

When Water Gourd was satisfied he had taken the boat far enough, he stopped and, to pass the time until night, used the point of his wrist knife to pry out the slivers in his knees. Now and again he paddled to keep his boat where he wanted it, but he decided it was safe to sleep away the afternoon, and when night fell to turn the boat toward land and paddle in. If the Bear-god People had taken the neighboring village—and he would surely know by the smoke that would rise from the ruins—he would go back out to sea before they noticed him, then continue south to the next village.

He gave the child some water, sang her bits of songs he remembered from his own childhood, and told her they would sleep a little while. She stuck two fingers into her mouth, looked at him solemnly, and nodded her agreement, then pulled with determination at the blanket he still had wrapped around his legs. He gave her the smaller deerskin, but she would not take it. Finally he shook a finger at her, giving a stern admonition. Since when did children tell grown men what to do?

She pulled the fingers out of her mouth, bared her teeth, and growled. It was good that he remembered her as Fire Mountain Man's daughter, or he might believe she was a Bear-god child. Then surely he *would* drop her into the sea.

He sighed and again cursed his bad luck, then gave her the largest deerskin. She stuck her fingers back into her mouth and lay down beside him, reached over to pat his leg. He bared his yellow teeth at her, gaping though they were, four in front where eight should be. Her lips trembled and she closed her eyes, covered her little face with one hand. Water Gourd hawked and spat over the side of the boat. Was any man ever so tested?

He began a song, and though it was a hunter's song, he tried to sing it softly, patting her as he crooned out the words, until finally they were both asleep.

When Water Gourd woke at dusk, he could no longer see the land. He breathed in hard to fill his nose with air and told himself that he could smell the earth. The girl was still asleep, and so when he began to paddle, turning the boat west, he used a gentle rhythm.

By the time the sky was completely dark, the child awoke. Her dreams must have frightened her, for suddenly she was shrieking so loudly that Water Gourd had to set aside the paddle and gather her into his arms. He gave her water and half a chestnut cake, wiped her eyes and nose on a corner of her blanket. He could not remember what her parents called her, so he soothed her with the name of Daughter, and once again changed the rag between her legs. Then he set her down so he could paddle.

He watched the horizon for signs of a village—beach torches, hearth fires, or the smoke of destruction—but though he paddled long into the night, muttering prayers to the boat and the earth, there was nothing but the sea. Finally his arms were so heavy he could no longer lift them. So he sat, watching until dawn, comforting himself with assurances that the morning light would bring sight of land, and if he had to wait another night, what hardship was there in that? He had water and food.

But when morning came, fear brought bile to his throat. There was nothing on any horizon, and only by the sun's place in the sky did he know in which direction the land lay. Daughter seemed to sense his fear, and began to cry, not with the shrieks that come with nightmares or the fussiness caused by urine burns, but a low throaty moan like an old woman mourning.

FOUR

Water Gourd paddled through the day and did not stop until he was able to see land toward the west. He took time to eat and feed Daughter, then he followed the sun as it set. By the time the moon rose, the land loomed dark and large, black against the purple of the sea.

He watched for the light of night fires, but there was nothing. Had the Bear-god warriors already destroyed every village? No, he assured himself. If they had, he would see smoke lifting from the ruins.

Perhaps someone else from his village had also escaped and was able to get to those people who lived south, warn them not to burn night fires so the Bear-gods would miss their villages if they passed in the darkness. But without night fires, Water Gourd was afraid to beach his boat. He could not tell where he was, and when a man does not know where shoals and rocks lurk, he is wise to stay in deep water until morning light reveals the danger. He kept himself awake by biting the insides of his cheeks.

Finally the sun broke the horizon, and he paddled until he came to a cove. The tide was low. A good thing if a beach was given to rips and hard currents, a bad thing if the sea lay shallow over reefs.

"Do you deceive me?" he shouted at the calm waters.

Daughter raised up and looked over the edge of the boat. "'Ceive me?" she echoed.

Water Gourd felt his lips curl into a smile, the first since the Bear-god warriors had attacked his village. He pulled the girl to sit between his knees and paddled the boat with strong strokes toward the shore. It moved easily, and in the shallows, Water Gourd could see that only sand and water plants lay beneath the surface. He did not stop paddling until the bow of the boat was well up on the beach, then he slowly unbent his old man legs and climbed out. Daughter raised her hands to him, so he lifted her, set her down on the beach, and motioned her away from the boat.

The boat was heavy, nearly impossible for an old man to drag, but he heaved and shoved and took advantage of the lift of small waves until even the stern was beyond reach of the sea. He sat down until his strength returned, then he and Daughter began to explore the land. They found a freshwater stream where they washed themselves. After refilling the empty water gourds, the old man lay belly down on the river bank, extended an arm into the water, and lay still and quiet until a fish swam over his fingers. With one deft movement Water Gourd flipped it to the shore, setting Daughter to chortle with delight. Though it was a freshwater fish, he did not bother to cook it. Why risk a fire? He sliced it thin, and they ate it raw. He gave Daughter the eyes, and watched with longing as she swallowed them, but he saved the cheeks for himself. A fair trade, more than fair, he reasoned.

They gathered sea urchins in tide pools until Daughter's blanket bulged with them, and they picked water plants: dulce and ribbon kelp and nori.

That night, after finding no sign of any village, not even a path or trail, they returned to the boat. Water Gourd placed several fist-sized stones in the bow—something of the earth to hold the boat ashore, so any sea-longings it possessed would be counteracted by the need of the rocks to stay on land. He stowed his water gourds, tying them in place in the stern, and set the sea urchins and plants in the bow. Then he made a bed for himself and Daughter in the center of the boat, the cedar walls close about them, the splintery bottom cushioned with beach grass.

The storm came suddenly. Wind and rain wrenched them from their dreams. Water Gourd considered tipping the boat belly up, but the storm cut at them from all sides—the rain coming from north, then south, and turning again. So even if he could tip the boat completely over—if he had the strength to do such a thing—the sea might rise and flood them.

Daughter began to cry, and he wrapped her in his arms, felt the warmth of her as comfort. For a time he sang songs, but he doubted she could hear him over the rage of the winds, and finally, his throat tight and sore, he stopped.

The rain soaked through their deerskin blankets, and he began to shake. The clattering of his teeth made his head ache. Then suddenly the boat lurched, and he knew the storm had taken them. He leaned forward over Daughter, flipped the largest blanket over the heap of sea urchins, and weighted it down with the rocks. He fumbled for the jar of dried meat, settled it under his buttocks, an uncomfortable seat, but better than losing their food. He split one gourd and used it to bail out the water that had begun to slap into the boat from the sea.

Daughter clung to him, her arms stretching to reach around his waist. With each wave that broke over them, Water Gourd was sure the boat would be swamped, but it managed to stay afloat. He bailed until his arms were heavy as stone, until an ache burned at the center of his chest, until finally he knew nothing but pain, fear, and darkness.

When day came, clouds lay heavy over the sun, but at least Water Gourd could see. He clung to the sides of the boat, bailed, and once, when the wind slacked, cracked a few sea urchins to get at the eggs. Rich and sweet, they warmed him from within, and even Daughter ate willingly when he offered her some on the flat of his thumbnail.

He had never spent much time thinking about small children. They were too fussy and smelly to have much importance. But he found himself marveling over her tiny perfect face, the black shining eyes, her fair and flawless skin. Her nose was only a bump, the space between her eyes perfectly flat, her ears like shells curled at the sides of her head. The rain had smoothed her hair, flattened it to her skull. She gripped his wrist with both hands as she licked his thumbnail, and he saw that one of her fingernails had been partially ripped away, a line of dark blood marking the tear. When she finished, he offered her more, but she turned her head, so he ate the eggs himself, pulled her back into the shelter of his legs, and continued to bail.

The storm lasted four days, and most of the time Water Gourd lived in a waking dream of bailing and paddling. He stopped only to drink a little rain water he caught in his bailing gourd, or to eat a share of the sea plants, chestnut cakes, or a thumbnail of urchin eggs. Sometime during the third day, he fell into a dreamless sleep. He woke feeling stronger, more hopeful, and lifted his eyes to see that a thin line of blue sky sliced the clouds. The wind had shifted to the south, was bringing warmer air, and the rain had stopped. He tried to smile, but a hardened rime of salt had molded his face into a mask of fear. He dug at his cheeks with his fingernails, peeled away the crust.

Daughter was curled on his feet, the girl so still that his breath caught. He reached down, lifted her, and she stretched out slowly, as though she were a stiff-jointed old woman. Water Gourd set her on his lap, grimaced at how cold she was. Her hair was frosted with salt, stiff as ice, and she lifted raw, red hands to swipe at her eyes, but when she looked up at him she smiled, and when he offered her a sea urchin, she ate willingly.

He ate also, then reached for the paddle he had wedged between his leg and the side of the boat. The sea was nearly calm, and he could see the place of the sun behind the clouds. He would paddle west toward his home, and even if the storm winds rose again, at least he would have gained back a little of the distance he had lost.

His hand closed over nothing, and he grasped again before he looked and saw that the paddle was gone. He clambered into the bow, dumping Daughter from his lap, did not even hear her cries of protest. He pushed his hands into the pile of sea urchins, ignored the prickling of their shells, then scrambled into the back of the boat, even over the outrigger rails to the small shaped log that kept them from capsizing in the waves.

The paddle wasn't in the boat. He stood, looked out in all directions. It wasn't even floating nearby. His despair was so great that he considered flinging himself into the sea. Why continue to fight when the storm had managed to take his best weapon? But as he looked into the cold depths, he lost his courage or perhaps regained it. The sea might take him, but he would not give up willingly.

He pulled the bailing gourd from inside his woven rush shirt, filled it from the bottom of the boat, and drank. The water was brackish and tasted of burnt wood, dark from the char that had not been carved away, salty, but not as salty as sea water—rain mixed with what the waves had brought in. He offered some to Daughter, then began to bail.

It seemed as though he had bailed forever. Four days since the storm had begun. How many days since he had left his village? Seven? Eight?

As he bailed, he watched the sky and realized that the sea was taking them north. But then the storm again howled down upon them, this time from the south and the east. He wrapped himself and Daughter in a deerskin blanket, and he continued to bail, working through that day and the next.

The morning of the sixth day, the sky divided, the clouds cut asunder as though by a knife, and Water Gourd knew that the storm's back had been broken. At midday the sun shone down on them.

The boat and outrigger, the blankets, even the bottle

gourds were coated with ice. The storm had driven them north, far beyond their own village, or any of the Boat People's villages. Perhaps he and Daughter were not meant to survive, for surely the storm had brought them to the small northern islands of the Bear-god People. Without a paddle. With a dwindling supply of sea urchins. With only ice rime and the water in the gourds. What hope did they have?

As the days passed, Water Gourd's hands went through the motions of keeping himself and Daughter alive. He carefully scraped the ice from the boat and blankets each morning, placed it in the split gourd, and held the gourd between his legs until the ice melted. Then he divided it between Daughter and himself, taking care to share it equally. Each night, they both took a swallow of water from the gourds.

In his thirst he thought much about water. As water carrier, it had been his life, but his first days hauling spring water had been filled with resentment. All the years hunting and fishing had brought him only the dishonor of doing boy's work. Anger had filled him so full that he didn't have room to swallow his own spit. He had seen other old men like that, drooling until chins were wet and crusted with saliva. He did not want to be like them, but still his hatred grew.

He hated the water he carried. He hated the bottle gourds. He hated the path that wound its way to the spring, slippery in winter, prickly with sharp-edged grass in summer. How much easier to hate than to look honestly at his own weak legs, his bent and gnarled fingers. But now in the boat, mouth parched, he thought longingly of those gourds, water beads on their tough, smooth shells. He remembered the smiles women gave him when he filled their water pots. He thought of the small gifts they offered in return—chestnut cakes, mussels and sea urchins, seeds roasted on hearthstones.

He began to realize that his work of carrying water had not been without honor. He had done what he was able to do, and maybe in some ways that was even more respectable than having a place as a wise elder, sitting and talking, expecting others to bring him food and water.

"Why didn't I realize that my life was good?" he asked Daughter.

She looked up at him with solemn eyes, perhaps surprised that he had spoken to her. Their world was mostly one of silence. He crooned a little when he wanted her to sleep, but his voice was ragged and harsh, brittle with age. Sometimes he heard her singing a song, muffled by the fingers that were always in her mouth, and sometimes she cried, but she had stopped asking for her mother.

Water Gourd no longer attempted to count the days. He was past numbering them. Too many days without enough food, without fire for warmth, without good water.

The storm had filled the earthenware pot, so the dried meat and fish inside had rotted. Each day he forced himself to choke down a little, and each day he tried to get Daughter to eat some, too, but usually she refused. He could not say he was sad when the food in that pot was finally gone.

Besides the spoiled meat, he allowed Daughter one sea urchin a day, himself two, but the morning finally came when there was only one left. He ate the eggs from three of the ovaries, gave Daughter the rest.

As Water Gourd licked the last of them from his thumbnail, his eyes began to prickle. He squeezed them shut, then rubbed the heels of his hands against the lids, was startled to find that his cheeks were wet with tears. I cry for Daughter, he told himself. Why waste pity on myself? He had lived well, had wives and sons. Daughter was the one who deserved a longer life. He looked down at her small face—at the eyes, once so bright, now sunken and dull with hunger—and sorrow burned at the center of his chest.

She is only a girl, he reminded himself. A girl's life was not easy, nor even necessarily good. As wife, she would spend her days working hard, her nights serving a husband who might not be easy to please.

He had been good to his own wives, Water Gourd assured

himself. Most of the time, anyway. Perhaps in his youth he had been more impatient with his first wife than he should have been. Demanding. But surely he had made up for that over the years, and paid for it with his fourth wife, wicked and self-centered as she had been.

Perhaps, then, for both he and Daughter, it was good that the sea urchins were gone. Perhaps neither of them had much to live for. Now, he could give serious thought to dying. How can a man consider the necessity of death when he still has food?

He set his thoughts onto ways of dying. Starvation was certainly one, drowning another, but neither seemed appealing. Water Gourd still had his knife. He could cut into his veins, knotted like blue worms under his skin. But thinking of blood turned his thoughts to butchering, and for most of that first day after their food was gone, Water Gourd was lost in remembering the feasts of the past, times of celebration.

He filled his mind with the remembrance of sea urchins, split and ready to eat, rich as the boar fat that dripped from spits into the roasting fires. Delicate chestnut cakes, roasted nuts and tubers, grass seeds pounded fine and mixed with water, cooked on flat stones and rolled around a paste of fish. He closed his eyes and allowed himself to eat his way through such a meal, finishing with flower blossoms, bitten and sucked to get at the nectar.

And it wasn't until Daughter's whimpering brought him from his feast back to the cold, wet hulk of the boat that he realized that instead of thinking about death, he had spent most of the day considering life.

He was disgusted with himself. If he wasted his time thinking about eating, how could he hope for an honorable death?

"There is nothing to eat," he told Daughter sadly, and she pulled her fingers out of her mouth and puckered her lips into a pout.

"Fish," she said.

"No fish," he told her.

She pointed at several empty sea urchin shells that littered the bottom of the boat. "Fish," she said again, in a more demanding way. He leaned down and picked up a shell, handed it to her. She licked at the inside, then played with it for a while, and for the first time he realized that she needed a toy. Didn't all children have toys? He considered cutting away the edge of one of the blankets, tying it into something that would look like a doll—legs and arms and head—but then he realized his foolishness. They needed the blankets much more than Daughter needed a doll. She was happy enough with the sea urchin shell, prickly though it was.

But the thought of cutting the blanket set another idea into his mind. Perhaps he could make some kind of line from the blanket, or better yet from the fiber of his shirt. He began to examine the edges of the jacket where stitches caught up a hem of sorts to keep the fabric from unraveling. He picked at the thread, wondered what it was made of. He had seen the women of the village pounding bark, perhaps to separate it into threads for sewing. Sometimes they twisted sinew, but what man paid attention to that? Curses were too easy to come by as it was. Why bring them on yourself with an inordinate interest in women's work?

By the time he had picked out the stitches, he had a section of thread as long as his arms stretched wide. Perhaps enough to catch a fish, he thought. He tugged at it, and decided it was strong enough to hold. He used his knife to cut away a section of wood from the edge of the boat, managed to take off a piece as long as his fist and as big around as two fingers. He smoothed the center of the wood, then tied one end of the line around it.

"A hand line," he said to Daughter, and she repeated the words. "For fish," he told her.

"Fish," she said, and clasped her hands to her belly and began to cry. "Fish," she said. "I want fish."

He gave her a little of his hoarded water, and it seemed to calm her. He held her tightly against the warmth of his stomach and watched as her eyes closed, fluttered open and closed again. Finally she slept, and he began to consider how to make a hook.

When the Bear-gods attacked his outrigger, two of their spears landed inside the boat. Water Gourd had nearly thrown them into the sea, fearful of the curse they might carry, but then he had decided to keep them. His first thought had been to use them on land to hunt small animals he and Daughter might come across, but now that they were so far out on the sea and their paddle was gone, how could he hope to hunt?

He had spent several days, when they still had sea urchins to eat, holding one of the spears poised over the edge of the boat, ready to thrust it at any fish that came close, but he had seen no fish, and finally gave up. What could he expect? he asked himself. It was a Bear-god spear, and what did the Bear-god People know about the sea? The fish had probably seen the spear as insult, and most likely thought he, himself, was a Bear-god.

He had tried to fashion a paddle using a spear as a shaft, but he couldn't gouge out a wide enough piece of wood from the boat to serve as blade. Besides, the spears were thrusting lances, the shafts too short for paddles unless he leaned far over the edge of the boat.

Before he made his decision, Daughter's warmth against his belly drew him into sleep, and in his dreams he was again a boy, idle for some reason and watching the village stone knapper. That stone knapper was long dead, and even in his dream, Water Gourd had a hard time remembering the man's name. Finally it came to him. Carver—probably not his true name, but a name, like Water Gourd, bestowed because of what the man did.

In that time long ago, Carver had made most of the spears, knives, and tools for the people of the village. For two years, Water Gourd had been his apprentice, learning the patient art of stone knapping, but then in the foolishness of his youth, he had decided he would rather hunt or fish.

But that night in the cedar boat, Water Gourd watched

Carver in his dreams, and he realized that he remembered much. There was the pad of leather used to protect the left hand as it cradled the stone; the deer antler punch and the fist-sized rock used as hammer; punches, drills, and incising tools to make arrow points from bone. All that night of sleeping, Water Gourd watched and learned.

In the morning, he unwound the sinew that bound the Bear-god spearhead to its shaft. He spoke in soothing tones to the stone as he freed it, so it would not be afraid of what he was about to do. He didn't want it to shatter in his hands.

He wrapped the sinew around his wrist and tied it, so he would not lose it. Then he carved himself a punch from the bone haft of his wrist knife, made a new handle from the shaft of the Bear-god spear. The knife wasn't as beautiful, but it was usable. He chose a ballast stone to be his hammer and padded his left hand with a corner of the smaller deer-skin blanket. He gripped the spearhead and began a careful reshaping, narrowing and thinning the base of the blade until he was able to chip away several long thin splinters of stone.

Water Gourd looked at his fingers in wonder, at the swollen, misshapen joints, and was amazed at what he was able to do. It seemed as though he could feel Carver's hands on his own, guiding, teaching, for surely the work was not Water Gourd's alone.

He knapped the narrow end of the largest stone splinter into a point, then cut another chunk of wood from the spear shaft, carved it down, and with his knife dug a hole where he inserted the blunt end of the splinter, the sharp end jutting up at an angle away from the wood. He bound the point in place with some of the sinew and used the rest as a leader to attach the completed hook to the length of line he had unraveled from his jacket.

It had taken him most of the day, for he had had to stop several times in his work to comfort Daughter, to wash out the rags that were now always wet between her legs. Her buttocks and the tiny woman's cleft between her legs were rough and red, swollen with a rash, and she fussed some, pulling at the rag now and again, but most of the time, she only sat, half asleep, so he wondered if she were considering death herself, a preparation to allow her spirit to slip easily from her body.

He considered what he would do with her if she died. The easiest thing would be to drop her into the sea, but would that be wise? Surely her flesh would be good and sweet, though he would not eat her himself. What man could risk a curse like that? But if he dropped her body into the sea, the fish would eat her. So what difference would it make if he used her for bait? The fish would still eat her, but he would have a chance to get himself some food.

He sat a long time watching her, and once she looked up at him, smiled around the fingers in her mouth. His heart squeezed tight, and he angrily batted at the tears that suddenly burned in his eyes. Ah ee! What foolishness, to care about a child so young that she could hardly talk!

Maybe he could catch a fish before she died, and the meat would give her the strength to live a little longer. He sat the girl down in the middle of the boat, in a place that was not too wet. With the remaining part of the spear shaft, he began to dig through the debris in the bow. Perhaps he would find something—a hard fin left from the smoked fish that had been in Daughter's pot, a glob of sea urchin eggs that he could rub on the hook.

A tatter from one of the deerskin blankets might attract a fish, but there were curses that came when a man put land animals in fish bellies. Surely he had enough bad luck as it was. Why ask for more?

He lifted each ballast stone, searched Daughter's pack. Finally he found half a sea urchin shell. Except for that shell, there was nothing, not even a bit of waste from one of Daughter's rags. That was what happened when a man went for too many years without a wife. He got used to cleaning up after himself.

He finally took the shell and tied it on the hook, lowered

the hand line into the water. He had thought he might need to attach a bit of stone to weight the line, but the stone hook was heavy enough to carry it down. He leaned over the boat and watched it drop as he unwound line from the wooden handle.

He watched for a long time, but saw no fish, and finally, his back aching, he sat up and scanned the sea. As swells lifted the boat, he looked out toward the horizon. Sometimes his eyes fooled him into thinking he saw land where there was none. Then the sea dropped the boat into a trough between the waves, and there was nothing but water rising, so that he marveled they had lived this long and not been swallowed up.

This day, with his hook and line and the hope of fish, Water Gourd decided that the sea was friend rather than enemy. He sang a fisherman's song in his old creaky voice, then told Daughter that the walls of water that rose smooth and green around them would soon bring a fish to his hook.

FIVE

Herendeen Bay, Alaska Peninsula
602 B.C.

A loud voice interrupted Qumalix's story. She closed her
eyes for a moment and shook her head as though she needed
to remind herself where she was. In the dim light of the ulax,
Yikaas could see she was searching for the one who had
called out.

A man rose to his feet. He crossed his arms over his chest,
puffed himself up with a full, long breath of air. He was First
Men. He wore an otterskin sax, a long hoodless parka favored by both men and women of the Traders' Beach, and
ivory labrets pierced his skin at the corners of his mouth.
Kuy'aa had explained to Yikaas that a man's labrets were
signs of his family's lineage and his place in their village.
This man's labrets were large circles, and from each, a blunt
tusk protruded the length of a finger joint. Vertical lines
darkened his chin, and a path of circles and dots crossed his
cheeks. No doubt he was a hunter from some powerful family. Did he not have a hunter's tattoos?

But to Yikaas's surprise Kuy'aa leaned close and whispered, "I know him. His name is Sky Catcher, and he's a sto-

ryteller from a First Men village a day's journey west of this Traders' Beach."

Sky Catcher spoke, and though Yikaas could not understand his First Men words, he heard the belligerence in the man's voice, and felt a sudden urge to protect the girl who had been telling them such a good story.

Yikaas hoped that she would translate Sky Catcher's words, but she did not. She answered him in a respectful voice, and their conversation went on, Sky Catcher's harsh comments, the girl's soft answers, until several River traders in the ulax spoke out to protest.

"What does he want?" one asked.

"Tell us what he's talking about," said another.

Finally Qumalix held up one hand, palm out, a request for silence. She lifted her eyes to the River traders and said, "He claims that he likes my story well enough, but that he has never heard of the Boat People. He wants to know if they are First Men or even River, and if not, he asks why I talk about them rather than tell stories of people we know, like Chakliux and K'os or Aqamdax—those people whose stories have come to us from times long ago."

Yikaas had to admit that he had wondered the same thing. Since Qumalix was from the Whale Hunter Islands, he had expected her stories to be about First Men, not Boat People. But still, he was not rude enough to interrupt and ask as Sky Catcher had.

"If you will be patient," Qumalix said, "you will see how the stories of Daughter and Water Gourd fit together with those about Chakliux and his family."

Sky Catcher asked another question. Qumalix answered, then said in the River language, "He wants to know if the Bear-god warriors are River people."

There was a murmur of agreement from other First Men, but the River traders raised their voices in outrage. "We're not like that. We would never attack a peaceful village. Perhaps the Bear-gods are First Men."

Then one of the First Men traders called out, "We have

heard your stories about the Near River and Cousin River people. They almost killed each other off. How can you claim to love peace? Besides, we First Men know how to build good boats. We would never make boats like those the Bear-god People used."

The argument grew worse, words flying. Men stood to shout at one another, and women screeched out insults. Yikaas huddled where he was, angry at all of them for interrupting a story he wanted to hear, angry most of all at Sky Catcher, who had started all the foolishness.

Kuy'aa pushed herself up to her feet and hobbled to the climbing log. Yikaas sighed and got up to follow her. Surely the storytelling had lasted long enough so that the sun had set, even on this short summer night, and he didn't want Kuy'aa to wander around the village alone, lost, as she looked for the ulax where she was supposed to stay. But to his surprise, once she had ascended several notches on the climbing log, she turned back to face the people and, setting two fingers at the corners of her lips, blew out a long, shrill whistle.

The arguing stopped, and mouths dropped opened in surprise as the people realized that the whistle had come from an old River woman.

"Be quiet!" she shouted at them. Then she lifted her chin toward Qumalix. The girl still stood in the storyteller's place, her hands clenched together so tightly that her knuckles were white. "Tell your story," said Kuy'aa. "Those who do not want to hear it can leave."

There was a mumble of agreement among the River traders, and questions from the First Men until someone translated Kuy'aa's words. Several men and one woman left the ulax, among them Sky Catcher, but the others settled down and urged the girl to continue.

Yikaas wondered if she would after so much arguing and rudeness. She rubbed her fingers against her eyes, and he saw the tiredness in her face, but she started to speak, at first so quietly that he could hardly hear her. Her voice trembled, and Yikaas lowered his head, embarrassed to look at her, but as she spoke, her words grew stronger.

Soon Yikaas was caught again in her story. Once more he was Water Gourd, an old man trying to cheat death as he and Daughter drifted north on a sea that seemed to stretch to the end of the earth.

The North Pacific
6447 B.C.

DAUGHTER'S STORY

Water Gourd fished two days without a bite. Each morning was gray with fog, the sun little more than a patch of brightness, scarcely strong enough to coax away the night. When a fish finally did take his hook, Water Gourd's fingers were so numb with the cold that at first he wasn't sure he had felt anything at all, but he bent quickly and set Daughter in the bottom of the boat, shushed her protest at being taken from the warmth of his lap.

"Fish," he whispered to her, and she was quiet.

The nibble came again, and Water Gourd tensed his arms, ready to snap the line and set the hook, knowing that if he moved too soon, he would scare the fish away. For a long time, he felt nothing, and the fear that he had not moved quickly enough settled in his stomach like a rock. He was suddenly dizzy, too long without food, too weak, and he wondered whether he would be strong enough to bring a fish in even if it did swallow the hook.

Thoughts of death again blackened his mind, and he shook his head to drive them away. What fisherman gives up after one nibble? He jiggled the hand line, lowering it slowly and then jerking it up, allowing it to fall again. Suddenly the line was tugged so hard that it nearly jumped from his fingers.

He cried out and began to sing one of the chants fishermen use to charm fish. It was a song for nets and not hand lines, but at least the fish would hear his Boat People words and know that he was a man who honored the sea and those who lived in it.

The fish was strong, and as it sped away from the outrigger, it began to pull them. Water Gourd held tightly to the wooden hand grip and contemplated the strength of his line. He interrupted his song to speak to it, begging it to hold, to stay strong.

"Strong," Daughter echoed from where she sat in the bottom of the boat. Then she looked up at Water Gourd and asked, "Fish?"

"Fish," Water Gourd told her. "A big fish."

"A big fish," she said solemnly.

A shadow moved in from the sea, changed from shadow to fish, swam until it neared the boat. Water Gourd's breath caught so hard in his throat that he nearly choked. It was huge, that fish. Surely too large to catch. Should he hang on, use up what little strength he had, or cut the line?

He had stone and wood for another hook, but what good were they if his line was too short to be of use?

Suddenly he was angry. No, he wouldn't cut the line! If the fish would not offer itself as meat, then it should leave them alone, let them catch another who was willing to be eaten. Surely it had recognized his song, knew they were Boat People and that Water Gourd would drop its bones into the sea so the fish could live again.

It pulled the line under the boat and came up beyond the outrigger, then dove again, carried the line down so far that Water Gourd had to extend his hands into the waves. The fish turned and rose so quickly, releasing the tension on the line, that Water Gourd fell backwards into the boat. The fish jumped and Water Gourd saw it, blunt-nosed, green and black against the misted sky, the mottled skin as shiny as wet rock. It was a fish he did not know, one he had never seen before, nearly as large as a man. Then, as the fish slipped into the water, twisting, the line suddenly went slack.

Water Gourd cried out at the loss, but quickly wound the remaining line back onto the hand grip.

"Fish?" Daughter asked.

"He was too big," Water Gourd told her.

"Fish," Daughter said again and began to cry. "Fish, fish, fish."

"Be quiet," he said.

He looked up into the gray sky, and wondered whether he were already dead. Was death this: riding forever in a boat that went nowhere? Without food, without water, and all the while watching a child die? Had he been a terrible person to deserve such a death? Had he not respected the small gods and the large ones, the spirits that lived in the grass and earth and sea?

He remembered times when he had been selfish, had taken more than his share of food or attention. How often had he demanded that his wives do something more than necessary? He remembered waking them in the night to satisfy his needs, for food, for sex, when they had already been up many times with babies. He remembered complaining about food prepared and clothing made.

But wasn't that what women were for? And didn't men work as hard, risking their lives to feed those women and their children? How could a few minutes in the middle of the night even begin to compare?

And what about Daughter? What had she done that was so terrible to deserve a death of parched mouth and empty belly, of bleeding sores and cracked lips?

But finally he decided that they were not dead. How could they be? In death a man would see spirits. He would see others who had died before him. Where were Knot Maker and Long Head? Surely they would be here in their own boats, for they, too, had been lost on the sea.

He was alive, and so was Daughter. The fish had taken one hook. Well, then, he would make another.

A quiet voice spoke from within his head. "You need bait," it said, no more than that. No other wisdom.

Water Gourd had scoured the boat well enough to know there was nothing edible lurking among the shells and ballast stones, but he searched again. There was nothing, not the smallest, hardest bit of fish bone, not even a smear of sea urchin eggs.

Water Gourd looked at his feet. Surely a man would not miss a little toe. And the pain of cutting it off would be quick. He took a long breath, released it. He had bait.

Before night fell and clouds darkened the moon so that Water Gourd could not see his own hands, he had finished another hook. He picked up his knife, settled one bare foot hard against the wood of the boat, and prepared to cut.

But that voice came again, louder this time, and said, "The girl's toe would be better. It is smaller and so will not hurt as much when it is cut off. Besides, any fish would come more readily to the soft flesh of a baby than to the hard, callused toe of an old man."

Water Gourd considered the advice, and thought that it was probably right, but either way, with his toe or Daughter's, he decided it was better to wait until morning. He did not want to fish at night when he could not see what had taken his line, and a fresh toe was more likely to attract fish than one that had sat with its blood hardening all night.

Morning then, Water Gourd told himself. Perhaps his mind would be clearer after sleep, though each day without food seemed to muddle his thoughts a little more.

"I will sleep first," he told the voice in his head. "Decisions always come more easily after sleep."

In the morning, Water Gourd studied Daughter's little pink feet. Her skin was shriveled by the salt water that always seemed to lie in the bottom of the boat no matter how much he bailed. The toe was so small he knew it would come off quickly. His own feet were hard and bunyoned, crusted with calluses. A toe, even his smallest, would not yield easily to a blade.

He stuck his little finger in his mouth and bit. The pain

was not terrible. He bit harder, until he tasted the salt of his own blood. Still, not terrible. Certainly he could bear the pain of losing a toe. But what if the wound drew spirits of illness? Everyone knew that each opening into the body could allow evil spirits to enter. The nostrils, the ears, the mouth, the anus, the hole in the end of a man's penis, even the tiny needle dots that let tears come from the corners of the eyes. And, of course, all cuts. How many times in his long life had he seen a person grow sick, burn with fever, and die, simply from a tiny cut in foot or hand?

What protection did he have in this boat against such spirits? He could not burn sacred grass. He could not have the herb doctor mix medicine for him, or the spirit-chanter sing. And if he died, so would Daughter. Without him, there was no chance for her survival.

On the other hand, if he took Daughter's small toe, he himself might be able to offer chants for protection, and if Daughter died, he would still live. With her gone, life for him would be easier. She wouldn't take a share of the water he melted from rime ice, and he would have her body for bait.

He tied the new hook tightly to the line, then gathered her left foot into his hand. She curled her toes and turned to look up at him, smiled, and reached to lay one hand against the side of his face.

It will be quick, Water Gourd reassured himself. He took his knife from its scabbard. Daughter sighed and snuggled back against his chest. He leaned down, set the foot in place against the bottom of the boat, and chopped, hard.

The stone blade caught for a moment on the bone, and the pain screamed in Water Gourd's head. He cried out, could barely make himself finish the cut. Daughter looked at him, her eyes round in horror. She began to weep, and Water Gourd reached into the growing puddle of blood, found the toe, old and bent and hard, then pressed a pad of rags against his wound.

"It ached every time it rained anyway," he said. Then he

rocked a little, turning his mind from the pain. He looked down at Daughter's two small perfect feet and was glad.

Two days passed. Water Gourd did not catch a fish with the first toe or the second, though they bit at his line, nibbled until the toes were nothing but bone. Finally, as he prepared to cut away another toe, Daughter held her little foot up to his face. She was very weak, and he knew that he would lose her soon. A baby could not live so many days without food. His own mind was nearly gone, lost in foolish dreams. The second toe had cost him too much blood, and the water he made from rime ice was not enough to soothe the raging thirst that came with the blood loss.

"My," she said to him in a soft, tired voice and lay her hands over his knife, shook her head. "Not your. My."

He had heard old women whisper that babies carried wisdom from the spirit world. Perhaps Daughter knew better than he did. Perhaps his old flesh could not catch a fish.

"It will hurt, Daughter," he told her.

"My," she said again.

"Sleep first," he said, thinking that it would be easier for him to cut if she were asleep, and perhaps her pain would be blunted.

He tried to sing, but his parched throat broke around the song, scattering the words into shards of nonsense. But finally as the sea swells rocked the boat, she slept, and then with tears nearly blocking his sight, Water Gourd raised his knife and took off Daughter's smallest toe.

At the pain, her eyes flew open. He looked into their brown depths and saw only understanding. She cried when he pinched the wound to stop the flow of blood, but she clung hard to him, and when he tied the toe on the stone barb of his hook, she raised her tiny chin and said, "My."

A fish bit nearly as soon as he lowered the bait into the sea, and Water Gourd jerked the hook, felt it lodge solidly into flesh. He played it for a time, allowed the fish to exhaust itself against the line, then he pulled it to the edge of the boat. The fish flipped once and was still. It was a hake, black and silver, as long and big around as his forearm. Water Gourd lowered a shaking hand into the water, the breath tight in his chest until he was able to hook his fingers into the gills.

"Now," he whispered, and tried to heave the fish into the boat. But it was heavy and beyond his strength.

"My," Daughter said in a quiet voice, looking over the edge of the boat at the fish. She patted her little foot, bound in bloody rags.

Water Gourd drew in another breath, pulled again, and this time was able to lift the hake, though not high enough to bring it over the edge. Then Daughter's small hands were at the bend of his elbow, her fingers splayed out over the sleeve of his coat.

"Now!" he said again. They pulled, and the fish fell into the boat at their feet.

"Yours," Water Gourd told her, and in the foolishness of his old age, he began to weep.

SIX

Water Gourd used the hake's innards to catch more fish, and after a few days of eating, he and Daughter both regained their strength. The currents still moved them north, and each night the water at the bottom of their boat turned into slush.

Water Gourd began to wonder if perhaps the sea was carrying them to that land where it was always winter. He had heard stories about such a place. Traders claimed it lay north of the Bear-god islands, but others said it did not exist. How could anything live where it was always winter?

The icy chill of the air seemed to live in fog, and Water Gourd could seldom see much beyond the bow of the boat. The fog not only battened his eyes, but also seemed to press against his ears, and sometimes he thought he could not bear another moment without sun and sky and sound. But one night the fog lifted, the clouds parted, and Water Gourd was able to see the stars. They looked nearly the same as they had from his village, and that comforted him, but there was some difference in their placement—more than just the turning that comes with the seasons.

They had several days where the sun shone, and he began to hope that the sea had not carried them to the far shores of the winter land, and that summer had actually come.

Though Water Gourd and Daughter had to huddle together for warmth during the nights, the sun, even on overcast days, warmed their bones back to living, and the morning frosts were so thin that he could scarcely add to their supply of water.

He watched for land, and the watching made his head ache, his eyes burn. The pain of his toes had nearly gone, and Daughter's small wound had healed well, but Water Gourd's eyes grew steadily worse. He carved a chunk of wood from the inside of the boat, whittled himself a pair of slitted goggles to combat the glare of sun on water, and often, if he was not fishing, he sat with his eyes closed, droning out stories that for a few moments carried him and Daughter back to their own village.

Daughter, too, was changing. Her delicate baby skin turned dark, and her legs grew thin. Her straight black hair, though tangled and knotted by the wind, now hung nearly to her shoulders. She had learned more words, and sometime during their days together, she had begun to call him Grandfather. He liked the sound of that in her mouth, her little girl voice crowing out when she saw something of interest, or slurring into baby words when she was tired and needed to sleep.

Though he longed for his village, for old friends and even the sweet-water spring, he could no longer imagine himself without Daughter: her face tipped up to his, her lisping words and bubbling laughter filling his days.

Sometimes in dreams he saw himself cut and mutilated beyond recognition as he pared himself away into bait. Toes, fingers, nose, and tongue, long slices of flesh all gone, eaten by fish too greedy and selfish to be caught.

Then he would wake, in gratitude stretch his fingers before him, bent and gnarled, but whole, his feet missing just the smallest toes, his nose and tongue still a part of him, and his body scarred only from the mishaps of a long life. And Daughter, too, was whole, save for that one small toe.

*   *   *

The morning they woke to see their boat flanked on all sides by sea otters, Water Gourd began to hope that they were near land. They had only three gourds of water left. How many days could they survive once that was gone?

The otters spread away from their boat in the fog like a brown sea, some jumping and playing, others lying on their backs, babies nursing. One otter, gray of face, swam very near their boat, a rock balanced on its chest, a mussel clamped tightly in its webbed fingers. The otter smacked the mussel against the rock until the shell cracked, then picked out the flesh, ate it in noisy slurps.

Daughter held one hand out to the otter, said, "My."

The animal flipped and slid quickly under the surface, and several otters nearest him did the same. Daughter looked up at Water Gourd, and he laid a finger against his lips to shush her.

Carefully, slowly, he began moving toward the remaining Bear-god spear that lay in the bottom of the boat. If he could affix his hand line to the spear, perhaps he could use it as a harpoon and kill an otter. He and Daughter were no longer starving, but an otter would have a lot of meat, not to speak of blood they could drink. And then there was the fur. Surely he could scrape a pelt clean enough to use for a blanket at night. There would be sinew also, to make fish line, and bones and teeth to carve into hooks.

Finally he managed to draw both hand line and spear to his lap, and again, motioning for Daughter to be quiet, knotted the line around the butt end of the spear shaft. It was a thrusting spear and not balanced to throw, but Water Gourd had cast enough spears during his life to compensate for the clumsiness, and if he missed, he would draw the spear back to himself with the line.

The gray-faced otter again surfaced beside their boat, another mussel clutched in his paws. Daughter was on her knees at the side of the boat, looking over the edge.

"My," she whispered and reached toward the mussel.

Like a child, the otter turned away, hugging the mussel to

his side. Moving slowly, Water Gourd set a hand on Daughter's shoulder, tried to pull her back to sit in the center of the boat, but she jerked away and would not look at him. He saw that she had a section of fish in her hand, and she held it out, offering the fish to the otter. The otter lifted his head, and suddenly Water Gourd was afraid the animal would bite her. Water Gourd lunged forward, but before he could reach her, the otter had taken the piece of fish, and somehow Daughter had the mussel, dark and wet, clutched in her hand.

"My!" she cried, as the otter dove beneath the surface and swam away. She held the mussel up so Water Gourd could see it.

He closed his eyes in relief. "Yours," he conceded.

As the day waned, Water Gourd watched the otters, waited in hopes that one would again come close enough for him to spear. As he watched, he found himself wondering whether he could use an otter's shoulder blade as a paddle. The remaining Bear-god spear could be the shaft. Though it was too short and thin for heavy seas, perhaps it would allow him to follow the otters back to land.

Several times since he and Daughter had begun their strange journey, he had tried to carve a slice of wood from the inside of the boat and make a paddle blade, but the cedar had grown soft and punky in the salt water, and no piece came away large enough.

Then he had another thought. Perhaps if he harpooned an otter, a strong animal that wouldn't die from one wound, it would flee toward the safety of land. And as it swam, still tied to them with Water Gourd's line, its fear would give it the strength to tow their boat.

Water Gourd watched and waited until the sun, a circle of yellow above the haze, had begun to set. No otters came near, and he had decided to put away his harpoon, pray that the animals would still be with them in the morning. But then a large otter swam close. It was strong and healthy-looking, nearly as long as a man is tall. The animal slipped down into the sea, and Water Gourd watched, leaning over the edge of the boat, finally losing the otter in the depths. But then, suddenly, it emerged, fur streaming, on the other side of the outrigger. It flipped to its back and swam slowly toward the bow.

Water Gourd bound the harpoon line to his wrist and hefted the spear, ground his teeth at the poor balance of the thing. He needed a stone counterweight for the spearhead. But why wish for what he did not have? He rubbed the hunting amulet he had worn at his neck since he was a boy.

As he was ready to throw, Daughter lay a hand on his leg, looked up at him. He thought he saw fear in her eyes, but what did a little girl know about hunting? He shook his head at her, upset that she had broken his concentration. No animal would give itself to a man who did not have respect enough to keep his thoughts on the hunt.

In his mind, he began a chant, a slow rhythm to help still his heart as he waited for the moment of throwing. He shut out Daughter and the boat, all things but harpoon and otter.

He threw.

The spear hit and the otter dove.

The line grew taut, and Water Gourd gripped his right wrist with his left hand, braced his feet, and felt the boat begin to move. The other otters began to dive until the sea was empty.

Daughter stabbed a finger into the air. "My! My! My!" she shouted and pursed her lips into a pout.

Water Gourd found the hand grip from his fishing line and managed to twist the line around it once, relieving some of the pressure from his wrist.

"A foolish thing to do, tying the line to your wrist," the pestering voice in his head told him. "You should have tied it to the outrigger poles. Now you will lose both spear and fishing line, and maybe your hand. Then what will you do?"

The line suddenly grew slack and Water Gourd again twisted it around the hand grip. Then the line was taut again, this time pulled straight down from the side of the boat. Water Gourd leaned over the edge. He could see the otter, large and dark, distorted in the depths. Suddenly it sped up through the water, moved so quickly that Water Gourd's only reaction was to raise his hands and cover his face. The otter reached the surface, flat nose bubbling out spent air, dark lips drawn back from yellow teeth. The animal leaped at him, and Water Gourd, without thought or reason, clenched his hands into the otter's thick pelt. The otter, twisting and snarling, drew in great breaths of air and curled to snap at the bloody spear protruding from its side.

Daughter began to scream, and Water Gourd felt the pain of the otter's teeth as it bit his arm, once and again, then too many times to count. Water Gourd tried to drop the animal into the sea, but it embedded its teeth into his forearm, locked them there, and would not release its grip. Dark clots of blood gouted from the otter's wound, and finally Water Gourd was able to reach his knife.

He plunged it into the otter's throat, but it took the animal a long time to die. Finally, as the otter's blood ebbed, so did its strength, and Water Gourd was able to use the blade to pry the jaws from his arm. He dropped the otter into the bottom of the boat where it lay with jaws clenched, feet scrabbling, gouging out wet splinters of cedar with its claws.

"Stay away," Water Gourd shouted to Daughter, and she kept her distance, staring with rounded eyes, one finger plugging the circle of her mouth. When the animal's death throes ended and it was still, she pointed at Water Gourd's arm, at the shredded skin that hung like a fringe from a wound that gaped from elbow to wrist.

"He eat you," she said.

Water Gourd's legs gave way, and he slumped to the bottom of the boat. A wound that horrible would attract spirits of illness. Fever would take him, and he would die. But he looked at Daughter and said in a loud voice, "No, he did not eat me. We will eat him."

SEVEN

Water Gourd's rush fiber coat was beyond repair. Seams, stressed by days in salt spray and nights without a woman's needle, had frayed and split. The otter's teeth had shredded the sleeve into tatters so fine that they were good for nothing but hook streamers—false promises of minnows swimming. Water Gourd bound the coat around him as best as he could using strips of fish skin.

Worse, far worse, his arm was nearly as shredded as his jacket, the muscle bared and bloody.

He washed his wounds in sea water, grinding his teeth closed over the scream that rose into his throat at the bite of the salt. What skin he could salvage he stretched over the wound; the rest—chewed into frothy strands—he pared away with his knife and added to his bait pile.

The deeper toothmarks and gouges still bled, and when Water Gourd had done all he could to clean them, he sat for a moment to calm his breathing, mindlessly watching the swirl of patterns made by blood in the water at the bottom of the boat.

Most of it was otter blood, he assured himself. He stretched his good hand toward the mess and spoke those words to Daughter.

She nodded her head, said, "Otter, him blood," in a soothing voice, as though she understood Water Gourd's need to believe what he told her.

He sat until his heart had slowed, until he felt a sleepiness begin to steal over him. His thoughts descended into a comfortable haze, then, for a moment, cleared, and he realized the trap of that sleepiness, brought on by shock and loss of blood. He forced himself to once again use his knife, this time on the dead otter.

He stretched the animal out in the bottom of the boat. He was too tired, too hurt to care about what the bloody water would do to the pelt.

Suddenly, foolishly, he couldn't remember how to butcher an otter. Should he cut off the head, like hunters did with seals, towing them behind their boats until the longworms that lived in the animal's intestines had fled the cooling body? Or should he cut from chin to anus, peel away the pelt, then empty the body cavity and squeeze out the contents of the gut into the sea? He finally decided on the latter. If there were longworms, he would deal with them when he found them.

He used his feet and his good arm to rip the hide away, did not bother to skin paws, head, or tail. He chopped each of these off whole, put them over the side of the boat with broken prayers, muddled and confused. He hoped that the otter's spirit would recognize his gratitude, in spite of his arm, and that the pieces would come together again as a whole animal, to swim in the sea. He stripped away thin slices of the muscle, gave some to Daughter, and ate one himself.

The flesh was thick and muddy-tasting, as salty as the sea, but when it had rested in his belly for a while, he felt some of his strength return. He lay the pelt, skin side up, over his lap, scraped away flesh and blood vessels and bits of fat, working slowly, stopping often to rest. Daughter sat watching him, her fingers in her mouth.

"Him blood," she said once, removing her fingers to point

at the bottom of the boat. Beyond that, she was silent, brow furrowed, eyes on Water Gourd's seeping wounds.

By the time night fell, Water Gourd had the hide scraped well enough to use as a blanket. He sluiced the water and gore from the fur, wrapped himself and Daughter, fur side in. For the first time since they had left the Boat People's land, Water Gourd was warm enough to sleep well, and in the morning, though his arm was stiff, he felt stronger.

He butchered the otter, sliced the meat thin, and plastered it up the sides of the boat to catch salt from the sea spray. He cleaned out the guts, sliced some into bait, left other pieces long to dry and braid. He saved tendons and sinew to make fish line, and the shoulder blades in hopes they could be fashioned into a paddle. He had forgotten to save the teeth before he gave the otter's head to the sea. How foolish! They would have made good fish hooks. At least he had the bones.

He and Daughter ate again. The meat wasn't good, but it was filling, and it gave strength, and being otter, it might even help guide them toward land. Perhaps by always eating fish they had prolonged their journey, content as fish were to stay in the depths.

Water Gourd's wound still bled, but a hard crust had begun to form over the muscle, making the arm less painful. He used a bit of otter gut to bait a hook, and fished most of the day. He caught nothing. Once, gazing out at the horizon, he thought he saw land, but with the haze of fog that rose from the water, he could not be sure.

The wind was calm, and he tried to be thankful for that, though he thought that a storm, if it did not swamp their boat, might drive them to some shore.

By night, his thoughts were tangling themselves into strangeness, as though he dreamed with eyes open. He wondered if he had given Daughter anything to eat. Yes, otter meat, he remembered.

And water? They had so little. He untied the gourd that hung from his waist and allowed her a sip, then took a drink for himself. When the sun set for its short night, he saw that

Daughter was shivering. Strange, Water Gourd thought. He himself was too warm. He wrapped Daughter into the otter pelt, felt her relax in his lap as sleep claimed her.

Surely his mind would clear if he could sleep, he reasoned, but his arm throbbed, and though he had loosened the ties that bound his tattered jacket to his body, he was still too hot. Finally he moved to one side of the boat, leaned over so he could settle his wounded arm into the seawater. The salt no longer burned, and the water pulled the heat from his body. He shivered, was suddenly too cold, and with the shivering finally understood that the wound had begun to draw spirits of sickness. He thought of laying Daughter in the bow of the boat where whatever evil he had drawn to himself would not touch her, but he was shaking too hard to let her go.

Finally his trembling woke the child, and she pulled herself away from him, stood up on spindly legs, her feet splayed. She stepped out of the otter skin and tried to cover him with it. He pulled her to his lap, wrapped them both in the pelt, and was finally able to sleep.

In his dreams, Water Gourd again battled the otter, but when he raised his knife to kill the animal, it changed suddenly from otter into Bear-god warrior. The warrior lunged at Water Gourd's throat, drawing back his lips so Water Gourd could see that the man's mouth was filled with otter teeth. He screamed himself awake and realized that Daughter, too, was screaming, shaking as hard as Water Gourd had been before he fell asleep. At first, he was afraid his sickness had claimed her as well, but when he soothed her with gentle words, told her he had only been dreaming, she stopped shaking. He cradled her on his lap until she again fell asleep.

The sky was still dark with no hint of dawn, and so Water Gourd knew he had slept only a little while. The longer they traveled, the shorter the nights had become. If he was home, in his own village, Long-day Celebration would be near. For a moment his thoughts strayed to the feasts that would be held in the Boat People's villages, but then he remembered the Bear-gods. There would be no celebration at his village, and who could guess what the Bear-god men had done to other Boat villages?

What if there were no celebrations at all? What would happen? Perhaps the sun, insulted by their negligence, would not linger the next year. Then winter would return too quickly, and the people would go hungry.

The Bear-gods were heathens and fools. Who could expect them to understand that all the ways of the earth must be kept in balance, one season with another, one village with another?

Water Gourd's anger rose, and he moaned in his helplessness. Perhaps he was the only Boat man alive on the earth, the only one who knew the ceremonies and the proper ways of life, and he was here in this outrigger, destined to go where the current took him, and now at the mercy of fever and illness.

He lowered his arm again into the sea. The elbow was swollen and impossible to straighten. Angry red lines streaked up toward his shoulder. The cold water helped deaden the pain. He wrapped his uninjured arm around Daughter and lifted prayers for a heavy rime ice on their boat by morning, enough to help refill the water gourds. He was so thirsty.

His prayers were answered. He and Daughter were awakened by the clattering sound of frozen rain, the stinging pelt of tiny ice balls.

Water Gourd, the ache of his arm so huge that it seemed to swallow his entire body, roused himself from dream-tortured sleep and began scraping up handfuls of ice, filling his mouth over and over until he realized that he must give Daughter ice as well, and collect enough to melt and fill his gourds. He lifted his head and opened his mouth, then pointed and nodded until Daughter did the same. She closed her eyes against the sleet, but kept her mouth open.

Like a little bird, Water Gourd thought, and tried to remember some prayer he could say in gratitude for what she meant to him. But all he could think of was a song men sing when the juice of fermented fruits and grains makes them foolish. That song was more about women than gratitude.

The ice melted to slush in the bottom of the boat. Water Gourd scooped it up until the fingers of his good right hand were numbed into a claw. He found his bailing gourd and used that, then with a ballast rock beat the ice from the edges of the boat. When he had filled all his gourds, he began to throw chunks into the bow, but finally, afraid the weight would sink them, he started to heave the ice into the sea.

The work drained his strength until he could do nothing but huddle with Daughter under the otter pelt, holding a deer hide blanket over their heads.

"Enough!" he finally bellowed, startling Daughter into tears. "We have longed for fresh water, begged for it until our mouths were cracked and parched, and now you give us so much that our boat sinks? What kind of gift is that?"

Thunder roared from the clouds, and Water Gourd cowered, afraid. How foolish of him to question the sky! Surely the spirits of pain spoke through him, for he was a man who knew the ways of respect.

The thunder came again, and again, then a crack of sound and lightening, the brightness so quick that Water Gourd would not allow himself to believe what his eyes had seen— a mountain in the distance.

"I dream," he said, and made himself small under the dark fur of the otter pelt.

EIGHT

His arm had cracked and was leaking pus. Water Gourd kept it now almost always in the sea, and once in the middle of a dream considered cutting it off, letting it float away. Perhaps then it would carry off the evil spirits of illness, but the thought never became more than that, an idea that he did not have the strength to act upon. If Daughter had been older, he might have asked her to do it, to cut the arm off and release him from the agony of putrefaction into the cleaner pain of the knife.

Thoughts of knives and cutting became so great that they pushed away all other dreams, and each time he awoke, Water Gourd was surprised to see the arm still with him, misshapen and discolored, skinned like the carcass of an animal.

Three days after the ice storm, he could no longer hold down food. The fever gripped his mind, and he grew to hate the sun as it burned through the fog and into his eyes. He dreaded night when the darkness confused him, tormented his thoughts with images of death.

Daughter's small face, pinched with concern, floated before him, and sometimes he felt her cool hands against his skin. But other times it seemed as though he had not seen her for days, and he worried that she had fallen into the sea. Did she know enough to stay away from the edges of the boat? Weren't children always falling—into water, on stony beaches, into hearth fires?

Then he would see her once again, her presence comfort enough that he would allow himself to sleep.

Daughter squatted on her haunches in front of the grandfather. She didn't know much about sickness, only that it frightened her, and she was afraid now. Sometimes the grandfather grew so hot that his skin almost burned her hands when she touched him, and at other times he was so cold that he shook the outrigger with his shivering.

She pulled a piece of otter flesh from the side of the boat and chewed at it. Most of the slices the grandfather had put there had frozen to the wood during the ice storm, and when the ice finally turned to water, the meat remained, hardened and stuck, as though it had melted into the boat. It tasted bad—sharp, bitter—and sometimes her stomach ached after she ate it.

They still had fish, gutted and tied to the outrigger poles, but Daughter was too small to reach them. Gulls had begun to swoop down and tear them away, battling with one another over each piece. They made her angry, those birds, stealing her food. What would the grandfather do when he woke up and saw that his fish were gone? Would he think she had been greedy enough to eat them all herself?

She found a water gourd and took several swallows, then held it up toward the grandfather so he would see it, but he didn't wake up. She pulled a little at the otter pelt he had wrapped around himself, but though he mumbled something, he did not open his eyes. She set the gourd down in the bottom of the boat and crept onto the grandfather's lap, pulled a corner of the pelt over herself.

She had forgotten her mother's face, but she remembered the smell of her and the good milk that came from her breasts, warm and rich and sweet. Grandfathers didn't have milk; at least this one didn't. If he did, he never offered it to her, but he was warm and was good at catching fish.

She looked down at her left foot, at the red scar on the side where her little toe had once been. It had hurt when he cut it off, but it didn't hurt now. She had thought it might grow back, but so far it had not. She remembered the fish the grandfather had caught with her toe. Her stomach growled when she thought of that good fish, its fat, oily flesh.

She was tired, but she tried to keep her eyes open. She didn't want to be asleep when the grandfather woke up. She needed to tell him to catch more fish. She raised her maimed foot to his face, held it there as long as she could, hoping that if he woke and saw it, he would be reminded of fishing. But finally she was too sleepy to do even that.

Her eyes closed, and in her dreams her mother came to her, offered her a soft brown nipple, and when Daughter sucked, it tasted like fish.

The grandfather's voice woke her. At first Daughter thought that he was crying. He began to struggle as though to free himself from the otter pelt. He thrust his good arm up, then brought it down hard. His elbow caught Daughter on the side of the head. The blow stunned her, and she cried out, rolling herself into a ball and sliding from his lap. It was night, but the moon was full, and Daughter could see well enough to understand that whatever the grandfather struggled against was outside the boat. She backed away from him, put her fingers in her mouth, and watched.

Something had hold of his arm, the hurt arm, the one he kept in the water. She wanted to see what it was, but she was afraid. What if it was a fish so large that it pulled him right into the sea? What would she do then? She wasn't strong enough to keep the grandfather in the boat. She began to cry, but finally crept forward and grabbed one of the grandfather's ankles. If the fish wasn't too big, maybe her strength would be enough to hold him in.

She looked at the grandfather's face, saw to her surprise that his eyes were closed.

"Open eyes," she called to him. "Open eyes!"

His eyes popped open and he stared at her, but still, he seemed as though he were a man asleep.

"Pull!" she said. "Pull hard."

He shook his head, blinked.

"Pull," Daughter said again.

He opened his mouth and roared such a terrible sound that Daughter lost her grip on his ankle and sat down hard in the cold water at the bottom of the boat.

But as he roared, he pulled his arm from the sea. It came up dripping with long brown strands, which at first Daughter saw as rotted flesh. She scurried to the bow of the boat, sat there on ballast stones that poked hard into the bones of her rump.

Then suddenly, to her surprise, the grandfather was laughing, laughing as he had when they caught the first fish. She covered her face with her hands, but split her fingers so she could see between them. He was cradling his arm on his lap, unwinding the brown. Eating it! Daughter gagged.

Then the grandfather sang out, "Kelp! Kelp, Daughter."

Slowly Daughter removed her hands from her eyes, looked at what he had on his lap. Yes, she told herself, it was kelp. Kelp grew near beaches. She remembered her mother peeling the stipes and cutting off small pieces for Daughter to eat. She remembered the strong salty taste of it. She pushed herself off the ballast stones, held one hand out toward the grandfather. He gave her a wet, slimy leaf, tough, nearly too tough to eat, but she took a bite, chewed, and swallowed.

It was not as good as fish, but better than otter. She sat down beside the grandfather, watched as he used his knife to harvest more kelp, then peel the stipes. Looking out over the side of the boat, she saw that kelp surrounded them. The sea was greasy with it. All the way to the edge of the earth where the fog lived, there was kelp.

The grandfather gave her more, and she ate until her belly was full. Then, as he directed her, she lay the long strands of peeled stalks down the length of the boat, the bulbed ends at the bow.

When the boat was full, he stopped cutting, and cautiously Daughter lay a hand on his cheek. His face was still hot and his arm looked terrible, but his eyes were clear. He ate more of the kelp, then again lowered his arm into the sea. Daughter didn't want him to do that. She wanted him to sit upright so she could sleep on his lap. She tugged at him, but he pushed her away.

"Sit down," he said. "Don't touch me."

Daughter stayed beside him, standing there, and thrust her lip out into a pout. He didn't tell stories anymore. He didn't want to hold her. She had wrapped her deerskin blanket around her, but it was wet and cold. The grandfather had the otter pelt. She squatted on her haunches beside him and slowly crept nearer until she was leaning against him and could warm herself with some of the heat that burned in his body.

She was very still, hardly taking a breath, and the grandfather didn't push her away or scold. She raised her fingers to her mouth, sucked, humming to herself, a song her mother had sung when Daughter was tired.

Her eyes followed the long strands of kelp, lying like rope down the length of the boat and up into the bow. Then she studied the sky, hazy and starless, the moon a blur of silver. Even during the day, the sky was seldom clear, almost always full of gray clouds or fog. She wondered where the sun hid in this world of boat and sea, so different from the village where her mother and father lived. She wanted to go back to them. She had tried to tell the grandfather that, but he didn't seem to understand, though once he had lost his temper with her and shouted, "No paddle. See, no paddle!"

Then, in her mind, she had seen the fishermen of her village taking their boats out into the sea, backs and arms straining, paddles dipping and rising. For the first time, she realized that paddles were what moved boats through water. With some surprise, she had looked around their boat, even stood on her toes to study the outrigger log, and saw that it was true what the grandfather had told her. They didn't have a paddle.

So the boat was taking them wherever it wanted to go, and who knew where that was? She wished it would turn around and take them back to the village, to her mother and her father, to the sun, which almost always shone there. She had asked the boat to do that. Many times she had asked it, but the boat stayed in the fog, in the cold, far from land. It was a boat that loved the sea, a selfish boat that gave no thought to Daughter or the grandfather.

Daughter shivered her way through the night, pressing as close to the grandfather as she dared. She slept only a little, and when the first light brightened the southeastern sky, she cupped her hands in the murky water at the bottom of the boat and drank. It was salt and blood and melted ice, but she was used to the taste.

She raised her eyes as she did each day to look for the sun, and finally saw a brightness in the clouds. She decided the sun was there, though she could not understand why it chose to hide. The grandfather probably knew why, but he was still asleep, his mouth hanging open, his eyes closed.

She sighed, and at that moment, the clouds parted, so a shaft of light fell to the sea, brightening it from gray to blue. The clouds were moving quickly, running over the sky, tumbling like boys playing games. She wondered if the sun was the mother, the clouds her boys, so large that they towered over her, blocked her from sight, like the little grandmothers in Daughter's village, dwarfed by their sons, grown men, tall and strong.

Daughter's eyes followed another rift in the clouds, waited until it centered itself over the sun so more light could get through. But then within that rift, she saw the peak of a mountain.

"Grandfather!" she called, and grabbed his good arm, tried to shake him awake. "Grandfather! Look!"

But the grandfather only pushed her away, mumbled angry words. She went to the bow, crouched on the ballast stones and began to talk to the boat.

"See," she said softly, "go there, to the mountain." She pointed toward the peak that pierced the clouds and seemed to float above the sea like an island in the sky. "Look," she whispered to the boat. "Look. Do you see it?"

She wished the grandfather would wake up, for surely he would know where the boat kept its eyes.

NINE

Yunaska Island, The Aleutian Chain

"Old Woman!" Eye-Taker called. "Do not come back empty-handed. Our husband does not need a lazy wife."

Old Woman turned her back, as though she did not hear what had been said, but she moved her fingers in a silent curse against her sister-wife, then squatted beside a small plant that was struggling back from winter, a beach plant of some kind, one she had not seen before. For now she would leave it, watch it grow, so she would learn to recognize it during all seasons.

That was the trouble with living in a new village, among these First Men. There was so much to learn. But surely one of the grandmothers would know if the plant was good for anything, or if it was harmful. Poisonous plants were too dangerous not to recognize, and people who lived a long time in one place knew which plants could kill or cause illness.

She was still studying it—fixing in her mind the way the stems branched, the shape of the leaves, the smell of it— when the thin, bleating cry came out of the fog.

At first the voice did not break through into her thoughts. It was a child's voice, high and full of tears. Old Woman did not like children. How could she, when her own family had turned against her? She should be an honored grandmother, doing the easy jobs of the ulax, tending the cooking fire, telling stories, but here she was, the lesser wife, searching for firewood in a strange land where the soil could not even grow trees, where the largest animals were the otters and seals that came to the beaches from the sea. No, she did not need the problems of some whining child to interrupt her work.

She glanced up for landmarks so she could find the plant again, then continued down the gray sand beach, picking up driftwood as she walked. When her arms were full, she would swing the sealskin sling from her shoulders, add the wood she had been carrying, then bend once more to her task. One slingful would not be enough. Eye-Taker would send her out for more, but Old Woman was good at stacking her wood slowly so she could get warm inside the ulax before having to go back out into the wet fog of the day.

She rounded a narrow point of beach, a small finger of gravel that protected a cove where the waves were generous. She was bent over a heap of branches when she again heard the child's voice, more clearly this time.

Strange, she thought as she straightened, arched her shoulders against the weight of the wood on her back. The voice did not come from the direction of the village or the hills. Had some child, playing in his mother's fishing boat, been swept out to sea?

She might not like children, but to rescue one—or at least go for help—would win her favor in the village. She untied the wood from her back and set the sling on the beach. She shielded her eyes with one hand, squinting into the haze. At first she saw nothing unusual, but then a darkness she had thought to be only a thin spot in the fog grew larger.

Old Woman was wearing a puffin skin sax. The long hoodless parka hung past her knees, and she wore no leggings, no boots. She pulled up the sax, balled it in one hand, and waded into the water. The cold numbed her skin and made the bones of her feet ache. She called to the boat, but received no answer, then saw a small white face peek up from the bow.

The child held a hand toward Old Woman, and Old Woman forgot about her sax, allowed it to drop into the water. She turned sideways to more easily take the force of the waves, and waited until the sea brought the boat to her. She clasped an arm over the edge, began to tow it toward shore.

The child, a girl, patted Old Woman's shoulder, and Old Woman shook her head at the sores that covered the girl's body. The child wore only the remnants of a parka, hoodless and made of something that looked like woven grass. From the waist down she was bare, more bone than meat, and her legs and feet were mottled blue around raw sores.

She looked like a First Men child, with a round face and small nose, her hair dark and straight, but when she spoke, holding out both hands as though asking to be taken from the boat, Old Woman did not understand her words. They were not First Men, not Walrus, not even the language of the River People.

Old Woman shook her head, held one hand palm up, and again grasped the boat, tried to guide it to shore. There was an undertow along the cove, and several times she lost her footing, but managed to right herself.

The boat was a strange craft, neither raft nor iqyax, but made of two logs, the larger hollowed out like the dugout canoes some River People used, and the other, much smaller, left whole, but shaped to a point at both ends. The logs were held several arm's lengths apart by four heavy poles that were lashed to the logs with bindings made of heavy rope.

Old Woman remembered how First Men hunters, when caught in storms on the sea, bound their iqyan together with their paddles to make a more stable craft, one that was less likely to be capsized. The man who had made this boat was no fool, but the craft had seen hard use.

It stank of old fish and worse. Slices of meat lay against

the sides of the boat, and many of them had rotted into the wood, making their own stink. Long stipes of bull kelp extended from bow to stern. They were fresh, and from the smears on her face, it appeared that the child had been eating kelp blades, though perhaps, from the smell of her, she had also been eating rotten meat.

A bundle near the back of the dugout was covered with an otter skin and a haired blanket that looked a little like caribou. The otter skin had been poorly fleshed, the smell told her that, but she could also see that chunks of fur had begun to loosen and fall out.

The bottom of the dugout hit the slope of the beach, and Old Woman had to wait for the waves to lift the heavy waterlogged wood. With each wave she pulled, moving the boat-raft a little farther until she was satisfied that the sea could not easily reclaim it.

The girl again put her arms out, and Old Woman lifted her from the dugout. The child was nearly as light as Eye-Taker's new baby, though the length of her legs made Old Woman guess she had at least three summers.

"How did you get in the boat?" Old Woman asked her.

The girl babbled something, and her words seemed to carry the same rhythm as the First Men's language, so Old Woman tried again, speaking more slowly in First Men, and then in broken Walrus. The girl covered her face as though in despair, but finally, with a shuddering sigh, she lowered her hands and turned to point at the heap under the otter skin.

Old Woman did not want to see what it might reveal. The smell was too overpowering, but the girl began to cry, so Old Woman carried her to the stern. With two fingers, she pulled aside the otter skin, and she gasped when she saw the man.

At first she thought he was dead, he was so pale, his eyes so sunken. His left arm was propped awkwardly on the edge of the dugout, and the skin had been torn away from wrist to elbow.

The girl pointed to him and said something. A name, Old

Woman guessed. The man's chest moved in a shallow breath, as though in response to the sound of the girl's voice. Old Woman repeated the word, then laid a hand against the child's chest. She screwed up her face as though she had been insulted and said a different word. Old Woman repeated it, stroked the girl's head, then patted her own chest.

"They call me Old Woman," she said, "though that is not my true name." She pointed at herself and said, "K'os."

The girl looked into K'os's eyes, pointed one small finger at K'os's face. "K'os," she said solemnly.

PART
TWO

TEN

Herendeen Bay, Alaska Peninsula
602 B.C.

"K'os!" Yikaas hissed under his breath.

Kuy'aa shushed him, but the name rang out loud in the earthen lodge. Qumalix stopped her story and looked at him, arched her brows in question. Yikaas turned his head and pretended to be interested in something near the curtained alcoves at the side of the lodge, but the girl was not shy, and she called, "Why do you interrupt?"

Yikaas bristled. Had she never been taught the correct way to address a Dzuuggi? She should have said, "There is one here who may desire to speak." Or better yet, "Sitting here with us is a great storyteller, well-known among the River and the Sea Hunter peoples. Would that one wish to say something?"

The girl treated him as though he were a child. He paused to gather his thoughts and rise above the anger that urged him to address her rudely.

"Honored storyteller of the Sea Hunters," he said to her, "surely you do not speak to me?"

"Yes, I do." There was no respect in her words. "We are

not Sea Hunters or even Whale Hunters, as the River People call us. We are First Men, the first to come to this land and to live on these beaches."

That claim had long been disputed by the River People, as the girl obviously knew. Yikaas heard a murmur of protest from the River traders in the lodge, then, like a low growl, the response of the First Men. The power the girl had inadvertently given him brought a rush of joy. He could lead all the River People out of the lodge. They would follow him. He began to stand, but Kuy'aa jabbed him with her elbow and said, "A Dzuuggi defends peace, not discord."

He sighed and sat down again, heard a release of breath move through the lodge.

"My apologies," he said to the girl, his voice taut with anger.

She smiled and inclined her head as though bestowing a favor.

Sharp words rushed into his mouth, but he pressed his lips tightly against them, swallowed them whole. They lay in his belly like knives.

"You have heard of K'os?" the girl asked.

"She was a River woman who lived long ago," Yikaas answered, "though we River have no pride in claiming her."

"Our stories of K'os begin with Daughter," Qumalix said, "the little girl whom K'os would name Uuluk. Can you tell us more about K'os?" Qumalix was no longer taunting him, but seemed interested in what he had to say.

Yikaas sighed. Why K'os? There were so many stories about honorable people.

"There are better tales," he said.

"But K'os seems to belong to both your people and mine."

"Yes," he agreed, glad to have her claim the woman. He drew in a long breath, then said, "The first stories we have about K'os tell of three River hunters who attacked her. They injured her so badly that she could never have children. According to those stories, she spent her life seeking revenge."

Qumalix nodded. "I have heard those stories. The honored woman who sits beside you told them once when we had gathered at the Walrus Hunters' village." She lifted her chin toward Kuy'aa, and the old woman murmured a few First Men words that Yikaas did not understand.

"I have also heard the Chakliux stories. He was the child K'os adopted as her son. We have heard about the fighting between K'os's River village and a neighboring village, how Chakliux—a man by then and trained as Dzuuggi—tried to bring peace, but K'os tricked the people into war. We have also heard how K'os betrayed her own village, and that Chakliux was able to save many of the people of that village, even after their defeat. We know about the woman Aqamdax. She was one of our own, a great First Men storyteller. She loved Chakliux and became his wife, although she had once been a slave of the River People."

Qumalix said the last words spitefully, as if what happened long ago were still an insult. Why bring up such a thing? Yikaas wondered. Didn't First Men storytellers also take on the role of peacemaker?

"We, too, honor the woman Aqamdax," he said carefully. "Her stories have been passed on, storyteller to storyteller, among the River People, so we will not forget how to forgive."

When he said this, Yikaas looked boldly into Qumalix's eyes, and to his surprise, she blushed.

She glanced away, brushed at the feathers of her parka, then squatted on her haunches, feet flat on the floor, arms clasped around her upraised knees. She lifted her chin, as though encouraging him to stand, and said, "Like the River People, we usually tell our stories while sitting, but there are too many in the lodge who would not hear you. Would you tell us more about K'os?"

Yikaas was so surprised at her request that he turned to ask Kuy'aa what he should do. From the corners of his eyes he saw Qumalix smile, and he felt the blood rush to his face. Was he a child who had to ask permission? To hide his embarrassment, he leaned toward the old woman, brushed his cheek against hers, and whispered, "Will I insult anyone by doing this?"

She smiled at him, her teeth no more than nubs above her gums. "Tell your story," she said.

He made his way to the girl's side, and with all politeness asked her to translate for him. She stood reluctantly, but Yikaas began his story without apology. She was the one who had asked him to speak. He had not begged for the opportunity.

"My story begins a few years before Daughter's story, and of course, it begins with K'os," Yikaas said. He spoke in a storyteller's voice, pitched deep to reach everyone in the lodge. "The evil in K'os had been there so long that it had rotted its way into her spirit," he said. "Like the otter meat in Daughter's boat, it had melded into her flesh."

A hiss of appreciation rose from the River People, and Yikaas smiled. He paused, and Qumalix spoke, translating his words into her people's language. The First Men nodded their interest, murmured their approval, and so the story continued, First Men and River words twisting around one another, twining like the weaver strands of a fine grass basket.

The River People's Village, Near Iliamna Lake, Alaska
Early Spring, 6452 B.C.

K'OS'S STORY

K'os stood in front of the elders' council, held her trembling so tightly within her heart that she could smile in spite of her anger.

"She has been a good slave for you?" Chakliux asked Gull Beak.

Gull Beak shrugged. "She taught me much about plants, but . . ." The old woman paused.

It seemed to K'os that through the years Gull Beak had come to look even more like a bird, with her small close-set eyes and a nose that hung nearly to her chin. Her back had narrowed and sprouted a hump, and her arms and legs, always too large for her body, seemed grotesquely so.

"But?" Chakliux asked.

"But it is sometimes frightening when a slave knows more than you do."

He gestured toward K'os's hands. They were misshapen, the knuckles swollen, fingers bent like claws. "Is she still able to sew?" he asked.

"Yes. She makes beautiful parkas."

K'os locked her eyes onto Chakliux's face. Sometime during this discussion he would look at her. She conjured tears to soften her gaze.

"I'm not a man who condones slavery," Chakliux said. "I think it is better for us that we own no slaves."

There was a murmur of protest from two of the elders: Gull Beak herself and the stuttering Sun Caller.

Wolf Head stood. He was tall; the thick thatch of his black and gray hair nearly brushed the domed caribou hide roof. "You would set her free?" he asked. "You can't trust her. Remember what she did to that young man whom I once called son? She bewitched him into taking her as wife, then made him steal everything from my cache. Now he is dead, as *she* should be."

K'os opened her mouth to protest. Was it her fault that men wanted her? Who could have guessed that the boy would steal a bride price from his father? Who could have guessed that someone would kill him so soon after he became her husband?

"I know as much about this woman as anyone," Chakliux said, "the evil she has done. My own wife was her slave, but there is one thing I cannot forget. Without her, I would be dead, sent to the spirit world as a baby because of my foot. I owe her a life."

"Chakliux," K'os murmured, extended her hands in supplication, blinked so the tears she had been holding in her eyes would fall. "What mother could love a son more than I love you?"

"Don't listen to her, brother," the man named Sok called out. "She has nothing in her heart but hatred."

Sok and Chakliux were full brothers by blood, but they did not look alike. Sok's face was wide-boned, thick-featured, while Chakliux's was narrow, refined. Sok's dark eyes slanted down at the outside corners and Chakliux's slanted up. Only now and again in the tilt of the head, in a full-throated laugh, could K'os see much likeness between them. For a moment, her thoughts went to that day when she had killed their father. With satisfaction she remembered the knife entering his heart, the surprise in his eyes. But that death was not nearly enough to pay for what he and his friends had done to her, what they had taken from her.

He had been a large man, and Sok was even larger, larger by far than Chakliux, wide of shoulder and as strong as any man K'os had ever known. But Chakliux was strong also, and his strength was that of the spirit, something that K'os in all her years of raising him had not been able to break. She had killed his first wife and their baby, had rejoiced when she heard of the death of his second wife. Now he had the Sea Hunter woman Aqamdax. Together they had made a son—a fine, healthy boy—and though K'os spoke curses against all three of them each day, some greater power seemed to protect them.

"You do not really know me, Sok," K'os said. "You have heard from others that I am evil, but I am not. As Chakliux said, I saved his life. His mother—your mother—didn't want him. He would have died on the Grandfather Rock where she left him as an infant if I had not decided to take him as my own son.

"It seems you will not listen to your own brother. Listen then to those people in this village who have benefited from my medicines. Would an evil woman heal people who keep her as slave?"

"Be quiet," Chakliux told her, and there was no softness in his voice.

She tried to force tears again, but anger had dried her

eyes, and she had to clench her teeth to keep curses from spilling out in words she might regret.

"My wife and I do not want to live in the same village as K'os," Sok said.

A murmur spun through the circle of elders.

Sok had more power than he deserved, K'os thought. Now that he and Chakliux had decided to return to this village, Sok was considered the people's chief hunter, though many of the Near River men coveted that honor. The Near River People had endured too many starving winters after the fighting. Though they had been the victors over the Cousin River People, many of their young men had died, and there were not enough hunters to feed everyone.

As a slave, K'os dreaded the deep cold of midwinter. She had fish to fill her belly, but fish is never enough to keep the cold from eating a woman's bones. Each night K'os could hardly sleep with the shivering that racked her body, and if dreams finally came, they were filled with the taste of caribou meat, dripping fat.

When Sok and Chakliux and the Cousin River men had visited the Near River village at the end of the winter just passed, they seemed to bring luck with them. It was the starving time of the year, yet the hunters took caribou and bear and even a moose. Then the people allowed their bellies to think for them, and they asked Chakliux and his people to live in their village. They began to call Sok their chief hunter, to honor him even above their own men.

Who wanted to live among a people so foolish that they could not think beyond a full cache and a boiling bag of meat?

"Set me free, and I will go," she said to the elders. "You will not see me again."

Sok shook his head, and Chakliux raised a hand toward K'os in warning. "I told you to be quiet," he said.

Then Gull Beak cleared her throat and said, "I'm an old woman, a widow without a husband. How can I survive without my slave to help me fish and gather wood?"

For a long time Sok and Chakliux whispered together, and though K'os could hear some of Sok's words, she could make no sense of them. He seemed to be talking about his wife. What foolishness! As if he must consider a young woman during a council of the elders.

Finally Sok raised his head, nodded at Gull Beak. "Many people have told me that you are a hard worker. They say there is no laziness in you. As you know, my wife is young, and I have three sons, one nearly grown and ready to take a wife of his own, but the other two . . ." He stopped and smiled. "Who, in passing my lodge, does not hear Carries Much complaining about the work he has to do? Who does not hear our baby crying most of the day? Would you consider being my second wife?"

The shock of the question shone in Gull Beak's eyes but did not still her tongue. "Could I keep my lodge?" she asked.

"If you are willing to sew for me," Sok said, and looked down at the parka he was wearing. The caribou skins were well-scraped and soft, but there was no beauty in the seamwork. "My wife has many gifts, but she has something yet to learn about sewing."

Gull Beak smiled, the smile of a woman suddenly worth something, and bile rose into K'os's throat, nearly choked her. Who in this whole village was better with needle and awl than she? Even Gull Beak's fine parkas could not begin to compare with what K'os could make, and everyone knew that.

As though Chakliux could hear the bitter thoughts in her mind, he stared at her until she lowered her eyes.

"Then there is no reason to wait," he said. "The sooner we get this settled, the sooner we can leave the winter village for our fish camps."

When the Cousin River People had agreed to come and live in the Near River village, they claimed and repaired empty lodges or lived with Near River families until they could make their own. They came with laden travois, with caribou fat and moose meat, dried fish and birds bagged whole in grease. Even their dogs were fat, and their children's faces were bright and round. The Near Rivers welcomed them into their warm, well-made lodges, and once again village caches were full.

But come spring, the people had decided to keep to their own traditions, to return to their own fish camps, though K'os had heard the council of elders encourage the men to visit one another, so friendships forged during winter would not die.

K'os shook her head at the marvel Chakliux had wrought in bringing the two villages together. Where did he get his power, her son Chakliux? Not from his worthless father, or the sniveling woman who had given him birth, not even from the man who raised him, K'os's dead husband, Ground Beater. Ground Beater had valued peace, but he had been a coward. Perhaps Chakliux had taken his power from K'os, his courage also, and the need for peace from Ground Beater. Why not? Most children hold some part of each parent in their faces—the eyes of a mother, the smile of a father—why not also a portion of the spirits of those who have raised them?

Chakliux left his place in the elders' circle and pulled aside the doorflap, but Sok followed him, whispered something into his ear. K'os hid her right hand within her left and signed curses against Sok's tongue.

Chakliux clasped Sok's arm as though in reassurance, and called out from the lodge. The young man, Cries-loud, came inside. If it had been some other boy, K'os might have hoped that they had decided to give her a husband, but Cries-loud was Sok's son.

"My son and his friends will take you to the Walrus Hunters' village and trade you as slave," Sok said to her.

"The Walrus?" K'os said stupidly, and stuttered on the name as though Sun Caller's broken voice had invaded her throat.

"If they do not want you," he said, "they can give you to the Sea Hunters."

The contents of K'os's stomach rose into her throat. She had heard stories about those Sea Hunters, how women and slaves spent days, months, tucked inside hide-covered boats to travel to their villages. How could she bear to stay within the close sealskin walls of a Sea Hunter's boat, tossed by waves, ever fearful of sea animals? What would happen to her spirit if she drowned? Would she live forever in the sea, never find her way back to the River People?

Fear brought anger, but then a soft voice came to her, a reminder of stories she had heard years before. Something had happened with the Walrus Hunters. Sok had stolen . . . no, killed . . . What was it? Then, suddenly pushing down from the smokehole, wind filled the lodge, brought with it the gift of remembrance. Again K'os heard Aqamdax's story voice. It came to her from the past, a day when Aqamdax had spun tales at some celebration.

She had told the people that she, Sok, and Chakliux had stopped at the Walrus Hunters' village, and while they were there, the Walrus's great shaman Yehl had died. The people had blamed Sok, Aqamdax as well, but Chakliux had worked his magic to bring them safely home to the River Village.

If the Walrus discovered that Cries-loud was Sok's son . . . Laughter bubbled into K'os's throat. Ah, but why let Sok know about the fine weapon she would take with her on this trading trip? She lowered her head, made herself shudder, then spat out careful insults, hatred bound by cunning.

Yaa sat outside in the lee of Aqamdax's lodge and tried to keep her mind on the sinew thread she was making, but with each twist of her hand, her belly also knotted until she could do nothing but stare at the elders' lodge, sit and wait for Cries-loud to come out. She knew what Chakliux had planned. During the night, she had heard his whispers as he spoke to Aqamdax. Usually she did not listen to their night conversations, those quiet words that often led to the joyous tossing and twisting of the two under their robes, for Aqamdax seldom slept on the women's side of the lodge.

Yaa's brother Ghaden, now with eleven summers, also slept on the men's side with his old dog, Biter. Yaa and Angax were left to sleep on the women's side, but Yaa did not mind that. Angax was a good boy with Aqamdax's round face, Chakliux's eyes, nose, and mouth. They had given him the name that had belonged to Aqamdax's first baby—the son that had been fathered and drowned by Night Man. He had five summers and was full of words, talking Yaa to sleep nearly every night. But the night before the elders' meeting, Angax had fallen asleep quickly. Then Yaa had heard Chakliux speaking to Aqamdax. There had been no teasing in his voice, and though Yaa had turned away from them on her bedding mats, pulled her robe up over her ears, some small part of her still listened. When she heard Cries-loud's name, she had shamelessly pushed her sleeping robe away so she could hear what Chakliux said.

She and Cries-loud were promised to one another, and by the end of the late fall caribou hunts, they had had enough hides for a lodge cover. Each day during that long winter, when her other work was completed, Yaa scraped and cleaned those hides. During the coming summer, when she wasn't cleaning and slicing fish, she would stitch the hides together into a lodge cover so that when she and Cries-loud returned from fish camp, they could live together as husband and wife.

Cries-loud wanted to give a bride gift for her, though in the Cousin River village, before the Cousin People came to live with the Near Rivers, the custom of bride prices and bride gifts had largely disappeared. With the village destroyed, nearly every lodge burned, with more women left than men, what father would demand a bride price? It was enough to find a hunter willing to take another wife to feed.

In the village they were already considered husband and wife, for sometimes Cries-loud stayed the night in Aqamdax's lodge, slept in Yaa's bed, though they did not do much sleeping. But they had not yet given a feast to celebrate. It would be foolish to do such a thing in the spring. Why consume all that was left in the caches during one day and night of eating? Better to portion it out carefully so the men had the strength they needed to hunt.

It was enough that when she and Cries-loud were together, he could not keep from touching her, always lifting a hand to brush at her hair, to cup her chin, to squeeze a breast. More than once they had endured the taunting of a group of children who caught them holding one another, or the tittering of an old woman who came upon them in one of the nearby willow brakes.

But Chakliux had decided that Cries-loud should be one of the young men to take K'os to the Walrus Hunters, to trade her there for whatever they could get.

Yaa lay in her bed that night, wishing for Cries-loud's arms around her, for his assurances that no matter what Chakliux wanted, he would stay in the village. Who could trust K'os? Even as a slave she could do damage. They had been with the Near Rivers only a few moons, and already Cries-loud's old aunt Ligige' seemed much weaker, and Twisted Stalk, that old woman sharp of tongue, had died, though she had seemed to be healthy and strong in spite of her age.

Yaa could not help but wonder if K'os, with her plant poisons or her curses, had caused that death. Apparently others felt the same way for the elders had decided K'os must leave. But why did Cries-loud have to be one of those who took her?

In the morning before the elders met, Yaa found Chakliux with his dogs. He had the best dogs in the village. Most were golden-eyed—those wise dogs long coveted by River men—and most could claim the brave dog Snow Hawk, dead now two summers, as mother or grandmother.

"Brother," she said quietly, and Chakliux, crouching beside one of the dogs, had startled.

"I didn't know you had left the lodge," he said, looking up at her.

She tossed her head, an insolence not of words. Her parka hood was pushed back to her ears, and the wind caught a strand of her hair, pulled it loose. "I need to talk to you."

"Here?" Chakliux asked, and stood to face her, brushing at a blaze of mud a dog's foot had left on his caribou hide pants.

"Here is good," she said. "I know you have to go to the elders' council." His eyes were a clear brown, and when Yaa looked at him, she always felt as if she could see into the goodness of his soul. "The council is about K'os, nae'?" she asked.

"Yes," he said, "mostly that."

"They will kill her?"

"I owe her my life, you know that," Chakliux said. "She was mother to me when no one else would be, but I think we are all agreed that she can no longer live in this village."

"So you will sell her?"

"Possibly."

"Where?"

"Not to any River People."

"The Walrus," Yaa said, and, lowering her head, admitted, "I heard you talking to Aqamdax last night."

She glanced at him to see what he would say, but the kindness had not left his eyes.

"Don't let Cries-loud go," she said. "K'os will try to do something to him to get back at you and Sok."

"Cries-loud is stronger than you think, Yaa," he said. "You cannot be a good wife to him if you also try to be his mother. Let him make the decision. I will not force him to go."

He told her to feed the dogs and left her standing there. Later, she took a chunk of caribou sinew outside and squatted in the lee of the lodge to twist the sinew into thread. When Cries-loud was called to the elders, she was there watching.

The wait seemed forever, but finally the doorflap of the

elders' lodge was flung open and Cries-loud came outside. Yaa stood, and the movement caught his eye. He motioned, and she hurried to him.

They walked out of the village, into the trees that overlooked the winter lodges. Cries-loud had grown into a tall man, as big as Sok. When Yaa thought about his mother, Red Leaf, she realized how much Cries-loud looked like her. Red Leaf's face, with strong features, was more like a man's than a woman's. She had been so gifted with needle and awl that people said her parkas could feed a village for a winter, they could bring so much in trade. But where Red Leaf's heart had been hard and evil, so that killing was nothing to her, Cries-loud was more like his father—though brusque and sometimes thoughtless, a good and fair man.

Cries-loud found a dry piece of ground, orange with shed spruce needles, and pulled her down to sit beside him.

"Wife," he said, "there is something I have to tell you."

"You plan to take K'os to the Walrus Hunters' village," she answered. The words fell heavy from her mouth. "I heard Chakliux talking to Aqamdax about it. Just you and K'os?"

"No. Squirrel and Black Stick and Wolf Head will go with us."

When she heard Wolf Head's name, some of her fear lifted. Squirrel and Black Stick were little more than boys, but Wolf Head was an elder still in the strength of his middle years. He would have more wisdom when dealing with someone like K'os. Perhaps, to avenge the death of his son River Ice Dancer, he would even kill K'os before they got to the Walrus village, and then the journey would be only a trading trip.

"I have always wanted to go to the Walrus village," Cries-loud said. He didn't look at her, but gazed out into the forest, as if he could see beyond the trees to the distant beach where the Walrus Hunters lived.

"K'os will try to trick you, or do something terrible," Yaa said. "Remember the curses she made against all of us when

Chakliux forced her to leave the caribou camp?"

"I have amulets to protect me, and my weapons."

"Don't eat anything she gives you," Yaa said.

"I'm not a fool."

His words were tinged with exasperation, like a boy speaking to his mother, and Yaa remembered what Chakliux had told her. She hung her head, angry with herself. Cries-loud reached for her, slipped his hands under her parka, and sought her breasts. He was impatient in his lovemaking, and Yaa had spoken to Aqamdax about that, how his hands were too hard and moved too quickly to bring her much pleasure, and how once he entered her, he worked only for his own satisfaction.

"Tell him what you want," Aqamdax said to her, as though she were surprised Yaa had not thought of that herself.

But as Cries-loud laid her back on the ground, as he pulled at the drawstring of her pants, she decided this was not the time to tell him. She had been mother enough for one day.

ELEVEN

Sok shouted out his news as soon as he came into the lodge, his voice raised to be heard above the baby's cries. "I have taken another wife."

Dii, their baby squalling in her arms, was arguing with Sok's son Carries Much about feeding the dogs. She turned her back on Carries Much and stared at Sok.

"Without talking to me about it?" she said, her voice so low and controlled that at first Sok did not realize she was angry.

As a child, she had been taught to show politeness, to close her mouth over hasty retorts and sharp words. So now, as usually happened when she was upset, tears scalded her eyes, and she turned her anger in at herself. How foolish! Why did she always allow tears to close her throat over what needed to be said?

"Who?" Carries Much asked, and stood with his arms crossed, legs spread in imitation of his father.

The lodge was suddenly quiet; even the baby was still, as though he were listening to hear the name of the one his father had chosen. The hearth fire popped and sent a circle of sparks up toward the smokehole. Sok pulled the moosehide mitts from his hands and strode to his weapons corner, pulled out a throwing lance as well as several arrow shafts, his back to Dii and Carries Much as though he had not heard the question.

"Your son asked you something," Dii said, and her voice was steady.

"Gull Beak," Sok answered, his back still to them.

He set two shafts back into place but kept the others in his hands. He turned to face Dii and said again, "Gull Beak."

"Gull Beak?" Dii repeated stupidly, and her anger drained as quickly as it had come.

"Which one is Gull Beak?" Carries Much asked.

"The old woman who lives at the edge of the village, not far from the river," Dii told him. She raised a hand to her face, gestured the shape of Gull Beak's nose.

Carries Much hooted out a laugh, but then, with a quick look at his father, clamped his lips together and said solemnly, "She's a good woman for a wife."

The compliment, usually given to a young woman by an elder, seemed strange coming from a little boy's mouth, and Dii had the sudden urge to laugh. But for fear of insulting Sok, she did not. One thing she knew, Sok would have a good reason for making Gull Beak his wife. He might be a strict husband, little given to jokes or teasing, but he was not foolish.

"A gifted seamstress," Dii said, and she smiled ruefully at the parka her husband now wore—warm but with no skill in the seams or cut, the amulet charms awkward in placement.

"She will make a new parka for you? For me, too, and for Cries-loud?" Carries Much asked, always concerned about his older brother.

"Yes," said Sok, his voice gruff. "Have you fed the dogs? They're barking."

"He was just leaving to do that," Dii said, and raised her eyebrows at the boy.

He scuffed a foot against the floor mats, gave an exaggerated sigh, and put on his boots. The baby had begun to fuss again, and Dii raised her caribou hide shirt, lifted a breast until he had the nipple in his mouth, then sat down near the hearth fire, batting at the smoke sucked toward her when Carries Much opened the doorflap.

"An extra fish for the white female!" Sok called after his son, then said to Dii, "She's pregnant again."

Dii knew, but pretended surprise. "Perhaps she'll give you more golden-eyed dogs," she said.

Sok shrugged. "Her pups are usually strong and healthy" he told her. "I have men who want them, no matter what color their eyes."

Dii raised her chin, pursed her lips into a firm line. She wanted him to know that she was not totally pleased, that at least he owed her an explanation. "Why?" she asked him. "Other than for the parkas."

"I don't want another wife," Sok said to her. He crouched on his haunches, set down his arrows, and leaned forward to stroke the side of her face.

She turned her head away from his touch, saw him frown.

"I had no choice," he said. "Chakliux wants K'os out of the village."

"It would be better for all of us if she were dead."

"And what man would kill her?" Sok asked, his words too loud.

Dii lowered her head. It was a question no one could answer. Who would doubt that K'os, even dead, could still be a threat? Surely her spirit would avenge her death, destroy those who had destroyed her. They might be able to bring a shaman from another village, buy songs of protection, even cut her body apart at each joint so the spirit would be bound to the gravesite, but as evil as K'os was, who could be certain that all those things would be enough?

"Chakliux wants to take her to the Walrus village, sell her there as slave."

"Will you go?" she asked, and she held her breath until he told her no.

"The only problem is Gull Beak," Sok said. "She needs someone to fish for her, to carry wood. You know who her husband was and how little he did for his wives. He couldn't even give them sons."

His eyes rested for a moment on the baby at Dii's breast.

"Some husbands are better that way," Dii said, and smiled at him. She did not regret that Fox Barking—the husband she and Gull Beak once shared—had not left her with a baby. What if the child had turned out to be like his father, lazy and cruel? But she knew Gull Beak had mourned her whole life for want of a son or even a daughter. What joy did an old woman have in living without children or grandchildren?

"She did not want K'os to be sold?" Dii asked.

"No. So I did what had to be done. Gull Beak will stay in her own lodge; she will sew, and in return I will hunt for her, as will our sons, and we will see she has enough wood and fish. She still keeps a trapline. Not even Ligige' does that anymore."

"And it will not be too much, to hunt for two old women?" Dii asked. Chakliux and Sok supplied meat not only for their own families but also for their aunt, Ligige'.

"It won't be easy, but Cries-loud is a man now, and Carries Much already has six summers. His strength will grow as Gull Beak's diminishes. And even that one," he pointed with his chin at the baby, "he will soon be hunting." He grinned at her. "Maybe by then I will have given you a daughter to help you with your work."

"I would be glad for a daughter," Dii said.

"As would I." Sok leaned forward, rubbed his cheek against hers, cupped a hand over the baby's dark head, then picked up his arrow shafts.

"Is Chakliux going?" she asked as he started toward the door to the entrance tunnel.

"Where?"

"With K'os to the Walrus Hunters' village."

"No, not Chakliux," he said, and something in his voice made Dii's heart press into her ribs.

"Not Chakliux," she said softly.

The doorflap settled down behind Sok, let a gust of new

air into the smoke of the lodge. She clasped the baby to her chest with one hand and went after Sok, crawling and stumbling. She pulled aside the inner doorflap, called to him just as he was leaving the entrance tunnel.

"Who?" she asked and continued after him, standing up in the snow and mud at the entrance of the lodge, her caribou shirt rucked up over the baby, her side and belly bare to the wind.

"Who, Sok?" she called, her voice strong enough to make him turn.

"Squirrel," he said, "and his brother Black Stick, and Wolf Head."

He paused, and she said, "Who else?" But she knew, she knew even before he told her.

"You have heard?" Yaa said. She came into Aqamdax's lodge, and the condition of her parka told Aqamdax what Yaa and Cries-loud had been doing.

"About K'os and Cries-loud?" Aqamdax said, answering question with question. "I knew last night. Turn around. You have spruce needles all over the back of your parka."

Yaa turned and waited as Aqamdax picked off the needles and scattered them into the hearth fire.

"Why did you let Chakliux choose Cries-loud?" Yaa asked.

"You think Cries-loud is not strong enough to stand against K'os?"

Yaa did not answer.

Aqamdax clasped Yaa's arms and stared hard into her face, then spoke to her as though Yaa were still a child. "A man will not allow himself to truly belong to a woman unless that woman is ready to let him be a man. Chakliux did not force Cries-loud to take K'os. He gave him a choice. Honor that choice, Yaa."

Yaa opened her mouth to speak, but began to cry. "He will never be content in this village," she said, the words coming broken from her mouth. "He'll always be looking for his mother. That's why he wants to go to the Walrus village. He thinks she's still alive."

"Then pray that he finds her," Aqamdax said, "and that if he does, he's wise enough to realize what kind of a woman she is."

"She's his mother. He sees nothing beyond that. He will never see beyond that."

Aqamdax settled herself on a pad of fox pelts and picked up the mat she had been weaving. "I hope that Cries-loud soon fills your belly with a child, Yaa," she said, her head bent over her work. "It's time you became mother to someone other than your husband."

TWELVE

They waited through two days of sleet and rain. On the morning of the third day, the new spring sun returned to burn through the haze, lifting the cold from the earth in great clouds of fog. They began walking, four men, four dogs, and K'os.

By midday they had left the familiar spruce woods for dense alder thickets. Branches caught in the dogs' packs and plucked at parkas, scratched faces until Wolf Head led them to the edge of the river, to that path of mud cleared by the ice and debris of spring breakup.

By night, they had come to the strip of tundra that was the buffer between the North Sea beaches and the forests, felt the teeth of winter gnashing in the wind from that sea, saw distant mountains of ice, white peaks created by wind and waves, now diminishing each day under the onslaught of the spring sun.

Wolf Head did not seem to worry much about K'os. After all, she was old. What harm can an old woman do? K'os kept a smile hidden in her cheek as she fostered that opinion. She stopped often as they walked, complained about her feet and her back and the load they made her carry.

She had nothing against the brothers Squirrel and Black

Stick. Squirrel had been well named. He was small and quick, with dark, round eyes and a hank of black hair that hung down over one side of his forehead. He spoke in a high, chattering voice, and was usually ignored by his brother. Like Squirrel, Black Stick was short, but he was thick of bone, with a sturdiness that made K'os dream of sharing his bed.

But Cries-loud deserved more than her indifference or her daydreams. Sok's son. Chakliux's nephew. He called himself husband to the young woman Yaa, though they had not celebrated with a marriage feast. He wouldn't get much out of Yaa in his sleeping robes, proud as she was, an old woman in a girl's body. Perhaps, for all that Sok had done for her, K'os should teach Cries-loud the joy of taking a woman who appreciated him.

When they made camp, Wolf Head told K'os to stake the dogs and feed them. Then he sent her to gather wood for their fire, not an easy task at the edge of the tundra, and for all her work, she brought back only sticks of willow and alder, which would burn slowly with acrid smoke and give little heat, less light. They would probably have her gathering heather during their next day's walk, that and tundra willow. How else could they have a fire? She carried her load of wood back to camp, saw that men had put up two lean-tos, open sides facing one another. She dumped her wood and laid a fire between the lean-tos, used a fire-bow and club grass fluff to get a flame started.

She warmed herself by crouching close until Squirrel ordered her to get more wood before the short spring night darkened around them. She hissed at him and stayed where she was, hands cupped around the tiny flame. Cries-loud came to her, grasped her shoulders from behind, and pulled her to her feet.

"Go now as you are," he told her, "or go bloody from my walking stick."

She lifted a hand to the side of her face, cowered as if she were afraid of him, and left the warmth of the fire. When she had gathered another armful of sticks, she returned to the camp, saw that Cries-loud had stood at the back of one of the lean-tos to watch her as she worked.

"Do you need a woman tonight, Tigangiyaanen?" she asked him, keeping her voice low so the others would not hear.

He laughed. "*My* woman, yes."

K'os snorted. "She's a child. What does she know about pleasing a man? When you take her to your bed, how long does it last for you?" She snapped her fingers. "That long?" she asked.

She walked past him, dumped the load of wood, and without being told returned to the thickets to gather more. At least there was a good supply of ice-broken limbs on the ground, scoured by the dry winds of a cold winter, so they were not as green as they might have been. She brought in three more armfuls, enough for the night, and each time she gazed boldly into Cries-loud's face, and if she spoke to him, she called him Tigangiyaanen.

Finally, as she brought the third armful, Wolf Head told her to sit down and eat some of the dried meat Gull Beak had given her for the trip. She chose to sit beside Cries-loud, and as she ate, she spoke to him boldly as if she were not a slave.

He ignored her and tried to begin a conversation with Black Stick or Squirrel, but they were tired, and only grunted at him. He asked Wolf Head questions about the Walrus Hunters, and once or twice Wolf Head answered. At those times, K'os listened also. She hadn't yet decided whether she would stay with the Walrus. At least with them, there was less chance of being killed for running away. She was only an old woman. Who would care if she left? One less person to feed.

But if she had tried to leave the Near River village, Wolf Head would have come after her, would kill her in revenge for the loss of his son. Better alive and a slave than to die under Wolf Head's knife.

From what Wolf Head said about them, the Walrus seemed to be a good people, full of laughter and joking. If so, she would not bother to tell them that Cries-loud was Sok's son. Why cause problems when she might decide to stay with them? She would work her way from slave to wife and from wife to healer. Once she was their healer, there would be no limit to what she could do. In sending her away, Chakliux had given her more gift than he realized.

The fire, though smoky, warmed her, and the food comforted her belly, so that she began to relax, and she allowed herself to dream of weapons she might use to kill those who needed killing. Lost in her dreaming, she nearly missed Cries-loud's question.

"I'm sorry," she said to him. "I wasn't listening. What did you say?"

"Why do you call me Tigangiyaanen?"

"You're a man now," she said. "You should put away your boy's name. Who better deserves to be called a great hunter, a strong warrior? Squirrel?" She covered her mouth with her hand, but fanned her fingers so he could see that she was laughing.

He smirked. There was an innocence about him that appealed to her, but with his mouth in a half-smile, he looked too much like Sok.

"Think about it. A new name is always a good thing."

She took another bite of dried fish. It filled her mouth with the woodsmoke smell of a lodge.

"No," Cries-loud said. "I will keep the name I have. My mother gave it to me."

"And you would honor her, the one who killed your own grandfather?" She snorted. "There are those who deserve honor and those who do not."

He looked into her face, and she was suddenly uncomfortable under his gaze.

"Perhaps you are right," he said, "but I need a person of honor to give me that name. I'll ask Chakliux."

She gritted her teeth and turned her left side to the fire.

"Rather you should name yourself," she said. "And while you are thinking of a name, think also on this riddle."

She glanced back over her shoulder at him, and saw she had his interest. Riddles were a game played often among those people who had lived in the Cousin River village. More than a game, riddles could teach, but they were also a way for women to say what needed to be said when men were too stubborn to hear the words outright.

> "Look, what do I see?" she asked.
> "It falls in autumn, taken by the wind,
> but the tree still lives."

"A leaf," Squirrel said, interrupting their conversation.

"That's a simple one," Black Stick told her, curling his lips into a sneer.

"And so you are right," K'os said, but she looked hard into Cries-loud's face. "The wind is always simple, nae'? And we always understand where it comes from and whence it blows."

For a moment, Cries-loud's eyes widened, then he feigned indifference. Did he understand that the riddle was about his mother, Red Leaf? K'os was not sure. But there were still at least two days' walking to the Walrus village, probably more.

Perhaps during that time, she would tell him that his mother once lived in the Four Rivers village, and that she had been wife to the trader Cen. K'os might not let him know that Red Leaf was dead. But she would probably tell him that he had a sister there, Sok's daughter. The girl would have five or six summers by now. If Cries-loud knew about her, he might decide to visit the Four Rivers village.

What a delight if Sok found out that Cen had taken Red Leaf as his wife after Sok had driven her away to die. How would Sok feel if he knew that Cen had claimed Sok's daughter as his own? And what would Cen do when he discovered that Red Leaf was the Near River woman who had killed Daes, the woman Cen had loved above all others? K'os smiled as she thought of Cen raising Red Leaf's daughter as his own, the girl given Daes's name. Surely that name did not rest easily, bestowed as it was on Red Leaf's daughter. Too bad Red Leaf was dead. She deserved the agony of Cen's anger when he finally knew the truth.

K'os swallowed her smile and called out to Wolf Head, "Which lean-to is mine?"

"You will sleep here with me," he said to her.

She gave him no argument, though her night might be better spent with Squirrel or Black Stick. It was easy to win boys with new pleasures.

She crawled on hands and knees to the back of Wolf Head's lean-to, said to him, "Unless you want me near the front to tend the fire."

"I will take care of the fire," he told her.

"And have the warmest place to sleep," she muttered under her breath.

"I've heard enough of your complaints today, woman. It's your fault that we had to leave our warm lodges and take you to the Walrus."

He pulled a rope from his pack, bound her ankles a handbreadth apart to hobble her, then tied the other end of the rope to his left wrist. Once they lay down, she brazenly reached over to pat his groin. To her surprise, she found that his penis was full and hard.

He slapped her hands away and said, "Some things a man cannot control, but there are always choices."

"What will it hurt?" she asked. "Surely you have heard that I am good at pleasing men."

"I've heard the stories. Who has not? But you were wife to my son. There are taboos."

"Once, long ago, you told me you had no son."

"Once, long ago," he said, "I was wrong."

THIRTEEN

The Walrus village was set near the sea, and during their last day of walking, Wolf Head led them across the wide silt plain. It was soft and wet underfoot, full of hidden rivulets, cold water seeping from the ice that had been driven ashore during winter—thick gray and blue slabs ramping and grinding themselves into hills and mountains, now rotting in the sun.

The silt held secrets, bubbling springs and sinkholes that would drop them suddenly to their knees, suck them down until they had to fight their way out. The dogs whined under their breaths as they walked, and K'os wished for a cold north wind to freeze the ground. But the wind blew from the west and by midmorning brought rain. Then K'os's wishes changed from thoughts of firm ground to a longing for one of Aqamdax's fine waterproof gut parkas. When Aqamdax had been her slave, K'os had owned several.

How much their lives had changed from those days, K'os thought. Now she was the slave, and Aqamdax was wife, her husband leader of the elders. Their village was strong with the hunting prowess of the Near River men, and secured by the wisdom of the Cousin River People. Who else but Chakliux could have convinced two villages that had nearly destroyed one another to come together as one people and live in peace?

Then, in her wish-making, K'os realized that she held one desire above all others: to return to that day long ago when she had found Chakliux as a baby, abandoned on the Grandfather Rock, given to the wind because of his bent web-toed otter foot.

If she had known then what her life would become, she would have left him to die.

Her right foot sank into the mud, and she faltered, catching herself on hands and knees. The men did not offer to help her, and she fought against the weight of her pack. When she regained her feet, she set her mouth firmly, rolled her tongue over the curses that she did not allow herself to speak, and lived again in her thoughts.

She had heard stories of shamans who were able to visit the moon and had ways to kill people with words alone, but she had never heard of anyone who could return to days already lived. So there was no hope of changing what had happened with Chakliux. Perhaps what she really wanted was another chance to raise him, this time with the wisdom she had garnered during her long life.

She wiped her face, sluiced away the rain. Fog hovered on the horizon. She blinked and looked again. Fog or smoke? Were they that close to the Walrus village?

She quickened her pace until she caught up with Black Stick. He was walking with his head down, the back of his hood taking the brunt of the rain.

"My eyes are old," she told him. "Do I see smoke or only fog?"

He looked up, and after a moment he stopped, frowned, then called to his brother. "Squirrel, is that smoke?"

"It's the village," Wolf Head shouted back. "We're almost there."

Then K'os began to shiver, her teeth clattering so hard that the curses she had held silent began to bleed out from the corners of her mouth. The cloud of her breath turned dark with whispered hate, and her words spun in the wind until they reached Wolf Head's ears.

He strode back, fisted a hand, and shook it in her face. "If your curses continue, I will kill you now, no matter what Chakliux wants." He made a sign of protection against her, then fell back to walk behind her.

K'os raised a mittened hand to her lips, pressed against her teeth until she was able to force the curses down her throat. Then, to battle her unease, she fixed her mind on the possibilities that would be open to her in a new village.

The Walrus lodges were stone and hide, set with their backs toward the sea on bluffs well up from the beach, away from the reach of waves. Wolf Head told the others to wait as he went on alone. K'os's heart rattled like a stone caught in the cage of her ribs. She had been sure she would be able to lure one of the boys to her bed during this journey and prise his loyalty from the others, thus giving her a chance to escape if she needed to. But Wolf Head had been cautious and kept her tied each night.

The three boys stood together in the rain, their hands clasped around their throwing spears. K'os huddled behind them, in the lee of their bodies, struggling to keep the dogs from each other's throats. She noticed that Cries-loud and Black Stick looked like men, while Squirrel still had a boy's thin shoulders and meatless legs. Squirrel and Black Stick clutched their spears to their chests, but Cries-loud held his weapon casually at his side, as though he often came to new villages and was not afraid, ready for either friendship or enmity.

Black Stick made a nervous dance, shifting from one foot to the other, and Squirrel squeaked out complaints in words that broke in mockery of the man's voice he would some-day own.

K'os sidled close to Cries-loud and asked, "Did you figure out my riddle?"

"Your riddle?" he asked, his words edged with irritation.

"We have no time for riddles." He turned and looked at her, then sighed and said, "It's about my mother."

"You do not care that I know where she went when she left the Cousin River village?"

"I have a wife now. I don't need my mother."

"But what about a sister?" she asked him. "It's always a good thing for a man to have a sister."

"My sister is alive?" he asked.

"Last I knew," she said. "A man who lives in the Four Rivers village has claimed her as daughter. Perhaps you remember him. His name is Cen. He's a trader."

"Cen?"

K'os laughed. "You're surprised?" she asked. "Your mother was no fool. You could learn from her. Cunning like the wolf. You wonder how I know? When Chakliux drove me from your hunting camp, I walked to the nearest village. Think for a moment. What village would that be?"

"The Four Rivers village," he said softly.

"Don't listen to her, Cries-loud," said Squirrel. "She lies. Everything she says is a lie."

Cries-loud opened his mouth as if to reply, but he said nothing, and finally turned back to watch the village.

K'os spoke into the side of his hood, leaning close so Squirrel and Black Stick could not hear what she said. "You remember Cen?" she whispered.

Cries-loud spun, and she saw by the set of his jaw that he was angry. "I don't believe you. Why would Cen take her as wife? She killed Daes, the woman he loved, and she tried to kill his son Ghaden."

"Cen is a trader," K'os said. "Think how many women he sees, how many villages he visits. Why would he remember what Red Leaf looked like? The last time he saw her in the Near River village, no one knew she was the killer. He had no reason to remember your mother's face."

"He would remember her name."

K'os laughed at him. "In the Four Rivers village they call her Gheli."

"So she's not dead," Cries-loud said softly. And though K'os knew he was speaking to himself, she answered.

"She wasn't dead."

The anger in his eyes was replaced by dread, and he was suddenly still.

"She died," K'os said, and found her heart lifted by the pain in Cries-loud's face. "While I was still living in the village, she died."

"How?" he asked.

Almost, she told him. The words—an illness of belly and bowel—were already sliding up her throat. But she caught herself, held them back. Cries-loud would think of poison, and he would blame her for the death. Instead she told him, "From childbirth and an illness that followed."

"The birth of my sister?" he asked.

K'os hid a smile. He was good at riddles himself, this boy. Good at snares. He should be an old woman. He had the cunning to catch and strangle. "Your sister was born before I found my way to the Four Rivers village," she told him. "Cen put another baby in your mother's belly, too soon after your sister's birth. But what else would you expect from a man who measures life by what he owns? Your mother died, and the baby also, a son."

She saw the sorrow in his face, so made her voice low and sad. "I'm sorry. The loss of a mother is not an easy thing. Perhaps the knowledge that you have a sister will lift some of your pain."

He turned away from her, and K'os crouched down on her haunches, rested her elbows on her knees, waited for Wolf Head to return.

Yehl listened patiently to the River man who called himself Wolf Head. The man was a warrior, but he had begun to grow old, and there was a weariness in his eyes that spoke of loss.

Yehl could understand pain like that. He still mourned his father, a shaman, strong not only of mind, but of spirit.

Only once during all the years of the old man's life had his judgment been faulty. Yehl leaned toward Wolf Head as though he were listening, but his eyes were seeing that time when his father was still alive. Then men easily brought in enough walrus to feed everyone in the village, enough seals for oil and hides. Their children were healthy and strong, their women eager to please. But all things changed when his father had welcomed a group of River traders to the village.

Yehl seldom allowed himself to think about what had happened. With a woman as powerful as Aqamdax—no doubt a witch who carried evil as easily as other women carry amulets—surely her curses would come back to them if Yehl allowed her to live in his thoughts.

For a year he had mourned his father's death. For a year he had kept himself away from women, had cut his flesh and bled into the hearth of his lodge. Had cut his hair and torn his parkas. When that year had ended, he took his father's name, Yehl, and also took his place as shaman. What better way to keep the old man's spirit alive and in this village?

Even now, as he spoke with Wolf Head, Yehl felt his father hovering over them, and the old man's strength gave him confidence. After all, what could these River People do to harm this village? They were only traders, looking for a few baubles. There was a slave, too, Wolf Head had told him, a woman to carry their packs, a woman good in a man's bed. What would it hurt if they stayed a day or two? Weren't the Walrus Hunters known for their hospitality?

"Their chief hunter has given us permission to come into the village and trade," Wolf Head said.

Squirrel snorted out laughter. "And what did we bring to trade besides this old woman?"

"I told you to bring something to trade, nae'?" Wolf Head said. "You have dogs to carry your packs."

"Young men must save their caribou hides for bride prices," said Black Stick.

"That's your choice," Wolf Head told him. "Don't complain about it to me."

Black Stick scowled. Wolf Head lifted his chin at K'os, gestured for her to follow, then said to Cries-loud, "You three do what you want. Stay here or come. Don't make any trouble with their hunters."

Wolf Head led, and K'os was next with the dogs. Cries-loud, Squirrel, and Black Stick walked behind them, each holding weapons, eyes challenging anyone who came close.

The lodge was set near the center of the village, and when she saw it, K'os began to long for the heat of a hearthfire.

She tried to accompany Wolf Head into the entrance tunnel, but he pushed her back, made her wait while the boys crowded ahead. Finally, after she had staked the dogs and fed them, she was allowed in, told to bring her packs. Squirrel held the inside doorflap open as she stooped to maneuver the packs through the door.

Her knees creaked as she stepped into the lodge, and a cramp spasmed across her shoulders when she stood to her full height. But the warmth was wonderful, soft against her face after so many days walking the tundra.

Wolf Head spoke to the Walrus men in their language. He spoke slowly and with many pauses, but K'os knew only those Walrus words she had picked up as a young woman when she welcomed a Walrus trader into her bed, and those were not words men spoke to discuss trade goods.

The Walrus leader wore many necklaces, and his hair was strung with beads and feathers. He held himself straight and stiff, but K'os thought she could see something close to fear in his eyes. He was tall, thick both of arm and of belly. His nose was as narrow as a gull's bone and had been broken and poorly set. He squinted when he spoke, as if his words came not only through the efforts of his mouth but also his eyes.

He called himself Yehl. K'os knew she had heard the name before. Was there not some shaman from the Walrus people who had also used that name? But that had been years ago. Perhaps this new leader was son or grandson of the old shaman, and the power of that man's name had clouded the people's eyes, so they did not realize that this new Yehl was less than they thought.

K'os was so intent on watching him that she nearly missed Wolf Head's signal. He wanted her beside him. She tried to move gracefully under the weight of her pack, and when she came into the light from the smoke hole, she set a smile on her face. Wolf Head murmured for her to show Yehl one of the parkas she had made. She crouched, untied her pack, and pulled out a ground squirrel parka, soft and warm.

She watched Yehl as he unrolled it, clenched her teeth in triumph when she saw the wanting in his eyes. For the first time, he looked at her. She made her smile into a slave's smile, shy and humble, and she wondered how much of her young beauty still showed in a face that was growing old. Even her hair had begun to betray her with strands of white, and her hands grew more gnarled each year.

Yehl asked a question and Wolf Head grunted an answer. He nodded at K'os and told her, "He asks if you have ever been a wife."

In a quiet voice, K'os said, "I had two good husbands before I was taken as slave. One was chief hunter of the Cousin River village. Perhaps you have heard of those people."

Wolf Head translated her words, and Yehl spoke in reply. "He knows the village," Wolf Head said.

"Perhaps then he has heard of my husband Ground Beater."

When Wolf Head asked, Yehl inclined his head, considered for a moment, then raised his fingers in the traders' sign for *no*.

Wolf Head spoke, then explained, "I told him that Ground Beater was a good man."

"Thank you," said K'os, though she knew he thought only of himself. The more he could get for her, the better for him, the better for the River Village.

Yehl asked something, and Wolf Head said, "He wants to know what happened to your husbands."

It was a dangerous question. A woman who was widow might carry some curse from her dead husband to a new husband, and K'os had been widowed twice, three times counting River Ice Dancer, but why bring up a young man who had shared her bed for only a few nights? She spoke slowly, carefully.

"My first husband was given to me when I was a girl. My father chose him because he was an honored elder. He was very old, but he lived a long time after we married and died in his sleep, full of years and full of honor."

She waited while Wolf Head translated, then she continued. "As I told you, my second husband Ground Beater was chief hunter of our village. He had traveled to another village to trade. While there, he stayed with an old woman in her lodge. She was careless with her fire and during the night the lodge burned, killing my husband, and the old woman and her husband as well.

"Not long after that, my village, the Cousin River village, was destroyed by the Near River men. I was taken slave, and have been slave ever since."

Again she paused, and waited for Wolf Head. Yehl nodded, gave trader signs to say that he had heard of the fighting between the Near River and Cousin River villages. Who had not?

K'os lifted her shoulders in a shrug. "Many of us were taken as slaves," she said, "though now the villages are at peace, and most of the slaves have been adopted or taken as wives. But who in the Near River village can trust me? I was wife of the chief hunter. They fear I seek revenge. So I am still slave."

Wolf Head held one hand up as though to stop her words. This time when he spoke to Yehl, he spoke for a long time, so that K'os began to wonder whether he translated what she had said or made up some story of his own.

Her heart thumped hard in her chest, pulsing in her wrists and at the sides of her neck. She was angry at her fear. This Yehl would be easy enough to control. Why worry? Wolf

Head didn't want to kill her and risk a curse. He would leave her here. Her heart slowed, and she nearly smiled. No. Be still, be silent, she told herself. All your dread was foolishness, but do not tempt Wolf Head with a smile.

Yehl watched the slave woman as the River man spoke. Wolf Head's words were broken, and his accent was strange. More than once Yehl had to ask him to repeat what he had said. Yehl wanted the woman, but he tried to keep all evidence of that wanting from his eyes. She was old, perhaps beyond the years of bearing children, but any man could see that she still held the beauty of her youth. Her hair was thick, and her skin smooth. She kept her hands tucked up the sleeves of her parka, but once or twice as she spoke, she used them to emphasize her words, and he had noticed that they were misshapen, the knuckles swollen, the fingers twisted. Most men would be put off by those hands, but his own mother's fingers had been the same way, gnarled and bent and often painful, even when she was a young woman. She had still been able to sew and do all the things a woman must do.

If this woman could sew, if she truly had made the parka, as Wolf Head insisted, then she would be worth much, as slave or as wife. There seemed to be nothing to worry about in her husbands. One had lived to be a very old man, and that was good. The other was chief hunter of his village. Perhaps she had brought him bad luck, but more likely the bad luck had come with the old woman whose lodge had burned.

Finally Yehl interrupted Wolf Head's blathering to ask, "What do you want for her?"

Wolf Head seemed surprised by the question. When he did not answer, Yehl said, "She is old. I cannot give you much."

"Three sealskins of oil, and the split hide of a walrus," Wolf Head replied.

"The parka comes with her?"

"For that I need another sealskin of oil."

"I will give you the oil for the parka," Yehl said, "and though I am sure, as you told me, that she made this parka, her hands worry me. Perhaps she made it long ago, when she was young."

K'os saw the consternation on Wolf Head's face. "What's wrong?" she asked.

"He thinks you did not make the parka."

"Tell him to give me an awl and needles, a woman's knife, and skins to sew."

Wolf Head made the request, and Yehl spoke to one of the older women who had crowded in at the back of the lodge. She brought K'os a needle, knife, and awl, handed her a sealskin. Before she began to sew, K'os slipped off her own parka, gave it to Wolf Head.

"Show the women this one," she said. "Who else would make a slave's parka but the slave herself?"

There was nothing fancy about it, no shoulder tufts of fox fur, no insets of frost-whitened gut, no beads, no feathers. But anyone could see the quality of the work; anyone could see how well it fit her.

Several Walrus women studied the parka, turned it fur side in to check the seams. Finally the oldest raised her eyebrows in grudging admiration. K'os bent her head over the sealskin as the old woman spoke.

"She says it is a good parka, a fine parka," Wolf Head whispered to K'os.

K'os did not answer. She worked as quickly as she could, punching holes with the awl. Then she knotted the sinew thread around her needle and made her seam, the stitches small and even and tight. Without speaking she handed the sealskin to Wolf Head. He gave it to Yehl. Yehl looked at it, then glanced at K'os. His eyes stopped on her breasts, on her waist and the small bulge of her belly, peaking up from the drawstring of her pants.

He is mine, K'os thought, and she smiled at him. He nodded to the old woman, and she gave K'os back her parka.

K'os slipped it on over her head, passed her hands quickly over her breasts. He would take her as slave, no doubt. A slave cost less than a wife. But once she had won her way into his bed, there would be no end to her power.

FOURTEEN

Herendeen Bay, Alaska Peninsula
602 B.C.

Yikaas was so caught in his story that for a time he continued to speak over the words of those around him. Then he
realized that the comments were not the usual murmurs of
approval storytellers expect. Women were whining, old men
complaining; two young mothers, babies tied to their chests,
got up and left, shaking their heads as if to empty their ears
of his stories. A Sea Hunter man raised his voice in rudeness, shouted out something that sounded like an insult.

Yikaas looked at Qumalix, lifted his hands in question.

She spoke to her people, listened to their replies, and
when she finally turned to Yikaas, she said, "They are tired
of your story. They do not know the people you talk about,
and they do not like K'os."

"Of course they don't like K'os," Yikaas said. "She's selfish. She's evil."

Qumalix shrugged. "So they do not want to hear about
her. She makes them angry."

"Sometimes stories do make people angry," Yikaas said.

"If we don't hear about evil, how will we understand what is good? Besides, your story about Daughter ends with K'os."

"I am glad to learn about K'os," Qumalix said. "But that is because I am a storyteller, and the more I know, the better my stories become." She stretched a hand out toward the people sitting in the lodge. "My people say they have learned enough about K'os. Perhaps it is time to talk about Chakliux or Sok. They seem to be good men. Why not tell us their stories?"

An old Sea Hunter woman stood. Her face was as lined and brown as tree bark, and she spoke in a reasonable voice, without whining, without complaining. When she had finished, Qumalix said to Yikaas, "This old woman is known for her wisdom, and she has raised three strong sons. She says it is good to know and to understand a little more about a woman like K'os. But she also says that her ears are heavy with hearing about one so wicked, and now she would rather have another story about Daughter."

Though his heart burned with anger, Yikaas was polite, and he took his place with those who listened. But as Qumalix spoke about Daughter, her words were only words, and he could not lose himself in the story. Instead his mind strayed back to what he had told the people. His voice had been strong, his words well chosen, yet they did not like his story.

Maybe the fault was not with him but with the Sea Hunters themselves. Perhaps their minds were like the minds of children, and they needed simple stories that were easy to understand, stories like the one about Daughter.

He sighed and turned his thoughts back to Qumalix's tale, but still he found nothing good in it, and finally when he had listened long enough so that his departure would not seem impolite, he rose quietly and left the lodge.

He walked down to the inlet, crouched on his haunches, and stared out at the water. An eagle was perched on a sandbar, tearing at a fish it held in one claw. When it finished eating, the bird spread its wings and lifted itself into the sky until it disappeared into the clouds.

Yikaas wished he could as easily leave his memories of the storytelling. The wind blew sand into his face, scoured his skin like the Sea Hunters' criticism had scoured his heart. He felt as though he were a little boy, unsure of himself, and he not only doubted his stories but also began to wonder if Kuy'aa had been wrong in making him Dzuuggi. After all, she was an old woman. What did old women know? They did not hunt and so learned little from the animals. They seldom traveled to other villages. What was any woman's life but the lodge she kept for her husband and the children she gave him? How could you expect to gain wisdom from that?

He heard a scraping in the sand behind him, and turned to see that Kuy'aa had followed him to the beach. He was disgusted with her. Couldn't she see that he needed to be alone?

"Why are you here?" he asked, and his voice was rude.

She looked at him as though he were a naughty child, her eyes as hard as limpet shells. Slowly, she lowered herself to sit in the sand beside him, and the wind blew the sparse white strands of her hair back from her forehead.

"I came to talk to you about your story," she said.

"They don't know anything about storytelling, those Sea Hunters," said Yikaas.

"You're sure?" she asked. "How strange that they know nothing about storytelling when they've been listening to stories all their lives. They must be very stupid."

"I've been telling stories all my life," Yikaas said. "I know more than someone who has only listened."

"And you are so old," she said.

"If you have nothing more to offer than ridicule, then I waste my time here at this village," he said. "I know my way home. I don't have to wait until the traders are ready to return. I'll go alone."

"That would be foolish. You would miss all of Qumalix's stories."

Yikaas scowled at her. "Why should I listen to her stories? She doesn't want to hear mine."

Kuy'aa was quiet for a long time. She pulled a shaft of beach grass from the sand and began to shred it with her thumbnail. "You're wrong," she finally said. "Perhaps some of the Sea Hunter people do not want to hear you, but Qumalix does."

"She told you that?"

"What storyteller does not want to hear new stories? Old stories comfort us, and new stories teach us. We need both, but I think there is something here you do not understand. You and I, we are storytellers, and we listen so we can learn. The people listen so they can live the stories. Your tales of K'os are good, but who wants to become K'os? Would you?"

"Of course not," Yikaas said. "K'os is a woman. What man wants to become a woman?"

She chuckled. "What if all things were the same about K'os, except that she was a man?"

Yikaas was not so quick with his answer. He found a stiff strand of beach grass, set it between his thumbs, then blew against it until the grass whistled a long, clear sound into the wind.

He looked up to see Kuy'aa smiling, and in his heart he felt a stirring of anger at himself, at the child who lived too close within. He dropped the grass and watched as the wind caught it, made it dance across the beach.

"No," he answered. "I would not want to be K'os, even if she were a man."

"Now do you understand why the Sea Hunters do not want to listen to your story?"

"But they need to hear about K'os."

"Of course they do, but there are many ways to tell a story. That is both the problem and the joy of being a story-teller. And that is why I'm here. To tell you how to make your stories better."

"I'm a good storyteller. Better than Qumalix."

"Yes, you are a good storyteller," the old woman said. "I will not argue with you about that. But do not ask me to say that you are better than Qumalix or any other storyteller. How can storytellers be compared one to another?" She lifted her shoulders in a shrug. "We are all different. If a storyteller touches your heart, then his stories are the best for you. That's why one storyteller is good for one person, and not for another. You can't change that, so why worry about it? But if a storyteller closes his ears to other's stories, how will he grow?

"Each of us sees the world through different eyes, and that's the greatest gift any storyteller can bestow—the gift of vision, and the growth that comes in understanding that vision."

"So is Qumalix still telling her stories?" Yikaas asked, interrupting Kuy'aa.

She glanced at him from the sides of her eyes and sighed like a mother with a child. "People were tired and hungry," she said, "so the storytelling is over until tomorrow. But I hope you will come back with me then."

"To hear Qumalix?"

"No. The people have asked me to tell the stories of Chakliux and Aqamdax. Will you come?"

"Of course I will come."

Her pleased look brought a grudging smile to his lips, and he thought she would say more. She was usually a woman of many words. But she only said, "I'm hungry. Help me up."

He stood and offered his arm, held her until she was steady on her feet.

"Are you coming?" she asked.

"Later," he told her, and watched as she tottered away, awkward as a puffin on the sand.

Again the earthen lodge was full of people. Again Yikaas took one of the honored places reserved for storytellers, and as Kuy'aa began her stories, her voice carried him to times long ago. Once again he was captured by the tales of Chakliux and Aqamdax. He became the man who was animal-gift to the River People, and he found himself filled with Chakliux's wisdom, with his strength.

It was nearly dawn when the old woman completed her tales. By that time new people had come and others had left, but the lodge was still full. Yikaas could see the light of Kuy'aa's stories in the faces of those who listened. They had earned wisdom and new ideas. A fair exchange for a night of lost sleep.

He could see that Kuy'aa was tired, and he went to her so she could lean against him. He helped her up the notched log to the top of the lodge and down the slippery grass thatching of the roof.

"You need to sleep, Aunt," he told her.

"How can I sleep, boy?" she asked him. "Chakliux and Aqamdax still dance in my head. I will walk for a little while in the wind, and when I am ready, I will sleep." She lifted her chin at him and reached out with a wrinkled hand to stroke the wolf fur that rimmed his parka hood. "Go back and listen. Qumalix is the next storyteller. This time see what you can learn from her. Listen with a true heart, then come and tell me what you think."

She turned and walked away from him, and he watched to be sure that her step was steady. When she reached the path that led to the beach, he climbed up the roof of the lodge and let himself in through the square opening that was smokehole as well as entrance.

Qumalix was in the storyteller place, and she was telling the same tale—the one about Daughter. But Yikaas had promised that he would listen, and so he took a place in the lodge, not one of the storytellers' seats, but a cramped, dark niche near the climbing log. He listened not only as a storyteller but also as a man so he would learn without prejudice, so he would hear without jealousy.

Soon her voice pulled him away into another place. He forgot that he was sitting in a Sea Hunter lodge, listening to a Sea Hunter woman. Instead, he became Daughter. He became Water Gourd, and he saw the world anew.

FIFTEEN

Yunaska Island, The Aleutian Chain
6447 B.C.

DAUGHTER'S STORY
Daughter pulled the otter pelt more tightly around her shoulders and made herself as small as she could. They were out of the boat, and for that she was glad, but by some magic, the old woman had taken them inside the earth, and Daughter was afraid. By another kind of magic, the woman had made fire on a rock, and now she was doing something to the grandfather's arm with knives and cutting stones.

Daughter allowed herself a glance at the thick layer of earth above them, and she wondered if they were dead, she and the grandfather and this old woman. She had seen the death rites for one of her aunts, how they put her in the ground. Had someone given them death rites and buried them?

The floor was covered with grass, cut and scattered. Daughter had dug one foot through it and found hard-packed earth underneath, like the floor in her own father's *iori*. It gave her some comfort, that floor. To have dirt under her feet, not boat, not water.

As small as it was—a circle of flames dancing above a rock—the fire threw off a good amount of heat. Daughter, so long in the cold of their boat, shivered at the warmth. Over the stone, the old woman had hung a skin bag full of water. She had put all kinds of things into that water, though none of it seemed like food, unless dead people ate dust and leaves rather than fish.

The woman dipped into the bag with a bone ladle much like the one Daughter's own mother had used, then she lifted the grandfather's head and pressed the ladle to his mouth. The grandfather moaned, but though his eyes were closed, he drank. Suddenly he gasped, choked, and turned his head away. The old woman pinched his nose shut, and when he opened his mouth to take a breath, she poured the rest of the liquid down his throat. He gagged and choked again.

Daughter leapt to her feet and ran to his side, her small hands balled into fists, her teeth bared. The old woman looked at her, surprise rounding her eyes, but she tipped back her head and laughed. She spoke in words that Daughter did not understand, and as she spoke she used her hands to give the words meaning. She directed Daughter's eyes toward the grandfather's arm, swollen and purple and oozing pus. Then she raised a knife. The blade was so black and glossy that it looked like water frozen into stone. It caught the light from the fire and seemed to glow in the old woman's hand.

She motioned to show Daughter that she would use the knife on the festering arm. The old woman had fed Daughter a piece of fish, and now it rose into Daughter's throat. She leaned over and vomited on the floor. The woman hissed at her, shouted angrily, then pushed Daughter back toward her place against the earthen wall. Daughter hunkered on her haunches, and the old woman crouched beside the grandfather. Her knife flashed light. Daughter covered her eyes with her hands, tried to stop up her ears by hunching her shoulders as the grandfather cried out again and again.

When he finally stopped screaming, Daughter slowly took

her hands from her eyes. The old woman had removed her feathered coat and was bare from the waist up. Her face was wet, as shiny as her knife, and little rivers of sweat made paths between her breasts.

Daughter gathered her courage and said, "Do not hurt him anymore." But her voice was tiny, and it seemed as though the earth sucked up the sound of her words. The old woman did not even look up from what she was doing. There was a sharp crack, stone against bone, another garbled cry from the grandfather, and then the old woman lifted the severed arm.

Blood dripped to the grass on the floor, and Daughter turned her back, leaned her head against the cold earthen wall, and wept. What would the grandfather do without his arm? How could he carry water? How could he fish?

She stayed huddled beside the wall until the old woman came and pulled her away. Daughter kept her eyes squeezed shut to close out the remembrance of the blood and the knife. She wrapped her arms tightly around herself in fear that the old woman would decide to cut her as well, but the woman only picked her up and crooned a song in a voice that was rich and comforting.

At first Daughter held herself stiff and still, but finally she ventured to turn her head, look at the grandfather. He seemed to be asleep, his face peaceful, as if he dreamed good dreams. Daughter's eyes filled with tears as she thought of his sadness when he awoke and saw that his arm was gone. If she could find it and somehow save it, then maybe the grandfather could sew it back on, like her mother sewed sleeves on a coat.

She scanned the floor for the arm. The bloodstained bundle was lying near a notched log that rose from the floor to a square hole in the earth. Above the hole it was dark. Did the log lead out into the night, or was the darkness only more dirt above them? When the old woman had taken them from the boat, there were other people who helped her, but one of them had wrapped Daughter in a fur blanket, had covered her so completely that she had not seen how they got down into the earth.

When the old woman finished her song, she gave Daughter water and more fish. The fish smelled good, like the smoke of a cooking fire, and Daughter tried to eat, but her throat seemed too small, and it was difficult for her to swallow. Finally the old woman gave her a cup of broth, but after one sip, Daughter drank no more. The woman made her a bed, padded with furs and layered with otter skins, sweet smelling, like the skins her own mother used for their beds.

She took the wooden cup from Daughter's hands, said something that Daughter did not understand, then lifted her chin toward the bed. Daughter crept into the furs, made herself a nest, closed her eyes, and pretended to sleep. But as she lay there, she thought of how she and the grandfather could sew his arm back on. If the old woman had knives, she must have needles and sinew thread. Daughter had not yet learned to sew. Her mother had said she was too little for needles. But she had watched her mother and her grandmother, and she was sure she knew how. Perhaps even the grandfather knew a little. After all, when a man was away hunting or fishing, who else would repair his clothes but he himself?

She considered needles and thread, finger protectors made of hide, awls, and sewing knives, until finally they all danced together like wind-bent flowers. She watched them until it seemed as if she were again back in the boat, the sea rocking her, and she fell asleep.

Through the night, K'os kept vigil beside the old man. He was strong, that one. The arm had been so badly festered that he should have died days before. She placed a hand on his forehead. There were spirits of sickness in him, no doubt of that, but his pulse was steady.

She was glad that her husband Seal was away hunting. He probably would not have let her bring the man or his little girl into the ulax.

At least the chief hunter had not been so foolish. There were tales of others who had come to the First Men's islands from distant shores, brought by storm winds. The chief's own family was said to have ancestors who had arrived in such a way, so the storytellers said.

The old man's boat was strange, unlike anything River People would build. None of the First Men had seen one like it, but if you could get beyond the stink, you could see that there was some merit in the way it was made. Even several hunters had commented on its stability in sea waves. But who would waste two good logs on building one boat when there was enough wood in them to make four or five iqyan? A greedy man, this one must be, those hunters had decided.

K'os had stood up for him, had told of lands where there were enough trees to make two handfuls of log boats for every hunter. They had considered what she said, but none of them had traveled much beyond their island, and her husband, the only trader among them, was not there to take her side. Surprisingly, K'os's sister-wife Eye-Taker had. Boasting, she told of the many strange lands where their husband had traveled, of places where trees grew as thick as grass. And finally, with Eye-Taker's words to back her, K'os had won permission to try to save the old man.

She could also keep the girl, the chief hunter said. At least until Seal returned from his hunting trip. Then the whole village would gather and decided what to do with both man and child.

After all, even thin and scabbed as she was, and also missing a toe, the girl was not ugly, and perhaps someday she could be a wife for one of their sons. Of course by the time she had learned to speak their language, she would have forgotten what she knew of her own people, where they lived and why they built their boats in such a way, for she was not yet to the age of remembering. But the old man, he would know much, and the chief hunter was anxious to learn what he had to tell them. For the man was not River, nor even Caribou, and not North Tundra. All those people the First

Men knew or at least had heard about. So yes, the chief hunter and the elders agreed, K'os should try to save him, and they would find places for Eye-Taker and her children in their ulas, since Eye-Taker had decided that the old man probably carried some curse. As long as he was sick, she and her children would leave Seal's ulax and stay in a safer place.

But who would care if K'os were cursed? She was, after all, a River woman, old, and only a second wife.

When the gray of sunrise finally pushed back the night, K'os ate a chunk of dried fish and roused the old man enough to give him something to drink. He fought against her, but finally she managed to get some willow bark tea down his throat. The girl was still asleep, and for a moment K'os considered waking her, but then she decided to wait. She climbed out of the ulax into the dawn wind, and she walked to the beach, where the grandfather's boat still lay, its tail in the waves.

She used a strip of driftwood to scrape the rotted meat and fish from the inside of the boat, then went back to the village and found several boys to help her. They approached the boat with fingers pinched over their noses, and even K'os could not keep from puckering her lips in distaste as the wind carried the smell to them.

"I need you to help me lift it past the reach of storm waves and into the shelter of those rocks," K'os told them, raising her chin toward a hedge of rocks that sat above the rise of the beach.

"Why keep it?" one of the boys asked. "It will never lose its stink."

"Perhaps the old man will want it someday," K'os told him.

"My uncle says he will die, that his arm is too rotten."

K'os shrugged her shoulders. "If he dies, he dies," she said, "but for now we will move the boat."

They complained, but they helped her, groaning and whining until K'os began complimenting them on their strength. Then they worked all the harder, each vying for her praise, and finally the boat was behind the rocks. The boys left her and ran back to the village, but K'os sat beside the boat, laid a hand on the wet, sated wood, and considered the gifts the sea had brought her—a good boat, and a daughter to raise more wisely than she had raised Chakliux.

She thought of a riddle, and it made her smile. She spoke it to the sky and told the wind to carry it above the clouds to those few stars that lived over the Sea Hunters' islands. They seldom shone, those stars, and when they did, their light was faint, as if in finding their way through the clouds, they used up nearly all their brightness. But each dim star reminded her of the great dome of night sky that rose over the River People's villages. And now she had more hope that she would live under those bright stars again.

"Look! What do I see?" she called to those First Men stars. "A daughter of light to guide my iqyax."

SIXTEEN

In Daughter's dream, the otter jumped from the sea into their boat. It chewed off the grandfather's arm, then came toward her, its teeth bared. She screamed and woke herself up. She opened her eyes and saw that she was no longer in the boat, and the memories of what had happened returned. She was inside the earth, she and the grandfather and an old woman.

She unwrapped herself from the bedding furs and stood up, but the motion of the grandfather's boat seemed to be a part of her arms and legs, and she walked with a lurch that made her reach out toward the earthen walls to keep her balance.

Then she saw the grandfather. He was lying where the old woman had left him, on mats of woven grass that looked a little like the mats her own people used. Only a short stump, little more than the length of Daughter's hand, remained where his left arm had been. Daughter remembered the bundle beside the notched log and her hopes of sewing the arm back on, but when she went to the log, the bundle was gone, nothing left of it but a scattering of dried blood in the floor-grass where it had lain. The old woman was gone, too, and Daughter decided she must have taken the grandfather's arm with her.

The loss of that arm made an ache in Daughter's chest, and as she crouched beside the grandfather she crooned a song her mother had taught her. It was a song for grass cuts and scraped knees, probably not much good for the grandfather, but it was all Daughter knew. She laid a hand on his forehead and was surprised to discover that his skin was cool.

Had the arm itself made him sick? If so, maybe the old woman had been right in cutting it off. At least the grandfather was alive. Daughter looked at her own small arms, so thin that they seemed little more than bone. She tucked her left hand behind her back and thought about living with only one arm.

She could still eat, she told herself. She could still pick up things. It would be hard for the grandfather to carry something heavy, but she still had two good arms. She would carry what he could not.

Water Gourd slept for five days, and when he opened his eyes to the darkness of the ulax, his first thoughts were of death. He had died, of course, and they had laid him in the earth. They had given him more honor than he deserved, for his grave was large. He tried to remember what he might have done to earn such a grave, but no remembrance of bravery or wisdom came to him. Maybe it was only that he had been killed when the Bear-god men attacked their village, and all those who had died were given honor burials. But the memory of many days in the outrigger boat came to him, and he thought of Daughter.

Suddenly he realized that in the darkness above him he could see ribs. Bones, they were, he was sure. He remembered his fight with the sea otter; he remembered his arm swollen and so painful that finally he could bear it no longer, and he had escaped into a sleep of spirit-wandering.

A sea dragon, no doubt, had found them and swallowed them whole while Water Gourd slept. He was now within that monster's belly, for no grave he had ever seen was made with bone rafters. Where was Daughter? He thought of the little girl, and his heart crept into his throat. Why, in his cowardice, had he slept? Surely he was man enough to endure pain, and if he had stayed awake, he might have been able to save them both from the dragon.

His arm still hurt, shooting pains that began in his shoulder and ended at his wrist, but some of the spirits that had entered with the otter's teeth had left, for the pain was merely a nuisance, nothing compared to what it had been. He tried to sit up, but his head spun, and he sank again to the floor of the dragon's belly. He lay there for a time, drifted into thoughts that were nearly dreams, but finally tried again. This time he managed to do so, though an ache began at the top of his skull and ground into his teeth, so that he clenched his jaw and bit his tongue. He tasted blood, swallowed, and gagged. He felt unsteady, like a child just learning to keep his balance. He tipped to one side and reached to catch himself before he fell, but his arm did not respond. He looked down, and, in horror at what he saw, screamed.

He fell, his weight mashing what was left of the arm, so that his second scream was one of pain.

Then Daughter was beside him, her small cool hands patting his face, and there was a woman with her.

His first thought was of his favorite wife, that good woman, long dead. But how could it be? No sea dragon had swallowed her. She had died in a choking fit.

Then, as the woman eased him off his shoulder, laid him on his back, he saw her face, and knew that she was not even from his village. Her eyes were too round, her face too long, her nose too large.

Daughter was whimpering, and before he thought, Water Gourd reached out his right hand toward her, caught his breath in gratitude when he saw that the hand and arm were whole. But how would he carry water without his left arm?

Carry water, he thought, and mocked himself for his foolishness. He was dead! Did the dead need water?

"She cut it, Grandfather," Daughter said to him. "She cut

it. I not find it." There was fear in the girl's voice, but Water Gourd saw something more. She looked stronger, her eyes brighter, her face fuller.

"Where are we?" he asked.

"Little village," she said, and raised a finger to point at the huge ribs that stretched like rafters over their heads. "Inside the ground," she said. She poked a finger into her mouth, sucked for a moment, then popped it out and told him, "You sick." She lifted her head to look at the woman and said, "She feed you and me. Good fish."

The woman said something to him, her voice low and thick in her throat, the words scraping against her teeth with sounds that were more grumbling than talking. Was she Bear-god?

No, he didn't think so. Her skin was too dark, and her hair was black and straight. He realized that he smelled smoke, tasted fish oil each time he took a breath. The woman must be burning it, he decided. That fire, set somewhere behind his head, gave light so that he saw the glint of gray in her hair. She must be older than she looked, and though she was not what the Boat People would consider beautiful—her features were too strong for a woman—there was something about her face that caught the eye.

"We are inside the earth?" he asked Daughter.

She was sucking her fingers, and the woman had turned away from them, was doing something that blocked part of the light.

Daughter nodded.

"Can you go outside? Can you leave this place?"

Daughter twisted to point at an immense driftwood log propped up at an angle from floor to roof, and Water Gourd could see that it extended into the darkness beyond, through a square hole. His eyes were dim, but he thought he could see the sparkle of stars within that hole.

"Is it night?" he asked.

"Night," she said, the word slurring around her fingers. "We go outside in morning. Catch fish."

"There are other people?"

Daughter's eyes were suddenly wet with tears. "Not my mama," she said in a small voice.

"Other mamas?"

"Other mamas," she said. "And babies."

"Men? Hunters? Fishermen?"

"Mens," she said. "Lots of mens."

At first her answers brought him relief. They were not dead. Somehow their boat had found a village. But they were far from their own island, and these people, if they all spoke like the woman who was caring for him, did not know the Boat People's language.

He and Daughter would be worthless in this village. Two more mouths to feed: a girl many years away from motherhood and an old man, weak and sick, and with only one arm.

At the thought, his elbow began to ache, not the elbow of his good arm, but the elbow he no longer had. Would it haunt him, that arm, blame him for the foolishness of trying to catch an otter? Would it give him pain that nothing could soothe? As a young man, when his hunting or fishing had made his arms ache, his wife would rub his muscles, bring life back into the flesh with her hands, but how could anyone rub what was not there? Could a man who knew medicine cut into the dead skin to bleed out the spirits of pain? Could a priest who knew prayer songs sing to an arm that was buried or burned?

The woman came to him then, slid a hand under his head and lifted him gently so he could sip from a wooden cup. He had expected water, but it was a warm tea that tasted of earth and plants, and it soothed his throat. He clasped Daughter's hand, pulled her down to her knees. She snuggled against him, and the woman brought a robe to cover the girl.

There are worse things than being warm and dry with a woman to watch over me, Water Gourd told himself. There are worse things than having Daughter safe. Then, with

Daughter warm at his side and the tea filling his belly, Water Gourd slid into a gentle sleep.

When he woke again, light streamed through the square hole in the roof of the earth *iori*. The woman and Daughter were sewing, and to Water Gourd's surprise, when the woman spoke, Daughter answered. Sometimes the girl's words were in the Boat People language, but other times she seemed to mimic the woman's speech.

How long had he slept? Through the turning of the moon? Through the seasons of a year? Or was Daughter still baby enough that words came easily, and she understood all languages?

This time when he struggled to sit up, the world stayed still, and what little dizziness he felt soon passed. He leaned against his good right arm and thought about how to tell the woman that he needed to release his water, that his bladder was full to bursting.

When he was sure he had his balance, he lifted the blanket that covered him and saw that he was naked. He leaned forward to gather the blanket around his waist and tried to ease himself to his knees. The woman looked up from her sewing and hissed, then rushed to help him. She lifted his arm over her shoulders, and slowly pulled him up. The world darkened until Water Gourd could see only a pinpoint of light, but he clenched his teeth and made himself stand until the darkness receded.

He motioned toward his penis, covered as it was by the sleeping robe, said the word for urine, but the woman did not understand. Then he saw Daughter point to a gully that was dug where the floor met the earthen wall. Sunk into that gully was a large wooden trough. The woman helped him walk, moved with him step by step until he stood beside the trough. By the smell Water Gourd knew it held old urine.

The women in his village also stored urine. When it ripened to a sharpness that burned the nostrils, it was good for many things—cleaning away fat or oil, preserving hides, killing the molds that rot grass mats during the rainy times of the year. But Boat women did not store the urine in their houses.

He was used to privacy when he relieved himself, and though the woman turned her head, it took him some time to release his stream. Finally he was done, and she led him back to his bed, helped him sit.

She offered him a bowl of broth, and he drank it greedily, surprised at his own hunger. When he had drained a second bowl, she knelt behind him, bracing his back with her knees, and began to knead his neck, so that under the pressure of her hands even the pain from his ghost arm lessened.

She laid him gently against his bedding and stroked her fingers through his hair until finally he slept again, and this time his dreams were good.

When Seal returned from his hunting trip, the First Men gathered in the chief hunter's ulax. Though K'os usually sat in the least honored place—with the children, furthest from the seal oil lamp—this time she sat beside her husband, near the chief, beside his fat wife and her ugly daughter. K'os held herself straight and strong. She was old, but most men would rather come to her bed than to that of the chief's daughter. She smiled as she thought of the day she and her husband Seal arrived at his village.

The men, seeing her from a distance, had thought Seal had brought a young and beautiful woman to their village. Only when they came close did they realize that she was as old as a grandmother.

Though she had not understood their language, she heard the tone of their words and knew they were ridiculing Seal. In her mind, she had given words to their jests. Why had Seal taken an old woman as wife? Even a young hunter could not hope to breed children from an old woman.

Seal had responded with angry shouts and showed them the scars left from his wound. As he spoke, he gestured toward his rebuilt iqyax and often pointed at his leg, so K'os had known what he was telling them. Then he pulled her close, reached a hand down the neck of her parka, ignored the sudden laughter of the young men, and finally pulled out her river otter medicine bag. They were quiet then, those young men, stilled by the knowledge of the power she held in that bag, and their ridicule had stopped.

Now, in the chief hunter's lodge, she raised a hand and laid it against her chest where the bag hung, soft and dark, over her breasts. In the custom of the First Men, she had removed her sax when she entered the chief hunter's ulax. To do otherwise would be an insult, a sign that the lodge was not warm enough for her.

Yes, there was power in that otter bag, but she did not allow herself to think of how few packets of each medicine she still had, and how few of the plants she needed grew on this Sea Hunter island. She was learning the island foliage, but the women were reluctant to teach her, and none of them were well versed in plant medicines. She had learned about a poison from one of the young hunters, a gift of knowledge in exchange for an afternoon in her bed. The plant was deadly, and she had gathered some, dried it and kept it in packets marked with red string, knotted four times. There was a tall, heavy-stemmed green plant whose roots made a good poultice for sore muscles, and there were others that she had known before—yarrow and fireweed and ground-hugging willow—but she worried that her healing powers would diminish as her supplies were used. Then what would she do, an old woman, River as she was, and second wife?

Better second wife than slave, she told herself. Seal had come at a good time, when her days with the Walrus Hunters were numbered. How terrible to find that the Walrus's shaman Yehl did not want her. Even when she sneaked away from the slave's lodge, crept to the warmth of his bed, stroked him out of his sleep—no matter what she did with hands or tongue or lips—he showed no desire for her.

As her understanding of the Walrus language grew, she

heard the whispers from his wives, how he shunned all of them, had welcomed no woman to his bed since K'os had come to live in the village. She heard the stories about Aqamdax and Chakliux and Sok, and what had happened to Yehl's father because of them, and finally she understood that Yehl's response to her had nothing to do with his desires, but rather with his fear of River People.

Once a man could not hold his power over a woman, how would the spirits keep their respect? How long until the people did not want Yehl as their shaman? Then how long until Yehl decided that K'os had cursed him? Without doubt he would kill her. What hope did she have? Who would stand up for a slave?

K'os chose a night of full moon to leave the Walrus Hunters' village, and she had walked many days in the direction of the Traders' Beach. Where else could she have gone? Not back to the River village. Not to the Four Rivers People. Only death awaited her at those places. What else was left but to go to the Sea Hunters? There she had the chance to earn herself some power. Perhaps she could find a shaman who might agree to use his own magic to destroy those who had tried to destroy her.

She had been scouring a beach for driftwood when she heard Seal's death song rising above the noise of the waves. She had followed that song up a slope of shale to a cave tucked into a cliff not far from the beach.

A spirit of sickness had come into his body, given entrance by a gash that had laid his leg open to the bone. She had given him medicines, sewn up the wound, tended his fire, brought food and water. Sometime during the long days of his illness, he had begun to call her wife, and when he was well enough, she showed him that she had found the skin covering for his iqyax, had saved many of the pieces of its frame. They rebuilt it together, Seal carving the frame and K'os repairing the cover, and when he left to return to his own people's village—a long journey of many days—he had asked K'os to come with him.

Until then, she had been the strong one, the warrior, the shaman, but once they were in the First Men village, she needed him much more than he needed her. She still struggled with the First Men's language, and it did not help that they were a people stingy with their words, spending long days saying nothing, the men watching the sea for seals and sea lions and fish, the women working in silence.

She despaired over the few plants on the island, and she had to wait through a long winter before even beginning to gather the plants she did know and to learn about those she did not. She used her supply of medicines sparingly and hoped for broken bones and dislocated joints, but some spirit had cursed her. The First Men she lived among were a healthy people. Even in giving birth, the women seldom had need of her advice. All the babies that had been born since she arrived at the village had come head first, face down, as babies should.

The First Men were short-legged, with thicker bones than the River People, with rounder heads and smaller noses. The women grew their hair long and bound it into tight buns at their necks or ears. They used a needle and charcoaled thread to draw broken lines across their cheeks and patterns of triangles on their thighs. The men marked their chins with long lines from lips to chins and wore thin ivory pins through the septums of their noses. They also pierced the skin at the corners of their mouths and set circles of ivory there, some nearly as large around as walrus tusks.

Their faces, marked as such, were at first strange to her, but now she was able to see the beauty in the women's marks, the fierceness in the men's. So that if by chance she saw the reflection of her own face in a still tide pool, it seemed to be the face of a child, not yet complete.

Though she was ranked as the lowest woman in the village, she was not a slave, and Seal treated her well. But with the arrival of the old man and the girl, her status had grown, and she sensed that both men and women watched her with no little fear, as though waiting to see whether she would fall under some curse or perhaps even a blessing. For after all, if their chief hunter carried the blood of people like these, could they truly be evil? And if K'os's medicines had saved their lives, then she, too, must have more power than they had thought.

K'os listened carefully as the First Men discussed what to do. They seemed in agreement that the girl should be allowed to grow up among them, though most women were afraid to take her into their own ulas. Finally the chief hunter spoke to Seal, asked if he were willing to keep her. Seal shrugged, glanced at K'os, and when K'os nodded, he ignored Eye-Taker's anger and agreed.

"As slave," he said, "for my wife Old Woman."

Then K'os did what no second wife should do, spoke without asking her husband.

"I will take her as daughter," she said, and when Seal looked at her, his mouth and eyes opened wide in surprise, she bowed her head in deference, but quickly added, "I need someone to help me with my medicines. I am an old woman, and the healing powers I bring are River. These powers have been a good thing in your village." She nodded toward her husband's leg, and lifted her eyes at the chief hunter's youngest son, who had cut his face in a fall against a rock. "But who can say what will happen to your children if I try to pass this knowledge on to one of them? River medicine might curse them. Better to take such a chance with this girl."

A murmur of agreement passed among the people, and Seal smiled at K'os. Eye-Taker hid her anger with a quick nod, and K'os again bowed her head in respect.

"And the old man?" the chief hunter asked.

An argument began among the hunters. Some wanted to kill him, others claimed he was a gift from the sea. Finally Seal spoke, and though he was a young man, he was known for having some wisdom, so even the elders stopped their grumbling to listen.

"My wife tells me that he will most likely die. She has already had to cut off his arm, and he is old and weak. Why take the chance of cursing ourselves by making such a decision? Why not wait and see what happens? If he is a gift from the sea, then the sea will give him the strength to live. If he is not a gift, then he will die, for surely a man as old and sick as this one will not have the strength within himself to survive."

So in wisdom the decision was made, that both man and child would live, accepted as gifts. K'os hid her joy in her heart, and from that day began to teach Daughter the many ways of River medicine.

SEVENTEEN

Herendeen Bay, Alaska Peninsula
602 B.C.

The story was short, but after Kuy'aa's long stories about
Chakliux and Aqamdax, Yikaas could understand the reason
behind Qumalix's brevity. The people began leaving the
ulax, most pausing to speak to Qumalix.

Yikaas pushed through to the back of the crowd. What
better way to understand these Sea Hunters than to spend
time alone here once everyone had left? Then he could try to
see the world as they did, bound by the earthen walls of one
of their lodges.

He settled himself in the darkness behind the climbing
log, pressed a hand against that log. Stripped of bark during
its long sea journey to this island, the log must have its own
tales to tell. Perhaps it longed to do so, listening as it must
each day to stories from other mouths. But since a tree kept
its voice within its leaves, maybe as a log it was content to
be silent, preferring to listen rather than tell.

He turned his thoughts to the Sea Hunters, and he wondered what it would be like to live so close to the sea, water
that was both boundary and passage.

He considered Qumalix's stories. They were good, but not as fine as Kuy'aa's. Yikaas closed his eyes and tried to imagine the old woman as a girl, how she must have looked and sounded. He wondered if she had been as good a storyteller then as Qumalix was now. Better, he told himself. She must have been better. How else could she be so good today, old as she was? Her skin seemed to be as thin as sea lion gut that had been softened by a woman's knuckles into wrinkles beyond count, and her voice was as scored by age as her face.

"Would you like some water?"

The voice startled Yikaas, and he opened his eyes to see Qumalix standing before him, no longer storyteller, but only a woman, offering an ivory-stoppered seal bladder.

He took it, pulled out the stopper, and drank. The water was good, so fresh that it barely carried the taste of the bladder. He handed it back, and she, too, drank, then sealed the bladder and hung it from a peg. She sat down on her haunches beside him, waved a hand before her face to clear away the oil lamp smoke that was sliding up the climbing log to the square hole in the ulax roof.

"You are leaving now?" she asked, though he had not risen from his place behind the log.

He had the advantage over her, since she sat in the light of the entrance hole while he was in darkness.

"No," he said, and asked, "are *you* leaving?"

She focused her eyes on the climbing log, as if she had spoken to it rather than to him, as if it were a storyteller worthy of respect. "It is good, sometimes, to sit in this ulax alone," she said. "In my village we do not have an ulax set aside for storytelling. I suppose here at the Traders' Beach they have need of such a place with so many people visiting in spring and summer."

She paused as though she expected him to reply, but since she was talking to the log, he did not. Let the log say something, storyteller that it was.

"The quietness gives me ideas," she said. "Sometimes when the ulax is so crowded with people, it seems I hear their clamoring thoughts in my head, so that I forget what I had planned to say."

Her words surprised him. They so nearly echoed his own thoughts. "That's why I'm here," he said. "To better understand your people. I had hoped to catch some of the thoughts and ideas they left behind."

Again Qumalix waved a hand before her face, coughed, and moved back out of the flow of smoke. "The lamp should be filled with whale oil," she said. "It burns more cleanly, especially the oil of toothed whales."

Yikaas raised his eyebrows at her. He knew nothing about whales or whale oil lamps, and the realization of the many differences between them suddenly made him uncomfortable. "Wood fires smell better," he said.

"Sometimes we have beach fires," she told him. "They do smell good, but usually we save the driftwood to build our ulas and for the men's iqyax frames."

"You have no trees on your island?" he asked. Kuy'aa had told him that, but he could not imagine such a thing. How did people live without trees?

"Only willow, and they are not like the willow here." She held a hand close to the floor. "They grow only this high and along the ground, but we use the bark for medicines, and the old women say that long ago the people sometimes split the roots to make gathering baskets. Grass baskets are better."

He merely grunted a reply. Why should a man think about baskets?

Qumalix stood and said, "If you want to be alone here, I will go . . ."

But Yikaas clasped her wrist and pulled her down beside him. "In the next storytelling will you speak about Daughter and how K'os raised her?" he asked.

"No one wants to hear about that," Qumalix said.

"I do," he told her.

"The First Men have heard it before, and it is not very exciting. The best stories about Daughter and K'os happen later, when Daughter has become a woman, and K'os is so old that only the evil in her heart keeps her spirit tied to her body."

"If I hear a story about K'os raising Daughter, then perhaps I will better understand the enmity between K'os and Chakliux."

Qumalix tipped back her head as though she were studying the ulax rafters. She was pleasant to look at, once a man was used to Sea Hunter women with their round faces and small noses, their tattooed cheeks.

"What can I tell you?" she asked, the question more to herself than to Yikaas. "Water Gourd, though he was not a man given to new and wise thoughts, was good at remembering the wisdom of others. Once he learned the First Men's language—and he was more than a year in the learning—he shared the stories and wisdom that he had heard in the Boat People's village. To the First Men, this was new wisdom, so Water Gourd earned a place with the elders, and though he had but one arm, he began to see himself as being more whole than he ever was as a young man.

"K'os gave Daughter a new name—*Uutuk,* which means *sea urchin,* for K'os had found her washed up on the beach, a gift of the tides. K'os taught Uutuk plant medicine and how to set bones and pull broken teeth and ease fevers. Daughter grew in her own beauty, but K'os planned and worked to bend her into evil ways."

"So Daughter became evil, like K'os."

"Oh, I did not say that," Qumalix replied. She sucked at her bottom lip as though considering something and finally said, "Perhaps there is a story about Daughter you should hear. I could tell you now, if you like, here in this ulax, or we could go to a place where we can see the beach and the water and the sky."

Yikaas looked into the dark corners of the ulax, at the earthen walls that rose warm and thick against the wind, but suddenly he wanted to be outside. He slipped on his caribou hide parka and waited as Qumalix pulled on her sax. The sax was made from many cormorant skins, the feathers shining black and sleek. Qumalix was unmarried, and so wore her hair long and loose rather than bound at the back of her head, but when she put on the sax, she tucked her hair into the collar rim.

She led him to a sheltered place in a valley between two hills, a walk that took them beyond sight of the village. They sat down behind a hummock of grass, and the blades of that grass cut the wind so it came to them in tatters, too weak to pull away their words.

When Qumalix began to speak, it was still light; clouds stretched across the sky in strips like storyteller strings ready for quick fingers to twist them into animals, people, and birds. Yikaas watched as the wind pulled the cloud strings into pictures, and when the day dimmed into night, even the stars seemed to hover close.

Yunaska Island, The Aleutian Chain
6440 B.C.

DAUGHTER'S STORY

"You cannot expect them to like you, Uutuk," K'os said. "Look at you. You're still a girl, but you know more than most women. Even their grandmothers do not know how to use plants like you do. Your fingers are quick with a needle, and your voice is the voice of a storyteller. When the young women are with you, they feel like children. Can you blame them for leaving you out of their games?"

K'os's words fell soft on Daughter's ears, and again gave her a place in the world. K'os handed Daughter a cup of yellow root tea and said, "Give this to your grandfather. It will lend him a little strength."

Over the winter Water Gourd had grown weak. Many days he was not strong enough to climb into the wind and sit at the top of the ulax to visit with the elders. They missed his wisdom, they told Daughter. What other man knew so much about life yet gave his advice with such a gentle spirit?

He took the cup from Daughter's hands, and she held her

breath until he managed to raise the tea to his lips. When he had finished, she leaned close to take the cup, and he whispered into her ear, speaking the language that they alone shared.

"I have had a good life, Daughter, but I am old and soon will leave you to go back to our people. Do not cry for me. I have been honored as an elder. Seal and K'os have been generous to me, and you have been a wonderful daughter. I have nothing more to ask for."

"You could ask for another summer," Daughter said to him, her thoughts suddenly selfish, wanting the grandfather to live, though he was ready to die.

They whispered as they spoke together so K'os would not hear. She had tried to learn the Boat People's tongue, but never managed to remember more than a handful of words. During the past few years, each time she heard Daughter and Water Gourd speak that language, K'os grew angry, so now they used it only when they were alone. But K'os had her own small ways of revenge. When Water Gourd did something to displease her, she spoke to Daughter in the River language, which he did not understand. Sometimes K'os went for days without using the First Men's tongue. But Water Gourd only shrugged off her obstinacy, and ignored her anger.

Usually they lived together happily. Seal had recently made another ulax for Eye-Taker. She was a strong woman, blessed with many children, a new baby almost every two years, so now there were eight, too many for the small ulax where Daughter and K'os and the grandfather lived. But K'os was still Seal's wife, and with his trading and hunting there was always enough food.

Though Daughter was thankful to have K'os and the grandfather, there were times when she wished she were more like the other girls in the village, with uncles and aunts and cousins living close. Of course, they had Seal's family and Eye-Taker and her children, but Daughter had come to realize that that was not the same as having blood ties. K'os had honored the grandfather with a River name—Taadzi, which, she explained, referred to the deadfall trap River men used to capture an animal called the lynx. Lynx were known to hold great spirit powers.

Daughter had never seen a lynx, but K'os owned the brown-and-yellow-speckled hide of one, given to her by Seal after one of his trading trips. Daughter had studied that hide, stroked its long, soft fur, and she tried to set an image in her mind of what a lynx looked like. Finally she decided it must be a kind of boar—an animal she remembered from her childhood with the Boat People—though with a softer, more beautiful pelt.

It seemed to Daughter that K'os was a generous woman. She made clothing for the elders, and shared the abundance of meat that was given to the grandfather in appreciation for his wisdom. During the days when the grandfather was outside speaking to the elders and Seal was away hunting or trading, K'os even shared her bed, for she was willing to give what a man needed, even if he was not her husband.

"Someday you'll give the same joy yourself, Uutuk," K'os often told her, and then went on to explain how men liked to be touched and how a woman could get what she wanted, trading pleasure for many things.

When Daughter was with the other girls of the village, they sometimes spoke of the ways of men with women. None of the girls had yet come into their moon-blood times, and none had bedded a man, so they knew only what they had managed to glimpse or hear. During this giggling and foolishness, Daughter pretended to be one of them, to know little and wonder much, and she did not tell them anything K'os had said to her, for she had learned as a child that the ways of the village were not K'os's ways, nor were K'os's ways always accepted. It was better to be quiet; it was better to hold what she knew within herself, because once words left her mouth she could never hide them again under her tongue.

* * *

One night when the grandfather was asleep and Daughter was sewing by the light from the whale oil lamp, K'os came and sat down beside her.

"I'm worried about your grandfather," K'os said. "I have a small amount of caribou leaf, a plant I brought with me when I came here from the River People years ago. It's a strong plant, with many powers for good, and I have saved it for someone special. Now is the time to use it. Otherwise I think he will die before summer."

She crouched beside Daughter on her haunches and opened the River otter medicine bag. She pulled out the familiar packets of plant medicines, each tied with colored sinew. Finally she brought out one so old that the hide packet had become brittle. K'os cut the knots and dumped the contents of the packet into her hand. The caribou leaves were merely dust, so light that a breath would take them away. She divided the powder between three wooden cups, handed one to Daughter and told her to mix it with oil and smooth it over Water Gourd's face.

They kept a sealskin of fat in a storage niche in the ulax wall. The sealskin was turned hair side in, and the summer before, Daughter had stuffed it full of seal fat cut in strips, all meat removed. Over time, the heat from the fat rendered out the oil.

Daughter got the sealskin, opened the neckflap, and tipped the skin to pour out some oil. She used her fingers to blend in the caribou leaf powder, then went to the grandfather, to his sleeping place at the back of the ulax, pulled aside his curtain, and began to smooth the oil into his face. He snorted a little, but did not awaken, and after a moment, he even smiled.

His body had grown gaunt over the years, his face pinched and lined, and his eyes had sunk deep into his face. He had never agreed to have his skin tattooed, nor did he pierce his lips for labrets. Instead, he wore long, thin mustaches that hung down over his mouth, the custom of the Boat People, whose faces came to Daughter like ghosts in a dream, scarcely remembered.

K'os had had her own cheeks tattooed, and even the tops of her thighs. Often she and the grandfather argued about the tattoos that Daughter should receive, the lines across the cheeks, the circles and triangles to beautify her legs. Daughter wished for those tattoos, so she could be like the other girls in the village, but the grandfather said they would only make her ugly, and when she became old the lines would blur under her skin, become a darkness that would never wash clean.

"He is an old man and will not live forever, Uutuk," K'os had said when Daughter complained. "When he dies and his mourning has passed, then we will begin your tattoos."

Daughter thought of K'os's promise as she smoothed the oil into the grandfather's skin. Gladly she would stay like a child, skin unmarked, if the grandfather would have more years of good health. She lifted small prayers of hope, and reminded herself that the other girls said the tattooing hurt, and that sometimes a woman was left with scars, ridges that marred the smoothness of her face and legs.

When Daughter had finished, she brought the rest of the oil back to K'os. "There is some left," she said. "Should I do his neck or hand?"

"Did he wake up?" she asked, ignoring Daughter's question.

"No," Daughter told her, but remembering the old man's smile, she also smiled and wondered what he dreamed about. Did he turn young again in his sleep, enjoy women and have success in hunts?

"Well, you will have to wake him. He must drink this tea. One cup now, and the other tomorrow."

Daughter set down the oil and took the tea. "Let him sleep until it cools," K'os told her, "then wake him and make him drink it all. I will leave you to do this, for I must go to Eye-

Taker's ulax. Seal has a sax he wants me to repair. It is his best, and he does not trust Eye-Taker's needle."

Daughter turned so her back was warmed by the oil lamp, but the cup was shielded from its heat. She was glad she had reason to wake the grandfather. Their best times together were when K'os was away, but since last summer, he slept so much that those times did not come often.

He told wondrous stories of the island where he and Daughter had once lived, and on occasion, he would even speak about Daughter's true parents, her beautiful mother and her strong young father. Daughter had given them First Men names so she could pretend they were a part of this village, that she had others here besides the grandfather. When the village girls were mean to her, the names helped, as did the grandfather's stories.

She dipped a finger into the tea. It had cooled, so she carried it carefully to the grandfather's sleeping place. She opened the grass curtain and knelt beside him, called to him in a whisper until slowly his eyes opened. He stared at her as if he were seeing someone else, but then he smiled.

"I dreamed that we were in our village, Daughter," he said in a voice clouded with phlegm. "Your mother was there and your father and that lazy woman, my niece. We were having the feast of moon promises, and one of the women was pledging herself to a young hunter as wife. There were chestnut cakes, Daughter, and I had lifted one to my mouth. You woke me just as I was going to take a bite. Do you know how long it has been since I tasted chestnut cake?"

"I'm sorry, Grandfather," Daughter said.

"No need to be sorry. I will go back to sleep and eat all the chestnut cakes I can hold." Laughter crackled in his throat.

Daughter lifted the tea so he could see it. "Mother left medicine for you. She says it will make you strong."

"She had you wake me from a good sleep to give me this?" he grumbled. "What does she know? Sleep and good dreams, those things make an old man strong." But he propped himself up on his elbow and leaned forward to drink. When he had finished the tea, Daughter set down the cup and tucked her hands behind his head, laid him gently back on his sleeping mats. The grandfather closed his eyes, but then he opened them and looked at her. He blinked and whispered, "Where is K'os?"

"She went to Seal's ulax."

The grandfather smiled. "Then perhaps I have time to tell you a story." He spoke in the language of the Boat People, and his voice seemed stronger. "Have I ever told you about the time when I was fishing far from shore and a storm arose?"

He had told Daughter the story many times, but she held her eyes open wide to show her interest. "If you have, Grandfather," she said, "I have forgotten most of it. Please tell me again."

He reached out to clasp her hand, and she settled down beside him and listened as he told the story.

K'os curled herself around Chiton's body and leaned forward to touch the tip of her tongue to each of his nipples. His wife had just given him a new daughter and was still living in the birthing lodge.

When K'os went to Eye-Taker's ulax, Chiton's sister and aunt were visiting there, and they told K'os about the birth. K'os had stayed only long enough to get the sax, then pretended that she needed to return to Water Gourd. Instead, she went to Chiton's ulax.

As she had hoped, he was alone. She had congratulated him on his daughter, but he scowled and said, "Every man wants a son."

"Once long ago when I lived with the River People, I had a son," K'os told him. "I was a good mother, gave him everything, sewed all his clothing and got him a beautiful wife. But when another village attacked our own, he betrayed us and went to live with our attackers because they were stronger, and he knew they would win. When nearly all our men were killed and our village was burned, I was sold as slave to the Walrus Hunters, and my son did not lift a hand to help me. Only by good luck did I come to this village, where once again I am wife and mother. If I had to choose between my son and my daughter, I would choose my daughter. Be thankful you have a healthy child. Daughters are good luck, and sometimes sons are not."

He did not reply, merely turned his back on her and grunted. She went to him, stood close. He was wearing only an otter skin breechcloth, and she slipped her hands around his waist, tucked her fingers under the edges of the otter skin.

"I have a wife," he told her, but he turned to face her and knelt to slip his hands under her sax. She pulled the sax off up over her head, then moved his hands to her breasts.

"Why should I give you my seed?" he asked. "You are too old to make children." His fingers strayed to the band of the woven grass apron that hung from her waist.

"I make no claim to be young," K'os said. "But I am not ugly." She cupped her hands around her breasts. "Are these the breasts of an old woman?"

"You must have some medicine that keeps you young," he told her. "Though it does not work for your hands, and perhaps not for your hair." He pulled several gray strands from the bun at the back of her head.

She smiled at him. "It is good medicine," she said. "How else do you think I have kept that old man Taadzi alive so many years? Whatever hunter I choose will keep his youth for a long time. I cannot give you children—you have a wife to do that—but my medicine will make you strong."

"I am strong," he said, and scowled at her.

"I only meant that I would help you stay strong," she told him. Then she said, "Enough talking." She pushed him back toward the curtained niche that was his sleeping place.

He clasped her arms, laid her on the furs, and fell over her. "It has been too long since I had a woman," he groaned, "and all that waiting just for a daughter."

* * *

The grandfather's words suddenly stopped, and Daughter, crouched with her eyes closed so she could see the story, waited. It was the most exciting part, where the storm waves had torn the outrigger from the boat, but she supposed that he had fallen asleep.

The longer he lived, the more easily sleep came to him. What had K'os told her? Life was a circle, and old people move toward that time when they were infants. They sleep as often as babies, and sometimes, like babies, their thoughts and words are garbled. Of course, the grandfather's mind was clear. No one in the village doubted that he was still the wisest of all the elders.

Daughter opened her eyes. To her surprise, she saw that the grandfather was staring at the top of his sleeping place. In curiosity, she bent close and looked up. There was nothing but darkness.

"Look, what do I see?" she asked, and waited for him to supply the rest of the riddle. Riddles were a River People game, but K'os had taught them both the joy of those word puzzles.

When he did not answer, Daughter clasped his hand. "Grandfather?"

A groan came from his throat, and suddenly Daughter was afraid. She slipped an arm under his shoulders and slid into the sleeping place so that his head was on her lap. She placed the palm of her hand on the center of his chest. His heart had always been strong, but now she felt only a faint fluttering.

"Grandfather!" she shouted at him. "Grandfather, don't leave me! I need you."

Daughter grabbed pelts from his sleeping place—any she could reach that were not tucked under him—and rolled them into a ball that she placed under his head and shoulders. She slipped away and grabbed a water bladder from the rafters, filled a cup and tried to make him drink. He choked, and she wiped the dribbled water from his chin, told him she would get K'os. Surely K'os would have medicine to help him.

She did not realize she had forgotten her sax until she was outside and felt the bite of the wind against her bare skin, but she did not go back. She ran to Eye-Taker's ulax, and without pause for politeness, started down the climbing log.

"My grandfather . . ." she gasped, trying to catch her breath.

"Where is your sax?" Eye-Taker asked her. Seal looked up from the spear shaft he was smoothing and frowned.

"You should protect yourself better," he said. "Wind spirits will get into your belly."

One of their sons farted, and the other children began to laugh. Daughter shook her head at them, and her eyes flooded with tears.

"My mother," said Daughter, "she was supposed to be here. My grandfather is very sick."

She saw the sudden concern in their faces, and the children closed around her, so that it was all she could do not to push them away. "My mother?" she asked again.

"She was here," Seal said, "but she left a long time ago. She must be visiting."

He told his two sons, boys of eight and ten summers, to go to all the ulas, to find K'os and send her home. Then Eye-Taker ordered one of the girls to bring a sax. They slid it over Daughter's head, and not until she felt the weight of the garment on her shoulders did she realize how cold she was. She began to shiver, her teeth clattering so hard that she could not say anything without chopping up the words.

"I will go with you back to your ulax," Eye-Taker said, and pushed Daughter toward the climbing log, hurried her outside. "My father was a shaman. I know chants that might help."

Daughter nodded. She remembered the woman's father. He had died shortly after she and the grandfather had come to the village. The shaman had worn three labrets, one at each corner of his mouth and a third below his bottom lip.

The weight of that labret had made his whole lip hang forward so his teeth were always bared in a grimace that sometimes still came to Daughter in nightmares. He had been a man of loud voice and many words, and at his death it seemed that those words had moved from his tongue into Eye-Taker's mouth. Always the woman was boasting about him, and when she spoke, she spoke as boldly as a man.

When they got back to the ulax, Water Gourd was moaning. His eyes were closed, and his breath bubbled from his mouth as though a river had suddenly decided to live in his lungs. The roll of pelts Daughter had left under his head had slipped to one side, and he was lying crooked in his bed. She knelt and again slid herself under the grandfather's shoulders, raising him until he seemed to breathe more easily.

Eye-Taker began to chant, and her words hammered in Daughter's ears. Daughter leaned forward and, in hopes that her need was strong enough to tie him to the earth, she whispered to the grandfather, told him how much she would miss him if he died.

Finally Eye-Taker's sons clambered into the ulax, each shouting and yelling, telling the story of where they had found K'os.

Their words were difficult to hear over the chants, and Eye-Taker did not stop, but began to dance and hop until Daughter felt that the whole ulax was filled with foolishness, and that she alone was there to protect her grandfather. But finally, in spite of Eye-Taker's loud voice, she understood what the boys were saying.

Her mother had been in bed with Chiton, a man whose wife had just given birth. Surely there was a curse in doing something like that. Daughter's cheeks burned in shame, and she tried not to think of what the other girls in the village would say to her.

Anger clasped her throat like a hand and squeezed until she could not breathe, could not speak no matter how hard she tried. She leaned forward and lay her cheek against the grandfather's forehead, allowed tears to drop from her eyes to his face.

Then K'os was in the ulax, and the boys were quiet. Even Eye-Taker stopped her chanting. K'os threw off her sax. Her medicine bag hung from her waist, and she pulled out a packet bound with blue string knotted twice. She used her teeth to untie it, and spilled its contents into the palm of her hand. She licked her fingertips, dipped them into the gray powder, and stuck her fingers into the grandfather's mouth, into his nostrils and the corners of his eyes. She did this twice, and it seemed to Daughter that the grandfather's breathing eased.

Daughter sucked large gulps of air into her mouth as though her lungs worked for both of them. The grandfather's eyes opened, and Daughter again found her voice.

"Grandfather," she said, "Mother has made medicine for you. Soon you will be well."

Daughter smiled and glanced up at K'os. The woman had a strange look on her face, almost regret, nearly sorrow, and the fist returned to Daughter's throat, again squeezed off her words. Eye-Taker pushed in to stand beside the grandfather. The woman nodded her head in a hard rhythm, as though her skull were a drum. Her lips moved, but no sound came out. A chant without words? What good was that? Then Eye-Taker gave voice to the words, and Daughter realized she was not making a chant for healing but sang in mourning, a death song.

"No!" Daughter said.

The word was like a knife, and it opened her throat, escaped as a scream that made Eye-Taker's sons raise the flats of their hands to their ears.

"No-o-o-o! No, Grandfather! No! No! No!"

She leaned forward over his body, and when Eye-Taker and K'os tried to pull her away, she kicked and scratched until finally they allowed her to stay where she was.

"Leave her there for the night," Eye-Taker told K'os.

"Maybe tomorrow she will regain her reason and grieve as a granddaughter should."

So all night Daughter stayed with the grandfather, guarded his body with prayers and chants.

In the morning, when she finally allowed the village women to come near, they saw with horror that she had cut off another toe, the smallest on her other foot, and that she had placed it in the old man's hand. When they tried to pry it from his fingers, Daughter growled at them like an otter, stood with teeth bared until K'os asked them to leave the toe where it was.

"I knew a man who cut off a finger and offered it to the spirits in exchange for his son's life," K'os told the First Men women.

"The son was dying?" one of the women asked.

"Nearly dead."

"And did he live?"

"He lived," K'os said.

Then the women made no further protests, only whispered among themselves about the strange customs and foolishness of other people. K'os herself sewed up Daughter's wound, and from that day said nothing about it, offered no comfort or admonition.

"After all, what do we know about these Boat People?" K'os asked Eye-Taker. "I shared an ulax with Taadzi, and still could not understand everything he did, but he was a wise man. A good grandfather to Uutuk."

And though for several days after the death, people spoke of K'os's visit to Chiton's ulax, she was so faithful in mourning Water Gourd that the whispers soon died. And when Seal took K'os back to his own bed, all the village honored him for his selflessness. What other man would keep a woman who had dishonored him, was nearly old, and could give him no children?

EIGHTEEN

Herendeen Bay, Alaska Peninsula
602 B.C.

"Thank you," Yikaas said softly.

Qumalix smiled at him, and the wind took a strand of her hair, pulled it from the collar of her sax, and carried it to Yikaas's cheek. Qumalix caught it with long fingers, tucked it back into her sax.

"It's a good story," she told him, "but I do not tell it as well as the one who taught me."

"The old man who is with you?" he asked.

"No, he's my grandfather. He was never a storyteller. Words do not come easily to him. Though he holds many stories in his mind, he has trouble telling them." She laughed and tipped her head as though remembering.

"Who taught you then?"

"His father."

Yikaas drew in his breath. "A man so old?" he asked.

"He's dead now. Dead many years. So you see, I had to learn quickly and when I was very young. When he no longer had strength to do anything but lie still, I used to sit beside his bed, and he would tell me stories. Each word came from his mouth as slowly as a woman punches awl holes to make a seam."

"A good way to learn patience," he said.

She nodded, her eyes turned toward the sky, and he knew that she had left him for a moment to revisit those days of learning.

"I gathered his words like an old woman who picks up spilled beads, and his slowness gave me opportunity to consider the light and color and life in each."

She plucked two blades of grass, let the wind take them from her fingers. Yikaas felt the warmth of her body like comfort, and he knew she must be tired, but he did not want her to leave. He opened his mouth to say something, hoping words might bind her, but she spoke also, their voices tumbling together so that he did not know what she had said.

She laughed, and he could hear the embarrassment in her laughter. What had the grandmother told him? The Sea Hunters—the First Men—were a people who did not need to fill the air with words. When they spoke it was because something needed to be said.

"I'm sorry. What did you say?" he asked.

"Only that I have talked enough today. Now it's your turn. I told you a story, so you must tell me one. Storytellers are traders, nae'? Journey for journey."

Aaa, she would stay, but Yikaas warned himself to see nothing more in her request than a storyteller's need to learn. Perhaps she felt as he did when he had told too many stories, and the sound of his own voice grew so wearisome that he could not tell whether his words were strong or weak. Those were the times to listen to others, to allow their tales to stir his own spirit and again give him delight in storytelling.

"Do you have something you'd like to hear?" he asked.

"I do not know many River stories. Tell me one that you like."

He thought for a moment, then said, "Do you remember when you were talking about Daughter, how K'os mentioned a father who cut off a finger to save his son's life?"

"Yes."

"Would you like to hear a story about that boy?"

"The son?"

"Yes. His name was Ghaden, and he grew to be a man who was known for his strength and wisdom."

"I would like to hear about Ghaden," she said.

She tucked her legs up into her sax and leaned against a hillock of grass. She pulled a strip of dried fish from her sleeve and handed it to him, then took one out for herself and said, "I'm ready. Tell me a story."

Yikaas took a bite from the fish and, looking out at the star-filled sky, pictured his own village: the domed caribou hide winter lodges, the meat caches, the wide river that flowed nearby. Ghaden had lived in a village much like that. A little closer to the sea, the elders said, but Ghaden had lived so long ago that no one knew for sure.

In those days, animals could turn themselves into people, and the stories that Yikaas now told as Dzuuggi were being lived.

He closed his eyes and saw Ghaden, son of a Sea Hunter mother and wide of shoulder like her people. Tall like his father, who was part River and claimed some Walrus blood, a people known for their bravery, those Walrus Hunters. Walrus Hunters still lived not far from the Traders' Beach, but they were a different people, had come from the north, were fierce and strong, sometimes friends, sometimes enemies. Those first Walrus Hunters were gone now, and no one knew where, though some of the storytellers said they had taken their iqyan far to the south and lived there on distant shores and islands, hunting not walrus but whale. It seemed a foolish story. Why would anyone leave the rich waters of the North Sea for that land where monsters lived, cet'aeni, nuhu'anh, and more? But enough of wondering. Qumalix had asked for a story.

Yikaas opened his eyes and began. "As a boy, Ghaden had learned to live with sorrow," he said. "His mother had been killed by a woman named Red Leaf when Ghaden was hardly to the age of remembering. Red Leaf had also tried to kill Ghaden, but he survived, though no one had expected him to live. Red Leaf had used a knife, and Ghaden's wounds were deep."

"Was that when the father offered his finger in exchange for Ghaden's life?" Qumalix interrupted to ask.

"Yes. And Cen was given his son's life in trade. Later, Cen moved to another village and took a wife named Gheli."

"Aaa, yes, Gheli," Qumalix said.

"That's another story for another day," said Yikaas, speaking to her as if she were a child. But she took no offense, only laughed, and so Yikaas continued.

"Cen and Gheli had two daughters, and though Cen was a trader and traveled much, and Ghaden was his only son, for a long time, Cen dared not come to the village where Ghaden lived because he was afraid the men there would kill him."

"Why?" Qumalix asked. "He was a River man, nae'?"

"Remember in the story I told about K'os how two of the River villages had fought against one another until one was destroyed with only a few hunters left?"

"I remember."

"Even the village that won the battle had many of their young men killed, and so after a few years, they decided to forget their anger and become one people. In that way they combined the strength of those hunters they had left."

"What does that have to do with Cen and Ghaden?"

"Before Cen married Gheli, he and Ghaden had lived in the village that had lost the battle. The problem came when Cen and the hunters of that village went to fight. Cen saw that they were outnumbered, and he left them in the night, and did not return."

"He was a coward," Qumalix said.

"Yet brave enough to cut off his finger when he thought the spirits might accept it as a gift and spare Ghaden's life."

"It's all very confusing."

"You will understand my story," Yikaas told her.

"It would help me if you spoke my language, and I did not have to listen to River words."

Her complaint angered Yikaas, but he shrugged and said, "Then I would need a teacher."

"Your aunt, Kuy'aa, speaks the language. At least a little," she said.

Anger took control of his tongue, and Yikaas answered, "Well, go get her. She can teach me now, quickly, so I can speak this story in words more gentle to your ears."

He saw her jaw tighten, and she jammed a large piece of fish into her mouth, as though to prevent herself from a sharp reply. Finally, speaking through the fish, she said, "I will listen to your River words."

"Stop me if you don't understand something," he told her. "I would be glad to teach you new words."

He waited, wondering if she would offer to teach him her language in exchange, but she did not, and so when he began, Yikaas spoke in a hard voice, touched with disappointment—a good voice for Ghaden's story.

Near Iliamna Lake, Alaska
Late Winter, 6447 B.C.

GHADEN'S STORY

"You're wasting food, feeding him," the hunter Sok said.

Ghaden squatted beside Biter, ran a hand through the dog's dark fur.

"He's old, Ghaden. He doesn't hunt anymore, and he won't be able to keep up with us when we travel to our fish camps."

Ghaden didn't have an answer. Sok was right. Biter was a dog celebrated for his wisdom, but now he was old and in pain.

"I'll take him," Sok said. "My aim is true. He will die before he even feels the bite of the spear."

Ghaden kept his head down. With sixteen summers, he had long been a man, and what man shed tears for a dog? He could not let Sok see his eyes.

"I'll do it," Ghaden said, and his voice was firm, hard.

Sok grunted and walked away. Ghaden stayed beside the dog, spent a long time combing his hands through Biter's fur.

Finally he said, "We should hunt today, Biter. See, look at the sky. Before long, clouds will settle in, and tomorrow we will get more snow. But the river ice is solid, and it will be easy walking. Wouldn't a fresh hare taste good tonight? If we get two we can give one to Yaa. Cries-loud has not yet returned from following those early caribou that left their tracks so near the village."

He thought of all the dogs he had known. Ligige's dog that even in his old age had helped kill that evil one, Night Man. Ligige' had been dead for two winters now, even in her last days full of wisdom and mischief.

The summer before her death, she had traded for another dog, and during her last sickness had given the dog to Ghaden. It was a female, and he had mated her with Biter, gotten himself three good pups. One had the look of Biter, the same dark brown markings and some of Biter's wisdom, though with a young dog, it was hard to tell. Ghaden had kept that pup for himself, given one of the others to Yaa's husband Cries-loud, and traded another to Cries-loud's younger brother, Carries Much, for fox pelts—less than the pup was worth, but Carries Much needed his own dog.

Sok had grumbled when Ghaden gave the dog to the boy, though Carries Much was Sok's own son. Sok had wanted the dog himself, but he was harsh with his animals, a good man with his wives and his children, but not so good with dogs—ignoring them for too long when he did not need them, stingy with their food.

Ghaden slipped into his sister's lodge, gathered snowshoes, two thrusting spears, and a bow. It was still winter, but the day was warm enough so that the bow, when pulled taut, would not break, and for taking small animals, Ghaden was better with an arrow than a spear.

Aqamdax was sitting with her young daughter, helping the girl string sinew thread through awl holes widely spaced in a piece of caribou hide. The girl's tongue was thrust from the corner of her mouth as she concentrated. She grunted in frustration when the thread twisted, and Aqamdax, though her eyes were on Ghaden, said to her daughter, "Remember what you do?"

The little girl let the needle hang loose, watched as the thread spun to untangle itself.

"Sometimes when you try too hard," Aqamdax explained, "things get tangled, and the only way to untangle them is to let go."

For a moment Ghaden closed his eyes. It was difficult to have a sister who always knew his thoughts.

"Be safe," she said to him as he left.

Unlike other dogs in the village, Biter usually slept in the lodge, but during feeding times, Ghaden staked him outside. He untied the dog, urged him with a shout and promises of good hunting. Biter groaned, heaved himself to his feet.

They walked the packed paths of the village, wove their way between the winter lodges and down to the river. Snow covered the ice in a strong, hard crust, but as Ghaden walked, he used the butt end of a spear to test the surface. Even small cracks could release water that would remain trapped and unfrozen under a layer of snow. If a man broke through into that water, he would soak his boots and freeze his feet. More than one hunter had been lost that way.

He walked until he came to a path that angled up from the river, a woman's trail that led to traplines. He cut up to the path, then stopped and put on his snowshoes. He trudged through the snow, loose in the shelter of willows and alders. He did not plan to go far. The walking was too difficult for Biter, but each of his steps seemed to lead to another, and finally Ghaden realized that he was walking only because he did not want to stop.

He turned and looked back at Biter. The dog was struggling, walking with his head down, tongue out. Ghaden crouched beside the dog, flung an arm around his neck.

How often had they sat in just this way, Biter's warmth and strength a comfort to a little boy afraid of so many things?

"I will never have a better dog," he told Biter. Biter wagged his tail, and Ghaden said, "I don't know where dogs go in the spirit world." His throat closed around his words, and Ghaden had to stop, take a breath. "But if you can, wait for me."

Biter whined low in his throat, and Ghaden knew that the cold was making the animal's legs ache. Had Ligige' herself not complained of the cold, what it did to her knees and ankles?

Enough waiting, Ghaden told himself, and for the last time, he leaned his head against Biter's neck, buried his face in the soft fur there. Yaa had promised that when Biter died, she would make a parka ruff for Ghaden from the dog's fur. At least that would be a comfort, and perhaps also give Ghaden some of Biter's strength.

Biter was too old to run ahead of Ghaden on the trail, giving opportunity to use a quick spear from behind. The easiest way to kill him would be to cut his throat and hold him as he died. Ghaden pulled his sleeve knife from the sheath on his arm, moving slowly so Biter would not jump away. Ghaden clasped the blade tightly, prepared to sink it deep, but suddenly Biter leaped up, his eyes fixed on something hidden in the brush. The whine in his throat changed into a deep growl, and the dog jumped away.

Ghaden lunged forward, trying to catch the braided babiche cord that was around Biter's neck, but, hampered by his snowshoes, he came up with only a handful of fur.

As though his legs were suddenly young again, Biter jumped through the snow, his frenzied yips laced with howls and cries. Ghaden followed the dog into a thick growth of black spruce. Two ptarmigan flew up from their hiding places in the snow, startling Ghaden into covering his face with his arms. Then he heard a growl—not dog, but bear— and he stopped, shifted his knife into his left hand, and pulled out one of his spears. He moved his head until he could see the animal through the trees, a glimpse of dark fur. Biter was still barking, and Ghaden slowly walked forward, pushed his way through a tangle of alders, then stopped in surprise.

It was a brown bear, the largest he had ever seen.

The warmth of the day must have pulled the animal from its winter den, Ghaden thought, though it was early yet for bears to be out. It stood as tall as two men, as wide as three, and was angry, as bears often are in late winter, their bellies empty, and the rivers still too thick with ice for fishing, winter berries stripped by children from the village.

If Biter had not alerted Ghaden, the bear would have come upon them as they sat together in the snow. Then what chance would they have had?

Like all River dogs, Biter had been trained in hunting bear, but the River hunters took black bear—smaller and less likely to attack, more predictable in their actions. Brown bears, twice, even three times as large as black, showed no fear of men, and why should they? What man, even armed with spears, knives, and a bow, had a good chance against such an animal, especially if it was hungry or protecting cubs?

The bear was distracted by Biter's barking, and at first did not see Ghaden. It lunged toward the dog, but Biter jumped away.

Ghaden gripped his spear, and when the bear reared up, erect on its hind legs, he aimed for the heart, threw. The bear caught sight of the spear in its flight and thrust out a paw, the animal's brown and yellow claws as long as Ghaden's fingers. The point penetrated the right front leg, and the bear screamed, turning its attention from Biter to the stone spearhead that jutted from the inner side of the leg. Biter scooted around behind the bear to rip at the animal's hamstrings.

"Get away, Biter!" Ghaden shouted.

A dog so old was not quick enough to lunge in and bite, then escape beyond reach of the animal's claws or teeth. That Biter had been able to evade the bear during the first attack was surprising enough. Ghaden called again, but Biter continued to bark and lunge.

Escape, Ghaden told himself. Go now. What more honorable way for Biter to die? But Ghaden could not make himself leave.

The bear broke off the spear's wooden shaft, bit at the spearhead, lacerating its tongue and coloring its muzzle with blood. The animal turned, swatted again at Biter. Ghaden, heart pounding, threw his other spear. This time the weapon hit solidly just below the animal's breastbone.

Ghaden waited for the bear to drop, but it merely grunted and gripped the spear with both paws, raised the butt end to its mouth, and jerked until the spear was free.

The bear looked at Ghaden, its eyes as wise and knowing as a man's, then stepped forward and crushed the spear into the snow.

Ghaden moved his hands to his bow, pulled the tie string to release it from his back, jerked arrows from the sheath. The bear dropped to all fours, and Ghaden's breath caught hard, closing up his throat, so that blackness began to draw in from the sides of his eyes.

The animal was going to attack. What could an arrow do against a bear that even spears would not kill?

Suddenly Biter jumped from behind, set his teeth into the back of the animal's left leg. At first the bear merely shook the leg, but Biter braced his feet in the snow and began to jerk his head side to side. The bear stopped, and Ghaden nocked an arrow, let it fly.

It took the bear in the left shoulder, and before the animal could turn toward the pain, Ghaden released another. It found the bear's neck.

The bear roared, broke off both shafts with one swipe, then he twisted and raised a paw, brought it down hard on Biter's head. The dog yelped, released his grip, fell to the snow, and lay kicking, keening out a thin, high wail.

Ghaden aimed the third arrow for the bear's eye, waited to release it until the animal turned back toward him. But he missed his mark, and the arrow glanced off the bear's skull, leaving a bloody furrow. Then the animal was running, and there was no more time for arrows.

In deep snow, even with snowshoes, Ghaden had no chance. He dropped his bow and drew his knives, the sleeve knife in his left hand, the long-bladed hunting knife he kept strapped to his leg in his right. He rolled himself into a ball, shrugged his pack up over the back of his neck, and waited for the attack.

Ghaden felt the claws rake through the tough caribou hide of his parka, through the inner parka and into his skin. The bear's mouth smelled of rotten meat, of long winter sleep, of fresh blood. The animal's teeth scraped Ghaden's shoulder, then clamped over the pack on Ghaden's back. The bear reared and jerked the pack hard enough to break its straps.

All things around Ghaden slowed. Even the wind's voice dimmed, and Biter's whines were a distant sound, lost in the branches of spruce and alder. He had heard stories of hunters who, attacked by a bear, had pretended to be dead. But this bear was hungry, and even if it thought Ghaden were dead, the animal would eat.

Ghaden turned his head and saw through the ruff of his parka that the bear was still battling the pack. If he had any chance to save himself, he must do it now. He no longer had his bow, and his arrows lay scattered in the snow. Even if he managed to bury both his knives deep in the bear's neck, slice the huge vessels that fed blood to the head, the animal would take too long to die.

With the bear weak from blood loss, perhaps Ghaden would have a chance if he ran. The animal had its back to him, but was so close that Ghaden could hear the grumble that came from its throat as it ravaged the pack. Ghaden, jumped up and began running through the snow. The ice crust caught at his snowshoes with each step, clutching as though to hold him back. With every breath he gasped in a mouthful of cold air until his lungs burned.

He saw the river through the trees and began to hope. Then, suddenly, a rip of heat, pain. The bear's claws gouged into his side. Ghaden turned, felt the teeth again, this time in his left arm. He plunged his hunting knife into the animal's throat, bore down on the haft, cutting a bloody trench into the animal's neck.

The bear slammed a paw against Ghaden's shoulder, and Ghaden was suddenly flying through the air. He landed against a large spruce, heard the pop of his ribs, felt pain like a blade slice into his side.

Ghaden reached for the tree's lowest branches and clamped his legs around the bole, his snowshoes scraping and clattering against the rough bark. The animal's breath was on the back of his neck, but Ghaden could not pull himself up. He braced for the death blow, then heard the tortured cry of a dog.

Though he should have been trying to climb, Ghaden could not help but look, and he opened his mouth in disbelief when he saw Biter standing behind the bear. Flesh torn from the top of Biter's head hung in a bloody flap over his left ear, leaving his skull bare.

The dog's shrieks were terrible, and even the bear stopped, stared, but then it dropped to all fours and attacked, flipping Biter to his back, raking claws into Biter's side. Biter whipped his head to find purchase on the bear's throat. The bear reared, and Biter hung on, rending the flesh as the bear tried to shake him loose.

Blood poured over Biter's fur, and the bear's roars rebounded from the trees, so it sounded as though many animals fought. Ghaden saw his bow in the snow and, dropping from the tree, scuttled over to it. He nocked an arrow and took aim, screamed at the pain when he drew back the bowstring.

The arrow lodged in the bear's left eye. The animal opened its mouth and a flow of blood gouted out, slicked Biter's fur. The dog released his grip and fell to the ground. The bear cocked its head and batted at something Ghaden could not see, then it slowly toppled, crushing Biter into the earth.

Ghaden waited for the bear to shake itself back to life, but it remained where it was, and finally Ghaden took another arrow, released it into the animal's neck. The bear didn't move. Ghaden walked close, prodded it with the end of his bow. The bear was dead.

Ghaden's ribs pained him with each breath, and his left arm dripped blood, but he set his right shoulder against the carcass, took in as much air as he was able, and heaved the animal to its side, enough so he could get Biter out from under it.

Biter's eyes were open, and Ghaden knelt beside him, lifted a hand to push the dog's scalp back over the dome of his skull. Ghaden stroked his muzzle and began a quiet song of praise, something sung to honor warriors. For one quick moment the dog's spirit rested in those open eyes, looked out at Ghaden. Love there. Love.

NINETEEN

Herendeen Bay, Alaska Peninsula
602 B.C.

"A sad story," Qumalix said, but she laid a hand against her belly as if she had just eaten her fill of a good meal.

Yikaas shrugged. "What better way for a brave dog to die? Besides, he was old."

"What happened to Ghaden?"

"According to most storytellers, he had broken ribs, and he carried the scars of the bear's claws and teeth all his life. He must have been a man who understood how to show respect. A bear that powerful would have cursed him had he not followed all the taboos."

"Taboos? What taboos?"

Yikaas was surprised by her question. Anyone who did not respect a brown bear was a fool. "The same that all people follow," he said. "A hunter can scarcely say the animal's name, and as a woman, even though you are a storyteller, you dare not. Only an old woman is allowed to eat bear meat, and then just certain parts. The hide must be scraped out by a man, and left to hang for a summer or two before it can be used. Some people cut it into little pieces and bury it.

That's how much life is in the animal. Even the hairs can curse you. The First Men do not know these taboos?"

"On the island where I live there are no . . ." Qumalix paused. "Large animals," she finally said. "Perhaps the hunters who live on the Traders' Beach know about taboos. I have heard them say there are such animals in the mountains here, and some that even live beside the streams."

"You have no bears on your island?"

"None."

"Caribou?"

"No."

"What do your men hunt?"

As soon as he asked the question, Yikaas realized it was a foolish one. The First Men were sea hunters. They took seals and sea lions and walrus and sometimes even whales.

"Our hunters take sea mammals."

There was no hint of derision in her words, and he appreciated the gentleness of her answer.

"But tell me more about Ghaden," she said. "What happened to him after the fight?"

"Ghaden's sister scraped out the dog's skin, and for the rest of his life, he wore Biter's fur as trim for his parka hood. The old ones say that the dog continued to protect him, for Ghaden lived long and became chief hunter for his people."

Qumalix stood up and shook the sand from her sax. "That's a good ending. Too many stories end with sadness."

Yikaas shrugged. "Any story can end with happiness or sadness, depending on where the storyteller chooses to stop."

She smiled. "I see why they chose you as Dzuuggi," she told him. "You should tell Ghaden's story tonight. The men will like it."

"And not the women?"

"The women, too, but men are more difficult to please."

She spoke a few words in the First Men tongue, then switched to the River language to say, "Those are the First Men's words of leaving. I said, 'I am going now.' "

Yikaas repeated the phrase, purposely twisted some of the sounds. Qumalix cocked her head and said the words again. Yikaas hid a smile in his cheek at her patience, for she corrected him until he had them right.

As the next long day colored toward night and its promise of brief darkness, the people left their fishing, and those hunters who were not out in iqyan joined the women and children in the storyteller lodge. This time a hunter from another First Men village spoke first. He wore a whaling hat, brightly painted in reds and blues, with eyes drawn on each side and a long prow that extended beyond his forehead like the snout of an animal.

He did not have the River tongue, so Qumalix translated his words. Yikaas felt like a young man sharing his wife for the first time, and his skin prickled at the thought of the hunter's words flowing from Qumalix's mouth. Finally he could no longer watch, but had to close his eyes and only listen.

The stories were about hunting, and Yikaas waited in hope for the man to boast of his own success, but he seemed to have no faults, telling only the stories of others and telling them with great respect.

Some of the stories were funny and made the people laugh; others brought tears. If Qumalix paused in translating, Yikaas found himself holding his breath until he heard what was going to happen next. But even so, the Sea Hunter's success with his stories grated as harshly as lava rock against Yikaas's spirit.

Between stories, he thought back over all the tales he himself told. Most were about people who lived in ancient times. Sometimes those stories were not much to hear, but what Dzuuggi could allow that knowledge to die? None of his stories were funny, but it would be good to have tales that brought laughter rather than only solemn agreement or careful thought. Kuy'aa should have told him such stories; surely funny things had happened to River People, too.

At least the Sea Hunter man spoke only in his own voice, did not send his words to the top of the lodge to echo from the smokehole, did not speak harshly to mimic a hunter or raise his voice to show he spoke for a woman. These were all things that Yikaas did and did well. And there were no riddles. Of course only River People made riddles, but these Sea Hunters might enjoy them, too. They were thinkers. Their silence proved them so, and often they said something very wise, words that Yikaas took into his heart to remember.

Finally the Sea Hunter's stories ended, but before he left the center of the ulax, he reached into a pouch that hung at his waist and pulled out a necklace of bird bone beads, handed it to Qumalix. Yikaas had to turn his eyes away from her joy. He wondered if such giving was customary among the Sea Hunters. If so, his rudeness was already noticed. It would do little good to give her something now. Better to wait until all the storytelling was over, then give her a large gift, something a woman would value. He could ask Kuy'aa what that might be. Perhaps Qumalix would like one of the parkas he had brought to trade.

Kuy'aa was sitting beside him, and she bumped his arm to call him from his thoughts, then pointed with her chin toward Qumalix. Qumalix gestured for Yikaas to join her, and he made his way to the center of the ulax, took his place beside her. She spoke for a moment to the people in the lodge, then leaned close to whisper that she had explained about Ghaden's story, and they were ready to learn about this man and his brave dog Biter.

Yikaas used his voices to tell the story, and though he had no jokes, the people laughed when the dog's barks came from the ulax roof. Even Qumalix laughed, hard enough that she had to stop in her translating, and Yikaas thought that she might be showing a little more joy in his stories than she had with the Sea Hunter's tales.

He wondered for a moment what it would be like to have Qumalix as wife. She was good to look at, and they could share one another's stories, but he reminded himself that most Sea Hunter women would rather be wife to a First Men hunter than a River man. River People and First Men looked at life so differently. Then he remembered the stories of Aqamdax and Chakliux. What man and woman had ever been happier together? And Aqamdax had been Sea Hunter, Chakliux River. Perhaps their differences had not mattered so much because they had both been storytellers.

The thought lifted his heart, until some commotion at the back of the ulax interrupted Qumalix's translations. She stopped, and the grandfather who had come with her stood and began to scold a man and woman for their rudeness. Qumalix leaned toward Yikaas and told him that they were husband and wife, known for their squabbles.

The husband stomped up the climbing log, hissing insults as he left. Then Yikaas asked himself why he should even consider taking a wife. He was young yet and had many years before he had to make such a difficult decision, choosing one woman above all others. What if he and Qumalix turned out to be like that man and woman—a joke in their own village? Why not just see if she was willing to come to his bed? He was Dzuuggi. Women never refused him.

Suddenly he realized that he had paused in his story-telling. Qumalix was looking at him with questions in her eyes. He made an apology and continued, living the story again as the words passed from his mouth. When he told of the bear's attack, the people were so quiet, he could hear their breathing. When Biter died, some of the women wept, and men cleared their throats, made remarks about bears in gruff voices, low and soft.

Then the Sea Hunter storyteller rose from his seat and asked if he could tell another story. Yikaas wanted to hear one of Qumalix's stories, and several of the people in the lodge seemed to feel the same way, for two of the women nodded their heads toward her. But in politeness, Qumalix gave her place to the Sea Hunter storyteller and again translated his words so the River People could understand.

Yikaas sat down in disgust. The man had had his turn.

Qumalix deserved her chance. Yikaas's anger grew as he listened, but dissipated when the Sea Hunter tried to lift his voice to the top of the ulax as Yikaas had, tried to speak in various voices and so become animal, woman, or man. He was not good at it, and some of the people in the back of the ulax began to grumble. Others left, but Yikaas sat very still, listened very hard, and learned how not to tell a story.

Finally the man was done, and the people, as though speaking in one voice, asked for Qumalix. Yikaas saw the disappointment on the Sea Hunter's face, and he wondered if he had looked the same way when the people were dissatisfied with him. It was not a good thing for a storyteller to act like a child, pouting over criticism. How better to learn?

Kuy'aa leaned against him, and he thought perhaps that she was weary and wanted to leave. He felt his heart drop in disappointment, but he smiled gently at her and said, "Aunt, are you tired? I will take you to the lodge where you are staying."

"No, no," she said impatiently, as though he were a troublesome child. "What storyteller gets tired listening to others' tales?" Then she added, "You did a good job. I was proud of you. You see that Sea Hunter storyteller?" She tilted her head toward the man and lowered her voice to whisper, "He's jealous. He knows your story was better than his."

"His hunting stories were good," Yikaas said.

"Of course they were." When he told them, he was thinking more about the stories than himself. The second time he spoke, he was thinking about himself, and about you and about who was best.

"When a storyteller pushes himself forward like that, above what he is saying, then the story no longer lives. It is only told."

It was wise advice, as was nearly everything Kuy'aa told him, and Yikaas opened his mouth to thank her, but she lifted fingers to her lips and nodded toward Qumalix.

Qumalix had begun to speak, explaining that her new story about Daughter took place five summers after the grandfather's death. The people murmured their understanding, and she began.

TWENTY

Yunaska Island, The Aleutian Chain
6435 B.C.

DAUGHTER'S STORY
The wind blew over them, whining, keening. Early summer grass grew strong from the hummocks left by previous years' growth. Daughter's sax was still rucked up around her waist, White Salmon's broad back and strong arms bare to the cold. She tucked her head against his shoulder. Their lovemaking had been quick, distracted, and she knew he was thinking about the evening ahead when he would speak to K'os and Seal about her brideprice.

She had given herself to him nearly a year ago, and during that time had prayed to make a baby. She could think of no reason for K'os or Seal to refuse White Salmon's offer, but a child would bind them beyond any objections her parents might raise.

White Salmon's brideprice offer was generous, surely more than most young men would give. No one could deny that she was skilled with a needle, that she was a hard worker and quick to smile, but she was not truly First Men. Who could say what her children would be like?

When young men began claiming Daughter's friends—a year after their moon bloods had begun—Daughter herself had little hope that any hunter would consider her. Perhaps for a night, but as wife? No. She was too different. When White Salmon first came to her, she refused him. Why give herself to a man who would only use her? If he had been old, a poor hunter, weak in some way, she might have considered it, but why suffer the hope that his attentions would lay in her heart? Better to ignore him, pretend he had no interest. Then her soul would not be eaten with bitterness after he had forgotten her.

But he had persisted, and finally she had given in. They had climbed into the hills above the village, had lain together among the clumps of wide-bladed grass, the tall, thick stems of iitikaalux. She had used all the skills K'os had taught her, ways of pleasing a man, and she had seen that he was surprised, first at her knowledge, then, upon entering her, to discover that she had been unspoiled. He had been gentle with her that night, and Daughter had allowed herself the joy of their union. But the next day, she treated White Salmon as though nothing had happened between them. Only after he had come to her again and again, had begun visiting her in Seal's ulax and made no secret of his intentions, boasting of the brideprice he would pay for her, only then had she allowed herself to hope that she might have a young hunter like other girls in the village, that she would be more than some old man's second wife, slave in bed to her husband, slave in work to a sister-wife.

"I must go now. I have everything ready," White Salmon told her. His voice was firm, and scattered any doubts Daughter had. K'os and Seal would have a difficult time finding a better man for her.

He sat up and pulled on his birdskin sax. Daughter had sewn him a fur seal parka, something she had kept secret and would give him tonight after he and Seal decided on the day their marriage feast would be held. Soon, Daughter thought. In three or four days, long enough for her and K'os and Eye-

Taker to prepare the food. Long enough for Eye-Taker's children to gather enough sea urchins and dig enough clams, catch enough pogies.

Seal had had little luck this summer in his hunting—another reason to be glad for a son-by-marriage to help bring in enough meat for the winter to come. But White Salmon had promised to provide the seal and sea lion meat for the feast, even to give some of the whale he had taken that spring, a fine humpback.

Daughter stood to brush the grass from the back of White Salmon's sax. He clasped her hand quickly, then strode away. She watched until he disappeared in the fold of a valley, then turned and went the opposite way, to the place where she and K'os had buried her grandfather.

"He has gone to ask for me now, Grandfather," she said and knelt beside the mound of rock that covered his body. She had carried most of the gravestones herself, bringing them up from the beach, hoping that the water that had rounded and smoothed those stones had once touched the shores of the Boat People's island, hoping that her grandfather would feel some comfort in those sea-worn rocks. "Perhaps next time I come, I will be a wife."

The words added to her hope, and she felt the same fluttering tightness that came to her belly each time White Salmon looked at her. She lifted prayers—for White Salmon and their marriage, for her grandfather—but finally she stood and started toward the village, walking in the long shadows of the evening, back through the grasses and the wind.

Daughter waited at the top of the ulax. She could hear their voices rising, Seal's and White Salmon's. Once in a while K'os would speak, but Daughter could not make out their words. There were many things to settle in a marriage agreement, not only brideprice, but living arrangements and hunting agreements. Daughter had told White Salmon that she would rather live with his family, and he had agreed, promising that once she had given him a child they would have their own ulax. Until then Daughter wanted to be out of K'os's ulax, away from Seal and his groping hands, away from K'os's jealousy as the years stole her beauty, but added to Daughter's.

White Salmon was inside a long time, and while Daughter waited, the wind grew so strong it seemed to push the stars away, made them so small that they were mere pinpricks in the sky.

When White Salmon finally came up the climbing log, it was too dark for Daughter to see his face. She stood in the grass thatching and held out her hands, whispered his name, and when he did not respond, she clasped his arm. He said nothing, only jerked away from her grasp and jumped down from the ulax, strode into the night. Daughter stood in the wind trembling.

When she went inside, Seal bared clenched teeth in a smile that made her shudder. K'os had her back to the climbing log, but she must have heard Daughter, for she said without turning, "Some men think they can have what they want without paying its worth. Some men are foolish, and foolish men do not make good husbands."

Daughter's fear, her disappointment, changed into anger, and though usually she did not answer K'os's criticisms, this time she said, "Mother, do not speak about your husband in such a way. For at least he has brought us a seal to eat, two since winter."

She heard K'os hiss and was wise enough to leave. Even boys of ten or eleven summers had already taken five or six seals. K'os's angry, scolding voice followed Daughter as she slid down from the ulax roof. What could they do to her if she and White Salmon simply decided on their own to be husband and wife? No brideprice. No hunting agreement.

She went to White Salmon's ulax, stood outside for a long time, hoping that perhaps he would come out, that they could talk this through. He was a proud man, and she had no doubt that K'os and Seal had insulted him. How had K'os convinced Seal that he was better off without a son like White Salmon? Of course Seal's sons, now grown, were generous and, unlike their father, good hunters.

Daughter climbed up to the ulax roof, took long breaths, inviting the wind into her chest to give her courage, and called down to White Salmon's family. At first there was no response, but finally White Salmon's mother stuck her head out the roof hole. The light coming up from the ulax made her face look like a mask worn by dancers to ward off evil and scare away spirits. Something broken after use, burned to keep those spirits from returning.

"Why are you here?" she asked. Her voice was hard and angry.

"I need to speak to White Salmon," she said, nearly whispering.

"Leave him alone. He does not want to see you."

"Please . . ."

"Go away."

The woman climbed back down into her ulax, but Daughter stayed, waited, hoping that White Salmon's anger would fade, that he would come to her. When the cold of the night ate into her bones and she could do nothing but shake, she left. Why stay when she knew she could not even open her mouth to speak without shredding the words through chattering teeth?

She went to the chief hunter's ulax, slipped inside. During the years since the grandfather's death, K'os had joined her husband twice on trading trips. Both times, Daughter had stayed in the village. During the first trip, she had lived with Eye-Taker and her children, but during the second Daughter had stayed with the chief hunter and his large family. That summer, the chief hunter had lost a wife in childbirth and the remaining two wives said they needed Daughter's help in sewing clothing for their children, to make up for the lost needle of that dead wife.

Daughter had been happy there, so much did the chief hunter's wives treat her like one of their own, scolding and teaching and laughing.

In the chief hunter's ulax all things seemed easier. If something was not finished by night, well, then, it could be done the next day. If Daughter sewed a crooked seam, then she could fix it. If someone spilled oil, well, the smell of it would sweeten the crowberry heather that padded the floor. There was little anger, little regret, and no day was marred by Seal's heavy-lidded eyes watching her from the shadows.

Where else could Daughter go, now that White Salmon's family did not want her?

Only one lamp burned in the ulax. The chief and his wives and their children were already in their sleeping places, but the grandmother was still awake. In her old age, she found sleep difficult to capture. She smiled a welcome to Daughter, patted the floor beside her, and when Daughter sat down, she handed her a needle and a cormorant skin sax that needed mending.

So then, for that night, Daughter stayed awake, sewing, and when morning finally gave the old woman heavy eyes, Daughter tucked her into a sleeping place, and sat alone in the ulax until she heard one of the wives wake. Then Daughter crept up the climbing log, and out into the day. Her sorrow was blunted, both by lack of sleep and also because of the pretense she had lived as she sat up with the grandmother—that she belonged to the chief hunter, a daughter loved, one whose marriage would be celebrated rather than cursed.

For the next few days, Daughter stayed in Seal's ulax, kept her fingers busy with sewing. Once she returned to the chief hunter's ulax, but by then even the grandmother knew what had happened to her, and Daughter could not bear their pity. Better to be with K'os, who treated her brusquely as though all that had happened was Daughter's fault. She tried not to hope that White Salmon would come for her, but every footstep on the ulax roof set her heart racing.

The morning of the fifth day, Seal came inside, windblown and smelling of fish. "We are ready," he told K'os, lifting his chin toward Daughter and raising his eyebrows in question.

K'os shook her head, and Daughter's belly tightened in dread. Something was happening. Had they agreed to give her to some other man? Someone old who could offer a better brideprice?

She dropped her sewing and got to her feet, clutched her fingers around the amulet that hung from her neck. The ulax was warm, but suddenly she wished she was wearing more than just the woven grass panels that hung from the belt at her waist.

"What have you done?" she asked Seal.

"Nothing," he said and smiled at her, his mouth wide. "Your mother and I think it is a good time for you to be away from this village. We will make a trading trip. You are coming with us."

"No," she said. "You go, but I will not. Eye-Taker needs my help with her children."

"You think that if we leave you, White Salmon will claim you as wife while we are gone?" K'os said.

Daughter did not answer.

"He will not. Ask Green Twig's father how much White Salmon offered for her."

The words were as vicious as a slap, and it was all Daughter could do to stay on her feet. But K'os had lied to her before, in small things, in foolish ways. Daughter said nothing, merely took her sax from a peg on the wall and slipped it on.

"When do you leave?" she asked Seal.

"Tomorrow, if the weather is good. Perhaps the next day."

She climbed from the ulax, went to the beach, hoping to find White Salmon there, or at least one of his brothers. He was at the iqyax racks, laughing and talking with other young men. Once she would have joined them, stood behind White Salmon as a wife does, in respect, but this time, she interrupted what he was saying, boldly lay a hand on his sleeve, pulled him to face her.

"What I hear about Green Twig, is that true?" she asked.

He looked down the beach, then over his shoulder at the sea, up toward the sky as though she were not there. One of the other young men covered his laughter with a hand and turned away.

"I have pledged a brideprice," White Salmon finally said.

Anger controlled Daughter's tongue, and when she would rather have given gentle words, she could think of nothing but curses, so she turned away, let the wind take the men's laughter from her ears.

TWENTY-ONE

A rock had rolled down from the top of the grandfather's grave, and Daughter set it back in place. Who would take care of the grave once she was gone? Soon earth tremors and wind would move all the stones, and grass would grow over her grandfather's bones. Then, even if she did return, how would she know where he was? It seemed a cruel thing to leave him here with people who were not truly his own, but what else could she do?

"I will try to return, Grandfather," Daughter said to the grave. "But K'os wants to visit her own people, the River men, and I am not sure that she will come back to this island."

Daughter hunched her shoulders so that the stiff collar of her sax covered her ears. She should have worn the hooded otter fur parka K'os had made her for the trading trip, but Daughter needed the comfort of familiar clothes.

She lifted her head and spoke a few words in the River language, as though the wind could understand. Perhaps it did, she told herself. Perhaps the wind that blew over the First Men's islands also carried the clouds and rain to the River People.

K'os said that Daughter spoke the language well. Seal

pretended to speak it, but he knew only a few broken phrases, words that traders might use. He pronounced those in strange ways so that when he said them, boasting of his knowledge, Daughter had to think hard to know what he meant. More than once he had cuffed her when she did not understand.

"So, Grandfather, I have come to say good-bye, and to tell you that I will not forget you or your stories and your wisdom. I will teach my children about the Boat People and about you and how you saved me from the Bear-god warriors."

Tears tightened her throat, and she could say no more, so she ripped the grass away from the grave, making an edge of bare earth, then rearranged the rocks, pressing them against one another into a tight mound that would stand for a while against wind and ice and tremors. The island's two mountains stood high to the south and west of their village, and Daughter spoke to those mountains, asked protection for the grave. After all, the mountains had so much island they could shake, why disturb this small mound of rock and the man whose bones slept under it?

She turned away, her good-byes said, but then remembered something she had meant to do. She had made a necklace of wooden beads carved from the remains of the log boat she and the grandfather had ridden from their island. She lifted the necklace from under her sax and, moving several of the rocks at the top of the mound, let it fall down into the grave. She was replacing the rocks when she noticed a bit of hide, dark and nearly rotted, sticking out between two stones. It came easily into her hand, and she realized that it was an amulet, one that the grandfather had always carried.

The hide fell apart in her fingers, and she clutched at what was inside—sand, lighter in color than the sand of the First Men's island. She clenched her fist so the wind could not steal what she held. Without doubt, it was a gift from the grandfather.

As she walked back to the village, she clasped her hands

in front of her, holding the treasure. She climbed up Seal's ulax, and looked toward the beach. To her relief, he was near the iqyax rack, oiling his trader's boat. When she went inside, prepared for K'os's questions—a story on her tongue about taking sand from the island for luck—she found the ulax empty, a disarray of food containers and trade goods cluttering the center of the floor.

Daughter slipped into her sleeping place and used her teeth to tug a bedding fur, skin side up, into her lap, then dumped the sand on the skin.

Among the grains were tiny fragments of green stone, nearly translucent. She picked out a thin, curved shard, and finally realized it was a bit of water gourd. How could she forget those gourds that had kept them alive during their journey?

Daughter picked up the shard of gourd and caught her breath when she saw the tiny carved bead under it. It was small, only the size of a crowberry, and nearly as hard as rock, but not rock. When she looked at it closely, she could see that there was a tiny face on one side. The bead was pierced with a hole, and so, although Daughter poured the sand, stones, and the shard of water gourd into her own amulet, she threaded the face bead on a sinew string and tied it around her neck.

They left two days later, K'os at the front with a paddle, and Daughter behind her, tucked among the packs of food and trade goods. Daughter looked long at the island, the grass so green, the flowers bright in the low meadows—yellow cinquefoil, lupine, primola, and bluebells—and the mountains that still kept their caps of snow.

Some of the people had come out to the beach, and she looked for White Salmon, wondered if he would say goodbye. But he was not there. The chief hunter's wives and their children crowded the shore, the boys calling for her to bring them back gifts. They celebrated her leaving because they thought she would return. K'os's eyes said otherwise, and

Daughter knew that K'os planned to keep her close. What mother wanted to face old age alone?

But surely K'os wanted Daughter to have a husband, and a husband always protected his wife, even against her own mother. Most likely he would be a River man, and Daughter would have to learn new ways, but she already understood the River language, and K'os had told her many River People stories, had insisted that Daughter learn to tell the stories herself. She had sewn parkas and boots like the River People wore, but she made them out of fur seal or otter skins rather than caribou hide. She had learned plant medicines, and K'os had made her an otter fur medicine bag like K'os's own.

So in some ways she understood the River People, but she had never skinned a caribou, never helped on a hunt. She had never eaten fresh caribou meat, and she often wondered how people lived without the good taste of seal blubber, the warmth it put into a belly during the cold days and nights of winter.

When she wore the beautiful parka K'os had made her, she found the hood restricting. How did a woman turn her head? How did she see anything but what was right before her eyes?

"You think our winters here on this island are cold?" K'os once asked her. "You will find out how cold winter can be when we live with the River People."

Daughter had not answered. Since she was a little girl, she had understood that K'os liked to frighten her, and she had learned that she had the strength to meet all the problems that K'os predicted. Those few times when Daughter did doubt her abilities, she reminded herself that K'os had once been young, had faced the same worries, the same dangers, and she had survived. If K'os could, then she could.

Though at first all things seemed new, their traveling, like everything in life, settled into sameness. Their days started with the first rays of sun. Seal told them that traders did not eat in the mornings, only at night, but K'os did not listen to him, and always had dried fish and a water bladder ready. She would not repack the boat until she had eaten, and Daughter ate also, fearful at first of taboos broken, but after several days of Seal's sharp words and K'os's defiance, Seal, too, ate a share of the fish. It seemed to Daughter that the eating was a wise thing, that Seal was able to paddle harder and longer.

Each morning, she and K'os packed the boat while Seal studied the skies and decided if the tide was high enough or low enough to start out again. Their landings were usually easier in high tide, and Seal tried to avoid beaches where rips spun out from the shore. They left when the sea was right, sometimes well into the morning, at other times as soon as they had packed.

Seal paddled all day at the back of the boat while K'os and Daughter took turns at the front, and the one who did not paddle bailed.

The bailing tube was a hollow piece of bamboo driftwood, cut the length of a forearm with the bow of a joint in the center. A hunter placed one end of the bailing tube into the water at the bottom of the boat and sucked on the other end until the tube was full. Then he emptied the water over the side of the boat. A man with both hands on a paddle could use his mouth to bail, and the tube fit easily into small spaces between packs, even down into a cramped iqyax hatch.

Daughter had seen boys practicing with bailing tubes in shallow water at low tide. Then she had joined the other girls in laughing at them. Why practice something that was so simple? But now she found that she did not have enough breath to suck up much water. Seal mocked her, commented on the weakness of women, but she ignored him and tried until she was so dizzy the sky spun. As the days passed, her lungs grew stronger, and though she could never suck up as much water as Seal, she was soon better at it than K'os.

Gradually, as they traveled, the boat's sea lion covering

allowed water to seep in through the seams, and sometimes waves splashed over the sides. Then Seal would curse his trader's boat, tell K'os that if it weren't for her and Daughter, he would travel like a man in an iqyax.

K'os would pack the gaping seams with strips of fish fat, and remind Seal in harsh words that almost all traders used open boats. If he did a better job of securing sea lion skin covers to protect bow and stern, they would not have so many problems. Then Seal would set his mouth in anger and say no more, for when it came to arguing, who was better than K'os?

When they found a good beach, they stopped. Sometimes that happened early in the day, other times not until sunset. Twice they found no beach at all, no inlets, and so paddled on through the night.

Each time they stopped, they carried the boat and their packs high above the tide line. The boat was longer and wider than an iqyax and thus more stable in the water, but it was still light enough for K'os and Daughter to carry.

To make a shelter they tipped it to the side, faced its belly toward the wind, and arranged packs like walls on either end, then stretched sealskins over them to make a roof. If the beach had driftwood, they built a fire on the open side of their shelter.

Daughter searched for driftwood while Seal oiled the boat cover and K'os repaired its seams. That was Daughter's favorite time of day. Though her belly twisted in emptiness, she knew she would soon eat, and it was good to again feel the earth firm beneath her feet.

On some beaches the waves were generous, bringing more wood than they could use in many nights, but other beaches were bare, with nothing but a few shells. On those beaches Seal used his hunter's lamp for warmth. It was made of stone like all First Men lamps, and seal or whale oil fed its moss wick, but it was small, only the size of a man's hand, fingers spread, and did not give much heat. On especially cold nights, Seal hunkered near the lamp, sometimes even squatted over it, his sax funneling the heat up to his legs and groin, smoke coming from the neck hole. Daughter and K'os would be left to shiver in the cold, no warmth for them except from each other.

"We should have brought our own lamps and oil," Daughter told K'os the first night they could not make a fire.

K'os had only shrugged and said, "We must be careful, riding this sea as we do. What the sea allows from a man, it counts as disrespect from a woman."

"Hunters' lamps are taboo for women?" Daughter asked.

"Perhaps," K'os had told her. "Why take the chance? We will be colder in the River People's land than we are here. Do you want the sea to hear your complaints? Wear your parka."

During that night, the parka warmed her, so Daughter wore it in the boat the next day. But that was a day of wind and waves, and soon in the sea spray she was drenched, the parka sodden. By the time they made a camp for the night, Daughter was so wet and cold that she could not keep her teeth still. She looked with longing at the hooded waterproof parka Seal wore, but was careful not to complain or even express a wish for one. Though K'os did not say so, they must also be taboo for women. Otherwise, K'os would have one. But how strange that only hunters were allowed to wear a chigdax when it was a woman's hand that fashioned it from dried sea lion gut, and a woman's needle that sewed the watertight seams.

Seal and K'os wore seal flipper boots, but Daughter went barefoot as she had all her life. She had made herself boots in the manner of the River People, but she did not want to watch them rot a little more each day, her feet in the water that always lay in the bottom of the boat.

The first few days on the sea had frightened her, and at night her mind was tormented by dreams of otters that attacked with sharp and vicious teeth. In one dream, she had looked down at her feet, was amazed to see them whole, even with her smallest toes. Then the grandfather had picked up a knife, a large blade, dark with dried blood, and she had awakened screaming, had reached down to where her small toes had been, felt the ridged scars, and reminded herself that she had received a fair trade for that first toe, life, not only for herself but the grandfather.

During the second moon of traveling, a squall came on them, and though Daughter had little respect for Seal, he handled the waves and the wind with strength, speaking in a soothing voice to his wife and daughter. His calmness seemed to draw away their fear, and bailing became a rhythm bounded by his words.

He managed to get the boat to a beach. It was little more than a shelf of rock, without sand or driftwood, set against cliffs so high that in the rain and fog Daughter could not see their tops.

Though they were cold and wet, and the ground was hard beneath their sleeping mats, Daughter could feel only gratitude that they were no longer on the sea. And after that, through all their journey, Daughter's fear no longer lived so near her heart.

That night they huddled together with K'os in the middle, and sometime during her sleep, Daughter was awakened by the rhythm of K'os and Seal grinding against one another, K'os making payment for their safety.

The next day they stayed, though the weather was good, because K'os had seen birdholes in the cliffs. She and Daughter walked the narrow beach until they found a talus slope that allowed Daughter to climb to the top of the cliffs. If there had been a group of women, young men, or agile boys, they would have made a sling and lowered someone to reach in and steal the eggs, but with only K'os to stand against Daughter's weight, they did not. Instead, Daughter lay on her belly at the edge of the cliff, stuck her hands into the holes she could reach, and gathered eggs. By the time she had checked each hole, her hands were cut and bleeding, slashed by the birds' beaks, but she had managed to gather a basketful and catch several auklets, wringing their necks even as they fought her.

She and K'os took the eggs and birds back to their camp and found Seal waiting impatiently for them.

"High tide!" he exclaimed, and saying no more, he gestured toward the boat.

He sat sulking as Daughter and K'os worked to repack, and Daughter hid her resentment as Seal poked his thumbs into nearly half the eggs and sucked out the contents.

Once she lifted her chin toward him and said to K'os, "See what he does."

But K'os merely answered, "And who paddles all day? Not you."

She knew that K'os was right, but the realization only fed her anger. When they had lived in the First Men village, K'os and Seal fought all the time, but here on the sea, K'os had suddenly become a good wife, always worried about her husband, sitting up in the night to repair his sax or chigdax when her own garments needed more attention than his, always being sure that he got the best food and the heaviest sleeping robes.

As though she could hear Daughter's thoughts, K'os said, "Remember this, Uutuk, until we get to a village, without him, we are dead."

Then Daughter understood that her mother had not changed. K'os knew what she wanted and merely worked to get it.

After more than two moons of traveling, the earth began to grow trees—black spruce, Seal called them. K'os said they were poor and sickly, bent in their struggle against the wind, and she told Daughter that the trees that grew in the land of the River People were straight and strong. Though Daughter said nothing, she suddenly remembered the trees that had grown near the village where she and the grandfather once lived. Those trees had been so tall that it seemed that their branches should be able to scrape down the stars. Here, the black spruce were no bigger than a man, but at least they were trees, and she celebrated with K'os, singing a River song about trees dancing.

Seal complained about that song, and it was true that the salt of the sea had coated their throats, so even Daughter sang in an old woman's voice.

The sea had also scoured their faces, and all of them had bleeding sores on their lips and nostrils. Ko's's hands were cracked and rough, and some days after taking her turn with the paddle, her fingers curled themselves so tightly that she could not straighten them until the next morning.

The day after they first saw the trees, they also saw a village, and Daughter hoped they might stop. It was a First Men village, small, but even from the sea Daughter could pick out the mounds of the ulas, the iqyax racks, and children and elders walking the beaches, gathering wood and digging for clams. But Seal did not stop, only uttered an insult, vulgar and spiteful, against the women of that village.

K'os turned to look at her husband, and Daughter expected her to scold him, but she merely set her mouth into a grimace, and turned back to her paddling. After a moment of thought, Daughter realized that K'os had been hiding a smile, that she had been mocking her husband, and Daughter guessed that he had made poor trades there or, worse, had angered some husband.

The long day stretched into weariness, but before night, they paddled into an inlet and came to another village. This time Seal turned their boat toward the beach. The children ran out to meet them, shouting that a trader had come to visit. Then the young men and hunters were beside their boat, hauling it to shore. One of them helped Daughter out and offered her water from a seal belly. Daughter reached for the belly, her throat harsh and raw from the sea, but before she could raise it to her lips, K'os clasped her arm, shook her head.

"Be sure he offers the water in kindness, not in trade," she told Daughter, and she spoke in the River language so the young man would not understand.

"It is only water, Mother," Daughter said.

But K'os turned to the man and asked him what he expected in return. He answered with a joke and a request for Daughter to stay with him in his father's ulax.

Daughter shook her head at the young man, but smiled to soften her refusal. Then she and K'os helped Seal pull the boat beyond the reach of waves. They waited as Seal spoke to the chief hunter, and Daughter smiled shyly at the children who gathered around her, one bold enough to touch her hand.

She was tired and her legs ached from sitting in the boat all day, so when K'os gestured for her to follow, she went without thinking, fixing her eyes on the path that she walked. She found herself wishing they could enjoy the warmth of an ulax. They had spent so many nights on the beaches at the mercy of wind and rain and sea waves.

She was led to an old woman's ulax. It was small but warm, and the woman made her a bed behind the climbing log. Daughter had hoped to be able to sleep as soon as the bed was made, but the old woman wanted to talk. Daughter struggled to keep her eyes open, bit the insides of her cheeks so the pain would keep her from falling asleep.

Old age had withered the woman's flesh and darkened her face. A hump on her back nearly bent her double, and the sparse strands of her white hair were drawn up tightly and tied into a knot at the crown of her head.

"Your mother and father are staying with the chief hunter," she said and began to laugh. "He thinks he has the greatest honor, that hunter, but he is also a fool, for children are the best, and daughters are very good. I am glad to have you here."

She chattered on, speaking of village people that Daughter did not know. Finally she said, "Do you like being a trader?"

Daughter had been so lulled by the old woman's words that it took her a moment to realize that she expected an answer.

"This is my first trading trip," Daughter said.

"Do you know where you are?"

"No," Daughter admitted, "but this is the second village we passed today."

The old woman laughed. "How will you find this place again if you do not know where you are?" she asked, but she did not seem to be scolding, for then she added, "This is the Traders' Beach."

Her words made Daughter glad, for she had heard Seal speak of the place, and knew he planned to stay and trade.

The old woman tipped her head and stared at Daughter's face, then she asked, "You have always lived in your mother's village?"

Daughter was not sure how to answer. But after thinking for a while, she said, "There are those who say I once lived on another beach. There are those who say that storm winds brought me and my grandfather a long way to a First Men's village."

As though she were speaking to herself, the old woman mumbled, "I knew there was something different about the face. The eyes are not First Men eyes, and the nose is too small." Then she raised her voice to ask, "Do you remember this other place where you lived?"

"Sometimes in my dreams it comes back to me," Daughter told her.

"Then do not forget your dreams. That grandfather you spoke about, does he remember?"

"He remembered much, and told me many stories."

"I would like to talk to him," the old woman said, "but he must be like me, too old to travel."

"He died five summers ago," said Daughter. "But perhaps I could tell you some of his stories."

The old woman's face brightened.

"Tonight?" she asked, but Daughter shook her head.

"I am sorry, Grandmother," she said in politeness, "but I am too tired. Could you wait until morning?"

Then, as though the old woman realized for the first time that she had a guest, she offered apologies and pointed toward a water bladder hanging from a rafter. "You can reach it more easily than I," she told Daughter, "but surely you are also hungry, and here I am asking for stories."

She lifted her chin toward a basket of sea urchins, and Daughter brought the basket, sat down, and set it between them. The old woman took a sea urchin, cracked it open, and used a thumbnail to scrape out the eggs. She sucked them into her mouth, then said, "Long ago my husband died and then all my children as well, except for one daughter who lives in another village. There was a time when a girl came to live with me. I taught her my stories, but then she left me for a River man husband. But this year, a good thing has happened. That girl's brother has come to this village, he and his father, a trader. The boy tells me his sister is well, that she and her husband have three children now."

"That is good," Daughter told her.

"Yes, it is good," the old woman said. "And for a little while I have this trader and his son living with me. They bring all kinds of good things to eat, things that are hard for an old woman to get for herself." She pursed her lips to point at the sea urchins.

"Perhaps if I stay long enough with you," Daughter said, "I will be able to bring you sea urchins as well."

The old woman chuckled, and there was a sudden clattering on the ulax roof, a boisterous man's voice raised in laughter.

"Aa! They are here!" the old woman exclaimed and leaned on Daughter's shoulder to push herself to her feet.

"We are eating," she said to the man who came into the ulax.

He was taller than the men of Daughter's village, lean and narrower in his shoulders. He was followed by a younger man who looked much like him, though he had the stronger build of the First Men. They both had long noses, humped in the middle, and long faces. They wore their hair braided at the backs of their heads, with feathers and beads strung into the braids.

"Cen, the trader," the old woman said, "and his son Ghaden."

The younger man's eyes were dark and round, soft in the flickering light of the ulax lamps, and, to Daughter's embarrassment, she realized she was staring at him. But he gave her a lopsided grin and did not seem to mind her rudeness.

"Cen, Ghaden, this is the trader's daughter," the old woman said, and again laughed. "I do not know your name," she said.

"That does not surprise me," said Cen.

"I am Uutuk, but most people call me Daughter." Then she smiled at the old woman, allowed a teasing to come into her voice. "And if I am to tell you stories tomorrow, I should also know your name."

Then Cen and Ghaden both laughed, and squatted on their haunches close to the basket of sea urchins. Daughter, as though she were the mother of the house, lifted the basket closer to them, and when they had helped themselves, she also took an urchin, cracked it open, and gave it to the old woman.

"I did not tell you my name?" she asked. "I thought everyone knew. Who is older than me in all these First Men villages? I suppose I will live until finally I have found someone who wants to learn my stories, a storyteller who will stay with the First Men, and not go off with some River man."

Cen smiled at that, ducked his head, and cocked an eyebrow at Ghaden. "She is still mad at your sister," he said.

The old woman frowned at him. "I am still mad at you, but at least you brought Ghaden." Then she said to Daughter, "I am called Qung. I look forward to hearing your stories tomorrow."

She bumped Ghaden's arm with her elbow and said, "And

if they are good enough, perhaps I will decide that you should hear them, too."

"Perhaps I have already decided to listen, Aunt," Ghaden said. "What better gift to take back to my sister Aqamdax than new stories?"

Then Qung was suddenly solemn, and she said, "Just bring her with you the next time you come. It would be good to see her one last time before I die."

"Live long, Aunt," Ghaden said in a quiet voice, the laughter gone from his words. "We need your wisdom."

TWENTY-TWO

K'OS'S STORY

"Do not think about eating until you have finished repairing the seams," Seal told K'os.

She smiled sweetly at him. "Think about trading for a new cover, husband," she said, holding her voice soft, filling her words with respect. "We will not get much farther with this one."

"You know so much about boats?" he snapped.

"About hides, husband," she said under her breath once he had walked away. There were other traders watching, and she did not want to destroy Uutuk's chance of finding a good husband. Too often a daughter was judged by her mother's behavior.

K'os tied a sinew thread to the end of her needle, wetted her fingers with water from one of the drinking bladders stored in the boat, and moistened the seam. It was weak with too many awl holes, gaping where the cover had stretched under the assault of waves and water. Seal had set the boat near the iqyax racks, and as she worked, K'os studied the markings on each craft. Most belonged to hunters, but there were three large open-topped boats, each marked with yellow to show they belonged to traders. The iqyan also had owners' marks painted in various colors, some done with a careful hand, others applied haphazardly.

One fine iqyax stood out among the rest, made, without doubt, by a First Men hunter, but its ownership markings were River. K'os set her birdbone needle between her teeth and wetted down a particularly bad seam. She kneaded it with her knuckles to soften the hide and tried to draw up enough extra to lap a fold over the weakest side, but she had done the same thing too many times. There was no more give. She would have to use a patch.

She stuck her needle in a soft strip of birdskin she had tacked to the front of her sax and dug into her sewing basket. She pulled out a roll of seal hide, the width of three fingers. With her thumb and middle finger she measured enough to cover the worst of the seam, then cut the strip from the roll with her woman's knife.

The strip was stiff and hard, and she moistened it with water from the bladder, then rerolled it tightly and placed in her mouth, held it there, testing it with her tongue. When it was pliable, she began to chew the strip, working it with her teeth.

The wind was cold off the bay, and K'os drew her hands up into her sleeves, waited for warmth to pull the pain from her joints. Her hands had always hurt her, even from the time she was a child, but on this trip, paddling and hauling, the pain had become almost unbearable. Sometimes it kept her awake most of the night.

When she found the right husband for Uutuk, she would get rid of Seal, lazy man that he was, and build a warm lodge in some River village, sew herself many fur mittens. Her hands would never be cold again.

She would not have to wait long. How difficult could it be to find a husband for a daughter like Uutuk?

Uutuk had spent her first night in the Traders' village with Qung, the village storyteller, an old woman who lived alone. How better to keep Uutuk away from men? K'os had taught the girl how to please a man in bed, but there was no sense in wasting Uutuk's favors on those who did not deserve them.

Besides, K'os wanted her to have a River husband, and River men were stingy with their wives, did not like to share them with others. No doubt White Salmon had had Uutuk in his bed, but White Salmon was far away, bound as he was to his small island.

Even if K'os had decided on a First Men husband for Uutuk, she would not have chosen White Salmon. Better to select a man who lived here in the Traders' village. Even in its strongest days, the Near River village had not been as large. Of course, K'os would rather live in a River lodge than an ulax, but she understood the necessity for underground houses close to the North Sea, where the wind was often strong enough to knock down a grown man.

Too bad that when she escaped the Walrus Hunters, her journey had not brought her here. It would have been better to find herself a husband in this village—rich with all the things traders can bring, and not as far from the River People as Seal's village. But then, had she come here, she would not have Uutuk.

K'os rubbed the strip of sealskin between her knuckles, then placed it on the inside of the seam and stitched carefully, making sure the needle did not pierce completely through the outer layer of the boat cover. It was meticulous work, and sometimes she had to stop and stretch her fingers, they grew so numb, but finally she was done.

She straightened and arched her shoulders, then started checking the remaining seams. When her eyes needed a rest, she would stop and focus on something distant or again study the iqyan on the boat racks. The First Men iqyax marked with River colors seemed to draw her.

You are lonesome for your own people, she told herself, but then decided there was another reason the markings caught her attention. She had seen them before. But where?

Suddenly she knew, and the knowledge was like a fist to her belly. Not on an iqyax, no. On the sheath covering of a hunter's bow, on a trader's pack, on the side of a River lodge. Cen's ownership mark. Her heart hammered into her ribs.

Even if he had given the iqyax in trade, the new owner would have painted his colors over Cen's, and what were the chances that two men would choose the same mark of triple circles and slashing lines?

She would have to convince Seal to leave the village, and leave soon. Cen would have nothing but evil to say about her, and there was always the chance that he had discovered she was the one who had killed his wife Gheli.

Cen should be grateful. Gheli had been a fool, trying to hide who she was merely by changing her name. Gheli or Red Leaf, what difference did it make? She had been the same selfish woman, but Cen had known only the good part of her, had no idea that his wife could kill. K'os should have told him, but when had Cen ever believed anything she said?

So now, did Cen hold a debt of revenge against her? What would happen if he killed her?

K'os snorted out a laugh. A foolish question. She knew what would happen. Seal would take Uutuk as wife.

Even a child could see the lust in Seal's eyes every time he looked at the girl, especially when he thought K'os was not watching. Why else would Uutuk shrink away from the man every time he was close to her?

K'os shrugged her shoulders as if she were in a conversation with herself. Yes, if she died, Seal would take Uutuk. But that would not necessarily be so terrible. Surely in death K'os would have enough power to change Seal's luck, add some hard times to his life. Of course, she would not wish bad luck on Uutuk, but the girl was young and could get herself another husband, a River hunter who would take her to Chakliux's village.

Who did not know that spirits could enter dreams? If she were dead, K'os could whisper her wishes into Uutuk's ears, and the girl would carry out the revenge K'os planned, not only on Seal, but on Chakliux and Aqamdax.

So death was not the worst thing that could happen to her. Why worry about Cen? How could she hide from him when they were both in the same village? She had changed some, not enough. Even with the tattoos and her hair cut into a fringe across her forehead, even in First Men clothing, he would recognize her.

K'os lifted her chin, set her teeth. She seldom played the part of hare, changing from flesh into earth to fool her enemies. Most often she was wolf.

"You speak our River language well," Cen said.

Daughter lowered her eyes in politeness, but could not keep a smile from her lips. She leaned close to Qung and translated the compliment. Cen began to laugh, and Daughter looked up, confused.

"I understand what he says, child," Qung told her. "After all, I am a storyteller, and a gift of languages is one that every storyteller should seek to own."

They sat in Qung's ulax, eating fish, dried and smoked and dipped in seal oil. It was a flavor of Daughter's childhood, of her first days in K'os's ulax, and the taste set her at ease with these new people.

She had slept long into the morning, woken to find Cen and his son waiting. She knew K'os and Seal would have work for her, but how could she turn away too quickly from Qung's hospitality? K'os would understand, and Seal's anger would not last for long.

She listened as Cen spoke about the journey he had made to his son's village and then to this beach, but finally she picked up her sax and stood.

"I must find my mother. She will have work for me."

Qung reached up and clasped Daughter's wrist, pulled her down again to the floor mats.

"Your mother told me that you can stay here as long as you like," Qung said. "Besides, you promised me stories about the island where you lived as a child, before you became one of us."

Ghaden lifted his head, and Daughter saw his surprise.

"You're not First Men?" he asked.

"Does she look First Men?" Qung said.

Ghaden stared at Daughter and smiled, half of his mouth lifting as though he were hiding a joke. She felt her face grow hot under his gaze, and she covered her embarrassment with words.

"I come from a village far over the sea," she said, and looked at the floor, at Cen, anywhere but at Ghaden. "We named ourselves for the boats we made. I was very young so I have little memory of the village or my people. But my grandfather said that we were attacked by another village, by their warriors. He and I hid in a boat, and during the night, a storm came and took us out into the sea. I remember the long journey, and that each day seemed to grow colder, but eventually we found the First Men islands."

"Your grandfather is no longer living?" Cen asked.

Tears gathered in Daughter's throat, and she had to cough before she was able to speak. "He has been dead for five years now," she said. "But I hold his wisdom and his stories here." She laid a hand at the center of her chest, over her heart.

"Since you promised us stories," said Qung, "now would be a good time." She raised her eyebrows and looked at Cen. "Nae'?" She smiled as she said the River word.

"Yes," Cen replied. "Now would be good time for a story about these Boat People. Do you remember their ulas? Do you remember their island? Do you know how many days you were in the boat?"

Qung began to laugh. "A trader's questions, without doubt," she said.

"And what is wrong with that, Aunt?" he asked. "I am a trader."

Qung filled her mouth with a piece of fish and cut her eyes away from Cen, an insult but given in jest. She flicked her fingers at Daughter and said, "Begin, begin. We are listening."

Daughter bowed her head for a moment, thought about where she should start. With the Bear-god warriors' attack, she finally decided. Cen and Ghaden should enjoy that story.

Men seemed to like tales of fighting. She told them all she could remember, then answered their questions. She repeated stories that her grandfather had taught her about their village and their people, the men and their fishing. Cen had questions about outrigger boats, but Daughter could not remember them well enough to explain.

Finally she said, "Perhaps it would be better if you asked my mother. She is good at describing things and could probably make you a drawing in the sand. The boat rotted long ago, and I was a child the last time I saw it."

"You said your father's name is Seal?" Cen asked.

"Yes."

"I thought I knew most First Men traders, but I do not remember him."

"He does not make many trading trips. It is a long way to our island. Have you ever been there?"

"No. There are too few villages between here and there. The distance is not worth a trader's time."

Ghaden leaned forward as if to draw Daughter's eyes, and he said, "But my father has been to the Tundra People's villages, where the sun disappears for the whole winter and dances in the sky all summer. He has traded with the men of the Caribou villages, with Walrus and River and First Men." It was a gentle boasting, and it warmed Daughter's heart toward Ghaden.

"And are you also a trader?" she asked.

"No, I am a hunter," he said.

Daughter saw a flash of disappointment in Cen's eyes, but it was quickly gone, and Ghaden said, "Sometimes I pretend to be a trader. It is worth the hardship to spend time with my father."

Cen laughed, then said to Daughter, "Your mother is here with you?"

Most wives did not travel with their trader husbands. There were always women in each village willing to be wife for a little while, and what woman wanted to leave her ulax or her children for long nights on cold beaches, for long days on tundra trails?

"She likes to travel with him," Daughter said. "But this is my first trip. My mother is a River woman, and she brought me because she hopes to find me a River husband."

Qung snorted. "A River husband! What foolishness! A First Men husband is far better."

Daughter bit her cheeks to keep from mentioning White Salmon, and she carefully kept her eyes from Ghaden. She had already said more than what was considered polite, and her thoughts were still too full of White Salmon to think of another man as husband. Besides, Ghaden's River face was strange to her, his long hooked nose, his heavy brow. But she supposed any woman would get used to her husband's face, no matter what he looked like. After all, the stump of her grandfather's arm, shriveled as it had been, did not bother her. What was a large nose compared to that?

"Your mother is River," Cen said, his words quiet as though he were speaking to himself. "How did she get to the First Men islands?"

"That is something she never talks about," Daughter said. "But once one of the other women in the village mentioned that she was slave to the Walrus Hunters. Perhaps she ran away from them, or perhaps they traded her to the First Men."

"When you were still a child," Cen said to Daughter, "there was much fighting between two of the River villages. Women and children were taken as slaves. Perhaps she is from one of those villages, and if she is, then I might know her."

"Her First Men name is Old Woman," Daughter told him, "but among the River people she was known as K'os."

When Daughter said the name, she was handing a seal-skin of fish to Qung and did not see the look on Cen's face.

"K'os," Qung said. "I have heard that name before."

She glanced over Daughter's shoulder at Cen, then pursed

her lips into a puzzled frown. Daughter turned to look and saw that Cen had jumped to his feet and was walking toward the climbing log.

"You know her, Cen?" Qung asked.

He stopped and turned back, tried to laugh, but the laughter came out as though it were a curse. "Once," he said, "a very long time ago, she was nearly my wife." He lifted his chin and spoke to Ghaden. "Do you remember her?" he asked.

"Yes," Ghaden said. "When I was living in the Cousin River village, she lived there then. My sister Aqamdax was her slave." His words were bitter.

The line of Cen's jaw tightened, as though he had clenched his teeth, but he thanked Qung for the food, then made polite excuses to leave. "Ghaden, come with me," he said. "I have things for you to do. Perhaps there will be another time for storytelling." Then as though he had just remembered that Daughter was still with them, he added, "It has been good to hear about the Boat People."

They left, and Qung, shaking her head at all the food that still remained, shrugged her shoulders and said, "Men are always too busy to sit in one place for a long time."

When they were outside, away from Qung's ulax, Cen told Ghaden, "Uutuk is beautiful, but stay away from her. If she is like her mother, she will bring you nothing but bad luck." Then, looking at Ghaden with eyes flat and cold, he said, "You have trade goods to set out, nae'? Trade quickly. We will not remain in this village as long as I had thought." Then he strode away toward the chief hunter's ulax.

Ghaden had heard tales about K'os, whispered things. She had killed her own husbands, they said. When he had returned to the Near River village with Chakliux and Aqamdax, they had agreed to stay only if K'os—slave then to the old woman Gull Beak—were sold to another village. Chakliux's brother Sok had wanted to kill her, but Chakliux still claimed the woman as mother and would not have her blood on his hands.

She had also lived in Cen's village—the Four Rivers village—and Ghaden had heard rumors that Cen had forced her to leave. Ghaden had never been to that village, though Cen lived there with his wife and two daughters. This year he would go, Ghaden promised himself, and meet those two sisters he had never seen.

Soon after Biter's death, Ghaden had taken a young woman as wife. Three years later, she had died in childbirth. Since then, Ghaden had considered taking other women, but none had filled his heart, and so he had been content to stay in Chakliux and Aqamdax's lodge, to provide meat for widows and elders.

Sometimes his father teased him about taking a Four Rivers woman as wife and coming to live in his lodge, but Ghaden's spirit was with the people at Chakliux's village. They had few enough hunters as it was. Besides, how could he leave Yaa? She had been both sister and mother to him since Red Leaf had killed his true mother, Daes. How could he leave Aqamdax and Chakliux, or even Sok? No, he would stay in Chakliux's village, someday take another woman there as wife.

Uutuk's face was suddenly bright in Ghaden's mind, and he found himself thinking about the stories she had told. She did not speak like a storyteller but more like a mother telling tales to a child, and truly that was a gift any man would treasure in his wife.

No, Ghaden told himself. She was K'os's daughter. Was he such a fool that he could not understand the danger in that?

When Cen saw K'os, she was wearing a First Men sax. Her back was turned and her hair had begun to gray, but he recognized her. There was strength in the set of her shoulders, grace in her movements, and who would not know the cunning needlework of her sax? Cut like a First Men garment, it was decorated in the manner of the River People, with bird beaks and shells and fringes of brightly dyed sinew.

She was working on a trader's boat. The sewing basket at her side was one that Cen had given her, and the thought that she still owned it clutched at his heart. Sometimes she came back to him in dreams, as young and beautiful as when he first knew her, when he wanted nothing more in his life than to have her as wife.

Long ago, he had heard rumors that she had been sold as slave to the Walrus. He had avoided their village for that reason. But then she had begun to visit his dreams so often, he had decided that she was dead. He had not allowed himself to mourn, but instead rejoiced that there was no chance he would see her again.

She was evil beyond anything and anyone he had ever known. He shuddered to think of her raising Uutuk and wondered what horrors lived behind that girl's dark eyes.

As K'os worked, she lifted her head once in a while and studied the iqyan. Surely she had noticed his, and he doubted that she would have forgotten the colors and symbols he used to mark his belongings.

For a moment he shifted his eyes out to the inlet, a sheltered bay, perfect for a village, good fishing in calm waters, and easy access to the sea. Fog had begun to move in, fingers spreading up the valleys and into the hills that rose behind the bay.

As trader, he wore the clothing of the villages he visited, partly because it was usually the best choice for the weather, partly so the villagers would accept him as one of their own. The First Men's sax was a comfortable garment, loose in the shoulders for paddling, and the birdskins easily shed rain. But he had worn caribou hide pants for too many years to be warm when wearing only the long-skirted sax. The air was damp, and he felt the chill of it in his hips and knees.

He sighed and looked again at K'os. She bound her hair like a First Men wife, in a tight knot at the nape of her neck, and as she worked she raised a hand to twist several strands back into the bun. The gesture was too familiar. Suddenly he could feel the warmth of her hair lying over him as they lay naked together in his lodge. He could taste the woman smell of her.

Cen thought when he had found Gheli that K'os had lost her power over him, but how could he deny that there was still some part of her lodged in his heart? He was suddenly angry that he had so little control over what he felt. A man old enough to be a grandfather should not act like a young hunter, his lust ruling his mind.

He had been too long away from his wife. Perhaps there was a First Men woman who would trade favors for oil or dried caribou meat. If so, he needed to find her.

His disgust prodded him into movement, and he crossed the beach to the iqyax racks, purposely kept his back to K'os as he pretended to study the boats.

"I see you found yourself a First Men husband," he said in the River tongue, though he directed his words at the iqyan.

"And you, have you found a new wife?" K'os asked, as though she had been waiting for him, as though they spoke often and there was no greeting or politeness necessary between them.

"A new wife?" Cen asked, puzzled. Then he tilted his head back and nodded. Of course, when K'os had left the Four Rivers village, Gheli had been sick. He had to admit that K'os had been good to them, had given Gheli many different kinds of medicines, but K'os must have believed that there was no hope.

"You think I'd live without a woman?" He turned to look at her as he asked the question.

She had changed more than he thought she would. For years she had remained the same, her skin unlined, hair dark, eyes bright. Her life, after leaving the Four Rivers village, must have been difficult. Deep lines scored her cheeks from her nose to her chin. Folds webbed out from the corners of her eyes, and her skin still carried the scabs and sores of sea travel. Of course, even Uutuk's face had been marred with sores, and they would heal, but where Uutuk's cheeks were unmarked like a River woman's face, K'os had taken the tattoos of the First Men. Blue lines, nearly black, crossed the flats of her cheeks.

The wind had pushed up her sax, exposing a bit of her thigh, and there, too, he saw the marks that proclaimed her a First Men woman. Still—though she looked older, and in spite of the tattoos—she was beautiful. No man would pass her without looking again to enjoy that face, and he supposed that for a First Men hunter, the tattoos enhanced her beauty. He had a sudden and foolish urge to pull the sax down over her leg, a possessiveness that should belong only to a husband.

She's not mine, he told himself. She has never been mine, and I do not want her.

"But why would I need a new wife?" he asked. "It's difficult enough for a trader to care for one, and to find a woman who is loyal even when her husband spends long months away from their lodge."

"I didn't think you would want to raise Daes without a mother," K'os said. "I'd have been a good mother to her. You know I did not kill my young River husband. You above all people know that."

He took a step toward her, squatted, squinting his eyes against the grit the wind blew into his face. "I still think you killed him."

She smiled at him. "You're wrong. How terrible for me that you convinced the Four Rivers People I did."

"If I had convinced them, then you'd be dead. As it was, they only asked that you leave." He raised his hands and spread them wide. "It seems that you're doing well. I met your daughter Uutuk. She's a fine young woman, and she speaks well of you and your husband."

"Be glad for me, Cen," K'os said. "I'm old, but my life is good. Tell me about the Four Rivers village and your family.

Have you found a husband for Daes? She must be past the age of marrying."

"She's promised to a hunter, but she still lives in my lodge. Her mother says she's a good worker, and she helps care for her younger sister."

"So you've given Ghaden another sister," K'os said. "The last time I saw Ghaden, he was just a boy. He must be a man now. Is he married? Does he have children of his own?"

Cen did not answer, but instead turned back to his iqyax. It was one thing to speak about his daughters, who lived far from this Traders' Beach, beyond the reach of K'os's wickedness, another to think about Ghaden. Surely he had changed enough that K'os would not recognize him.

Cen ran a hand over his iqyax and K'os said, "It's by far the finest on the beach. Where did you get it?"

"In trade," he said. "There's a River hunter who makes iqyan in the way of the First Men." He faced her, met her eyes and said, "He has the gift of the sea otter." He looked down at his feet, just a flick of his eyelids, but he heard her hiss, and knew that she understood that her son, Chakliux, had made the iqyax.

K'os took a few quick stitches in her husband's boat cover. With her eyes on her work, she said, "So you found another wife."

"Your medicine was stronger than you thought. Gheli is alive."

Disbelief, anger, hatred twisted her face, each like a dancer's mask falling off to be replaced by another, but finally she smiled. "I'm glad. For you and for Gheli. Now tell me about your new daughter."

Cen shrugged. He wanted to be done with this conversation. K'os was like a deadfall trap, ready to catch and crush anyone who was not wary. "She's a baby," he replied. "What is there to say? She cries and she sleeps and she eats."

Before K'os could ask another question, he walked away, flexing his shoulders, brushing his hands through his hair, like a man in the tundra during the moon of flies and gnats.

TWENTY-THREE

The morning trading was slow, and after a time Ghaden asked if he might go with several of the First Men out into the inlet to fish.

Cen had shrugged his permission. Why keep Ghaden with him when one man could easily handle the trades? Besides, it would be good to give a few fish to Qung, especially if they decided to leave the village in the next day or two.

Ghaden caught several pogies, the delicate-flavored, green-fleshed fish so prized by the First Men, and Cen told him to give them to Qung, then come and take his place so Cen could spend some time on the ulax roofs talking to the elders. Often the best trades were made because of friendship. But by midafternoon, Ghaden had not yet returned, and finally Cen left his trade goods and went to Qung's ulax.

Ghaden was there, beside Uutuk, across from Qung, the three with their heads bent together. Playing some game, no doubt, Cen thought. Ghaden was always lucky with casting bones, and more than once had won some hunter's prized treasure.

Traders had to be careful about their luck in games. Good luck usually twisted itself into bad trades. But when Cen squatted beside them he realized that Ghaden was showing the women the scars left by the brown bear that had killed Ghaden's old dog Biter and nearly killed Ghaden as well. So, his son had been telling stories to storytellers. Why not? It was a good tale, and the boy told it without boasting, save about his dog. But there was too much sadness in the dog's death, and the pain in Ghaden's voice when he spoke of what had happened always tore at Cen's heart.

He saw this same pain on Uutuk's face, and suddenly felt as protective toward her as though she were his own daughter, so his voice was harsh when he spoke to his son.

"You sit here when I asked you to come and watch over our trade goods? I guess you would rather be a woman and stay in the ulax all day."

Ghaden's jaw tightened, but he got to his feet and pulled on his parka, then left without speaking except for a word of politeness to Qung.

Uutuk offered Cen a water bladder and then fish, gestured toward the mats, and asked him to sit down. He remained standing and waved away the fish, but lifted the bladder to his mouth, squeezed out a stream of water, and, when he had drunk his fill, wiped his hand across his lips.

Qung shook her head, rousing herself as though she were waking from a dream, and looked at him from slitted eyes. "You have not changed much, Cen. You still have more words than necessary. Your boy tells a good tale."

Cen opened his mouth as though to reply, but Qung held up one hand to silence him. "You have no reason for worry. He will never be a storyteller. He has the words and the gift, but not the desire." She struggled to her feet, and Cen leaned down to offer his hand. When she was standing, she lifted one finger and wagged it in his face, began to scold him as though he were a child. "Do not make him into a trader. Hunting is in his hands and his heart. If you have not yet realized that, then you are more foolish than your words." She turned her back on him and busied herself with women's work.

Cen had no answer for her, so rather than stand there trying to decide what to say, he left the ulax. He paused when he was on the roof and looked out toward the beach. He saw Ghaden pulling packs into place, arranging trade goods. For what little he had given the boy, Ghaden was a far better son than Cen deserved. Too often he had left Ghaden in the care of others, too often depended on Ghaden's sisters and their husbands to teach him and take care of him.

Cen had never even asked Ghaden to come to his own lodge in the Four Rivers village, but that was because of his wife Gheli. She was a shy woman, strong in many ways, but unsure when it came to her own worth. Cen saw the dread in her eyes every time he talked about Ghaden. And why not? He was the son of the woman Cen had loved above all others. Gheli, as fine a wife as she was, could not drive the dead Daes from Cen's heart. He wished he had not given Gheli's daughter Daes's name. She had grown into a fine woman, tall and strong like her mother, but too often Cen found himself comparing her with that first Daes, seeing his daughter's shortcomings rather than her abilities.

As he watched his son, Cen's heart seemed to grow until it ached in the tight spaces of his chest. Finally he turned his eyes away, looked off into the foothills, and thought of other things besides good sons and strong daughters.

K'os ran her hands over the sides of Seal's trading boat one last time. The seams were as good as she could make them. Perhaps the boat would get them to the River People's villages, but her stomach knotted when she thought of that journey. More than once Seal's stubbornness had brought them trouble.

She was wise enough to know that arguing with him about a new boat cover would only make him more determined to keep the old. She had seal bellies of oil that were her own, and she could trade those, but she hated to waste them on hides for a boat cover. Perhaps she could convince Seal to leave her and Uutuk here while he traded at some First Men's village a day or two down the coast. Surely he would not try to take the unwieldy boat by himself, but would invite another trader to travel with him. Without doubt, any man would be quick to point out that Seal needed a new cover, and Seal would listen to a stranger long before he would hear what she had to say.

K'os hated her helplessness. In many ways, her life would be easier without Seal, but how could she and Uutuk go by themselves to the River People? They could not paddle a boat all that way, and even if they could, she would not risk returning alone without a husband to the Walrus Hunters. What would keep them from reclaiming her as slave?

She was not welcome at Chakliux's village. Of course, there were other River villages, but they were farther away from the coast. It would be very difficult to travel that far, she and Daughter alone, walking the tundra. Too bad Cen held so much anger against her. He knew all the River villages.

She thought of Gheli. K'os had given the woman enough poison to kill more than three men. How had she survived?

Suddenly K'os found herself smiling. She would like to have another chance at that one. She and Gheli saw the world through the same eyes. Theirs would be a fine battle, and K'os would have the advantage because Gheli did not know K'os was still fighting. Women were warriors in ways that men would never understand.

K'os allowed herself a moment to think about the wars she had fought and won: with Chakliux's first wife, Gguzaakk; with Fox Barking; with Ground Beater. Each victory brought its own kind of power, and now, though she was years away from those conquests, she felt them strengthen her anew.

She lifted her eyes to the rise of land at the back of the beach and saw Uutuk standing there. K'os forced herself to smile. Uutuk lifted a hand in greeting and hurried toward her. The girl's dark hair blew free in the wind, and K'os's heart beat hard in fierce gladness. This daughter would bring K'os everything she wanted.

Perhaps that was the power that Gheli owned, the strength

she had held against K'os's poison—her hope in her daughter. K'os laughed. A daughter named for the woman Gheli herself had killed!

She pursed her lips in thought. And perhaps that was the way to weaken Gheli's power, by destroying that daughter. Of course, the easy way was to tell Cen that Gheli was Red Leaf. Then Cen would kill Gheli himself. But K'os's victory would be greater if she were the one to kill. Why deny herself joy? After all, there were many paths to the Four Rivers village.

K'os leaned down into Seal's boat. On trading trips she always tied several empty gathering bags to one of the boat's ribs. She chose the largest, tried to loosen the knot. Sea spray had tightened it beyond the strength of her fingers, so she used her teeth and waved away Uutuk's offers to help. By the time she had freed the bag, the salt-crusted cords had burned her lips. She scowled at the pain and carried the bag to a tide pool, gathered three sea urchins, and went on to another pool.

"You have been working all morning, Mother," Uutuk said. "Go to the storyteller's ulax. Qung is there alone. You will learn much about these people by listening to her."

K'os frowned. Did Uutuk think she was a child who needed instruction in the ways of the First Men? But then she realized that the girl was only worried that her mother was working too hard.

"Aa, Uutuk, you know what it is like when two old women get together. We would soon fill that ulax so full of words that no one else could get inside."

Uutuk laughed. "At least let me gather the sea urchins." She took the bag from K'os's hands, then, leaning close, she lifted her chin toward the traders who sat on the beach and whispered, "See the young man standing behind that stack of hides? He is a River hunter, and his father is a trader."

K'os lifted her head to look, but her eyes were not as strong as they had been, and she could see only that he was well built, taller than the First Men but short for a River hunter.

"He has the look of the First Men about him," she said.

"Qung says his mother was First Men."

K'os cleared her throat, steadied her voice. "Have you met his father?" she asked, and worked to keep her words low and quiet. She stooped to retrieve another sea urchin.

"Yes. His father's name is Cen. He is a River trader."

"Go see what he has," K'os told her. "Perhaps he will take a belly of seal oil for something you would like."

"Come with me, Mother," Uutuk said. "What do I know about making trades?"

"You said he was a hunter, not a trader. A young woman might be able to get more than she should from a man like that."

K'os saw the uncertainty in Uutuk's eyes, but the girl handed back the gathering bag and walked the length of the beach toward the traders. K'os pretended to work at gathering sea urchins but quickly went from tide pool to tide pool until she was close enough to see Cen's son.

Ghaden, yes, without a doubt. Though she was not sure she would have recognized him had she not been told who he was. He wore a First Men's sax. Wise. Cen might be a fool when it came to women, but he was the best trader K'os had ever known. Too bad they could not travel together so that Seal could learn from watching the man. Of course, Seal was so set in his ways, he would probably learn nothing at all.

The boy had Cen's nose, a pity that. But he also had his father's strong-boned face. There was something about his eyes that reminded her of the First Men. And who could doubt that his wide shoulders had come from his mother's people?

A livid scar curved down his neck from his left ear to somewhere inside the sax.

When Gheli had tried to kill the boy, she had used a knife,

but this scar was too new, still plump above the skin that surrounded it.

K'os watched as Uutuk approached him. The young man puffed out his chest as though he were getting ready to boast of some great deed. Uutuk waited while others made trades, her head lowered modestly. She fingered a caribou hide, stroked a fox pelt.

The familiar River things called K'os, and she found herself longing to be away from beaches and the sea, to once again walk forest trails, to hear the wind in black spruce branches.

She let herself dream of the plants she would gather, of the people she would choose to heal, and those she would not.

Even among the River People, Uutuk, with her beautiful face, would soon find a strong husband. Then what would prevent K'os from becoming the healer in that young husband's village? Soon she and Uutuk would gather so much strength for themselves that even Chakliux would not be able to stand against them.

Ghaden watched Uutuk from the corners of his eyes. It was difficult to remember that her mother was K'os. It brought him joy just to look at her. He wondered if all the women of her island, those Boat People women she had spoken about, were as beautiful as she was.

He missed what a First Men hunter was saying and forced his thoughts back to the trade the man was trying to make—sea lion skins for caribou hides. Ghaden pretended to consider the offer, but finally said, "I can get sea lion skins from Walrus Hunters, and even in those River villages nearest the North Sea."

But then Ghaden appeared to reconsider. He ran his hands over the hides the man was offering.

"They are good," he said, "large and well scraped." He spoke softly—as though he were arguing with himself—but loudly enough that the First Men hunter could hear him. "If

I give too good a deal, my father will not take me with him on the next trading trip."

"Three for two, then," the First Men hunter said.

"Three sea lion, two caribou?" Ghaden repeated and looked at the man with eyebrows raised.

"That is what I said."

Ghaden ran a hand over the top of his head, sighed as though he were frustrated. "You should be a trader yourself," he said. "You make good deals." Then he gave a grudging smile and pushed the pile of caribou hides toward the man. "Two for three," he said. "Choose the ones you want."

The First Men hunter reached out to clap a hand against Ghaden's arm. "I have been doing this a long time," he said. "You will learn. Your father will not regret bringing you."

The hunter chose his hides and left the sea lion skins. Ghaden set them out with the trade goods. Another hunter who had been considering a parka wandered away, and Daughter, now alone with Ghaden, said in the River tongue, "You got what you wanted in that trade, nae'?"

He smiled at her. "They're good hides," he said, "and the hunter will be back to trade again."

"You say this is the first trading trip you have made with your father?"

"To the Traders' Beach, yes, though I've traded in River villages with him and with my sister's husband, Chakliux."

Daughter frowned. The name was familiar to her, as though it were something she had heard as a child. She tried to place it, but let it go when Ghaden asked, "Do you have anything to trade?"

"No," she said, "but my mother has oil."

"What does she want?"

"She told me to choose something."

Daughter lifted a parka. It was made of caribou hide scraped until it was white. The seams around the arms and at the tops of the shoulders were inset with white fur.

Ghaden smoothed the fur with the tip of a finger and said,

"Winter weasel. They're small animals like lemmings, only thin and long with pointed noses and black-tipped tails. In the summer weasels are brown, and in the winter they turn white."

She smiled at him and shook her head. "There are so many animals that I do not know," she said. "I need to spend a year in a River village just to see what I have missed."

"There might be some River hunter who would like to show you his village," Ghaden said.

Daughter's face burned in sudden embarrassment. She was old enough to know better than to say such things. What had happened to her tongue? It was suddenly as though her mouth belonged to a child rather than a woman.

"I was hoping my father might decide to travel as trader among the River villages," she said and, glancing up at him, saw disappointment dim his eyes. She had only made it worse. "It would be good if we might travel together," she said, then wished she could pull back those words as well. She was First Men, and First Men knew how to stay quiet when something is best left unsaid.

To divert his attention, she lifted the parka, exclaimed at the gray and white fur that trimmed the hood.

"Wolf," Ghaden told her, and she saw that he was fighting to keep a smile from his lips.

Yes, why risk a smile that might lead another to believe that the trader thought he had the best side of the deal? But still Ghaden's mouth jerked up at one side, quivered as though he hid laughter from her. And why not? She was acting like a child, saying all things wrong.

"These . . ." Daughter said, and lifted a row of danglers sewn across the front of the parka.

"Flicker beaks and feathers. Flickers are a bird of spirit power, and very seldom seen. A man who takes a flicker brings himself good luck for the rest of his life. So you see, flicker beaks are not traded lightly."

She studied the seams. The stitches were as fine and even

as if K'os had made the garment. "The work is very good," she said.

"I should be the one to say that," Ghaden told her. "You should tell me what is wrong with it, and why you will not give me as much as I want."

A smile forced his eyes into thin crescents, like moons just reborn.

"It does not matter. I cannot trade for this parka," she told him. "My mother and I have only a few seal bellies of oil."

Daughter lifted the parka to her face and breathed in the clean smell of well-scraped hides. She laid it down, fingered the wolf fur ruff.

"It would be a good parka for a woman to own," Ghaden said.

"A woman with a husband who has more oil than he needs," said Daughter, then turned to walk away.

"What about the sax you are wearing?" Ghaden called to her. "Perhaps I would be willing to trade this parka for some oil, good seal oil stored in seal bellies, and for a First Men's sax."

"I need my sax," Daughter said. "How would I survive in my father's boat if I had only a parka to wear?"

She saw that her mother was still gathering sea urchins, and so hurried toward her, took the bag. It was heavy and full.

"Do you want these to go to the chief hunter's ulax?" Daughter asked.

"It would be a good gift for them," her mother said.

Daughter walked across the beach carrying the bag, and Ghaden again called out to her. "Perhaps there is something I might trade for sea urchins!"

Laughter bubbled from Daughter's throat, and she went to him, took a green-spined urchin from the gathering bag, and laid it on his trader's mat.

"A gift," she said.

He pulled a flicker feather from one of the danglers on the parka and gave it to her.

"For luck," he told her.

K'os watched Uutuk until she disappeared into the tall grasses at the rise of the beach, then hurried over to Ghaden. He was still staring at the path that led to the village, as though he could will Uutuk back. Finally he realized that K'os was standing in front of him.

"We have oil and caribou fat and dried caribou meat," he told her, "parkas and pants made of caribou hide. There are wolf pelts and fox furs, birdskins and dried fish, shafts for spears as straight as the edge of the sea where it meets the sky."

He spoke the words as traders do, in a rhythm that was nearly a song, and his voice was pleasing to the ear, like a storyteller's voice. Cen had said he was a hunter, and yet it appeared he could also be a trader if he wished, or even a storyteller. A young man given many choices. K'os wondered whether Ghaden had the wisdom to make the right decision for himself.

"I'm Uutuk's mother," K'os said, speaking in the River language. "I saw that she was looking at this parka." She bent close to study the seams. If she had doubted that Red Leaf was still alive, that parka lifted her doubt. Who else could sew like that?

"I told her that I would trade it for a First Men's sax, well made, and several bellies of seal oil."

"And she would not trade?"

"She said she needed her sax."

"She's a wise woman, my daughter."

K'os looked hard into Ghaden's face. "You do not know me, Ghaden?" she asked.

"I know you. I remember when my sister was your slave." His voice was quiet, but she heard his anger.

"You hate me for that?" she asked. "You've never had a slave? I myself was slave to the old woman Gull Beak in the Near River village. Perhaps you remember her. She was old then. She must be dead by now."

"Still alive when I left the village," Ghaden told her.

K'os smiled. "Good. I liked her. Though it was not easy being a slave."

"You could have treated my sister better."

"I realize that now," K'os said. "But I was ignorant then. As a girl I was the only daughter of a good hunter. As a woman my husbands were leaders of their people. I was respected as a healer, and I helped many. I didn't know what it was like to be slave. Now that I do, I would never own a slave again."

Ghaden studied her face as though trying to decide whether or not to believe her.

"Someone told me that the First Men don't have the same plants that we River People do," he said, as though they had never spoken about slaves. "Perhaps there are plants that you have found growing on First Men islands that River healers would find useful. My father brought caribou leaf to trade."

"I have plants," K'os said slowly, thinking over what was in her medicine bag.

Who would guess that Cen would bring medicines? But why be surprised? She had been a healer when Cen knew her. Surely during that time he had learned the value of plant medicines. She needed caribou leaf. A pity that most of the plants she had brought with her also grew in the River People's land.

"I have cixudangix," she told him. It was only the seagull flower, but the root had the power to clot blood. "It's difficult to get, even on First Men islands, and doesn't grow anywhere near our River villages." She was lying, but Ghaden would not know that. "A woman who has had a hard birth, or a man who is bleeding from a wound, these people should drink a tea made of the root."

"I need proof of what it is," he told her.

"You think because I was once slave that I will not trade in honesty?"

"How will I trade it to someone else if I don't know what I have?"

He was no fool, this boy. He reminded her of his half-sister Aqamdax, a woman who had given K'os much to regret.

"I'll give you a packet," she told him. "Show it to some of the First Men elders. They'll tell you what it is."

"And if the elders think it's a wise trade," he said, "then I'll give you caribou leaf in exchange."

"Good. I'll be back, and don't be too quick to trade away that parka. It would be beautiful on my daughter."

She went quickly to the chief hunter's ulax. She was relieved to find no one there except the hunter's old father, a man who spent most of his days living in a world that he had known as a child. When he saw her, he thought that she was his sister, a woman who was long dead. He called her that one's name, and K'os thought she felt the sister's spirit close. She shivered, and her arms pimpled with bumps.

She ladled him a bowl of broth and said, "Be quiet and eat. You do not know what you call down on us."

Then she sorted through her medicine bag, found the packet she wanted, also took one of her seal bellies of oil, and left the ulax.

When she handed the cixudangix to Ghaden, she said, "You claimed you would take oil and a First Men sax in trade for that parka." She lifted her chin toward the caribou parka, could not keep from touching the soft wolf fur that rimmed the hood. She had once made parkas like that, even more beautiful, but where had Red Leaf gotten all the flicker beaks? She had never seen so many. She and Uutuk could use the luck that a parka like that would bring.

She handed him the seal belly, and leaned over his trade goods to pull out the ivory stopper. She gently pressed a finger against the side of the belly until a fine spurt of oil erupted from the opening.

"Taste it," she told him. "It's new oil, and there's no seal hair in it. You won't find better."

He rubbed at the spilled oil with his hand, then licked his palm. "How many bellies do you have?" he asked.

"Six."

"Four and a sax," he told her.

"My daughter has made necklaces. Shells from our island that you can't find here."

"I have enough necklaces."

K'os shrugged, and held her hands palm up. "We don't have a sax to trade," she said. "But I'm sure there are ways to get one. I'll tell Uutuk what you have said. Will you put the parka away if I give you the oil now?"

"Bring it," he told her, then asked, "Where will you get the sax?" He picked up the parka and placed it in one of his packs.

"Young women as beautiful as Uutuk always have something to trade, and old men are willing to give more than they should."

She walked away and did not look back.

K'os found Uutuk sitting at the top of Qung's ulax. She climbed up and squatted on her haunches beside her. In the custom of the First Men, they did not speak for a time, but finally K'os said, "You should go back down to the beach. Ghaden might be willing to make a trade with you. Take three seal bellies of oil. They are in the chief hunter's ulax in the sleeping place closest to the climbing log. Take some necklaces and two sealskins, also some dried fish. Do not tell your father that you took them. I think Ghaden will be glad to trade."

K'os saw the joy on her daughter's face and hid a smile in her cheek. "Be wise, Daughter," she said to Uutuk. "You trade for more than a parka."

TWENTY-FOUR

Herendeen Bay, Alaska Peninsula
602 B.C.

Yikaas raised his voice to call out praise for Qumalix's stories, and others in the ulax did the same. Qumalix let her eyes rest for a moment on his face, and she smiled at him. He stood, stretched, then began to work his way toward her through the crowd, but suddenly a rough hand pushed him aside. A First Men storyteller—the one named Sky Catcher—stepped in front of him and, elbowing his way past elders and children, reached Qumalix first.

He spoke to her in the First Men language, interrupting others. Finally, as though the man were a boy, Qumalix raised a hand and made the sign for silence.

Yikaas felt a bubble of laughter rise into his throat, but then she leaned toward Sky Catcher and whispered into his ear. The man smiled and pressed his fingers against her shoulder as if he were a husband with a wife.

Then the old woman Kuy'aa was beside Yikaas and, standing on tiptoe, her head at his shoulder, she said, "Remember him? His name is Sky Catcher. There's a story he tells about the hunter who called the sun to the First Men's islands. He offered to tell Qumalix that story."

"Here? Now?"

Kuy'aa avoided his eyes, but said, "The First Men word he used means somewhere outside, in the wind. Away from here."

Yikaas glanced toward Qumalix. She and Sky Catcher were laughing, heads bent close. Pain and anger filled him to bursting, and he spoke to Kuy'aa through the edges of his teeth. "I'm going now. Do you want to leave, or will you stay and listen to more stories?" He offered his arm to help her up the climbing log, but she shook her head and settled down on her haunches as another storyteller began speaking.

Yikaas started up the climbing log, but could not keep from looking back one more time. Qumalix was pulling on her sax, and she was still speaking to Sky Catcher. Yikaas shrugged as though to tell himself that he did not care, and he climbed out into the wind.

Morning fog was down on the bay, and all things seemed cold and wet. The grayness entered at his heart and pushed up into his head, seemed to close off everything but his own thoughts, his own pain. He walked to the beach, to the mats where the traders had set their goods, and began to look for something he might buy with the caribou hides he had brought from his village. But the oil the traders offered had a sour smell, the pelts were dull and thin, and even the beads were misshapen.

The fog pressed against his ears like hands set at the sides of his head. Words spoken were lost before he understood them, and finally he turned away from the traders and walked across the beach to the iqyax racks. There he hunkered down on his haunches, arms around his knees like a First Men hunter, and thought about Qumalix and Sky Catcher. He shook his head as he remembered Sky Catcher's hand on her shoulder as if he already owned her.

What if he did?

The idea came so suddenly that it seemed as though someone had shouted it. What if Qumalix were promised to Sky Catcher? Perhaps that was why she had come so far to the Traders' Beach. After all, they were both First Men, and both storytellers.

Yikaas heard a giggle behind him and turned, his heart jumping at the sudden break in the silence. His first thought was Qumalix, but he laughed at himself over that. When had he ever heard her giggle? She was a woman, not a girl. Her laughter was full and strong, never foolish.

Two First Men girls walked out of the fog. They wore their hair loose, in the tradition of unmarried women, and their cheeks were marked with tattoos. One girl was plump and the other thin, but aside from that, they looked like twins, so much alike were their faces.

They swooped down on him like murrelets going into their burrow nests and both began to speak at once, using the First Men tongue. Suddenly the thin one stopped and held her hands over her mouth.

"You River," she said to him in his own language.

He could not help but smile at the way her First Men mouth bent the River words. "Yes, I'm River," he said.

"Speak First Men?"

He shook his head, and the girls sank to the sand together, giggling and whispering. Suddenly they leaped to their feet, grabbed his arms, and pulled him up, motioning that he should come with them.

He voiced a few protests, but made no effort to break free as they stumbled up the sand and gravel dunes toward the village. The fog blocked his view of their ulax until they were nearly upon it. He realized they were at the inland side of the village, where the ulas were smaller and backed tightly against the hills. The girls motioned for him to climb to the moss and grass roof, and he did so, then turned to look down at them.

They leaned their heads together, covered their mouths as they whispered to one another, then the sister who was plump, her eyes mere slits above her round, fat cheeks, smiled at him with her lips open, the tip of her tongue sliding over her teeth.

She spoke in the First Men language, but Yikaas had no trouble understanding what she meant. They joined him at the top of the ulax, then gestured for him to follow them inside. He threw one quick look toward the storyteller's ulax, thought of Qumalix and how they had shared stories hidden in the foothill grasses. Then he remembered Sky Catcher, his wide, broad face, his strong arms and shoulders, his short, powerful legs. He was a man of beads and feathers, of oiled hair and chin labret. When a man like that walks, the earth feels his steps. When a man like that speaks, what woman does not listen?

Yikaas lowered himself into the ulax.

Only the two girls were inside. Each had taken off her sax. They were small-breasted, but their skin was smooth and fragrant with oil. They looked at him from under half-closed lids. Why should he mourn over Qumalix? He pulled off his parka, and they each came to him with a bladder of oil. They began at his shoulders, rubbed his skin until they had driven the fog from his bones.

He closed his eyes and pushed Qumalix from his mind.

"So," Sky Catcher said to Qumalix, "I have told you the story of Sun Bringer. What do you have to give in exchange?"

Sky Catcher kept finding reason to touch her, to cup a hand over her knee or place an arm around her shoulders. She had finally wiggled so far away from him that he could not reach her without looking foolish, and as she had guessed, Sky Catcher was not a man to choose the part of a fool.

His story had been good, and he had given Qumalix permission to tell it. She had listened carefully, deciding even as he spoke where she would make changes so her listeners would feel as if they were the young man who had tricked the sun into coming so far north to a land of snow and ice.

Sky Catcher had told her that even yet, hunters in their iqyan could follow the path the sun had taken in coming to the First Men. What hunter—driven far out to sea by storms or drawn by whales—did not seek those warm rivers that flowed up from the south and along the edges of the First Men's islands? What hunter did not sing songs of gratitude for those trails the sun had left in its quest for the beautiful First Men women Sun Bringer had boasted about?

When Sky Catcher finished his story, he leaned toward her and looked into her eyes.

"Too bad you were not here in those long ago days," he said. "Then the sun would have lingered even into winter nights. How could it turn away from your face?"

It was as fine a compliment as Qumalix had ever received, but for some reason it sent her thoughts to the storyteller Yikaas, and she wondered if he would ever say such a thing. Then she was disgusted with herself. Why think about Yikaas? Anyone could see that Sky Catcher was more handsome, with his small straight nose and bright dark eyes. He was wider of shoulder and stronger of arm. Yikaas even walked with a limp. No wonder he was storyteller rather than hunter.

And what woman would choose a storyteller above a hunter? What hunter would trade caches with a storyteller? Far better to rely on yourself than on the generosity of others.

"You have not answered my question," Sky Catcher said, an edge of irritation in his voice.

Qumalix was used to a man whose temper came quickly. Her father was that way, though his was always an anger of words, spoken and quickly forgotten. He had not wanted her to return to this far village, the fear clear in his eyes until her grandfather had agreed to accompany her.

"If you bring back a husband," he had told her as they were leaving, partly in jest, a joke to cover the tremor in his voice, "be sure he is a hunter."

Her father would most likely be pleased if she brought back Sky Catcher, a man who was both hunter and storyteller. But what if she brought Yikaas? Aa, her father would be angry. A River man who could speak no First Men words. A River man who could not hunt from an iqyax. Nor would she be accepted in Yikaas's village. She had no River skills, had never even set a trapline, but surely it could not be too different from the bird traps she set at murrelet holes.

And making a parka, how difficult could that be for a woman who knew how to sew birdskins?

She was pulled from her thoughts by Sky Catcher's face too close to hers.

"A story, of course," she said in answer to his question. "What else do I have to give you?"

"What story do you know that I might like to hear?" he asked, his words coming from lips outthrust, as though he were pouting. "You think I want to hear stories about women? What man wants that?"

His words were as sharp as a slap, and his insult burned as though he had hit her, but she said, "I have whale hunting stories."

"Those would be better," he told her, "but I think I have heard all your whale hunting stories."

She shrugged. "Then I will tell you about Daughter. Listen if you want. Otherwise leave."

He allowed his eyes to rest at her hips and chest, and suddenly she wished she were not alone with him in this place too far from the village. She wrapped her arms around her knees, clasped her right hand over the crooked knife that she had strapped to her left forearm. It lent her courage, that small knife, and suddenly her mouth filled with words. As she began to talk, Daughter's story settled around her like the strong walls of an ulax, a protection against a man who wanted more than Qumalix was willing to give.

TWENTY-FIVE

Herendeen Bay, Alaska Peninsula
6435 B.C.

DAUGHTER'S STORY

K'os reached out and clasped Uutuk's hands. They crouched at the top of the chief hunter's ulax, alone except for the wind.

"One of the reasons we brought you with us on this trading trip was to find you a husband," K'os said. She released Uutuk's hands and stood, placed her fists at the small of her back, and leaned into the wind, flexing her shoulders. She laughed and said, "I am too old to spend so much time gathering sea urchins."

Uutuk stood up beside K'os, placed strong hands on her mother's shoulders, and kneaded the muscles. K'os closed her eyes.

"Aa, Uutuk, you are a good daughter," she said, and with eyes still closed she asked, "What do you think of the River man Ghaden?"

Uutuk's hands paused, but then she began to kneed even harder until K'os wrenched away from her grip.

"Uutuk, you are breaking my shoulders!"

Uutuk looked out over the village and murmured an apology, but she was facing the wind, so when her words came to K'os's ears, they were as twisted and tangled as beach grass. K'os reached to turn the girl toward her.

"I could not hear you."

"He is a good trader," Uutuk said, "and I hear luck favors him when he hunts, but he is River." She held her hands palm up as though to ask the sky what it thought.

"So am I," K'os said. They were speaking in the First Men language, and K'os changed her words to River. "Which means you are as well."

"Do you think if he took a First Men wife, he would be willing to go and live with her on her island?" Uutuk asked.

She crouched again and pulled her sax over her knees, down to her feet. K'os squatted also, and cupped a hand to her mouth so the wind would not blow away her words.

"No," she said. "He wouldn't come. He's not a trader. He's a hunter. You can't expect a grown man to become a boy again and learn to hunt sea animals when he already knows how to take caribou and moose and bear. But at least his father is a trader and has taught Ghaden how to use an iqyax. If his First Men woman was a very good wife, perhaps sometime before she grew old he would take her back to her island so she could visit her people."

"You want me to marry a River man."

"Only if he'll be a good husband to you and a good father for your children."

"White Salmon would have been a good husband and a good father."

There was a sharpness in Uutuk's voice that surprised K'os. The girl had barely complained when Seal refused White Salmon's brideprice.

"He offered too little for you," K'os told her. "What man values a wife when he can get her so easily? I don't always agree with your father, but that time he was right. If White Salmon had truly wanted you, he would've been willing to hunt another summer for your brideprice."

"I did not know he offered so little," Uutuk said. She spoke again in the First Men's language, and her voice was small, like a child's voice. "He told me he would give ten bellies of oil, ten otter skins, five thick pelts from fur seals, and many bellies of dried fish. He said if that was not enough his mother had a birdskin sax and three pairs of seal flipper boots she would be willing to give, but that I would have to sew for her during the first winter I was wife."

"He lied," K'os said.

Uutuk crossed her arms over her knees. "Why would he lie?" she asked, and her voice held the sound of tears.

"Who can say?" K'os answered. "Perhaps he thought you would be a better wife if you believed he had given so much for you."

"What did he offer?"

"You don't need to know. More than many young women would bring, but not enough for you."

K'os pushed herself back until she was sitting behind Uutuk, then gently pulled the girl's hair from the collar of her sax and began to comb it with her fingers, fighting the wind as it tried to steal the strands from her hands. "White Salmon is not gifted in his hunting. Even his iqyax and his weapons are poorly made. Do you think any sea animal is honored when he sees an iqyax with weak joints or a gaping cover? Do you think a harpoon with a crooked shaft will ever hit its mark? Perhaps the reason he said he offered so much for you was to hide the fact that his hunting skills are less than they should be."

K'os leaned forward over Uutuk's shoulder to look into her face. "Do you remember when you were a little girl, and I would braid your hair in the way of a River woman?"

Uutuk smiled. "I remember."

"Let me braid it for you."

"Do what you want," Uutuk said.

"There's too much wind up here." K'os lifted her chin to point toward the leeward side of the ulax.

Uutuk slid down the sod roof and reached up to help her

mother. Then she sat cross-legged like a River woman and let K'os weave her hair into braids.

"What would you take for the parka?" Ghaden asked Cen.

"You have someone who wants it?"

"Two women are interested."

"Good!" said Cen. "Play them off against one another. Get as much as you can."

"They've offered oil and a sax."

"See if you can also get a pair of seal flipper boots and a chigdax. They trade well among the River People. Their women don't know how to make either."

"In my village, all the River women know how to make a chigdax."

"Hayh!" Cen said, flicking his fingers in the air. "Your sister is more generous than she has a right to be." But he laughed, taking the sting from his words.

"Two handfuls of seal bellies?" Ghaden asked.

Cen nodded, then said, "And the sax and a chigdax. Maybe boots. I want to bring my wife a good price for this parka. It has much luck in it. Don't forget to explain about the flicker beaks."

"I told them."

"Good." Cen looked up at the sky, found the brightness that was the sun hidden behind a bank of high clouds. "The day is half gone. Are you hungry?"

"I could eat," Ghaden said.

"Qung will have something in her cooking bag."

Ghaden left the beach, turned to watch as Cen lifted his voice to beckon several hunters to his display of trade goods. Two groups of Walrus men had come that day. The Walrus were always greedy for weapons, and Cen had a good supply of birch spear shafts. He would make some fine trades.

Ghaden did not go immediately to Qung's ulax, but instead visited the cache where he and Cen stored food and extra trade goods. He had promised one of Aqamdax's parkas to a First Men hunter in exchange for six bellies of oil. He took the parka from the cache as well as a few wolf pelts, a packet of bear teeth, and several claw necklaces. Perhaps the man would be willing to trade a few more bellies of oil for a bear claw or a wolf pelt.

Ghaden rubbed at the scar on his neck. Sometimes it prickled, as though the bear's spirit now and again thought of him. Among the First Men a bear claw might bring much in trade, or perhaps nothing at all. As Cen often told him, the value of any one thing changed from man to man.

"That one, the River boy," K'os said, and pointed to Ghaden as he stood speaking to several First Men hunters. He was holding up a wolf pelt and dangled something from his left hand, but K'os was too far away to see what it was.

"As husband for Uutuk?" Seal asked.

"Only something to consider," she told him. "I know his family. His sister is married to the chief of the elders in one of the River villages, and his mother was First Men, so he speaks our language."

"It might be better for us if she married a hunter," Seal said. "Since I am a trader and can get anything we need. . . ."

"More than what we need," K'os interrupted him to say. "There are not many traders who are as gifted as you."

He pressed his mouth into a frown, and K'os could hear the boasting under his words when he said, "So what good will it do her to marry a trader?"

"He is a hunter," K'os said. "His father is a trader, and Ghaden sometimes travels with him."

"A good hunter?" Seal asked.

"Qung told me that he killed a brown bear when the animal attacked him."

Seal tilted his head and made a noise in his throat. Laughter or disdain? K'os was not sure.

"Should I tell Uutuk to stay away from him?" she asked.

Seal puffed out his chest with a long breath. "See what he offers in a brideprice. See if he is willing to come and stay on our island and hunt there."

K'os nearly explained that Ghaden would not know much about hunting sea animals, but she held her tongue. Let Seal believe what he wanted. Once Ghaden had Uutuk as wife, it would be too late for Seal to change things just because the man hunted caribou rather than sea lions.

She dipped her head in acknowledgment, then asked, "May I get you something to eat?"

"The chief's first wife fed me," he said. "But it has been a long time since I had you in my bed."

K'os curled her lips into a smile, allowed her eyes to drop briefly toward Seal's crotch. "When you have made enough trades, come and find me," she said. Then she walked away, swinging her hips.

When she knew Seal could no longer hear her, she looked up at the sun, hidden as it was behind a thick mat of clouds, and she said, "Look! What do I see? In giving it takes. In taking it lives. A riddle for you, my sister in the sky."

Ghaden hummed under his breath and considered the fur seal sax. It was beautiful and more practical for a River man than a birdskin sax, warmer and not easily torn, but River women did not sew feathered birdskins and so a birdskin sax would have more worth.

"Two teeth and a claw," the man said, "and for a wolf pelt, I will give you these seal flipper boots."

The boots were old, but they looked as if they had seldom been worn.

"I kept them oiled," the man said.

Ghaden traded the teeth and claw for the fur seal sax, gave him his choice of pelts for the boots, then asked if he knew of anyone else who had seal flipper boots to trade.

"Sometimes the old women make extra pairs and are willing to take food for them. You have caribou meat?"

"Some," Ghaden told him, his mind already on Qung. He and his father would give the old woman a good supply of dried meat for allowing them to stay in her ulax, but she might have boots to barter, or know of someone who did.

He went to her after he had completed his trades with the First Men hunter. Qung gave him the names of three women, and each had something worthwhile to trade, a pair of boots, delicate shell bead necklaces, a puffin skin sax, grass baskets so finely woven that Ghaden could scarcely believe a woman's fingers had made them.

He traded for all of them and stowed the goods in his cache. Then he went to Cen and offered to take his place at their trading mats.

Cen was gone for a good share of the afternoon, and during that time Ghaden went to his cache, brought out the seal oil bellies, the puffin skin sax, the seal flipper boots, the grass baskets, two caribou hides of his own, and a handful of shell necklaces. He piled these things with Cen's trade goods and took the caribou parka.

Ghaden had intended to tell Cen about the trade, but as soon as Cen returned a group of Walrus men crowded around him, began making offers for spear shafts and knapped points, so Ghaden let his father take over the trading and returned to Qung's ulax. There were questions he needed to ask her about First Men customs and brideprices.

He was still with Qung when Cen came in. Ghaden looked up, surprised to see that his father had left his trade goods. A man had little to worry about in this village as far as anyone taking what did not belong to him, but why leave the trading in the middle of the day when the best barters were often made?

"The parka is gone," Cen said, interrupting rudely, without greeting Qung.

"I am glad you have come to my ulax," Qung said, and rose to her feet. She was so bent by her humped back that she reminded Ghaden of a duck, waddling on widespread legs. She hobbled to a low-slung hook where she kept a water bladder and offered it to Cen.

Cen's face reddened. He took the water, murmured his thanks, then drank.

"Sit down," Qung said, the words like an order given to a child. "Are you hungry?"

"No." Cen bit out the word.

"Now, you have something to say to Ghaden?" she asked, raising her eyebrows into the wrinkles of her forehead.

"Yes, I have something to say to Ghaden. The white caribou parka is gone."

"I traded it," Ghaden told him.

Cen took in a mouthful of air, then blew it out between his teeth. "You should have told me," he said, his voice low and quiet.

"It was a good trade."

"What did you get?"

"A puffin sax and one of fur seal, two pair of seal flipper boots, necklaces and baskets, and eight bellies of oil. I put out the fur seal sax, the oil and boots, and some of the necklaces, but the puffin sax and the baskets are in my cache."

Cen was still angry, but Ghaden could see that he was pleased about the trade goods, and gradually his anger faded. But he held up one finger, and like an old woman shook it in Ghaden's face.

"You should have told me, and even though it was a good trade, you should have asked me before making it. The parka belongs to my wife."

"Grass baskets and a birdskin sax will not please her?" Qung asked.

Cen blinked and looked at the old woman as though he had forgotten she was with them. "She is not difficult to please," he said. "She would be happy with the baskets alone, but I want her to know . . ."

He stopped as if unsure how to say what he meant, and Qung said, "You want her to know that you missed her and that you think she is a good wife."

Cen merely grunted, and when he walked to the climbing log, his footsteps were heavy, as though he needed to remind himself of his own importance. At the top of the ulax he looked down at Qung and said, "See if you can teach him some wisdom, Aunt."

After Cen left, Qung put her hands over her mouth and began to laugh, but when Ghaden joined her laughter, she settled herself back onto her haunches and said, "Your father is right, you know. You should not have made that trade by yourself. What if you had taken too little?"

"It was not a problem," Ghaden told her.

She tilted her head, asking a question without speaking.

"I own the caribou hide parka," he said. "I traded it to myself. If my father was not pleased with the trade, then I would have given more."

"This Boat People woman—Uutuk, K'os's daughter— you plan to give it to her?" Qung asked.

"How did you know?"

"I am old, but I see well enough." She lifted her chin toward an ulax rafter and told him, "Bring down that seal belly for me. I need oil for the lamp."

He stood and reached for it, took out the stopper, and poured oil into the side of the stone lamp farthest from the clump of moss she used for a wick.

"Be careful," she said, "or you will douse the fire."

When the bowl of the lamp was full, she waved one hand at him and said, "Hang it up again."

He replaced the belly on its peg, then she pointed at the floor with pursed lips. "I think you had better sit down and talk to me."

He turned toward her but remained standing.

"Sit!"

He sat.

"You are making a brideprice," she said, "but you hardly know this girl. Her father is not much, and you have heard about her mother. What River man has not?"

"Yes, I know her mother," Ghaden said, "and I know what she did to my sister."

"Daughters are like their mothers. Surely you are old enough to have realized that."

"Uutuk is not like K'os."

Qung began nodding her head, keeping a rhythm as though she were listening to a drumbeat. Finally she said, "And what if you are wrong? Are you willing to chance that you might bring another K'os into your village?"

"I told you. She is not like K'os."

"You have seen her sewing?"

"It is very good."

"She has her own medicine bag, a sea otter. Did you know that?"

"No."

"You know that K'os is a healer?"

"I know."

"And she also uses her knowledge of plants to kill."

"Some people say that."

"Did you know that she sews very well?"

"I have seen parkas she made."

"Then how can you say Uutuk is not like her mother?"

"In these things—in the good ways—she might be like K'os."

"Only in good ways?"

"Uutuk is not K'os. There is no hatred in her."

Qung began nodding again, and finally even closed her eyes, so that Ghaden thought she had fallen asleep. He had nearly decided to get up when she said, "Uutuk seems to be a good woman, which means either that she *is* a good woman, or that she is very good at being evil."

Ghaden considered her words, then said, "She is a good woman. I know it."

"Then if you are sure, and you have decided to make her your wife, there are things you should know about First Men customs."

He waited, but Qung did not say anything more. Finally he asked, "Do you know someone who will talk to me about these customs?"

"Do you think there is anyone who knows more than I do?"

He smiled at her. "No, but I am not sure you want to tell me what you know."

"Better I should tell you than someone who will give you poor advice. But you are not the only one in this ulax who trades."

"I have oil," he said to her, "and caribou meat."

She waved a hand at him. "I have more than enough to keep me through the next winter and even beyond that, and I am still not too old to catch a few fish and gather sea urchins."

"Baskets? Necklaces? A parka. I have a parka my sister Yaa made, not as beautiful as some, but the caribou hide is well scraped and the seams are straight and strong."

Qung wrinkled her nose as she considered his offer; then on impulse he lifted one of the bear claws he had strung on sinew and hung at his neck. He untied the sinew and held out the claw, a long brown curl, polished to brightness with caribou fat. She squinted at it, reached out and took it, then cradled it in her lap, but she asked, "What would an old woman do with a bear claw?"

"Power is power," Ghaden told her.

She chortled to herself and wrapped her fingers around the claw, held it as she told Ghaden the First Men customs of taking wives.

"She is worth more than a few seal bellies of oil and six necklaces," Seal said to Ghaden.

They were sitting on the lee side of the chief hunter's ulax, away from the wind. Trail-walker, brother of one of the chief's wives, sat with them. He was thin, long of legs, and tall. His large nose and narrow face made him look out of place among the First Men. Like Seal, he had cut his hair in a fringe across his forehead, and large round labrets pierced his skin at the corners of his mouth.

"Get some caribou meat," Trail-walker said to Seal, the labrets clicking against his teeth.

"Trades are better made between two men," Seal told him. "Be quiet and let me think about this."

Trail-walker leaned close to whisper into Seal's ear, but Seal pushed the man away and said to Ghaden, "She sews well. Do you want to see one of the parkas she made?"

Ghaden agreed, though he knew that Seal was only trying to make the bargaining more difficult.

Seal climbed up to the ulax roof and went inside, returning with a large, square trader's pack. He untied the flap and pulled out a black-feathered birdskin sax, unrolled it and held it up. Ghaden grunted his approval, then noticed a few stitches of red sinew on the top edge of the collar rim.

"Your wife used to live in my village," Ghaden said. "She owned my oldest sister as slave. I know K'os's mark." He reached out and fingered the red stitches. "This is not Uutuk's work. Perhaps you are ashamed of what she sews . . ."

Trail-walker bumped Seal with his elbow and gave a quick shake of his head.

"Do not take me for a fool," Seal said to Trail-walker. "I did not notice that this was my wife's work. Wait."

He dug through the pack, pulled out another rolled sax, then two more, checking the collar rims on each. Finally he grunted and threw one toward Ghaden. Ghaden unrolled it. He knew little about stitching and cutting, but he had seen Cen turn a garment to the inside, run his fingers across the seams, and sniff the hides, so Ghaden did all these things. He noticed that the stitches were small and even, which seemed good. Birdskins smell different than caribou hides, so he could not be sure about the odor, whether good or bad, but they carried no stink of mold.

Thrusting out his chin as if he knew what he were talking about, Ghaden said, "Well made."

"She sews quickly. She can make a sax of puffin skins in just a few days."

Trail-walker rubbed his nose and commented, "What does he know about puffin skins? He is River."

"Puffin skins are smaller than cormorant," Seal explained to Ghaden. "It takes a woman more time to make a sax from puffins."

Ghaden did not answer. Trail-walker had insulted him, assuming his ignorance about puffins and cormorants, but Seal did not seem to notice Ghaden's silence. He continued to chatter about his daughter's abilities.

"Her mother has taught her about plants. It is useful to have a wife who knows something about healing."

"Would she be willing to live with the River People?" Ghaden asked.

"She wants a husband who will hunt for her family. How can you do that if you go back to live in a River village?"

At first Ghaden had no answer. Surely Seal was wise enough to realize that a man who had spent his life learning to hunt caribou would be of less use than a boy when it came to taking sea animals.

"I could make sure that my father always brought a good supply of dried caribou meat to the Traders' Beach each summer," Ghaden said. "You could claim it here. Surely with your own hunting skills, you do not need more seal or sea lion meat, and because you are a trader, you could make good deals with the caribou I provide for you."

Trail-walker spoke again into Seal's ear. This time Ghaden heard what he said. It was an insult, but Ghaden held in his anger and waited for Seal to speak.

"How do I know you will do such a thing?" Seal asked. "I do not come to this beach every year. It is too far to travel."

"I give you my word. Ask anyone who knows me, and they will tell you that I do not lie. I will send meat whether you are here or not. If you do not come, the chief hunter can use it and later exchange seal oil for what he and his people have eaten. You know that the men of this village can be trusted. They often do things like this for traders. Why do you think traders continue to come to their beach?"

Seal pinched his lips into a frown. "I will not be here next year," he said, "so perhaps you should give me now what I would have coming."

"What if she is not a good wife?" Ghaden countered. "A man cannot be expected to pay for a wife who does not please him."

Seal looked at Trail-walker, but Trail-walker only shrugged. "A caribou hide of dried meat," Seal finally said. "I will give her to you for two wolf pelts, the oil and necklaces, and a caribou hide of dried meat. She is yours as soon as you bring the oil and meat. Do not forget the necklaces, but give the most beautiful to my daughter. Tell her it is from me. Tell her that I expect grandsons in exchange."

Trail-walker leaned close again, and Seal listened, then smiled. "One last thing," said Seal and lifted his chin toward Ghaden's chest. "A bear claw."

Ghaden used his sleeve knife to cut the sinew that knotted the claw into a necklace. "Done," he said.

TWENTY-SIX

"There was something you needed to ask me?" Cen said to Ghaden. Impatience roughened his voice, and he glanced out at the bay where two Walrus traders waited in their iqyan. They had invited him to join them on a trading trip to several nearby First Men villages.

Ghaden drew in his breath, released it in a short laugh. "Nothing," he said.

"You're welcome to come."

Cen raised his eyebrows at his son, but Ghaden shook his head. The journey would not be long, depending on tides and weather, two or three days of travel, then a night or two at the village and the return trip to the Traders' Beach.

Too bad Ghaden didn't want to come, Cen thought. It would have been a good way to get him out of the village. But why worry? Ghaden had changed from child to man since K'os last saw him. She didn't even know he was here. If she did, Cen assured himself, you would have heard about it. She's not a woman to keep small victories to herself.

"You're sure, then? We might make some very good trades."

"You told me about that village once," Ghaden said. "Remember? It doesn't sound as if the women are very friendly."

"Aaa, always women," Cen said and laughed, but then his face grew stern. "Don't forget what I told you about K'os and her daughter."

Ghaden looked away, out toward the inlet where the traders were waiting. "I won't," he said.

Cen pushed his iqyax into the water and climbed inside, then shoved himself away from the shore with his paddle. It was a single-bladed cedar paddle, banded with Cen's colors. Ghaden had carved it himself, according to Chakliux's directions, and had given it to Cen as a gift.

Cen lifted the paddle in farewell, then turned his iqyax into the fog that lay over the bay.

Ghaden thought he would feel a release once his father was gone, a joy in being a man again, rather than the boy that Cen always seemed to see.

He stroked the bear claws that hung at his neck. No matter how much praise he received for his hunting success, no matter how cunning he was in making trades, to Cen he remained a child.

Ghaden's thoughts ran ahead to the day when Cen would return and discover that in his absence Ghaden had taken Uutuk as wife.

A man makes his own decisions, Ghaden reminded himself. Except for his first wife, now dead, no woman had held his eyes or lived in his dreams like Uutuk. How could he return to his people without her? Once he was back in Chakliux's village, he would take some old widow as second wife, placate Chakliux and Cen by keeping her fed.

And K'os? She would go back with her husband to his people and that distant island where they lived. What could be more simple than that?

K'os raised her voice and screamed, "You promised her to a River hunter! Who?"

Of course, she knew who, and she was pleased, but with

Seal the wisest course was to pretend disagreement; then any uncertainty he carried was lost in his need to defend himself.

"The trader's son, the one you yourself suggested," Seal told her, his voice loud and angry. "I thought you wanted that."

"It was only a consideration, something to think about. You said you would see what he offered as brideprice, not that you would accept his offer."

"Look." Seal held out the bear claw. "There is enough power in this to last me into old age."

"She is my daughter. You should have asked me first."

"What woman expects to have a say in the giving and taking of wives?" Seal countered, and kicked at the crowberry heather on the floor of the chief hunter's ulax.

The chief's third wife Spotted Leaf was there, and as soon as Seal and K'os had begun to fight, she had turned her back as though she were not listening, but when one of her young sons started climbing down the notched log into the ulax's main room, the woman had snapped her fingers above her head, motioning for him to leave. The boy had, but not before standing and listening to the argument, a wide grin on his face.

"I got eight bellies of oil, two wolf pelts, a caribou hide of dried meat and some necklaces. He has also promised to hunt for us."

"You expect a man trained as a caribou hunter to come to our island and hunt sea mammals from an iqyax? He will be a boy, worse than a boy, because we will have to feed him and he will eat like a man."

Seal's eyes widened, and K'os knew he had given no thought to the fact that Ghaden would not be able to hunt sea animals. But then he smiled, looked at her as though she were a child.

"You think I do not know that?"

K'os felt hope rise in her chest. Perhaps Ghaden, knowing he could not hunt sea mammals—at least not without several summers of hard work learning—had already convinced Seal to spend the winter with him, make a trading trip among the River People.

She bowed her head as though suddenly submissive. "When do we leave?" she asked.

Seal looked at her in surprise. "When I am done trading," he said. "But first I plan to take a few days and travel to a nearby First Men village with other traders. You and Uutuk can stay here if you like." He stopped. "Though by then she might have left with her River husband," he said. "She is a good daughter. I will miss her."

K'os felt a numbness creep into her arms. She tried to speak, but her anger at her husband's stupidity closed off her throat. How did he think Ghaden would hunt for them? Did Seal plan to make the long journey each year to the Traders' Beach? Could he be that foolish?

"You can come with me if you want," Seal said, a puzzled look on his face, as though she had just told him one of her riddles. "I know you will be lonely without Uutuk."

"We're going with her, nae'?" K'os asked, and in her distress, did not realize that she had spoken in the River tongue. Seal made a rude noise, and insulted her with fingers flapping—sign of the gull, a bird so lazy that it steals food.

She ignored the insult and repeated her words in the First Men language.

"How can we go with her?" Seal asked. "We have to return to our own village. Our chief hunter and my uncle gave me sealskins, fur seal pelts, and oil to trade. If I do not return, they will think I have cheated them."

"Or they will think we are dead, swallowed by the sea," K'os said. "Who could be angry about that? Then when we do return, they will be glad. You told me once that you had hoped to trade with River People. Why lose your chance? Now you have a son-by-marriage who can help you make those trades."

"I am wise enough to make my own trades."

"Of course," K'os said, and shrugged her shoulders. "You are right. You do not need him, but I do not want to see my daughter go off with a River husband by herself. What if the people in his village hate her? She is a First Men woman, and not only First Men but also Boat People. What hope does she have to be accepted as one of them?"

"You told me that Ghaden himself is part First Men. He lives among them without problems."

"Who would risk angering a young man who can kill a brown bear?"

Seal stroked the claw at his neck and raised his eyes to the ulax roof as though he would find wise answers there among the rafters and grass mats.

Finally he said, "You have trained Uutuk in plant medicines. All people are glad to have a healer."

"She knows First Men medicines."

"She can learn River."

"If she finds someone to teach her."

Seal narrowed his eyes. "You want to go with her so you can teach her."

"No one knows more about plant medicines than I do," K'os said. "In one year, summer to summer, I can teach her what would take a lifetime to learn without help."

Seal stood and reached up for a water bladder. He drank and offered it to K'os. She was not thirsty, but it was always wise to accept Seal's gifts, even those as small as a sip of water. She took the bladder, drank, and thanked him.

He returned it to the peg and said, "So you think I could make good trades?"

She smiled. "You always make good trades. I think you would have opportunity to barter for things we cannot get even here, perhaps something from the North Tundra People or the Caribou Hunters who live far to the east."

"It might not be terrible to spend a year with the River People," Seal said. "I will speak to Ghaden about it."

K'os tilted her head and ran her tongue over her lips,

making promises without words. "I was wrong," she told him. "You made a good decision in giving Uutuk to Ghaden."

Seal shrugged. "Wives are not expected to have much wisdom in choosing husbands for their daughters. But if we are to go with Ghaden and Uutuk, think about this. I will need a good parka."

Seal approached his daughter as she was digging bitterroot in the meadow on the mountain side of the village. She was carrying a net gathering bag, and it was nearly full.

"Bitterroot," she said, holding the bag up for him to see. Bitterroot, boiled and mixed with seal oil, was one of his favorite foods.

"It is early for bitterroot," he said.

"Here the summer is warmer and all plants are ahead of themselves."

As she spoke her eyes moved nervously, and he knew that she was deciding which way to run if he tried to touch her. The thought made him angry. He had never touched her more than any father touches a daughter. There were taboos. Of course, she was not daughter by blood, and bedding a woman like Uutuk would be worth a small curse. He lifted his hand to the bear claw, felt power course into his fingers, and he reminded himself that for now, at least, Uutuk would serve him better as daughter than as bedmate.

"I need to talk to you," he said.

She was using a piece of driftwood as a digging stick, and she lifted it from the ground, held the end high enough so that he could see she had sharpened it into a point. She raised her chin in the direction of the beach.

"The iqyax racks cut the wind," she said.

"There are too many people on the beach," he told her.

She set her mouth into a firm line and squatted on her haunches, laying the digging stick across her knees.

"Talk," she told him.

"I have accepted a brideprice for you."

She grimaced but said nothing, and her silence added to his anger.

"You are old enough to be a wife—beyond the age of becoming a wife," he told her. "You should have babies by now. Instead I have to feed you."

"Who?" Uutuk asked, ignoring his insults. "River or First Men?"

"River," Seal said harshly. He clasped the bear claw that hung from his neck, and he saw her eyes widen in understanding. "Be glad. I could have gotten more for you from some old man who would not even be able to fill your belly with children."

He did not wait to hear her protests. As he strode away from her, back toward the village, he passed two old women with gathering nets. They gave a greeting, but he snarled at them, pounding his feet into the ground as he walked so no one would doubt that he was a man who understood the powers of the earth and used them well.

TWENTY-SEVEN

Qung was napping as she often did during the middle of the day. When else could a storyteller sleep? Most people wanted to hear tales during the long twilight of summer nights. Daughter sat near Qung's oil lamp, crimping seal flipper boot soles with her teeth and thinking about being wife to a River man. When her fears seemed too large, she pulled Ghaden's face into her mind, his smile, and then the tight ache in her belly eased.

Her thoughts were interrupted by a voice calling from the top of the ulax. It was K'os. Daughter set down the boot sole and climbed partway up the log, whispered to her mother that Qung was asleep.

"I have fireweed leaves made into tea. Would you like some?" Daughter asked.

K'os waved a hand in refusal and said, "I have something to tell you."

Even after many years away from her own people, K'os was much more River than First Men, direct in her way of saying things, without the quiet joy of shared food or tea.

K'os climbed into the ulax, and Daughter put away the boot sole, squatted beside the oil lamp, and waited as her mother took off her parka and sat down.

"Your father has accepted a brideprice for you," K'os said, and she did not seem concerned about what Daughter thought or how she felt. "The man is Ghaden, and he is a hunter."

"So I have heard," said Daughter, leaving her mother to guess whether she meant she had heard about Ghaden's hunting or about Seal's choice. "I will miss you."

"You think I would let you go by yourself and live as wife to a man I do not even know?" K'os asked. "I am a better mother than that."

Daughter's relief was so great that she had to close her eyes against the burn of tears.

"And Seal?" she asked. "What does he say?"

"He is a good father," said K'os, but she looked away, as though she were embarrassed at making the claim. "He promised that we would spend a year with you. That way he will have opportunity to trade with the River People and perhaps the Caribou. While he trades, I will teach you River medicine so that you will not only be wife among the River People but also healer."

Questions filled Daughter's mind, but her throat was so thick with gratitude that she had to drink from her cup of fireweed tea before she could find her voice. "After that year you will return to our island?" she finally asked.

"Most likely," K'os said, "but a year is a long time, so we will wait and see what happens."

Daughter wanted to ask if she might return with them, but why request a promise that her mother might not be able to keep? Instead she thought of all the good things that come to a woman when she is a wife—her own ulax, children, and a man to share her bed. She thought of Ghaden's smile and the kindness that shone from his face. Then, to hold in her tears, she fixed her eyes on the flames that danced in the stone lamp and listened as K'os told her how to give joy to her husband during that first night they would spend together in Daughter's bed.

* * *

That evening in the chief hunter's ulax, K'os helped Daughter wash her hair, first with urine to strip out the old oil, then with three bladders of fresh water to rinse away the urine. They rubbed the hair dry with lemming skins, then K'os used an ivory comb—a marriage gift from the chief hunter's wives—to smooth out the tangles.

Daughter's hair hung to her waist, and was so dark that sometimes in the sunlight it seemed to shine blue. K'os combed fresh seal oil through the strands, then also oiled Daughter's face and arms and breasts. She stepped back and smiled, but when Daughter returned the smile, K'os's face changed—a quick tightening of the jaw, a clenching of teeth, a look too fleeting for Daughter to name.

"You are beautiful," K'os said, "and perhaps it is good that you do not have the First Men's tattoos, since you will be River."

"Even many of the Traders' Beach women do not mark their faces," Daughter told her, something she had noticed when they first came to the village.

K'os nodded and squinted her eyes, tipped her head to study Daughter's hair.

"A braid might be good, Uutuk," she finally said, "since you are marrying River. To let your husband know that you respect his people."

Daughter made a face. She liked the First Men custom of a bride going to her husband with her hair loose, then the next day binding it in a bun at the nape of her neck, a proud sign that she had been accepted as wife.

"A small braid," K'os told her, and knelt beside Daughter, used her fingers to divide a section of hair at the left side of Daughter's face.

When she had finished, she tied it with a bit of sinew thread, then lifted Daughter's hand to the braid. "Here, see?"

Daughter smiled. It was no bigger around than her smallest finger, but as K'os said, it would show respect for Ghaden's customs, even though most of her hair still fell loose over her shoulders, as a woman's hair should.

"You are beautiful," K'os said again, "and if you remember all the things I taught you about the ways a wife can please . . ."

She was interrupted by a voice crowing from the top of the ulax, one of the chief hunter's young sons. He hopped to the floor from the middle of the climbing log, carrying a pack nearly as large as he was. He thrust it at Daughter.

"Here, for you, from that River man. The one who is not a trader."

The pack was square and cut from hardened caribou hide, laced with babiche at each seam, much like a storage pack K'os had used during Daughter's childhood until the damp, foggy air of their island had rotted it. Daughter untied the cover flap and reached inside, gasped when she pulled out the white caribou parka.

"For you! For you!" the chief's son shouted, his thin arms jerking as he danced in a little circle, scuffing up the grass and heather on the hard dirt floor. "Leggings, too. Look inside."

Daughter took out the leggings. They were made of many small pelts, reddish in color. She stood and held up the parka and leggings so her mother could see.

"The parka is caribou," Daughter said, "but what are the leggings?"

"Red squirrel," her mother told her. "They will be warm and light and should last you for more than one winter."

The chief's third wife, a woman much given to necklaces and fancy clothing, came out of her sleeping place, and, seeing the parka, exclaimed her envy. She began to finger the fur ruff and count the flicker beaks. Daughter's joy bubbled into laughter.

"You are First Men, and used to your sax," K'os told Uutuk, "but you need to wear his gifts."

Daughter set a hand on her puffin skin sax. She had mended and cleaned it for this night, and it was a reminder of her island, but she knew K'os was right. She had to learn River ways.

She had not worn leggings since she was a little girl, and she soon had the chief's wife and son laughing as she tried to keep her balance, standing on one leg, then the other to pull on the garment. K'os helped her with the parka, then took a necklace she had been wearing and draped it over Daughter's head.

"Your father wants you to have this," she said.

Daughter thanked K'os, but the necklace seemed dark and old against the white of the parka, as if her father's hands once again lingered too close.

Qung's teeth were so worn with age that when she smiled, her mouth seemed like a wide, empty cave. Her laughter came from deep in her throat, and her happiness drew wrinkles in her cheeks.

"A wife!" she said to Ghaden. "Will you know what to do with her?" She made a series of coarse jokes, and it seemed so strange to hear them come from an old woman that Ghaden could not help but laugh.

"I have food enough for everyone," Qung said. "Or will you spend the night in the chief hunter's ulax? You and your bride are welcome here, you know."

Ghaden could see the hope in her eyes, and he made a joke of his own, saying, "There are more people than sleeping places in that ulax. Do you think my new wife would like to share our first bed with the chief hunter?"

Qung laughed. She crawled over to the floor cache that held her storage bags of dried meat and fish. She began pulling them out one by one, pawing through them and piling fish and caribou meat on the mats beside her oil lamp.

"You might go and see if anyone has sea urchins to trade," she told him as she arranged peeled stalks of fresh iitikaalux beside the meat.

He would rather have waited in the ulax for Seal to bring Uutuk, but Ghaden did as she asked. Thoughts of bedding Uutuk drove away his need for food, but he was sure that Seal would want to eat.

At least they were not in a River village. There the marriage would be celebrated with a feast and a long night of dances and songs and riddles. The First Men were more wise about taking wives and did little to celebrate other than the exchange of a brideprice.

It did not take him long to find someone with sea urchins, a girl willing to take a necklace in exchange for her morning of gathering. When Ghaden returned to the ulax, Seal and Uutuk were there.

Uutuk was wearing the caribou parka and leggings, her hair a dark and shining river over the white of the parka.

Praise for her beauty filled Ghaden's mouth, but a husband did not say such things to his wife, lest it seem he were praising himself, so he only lifted the bag of sea urchins and said, "Sea eggs for our celebration."

Seal squatted beside the food mats and accepted the fish and meat Qung offered him. She gave him a bowl of seal oil for dipping, and Uutuk ladled out soup from the caribou hide bag that hung over the oil lamp. She gave the first bowl to Seal. He lifted it to his mouth and slurped loudly in appreciation.

She filled another and gave it to Ghaden. He tried to catch her eyes, but she kept her face lowered. It was the custom to do so among First Men brides, but he was disappointed. He had hoped that she would show some joy in being his wife, or at least gratitude for the parka.

Seal leaned toward his daughter and ran a hand over the flicker beaks, lingering for a moment on the mounds of her breasts. Anger filled Ghaden's mouth, but he shut his lips tightly over it, swallowed it down, and accepted Seal's actions as compliment.

They ate, mostly in silence, and Uutuk continued to serve them as though she had long been his wife. When Seal and Ghaden had finished, Qung boldly helped herself to the remaining food.

"Where is your father?" she asked Ghaden, her mouth crammed with dried fish.

"I did not tell you?" Ghaden asked. "He and two other traders decided to travel to villages west of the Traders' Beach."

Qung raised a bowl of broth to her mouth and looked at him over the rim. "He should be here," she said.

"They plan to be away five or six days. I decided not to wait for him."

"A good decision," said Seal, his voice nearly too loud for politeness.

"He should be here," Qung said again.

"But he is not," Ghaden said firmly. Should a hunter let an old woman make his decisions?

Then Uutuk knelt beside Seal to ask, "Would you go get my mother now? She should not be left out of the feast."

"She is happy at the chief hunter's ulax," Seal said. "She does not need to be here."

"I want her here," Uutuk said.

"I will get her," Ghaden told them, grateful for something to take him out of the ulax, away from Qung's questions and demands.

Daughter let her eyes shine at him, and he felt his cheeks burn, as though he were a young boy having his first thoughts about bedding women.

When Ghaden left, Daughter busied herself rearranging the food on the mats while Qung continued to eat, and when Daughter heard voices from outside, saw bits of dirt sift down from the ulax rafters, she got to her feet and straightened her parka. For her mother, she told herself, but Ghaden was the first down the climbing log, and she had to lower her head when she saw the desire on his face.

She turned away, stood on her toes to reach a water bladder. Then Ghaden's hands were on hers, his body pressed close against her back, and he pulled down the bladder, held it until she looked up at him. His smile made Daughter's belly tighten, and her breath caught high in her throat.

K'os broke the silence with compliments about the food

and praise for Daughter's parka. She asked Ghaden about his hunting, and Ghaden squatted on his haunches beside her, answered her respectfully, as though she were his own mother.

But Daughter, watching them as she ate, saw the caution in Ghaden's eyes, heard the care in his answers, and saw that K'os, too, was careful, stiff and proper as she seldom was to a man.

When the women had eaten their fill, and Qung and Daughter were putting away the food, the truth came into Daughter's mind, prickled there like a stone inside a seal flipper boot.

Ghaden and her mother did not like each other. Then why had K'os been so eager for Daughter to become Ghaden's wife?

K'os turned away from Ghaden, spoke a blessing that Daughter had never heard before, something in the River language about wives and husbands and children.

"A marriage blessing," K'os said, and translated it for Seal.

He nodded his approval, and added a First Men blessing, then made a joke about sleeping places and the secrets women hold between their legs.

Ghaden laughed, as did Qung, but K'os did not join in. She held a smile on her face, and Daughter recognized it as a trader's smile, a guarded joy, held without words so the trading would continue to be good.

As Qung raised her old woman's voice into a song about getting children, K'os and Seal stood up, took Daughter's arms, and pushed her toward a sleeping place. Then the woven grass curtain closed behind her, and for a few moments Daughter was alone.

In the darkness she could still see her mother's smile, and she wondered what great treasure K'os planned to own in exchange for a daughter's life.

TWENTY-EIGHT

The summer before, Daughter had given herself to White Salmon. So many of the young women in her village, a year past their first moon blood time, had already been chosen as wives that Daughter had begun to worry she would be the only woman, save a few elderly widows, without a husband.

When White Salmon had shown some interest in her, she had welcomed him into her bed. After all, K'os had been diligent in teaching her how to please a man.

Now that she waited for Ghaden, she wished she had saved herself for her husband. He had been raised River. How often had K'os told her that River men did not like to share their wives, except with their hunting partners? When he found she had known another man, would he throw her away? Even in the warmth of the fur-lined sleeping place, she was suddenly cold.

A roar of laughter pushed at her from the ulax, and the dividing curtain was thrust aside. Ghaden was shoved in with her. Seal called out a coarse joke, but in the light that filtered through the woven grass of the curtain, Daughter saw that Ghaden was not laughing. His eyes were soft. He raised his hands, placed them on either side of her neck, then lifted her hair and ran gentle fingers up the back of her head.

"I have wanted to touch your hair for a long time," he said. "It is as soft as eiderdown." He spoke in the First Men language, and she felt even more honored by that than by his compliment.

He had taken off his parka, most likely the reason for the laughter, and she noticed that he had oiled his skin. She laid her hands on his chest. The warmth of him lifted the cold from her fingers and some of the fear from her heart. He looked into her face as though he were seeing her for the first time. She raised her fingers to his nose, and he began to laugh.

"First Men do not have much by way of noses," he said, and pressed his cheek to hers. She shivered, wrapped her arms around his shoulders. They were wide, his muscles tight and hard under his skin.

Then memories of White Salmon came to her, as if he had thrust his way between them. Daughter did not want to think about him, his fingers stroking her skin, his body within hers. Ghaden cupped her breasts in his hands, and Daughter's breath came hard into her throat. But in the close heat of the sleeping place, White Salmon again pushed his way between them, a ghost haunting.

"My husband," Daughter whispered, "there is something you must know."

Ghaden pressed his fingers to her lips, turned her so she was leaning against his chest, then lifted her into his lap as if she were child. His mouth was so close that his words were a soft wind against her ear.

"My little wife," he said, "I am sure Qung told you that my mother was First Men. Though I was raised by the River People, I understand First Men ways. You have had other men in your sleeping place."

It was not a question, and so Daughter knew she did not have to answer him, but she said, "Only one, and I thought he would be my husband, but Seal would not accept his brideprice."

Ghaden lifted his head from hers, and she raised her hand

to her eyes, pressed her fingers against the lids to hold in her tears. What would K'os say, what would Seal do, if Ghaden threw her away even before the night was over?

"Do you wish you were with him?" Ghaden asked.

"No!"

He made a sound in his throat, and Daughter was surprised to realize that he was laughing. "Speak quietly, wife. They will think you have refused me."

She turned herself to face him, straddling his lap, her legs wrapped around his waist. "I will miss my island." They were words that she had never thought to say to him, but as little as she knew him, she had already begun to understand that Ghaden was a man to whom you could tell secrets. "I will not miss him."

"You are sure?" he asked.

She raised her hands to stroke his face. "Forever I will be a good wife to you," she told him.

He leaned forward and laid her down against the sleeping furs, lowered himself over her. Then she could no longer see White Salmon's face or even remember what he looked like. There was only Ghaden.

When their lovemaking had ended, Ghaden fell asleep, a leg wrapped over her, a hand resting on her breast. For a time she lay awake, feeling her husband's seed leak from her body.

During all the advice K'os had given Daughter about bedding a man, she had never mentioned that a woman could also find pleasure. Perhaps it was a thing so rare that K'os herself had never experienced it.

In her joy, Daughter found herself thinking about the grandfather. He would be happy for her. She had no doubt of that, and somehow she knew what he would say.

"Do not question your joy, but be careful about telling K'os. She is not a woman who delights in the happiness of others."

Ever wise, Daughter thought as sleep claimed her. The

grandfather had always been gifted with more wisdom than other men. How good that death had not taken his wisdom from her.

Daughter's sleep was deep and hard, a sleep without dreams, and she did not wake until she felt Ghaden's arms tighten around her. She smiled, thinking that he wanted her again, but when she moved a hand toward his groin, he trapped her fingers in his own and said, "Listen."

Even through the thick ulax walls, Daughter could hear the moaning of the wind as it ripped at the sod.

"A storm," she said, and tucked herself close to Ghaden.

He pulled away from her and sat up. Her disappointment was a weight in her chest, and she could not help but remember White Salmon, how he always lost interest in her once their lovemaking was finished. Ghaden's gentleness had allowed her to hope that he would be different.

"My father," he said.

Then Daughter was ashamed of her selfishness. A wife should always consider her husband first.

"When did he leave?"

"Yesterday morning, early."

"They went to trade at another First Men village?" Daughter asked, and without giving him a chance to answer, said, "How many days travel to that village?"

"Two."

"They would have spent the night on a beach?"

"No," Ghaden said softly. "I have heard other traders talk of the journey. Unless you stop after a half-day's travel, there are no good beaches between this village and that. During the night they tie their iqyan together with their paddles so each man can have a little sleep while the others watch."

Daughter heard the fear in Ghaden's voice, and she clasped her amulet, cupped it in her hands, and pressed it close to her husband's chest.

In spite of the sand it held from the Boat People's beach,

it was still just a woman's charm, at best only strong enough to help her find a few sea urchins, to keep tussocks of basket grass alive through the winter, so new grass would grow up from the old. Nothing powerful enough to save a man's life.

But Ghaden curled his hands over hers and held the amulet with her, so Daughter began to hope that their prayers, rising together, would be stronger than either one could offer alone.

Herendeen Bay, Alaska Peninsula
602 B.C.

As soon as the last words were out of her mouth, Qumalix stood and stepped away from Sky Catcher. Before he could give voice to much complaint, Qumalix raised one hand and said, "You see those clouds? They are full of rain. You do not even have a wife here to take care of your sax if you get it wet."

"I am not helpless," he said, curling his lips into a pout. "I know how to take care of a wet sax." But he got to his feet, and when Qumalix started walking toward the village, he followed.

"I want to know what happened to Cen," he called to her. "Did he die in the storm?"

"That is something you will have to find out the next time it is my turn in the storytellers' ulax."

He caught up to her, nudged her aside into the longer grass so he was walking in the center of the path.

"You could always tell me the story. We can find a place to be alone. I have a trader's boat we can sit under and stay dry."

She cupped a hand over her mouth and coughed, cleared her throat, and spat into the grass. "I have done enough telling for one day," she said. "My voice needs a rest." She dropped back behind him on the path, felt a splatter of rain hit her face. "Hurry," she told him, though she was not much concerned about getting wet. The puffin skins of her sax shed water well.

Sky Catcher broke into a slow lope, and she did the same. The rain split the clouds, poured down heavy and cold. Sky Catcher began to run, but Qumalix kept her pace slow and thanked the skies.

Yikaas crawled out of the sleeping place, shook his head against the giggling foolishness of the two sisters. He had found release in their bodies, but he felt uneasy, an ache in his gut as if he had gorged himself beyond his needs, and shamed himself by his greed. How could he think he was wise enough to be a storyteller if he took more than his share, even of women?

Worse, how would he get rid of these two? Every night he spent during his visit here, every time he came to their village, they would have a claim on him. What if Qumalix found out?

He pulled on his parka and adjusted his caribou hide leggings. You worry about Qumalix? he asked himself. Why? She's a storyteller, nothing more. Besides, *she* had chosen to spend the day with Sky Catcher. Perhaps even as he himself was pushing his way into the fat sister's *chisum naga*, Sky Catcher was doing the same to Qumalix.

The thought thrust a spearpoint of anger into Yikaas's chest.

"You have no claim on her," he said, and did not realize that he had spoken aloud until the thin sister placed a hand on his back and leaned forward to look into his face. She asked some question in the First Men language. Yikaas shrugged and shook his head to show he did not understand. He was usually more polite to women who had allowed him in their beds, but what could he say to a girl who did not understand the River language?

He pulled two necklaces out of a packet at his waist. They were nothing special, birdbone beads cut long, and he could see a quick shadow of disappointment in her eyes, but he gave her the necklaces, and raised his hand toward the climbing log. He tried to smile, but his face felt stiff. He clambered up the log quickly, moaned when he saw that it was raining.

The grass growing on the ulax roof was slick, and when he walked to the edge, his feet went out from under him and he slid to the ground, landing hard on his buttocks. He heard laughter, turned his head, and saw Qumalix. Water dripped from the feathers of her sax.

"You're wet," he said to her, and she arched an eyebrow at him.

"I've been outside telling stories."

She looked up as the sisters peered over the edge of the ulax. They wore only their grass aprons. The thin one said something, thrusting out her narrow chest as though she were proud of herself.

Qumalix translated for Yikaas. "She says, it is too bad you are not as good on your feet as you are in a bed."

Yikaas stood, wiped a hand down the front of his parka. "You were with Sky Catcher," he said, but as soon as the words had come from his mouth, he wished he could take them back.

"What do you mean by that? If I would have been here, that I would have been the fortunate woman to share your bed?" Qumalix turned her back on him and the sisters and walked toward the storytellers' ulax.

The sisters called down to him, but he ignored them. "Qumalix!" he shouted. "Qumalix, wait!"

She did not slow her pace, only lifted her hands over her head as though her fingers could shield her from the rain.

Yikaas heard someone behind him and turned, ready to rebuff the sisters, but found himself looking into Sky Catcher's face.

"She is not worth your worry," he said, his words in the River language, stilted and broken. "That one thinks about nothing but stories."

Yikaas nodded grimly, but as soon as the man walked away, he could not help but let the smile that was lurking behind his teeth out of his mouth.

* * *

The heavy, cold rain brought the traders from the beach, and the place smelled of wet parkas and mud, for the men's feet had stirred the hard-packed floor into a thick dirt soup.

"Sit down!" Qumalix shouted, raising her voice into a screech. She was disappointed with Yikaas, and angry at herself for being so. What better way to shed some of that anger than in trying to make order out of the chaos in the storytellers' ulax? "Sit down," she shouted again. "Does anyone need water?"

As quickly as she started passing water bladders, others dug into packs and bags for smoked fish and sweet dried berries. Before long, the damp and the dirt were lost in the laughter of people who have decided to make a celebration out of misery. Qumalix raised an arm to gesture toward Yikaas, who had just entered the ulax.

"You need to tell a story," she said, then stood on her toes to look over the crowd. "If you don't want to, Kuy'aa is here also."

"I'll tell a story," said Yikaas.

"About bedding First Men women, no doubt," Qumalix snapped.

"We have mostly traders here," Yikaas said, ignoring the barb. "Perhaps they would like a story about one of their own. I know a good one."

Qumalix lifted her fingers and flicked them toward Yikaas, almost an insult. "Tell your story. I will be glad to hear it."

But the clamor in the ulax had again grown loud, so Yikaas pressed the biting edges of his front teeth together and blew out a short, sharp whistle.

The whistle brought silence, and Yikaas said, "The young woman beside me asks to hear a story about traders."

As if speaking in one voice, the men in the ulax shouted their agreement.

At that moment, Sky Catcher started down the climbing log. His sax was soaked, and his legs were spattered with mud. The men sitting near the log raised protests as he sluiced the water from the sax.

Sky Catcher acted as if he did not hear them. "Yikaas's story will be about River traders," he said. "How many of you are River?" He stood with his chin outthrust, labrets bristling like tusks. "You want a story. I will tell you a story, and it will be about First Men traders."

A low grumble swept through the ulax, First Men and River traders arguing. Qumalix's heart lurched in her chest. How could a woman handle a fight between men?

"Yikaas first," she called out. "Because he was asked first." But her voice was drowned in the arguing. Suddenly she was very angry. She made her way through the traders to the climbing log, grabbed one of Sky Catcher's dirty ankles, and yanked him down. It was not a far drop, and he landed easily on his feet. Before he could react, Qumalix scrambled up the log until she was a head taller than any man in the ulax. She cupped her hands around her mouth and shouted, but still no one seemed to hear.

Suddenly Yikaas's piercing whistle again cut its way through the noise, and in the moment of silence that followed, Qumalix said, "You traders have come to hear a story, but what you forget is that we are in this ulax because of other people's hospitality. We drink their water and muddy their floors and leave the stink of our parkas in these walls."

Though there had been a gruff laugh when she began, now the men were quiet, and one of the few traders' wives in the group batted her husband with the back of her hand and said loudly enough for everyone to hear, "How would you like it if all this mess was in your lodge?"

They began to give apologies, but Qumalix said, "No one asked you to be sorry, only to be polite. Yikaas was invited to tell the first story. After he is done, Sky Catcher will have his turn. The clouds are too thick for this rain to leave us quickly. We will have a long time for stories."

She nodded at Yikaas and said, "We are ready."

Yikaas saw the weariness in her face and wondered how long it had been since she had slept. Don't pity her, he told himself, fool that she was to go with Sky Catcher. Yikaas pulled his thoughts away from her and brought into his mind the remembrance of hard seas, lashing winds. He closed his eyes, waited until he could see the storm, hear it, feel it; and when he began the story, Yikaas had become Cen.

TWENTY-NINE

The Bering Sea
6435 B.C.

CEN'S STORY
They had lashed their iqyan into a raft of three, Dog Feet with his larger iqyax in the center, Cen and He-points-the-way with theirs tied to each side. When the only beaches were more treacherous than the sea, how else did traders ensure their safety for a night?

Theirs was the gift of clear skies, and they saw no sign that would lead them to fear a storm, no haze of approaching rain, no thin white lines at the edges of the sea to suggest a far-off wind kicking up whitecaps. Even the smell of the air was that of fish and sea animals rather than any taste of forests or strange lands brought by foreign winds.

They had chosen He-points-the-way to watch as Cen and Dog Feet slept. Well into the night, Cen heard him wake Dog Feet for the second watch. Cen roused himself enough to look out over the blackness of the sea. He rubbed his eyes and squinted up at the sky. There were no stars, but that was no surprise. What clouds did not hide, fog often did. A thin wind had begun to blow from what he assumed was the west—without stars or a clear vision of water currents, it was difficult to tell—but the sea was nearly calm, lifting and dropping in a gentle rhythm that lulled him back into sleep.

Later, when he heard Dog Feet's voice, he thought it was his turn to watch, and so he was surprised to see that the skies were still black, not even the hint of dawn to the east. Dog Feet must not have taken his full turn. Cen did not know the man well, but he must not be much if he cheated on the length of his watch. Still, Cen told himself, it was better to have slept a little than not at all. He had made the same journey alone, catching only a few blinks of sleep now and again during the long beachless night between the Traders' village and the cluster of First Men villages two days west.

"My turn?" he asked, and tried to keep the disgust out of his voice.

"No," Dog Feet answered, and in the darkness Cen heard the dripping of the man's paddle as he lifted the blade from the water. "What do you think of that?"

Cen pushed himself upright in his iqyax. He could see nothing but darkness.

"What?" he asked, and this time he did not try to hide his exasperation. Dog Feet was a young man, probably given to all kinds of fears. He had listened to too many stories about blue ice people and sea monsters.

"Listen."

At first Cen heard nothing but the waves against their iqyan, but then, rising over those gentle voices, came a howling, sprung from many throats.

"Wolves," he said. "We must be close to land."

"No, listen!" The young man's voice was tight with worry.

He-points-the-way called from the far iqyax, "What is the matter? Be quiet, both of you. I need to sleep."

"Listen, those are not wolves," Dog Feet said. He pointed toward a white blur coming at them across the water. "See?"

Cen's throat constricted, cut off his breath. If they had been in that sea that lies south of the First Men's islands, he would have thought it was a tidal wave, but there were no such waves here in the North Sea, though quakes could raise the water to a height that would swamp most boats.

He-points-the-way shouted, "The wind! Look! It drives the sea toward us."

Cen began to unlash the paddles that held his iqyax to the others, but Dog Feet protested.

"We will have a better chance against it if we stay together."

The wind had grown so loud that Cen could barely hear what Dog Feet said. "In a storm, yes," Cen shouted, "but with a wave like this, we are better to drive our iqyan through it rather than try to ride it."

"You are a fool!" He-points-the-way said, and in the noise of water and wave, his voice seemed to come from a long way off.

"Do what you want," Cen told them, "but I will face this alone."

In the darkness, it was difficult to judge how close the wave was—closer than Cen had first thought; that, or it was traveling much faster than any wave should. He cut the remaining lash, reclaimed his paddle, and thrust it into the water. He pushed back from Dog Feet and He-points-the-way. Cen knew he could never outrun the wave, but he paddled hard.

The water roiled under him, grew choppy, as if the sea itself were afraid. Cen looked back and saw that the sky had opened, the dark clouds split. He could see stars in the break, the last faint light that shines just as dawn brightens. They gave him his bearing, and he knew he was paddling toward land. Not good. The wave would smash him into the shallows or against a cliff. He turned and started out to sea. The wave was coming from the north, and he headed his iqyax west.

The chop became swells. Cen paddled over them, careful to keep his bow straight so he did not roll. He needed to stay upright until the moment the wave caught him. He looked back over his shoulder, hoping to see that Dog Feet and He-points-the-way had decided to cut their iqyan apart. A wave lifted them into view, and Cen realized that he had come farther than he thought. They were so small to his eyes that by raising a hand he could cover them with his palm.

"Cut loose! Cut loose!" Cen yelled at them, but he knew that his warning would not be heard above the wind.

He turned away. The wave was close enough that it looked like a mountain rising in the sea. Once on one of his trading trips, a whale had breached near his iqyax. Cen had been young and numbed with fear, but watched as the whale approached, pushing a mound of water ahead of it. Finally the animal had rolled and turned, one long flipper flailing at the sky. Its wake had caught Cen, skipped and skidded his iqyax across the water like a flat stone.

This wave was larger than the whale's swell, but it looked as if some power lived beneath it, forcing it forward.

"I'm too shallow," Cen hissed under his breath, and continued to paddle toward deeper seas. If the wave remained merely a mountain of water, there was some chance he could go up and over it, but if in gaining mass and speed, it grew so tall that its roots touched the bottom of the sea it would curl and break. Then Cen's only chance would be to turn his iqyax upside down, allow the bottom of the boat to take the brunt of the breaker.

Bound together as they were, Dog Feet and He-points-the-way would have no chance to do that, and even if the iqyan in their own wisdom turned, the men would never be able to right themselves before they drowned.

The swells grew, and Cen glanced one last time toward Dog Feet and He-points-the-way. What he saw made him scream in frustration, for they were paddling their bound iqyan hard toward the shore.

"Fools! Stay in deep water. It's your only chance! Cut loose, cut loose, cut loose!"

Suddenly the motion of the swells stopped, and Cen pulled his eyes from the men and stared in horror at the sea.

It was smooth, as though a giant hand had stretched it taut, and he realized that the water was being sucked toward the wave as though it were a maw, eating, filling its belly. He felt his iqyax drawn with the water, and he knew he would be swallowed.

He checked the bindings that lashed his spare paddle to the deck. If he survived the swallowing, he would not be able to turn himself upright without a paddle, and surely the one that he held in his hands would be torn from his grasp.

He realized that in his fear he was holding his breath, and he forced himself to look up at the sky, to draw in power from the air until his lungs were full to bursting.

Then for a moment it seemed that all the world stopped. He saw his wife, Gheli, and his daughters. He saw his parents, and worried that they called to him from the dead. He saw K'os as she had been when they were both young, and Daes, the woman he had loved above all others, she, too, dead. But Cen set his mind on Ghaden, as if his son, with all the strength of youth and the power he had gained from killing the brown bear, could lend him luck.

He tested the knot that bound his chigdax hood tight around his face, then braced his legs wide inside the iqyax. Once more he filled his chest with air, once more he filled his eyes with the sight of the sky, and as the wave loomed over him, as whitewater curled down the sheer green of its sides, he flipped his iqyax and drove the bow into its mouth.

Herendeen Bay, Alaska Peninsula
602 B.C.

Yikaas stopped. Sky Catcher had chosen to sit directly in front of him, and the longer Yikaas spoke, the more noise Sky Catcher made. First he merely sucked at his teeth; then he began clicking the blade of his sleeve knife against the flats of his fingernails. Now he was snorting and coughing and clearing his throat.

Yikaas had tried to keep his thoughts on the story, but Sky Catcher's small irritations began to thrust themselves between each of his words.

It is a good place to stop, Yikaas told himself. He had heard other storytellers do so. He nodded his head and repeated the traditional story ending: "That is the way it happened, so they say." Then he thanked Qumalix for her translation.

"You're done? The story is over?" she asked.

"You can't stop there," shouted a River man.

Several others protested, some in the River language, others shouting out First Men words.

Sky Catcher stood and swaggered into the storytellers' circle. "I will tell you a better story than that," he said, and Qumalix translated his words into River, flashed her eyes at Yikaas, as though he should do something to stop the man.

She leaned close to Yikaas and said, "Finish your story." But her words were more demand than request, so he told her, "It is finished."

The nearest trader stood up and shoved the flats of his hands against Sky Catcher's chest. "Sit down, go back and sit down," the trader said, then lifted his chin toward Yikaas and asked politely, "Will you tell us the rest of the story?"

"The story is told," Yikaas said, and glanced at Qumalix, saw that her face was pinched, her lips tight.

Then she smiled at him, a forced smile that showed her teeth, white as gull feathers. "Perhaps there is a story that follows this one," she said, "but if you have no more stories about Cen, then I guess we will listen to Sky Catcher."

Several First Men spoke, and Qumalix told Yikaas, "They say they would rather hear your story."

"Ask how many want to hear my story and how many want Sky Catcher's."

She asked, and every man in the ulax chose Yikaas. Sky Catcher puffed out his cheeks and spat a word of insult, then made his way to the climbing log and left the ulax.

"He's a child in a man's body," Qumalix said to Yikaas. "I'm glad that you are wiser than he."

"Sometimes I'm wise," Yikaas said. "Other times I'm as foolish as any child could be."

"Women have their own ways of foolishness," Qumalix said, and though neither had spoken words of apology, Yikaas felt his heart lighten.

"So, then, my friend," Qumalix said, "will you finish the story?"

"Tell them that in the River tradition this story is sometimes stopped at this place so the listeners can give ideas to the storyteller."

As she translated his words, there was a murmur of surprise among the traders, then one of the First Men, a hunter called Fish shouted out words in broken River, "Cen dead. No chance."

Several First Men began to quarrel. Qumalix laughed and told Yikaas, "They claim that Fish will curse Cen's chance to survive."

A River trader heard her translation and also began to argue, drawing in other River men. Two hunters discussed the best way to roll an iqyax, and several men told of their own experiences in heavy surf. The arguing began again, and Qumalix finally held both hands up, laughing. She pinched the bridge of her nose as though to say that her head was aching.

"Enough!" she said in the River language. "Arguments are too difficult to translate. Tell your story, Yikaas. Please."

Yikaas took his place again in the storyteller circle and held his arms out, hands palm up. "Perhaps the prayers of all those who have lived these many years since Cen fought that wave, perhaps those prayers have traveled back to make a difference for him."

There was a roar of approval from the men who thought Cen would survive, but then Yikaas said, "Of course, there is that chance that those prayers did not help at all."

Then the other the traders began to laugh, and Yikaas lifted his voice to finish Cen's story.

The Bering Sea
6435 B.C.

CEN'S STORY

He had been inside waves before, had turned his iqyax so the bottom of the craft, rather than his own head, took the brunt of a breaker. He expected the cold that suddenly enveloped his body. He did not worry when the noise of the wind was replaced by the sound of the water and by the hollow voice of his own heart pushing his blood.

But in this wave, he had expected darkness. What light could survive in the belly of the sea? To his surprise, although the sky scarcely held the first rays of dawn, somehow the wave had captured that brightness, and the water glowed.

Cen tried to right himself, arched his spine back over the hard wooden ridge of the iqyax coaming, thrust his upper body and his paddle forward with enough force to move quickly through the water. The sea grabbed Cen and his blade, slowed their thrust. Once, twice, he arched and pulled. The third time the iqyax rolled upright, but in numbing despair Cen realized that he was still trapped within the mountain of water.

He had misjudged his air, allowed the stored breath that expanded his lungs to hiss out between his teeth when the iqyax finally turned. Now his lungs begged for new breath.

There were currents within the wave. They caught Cen and fought to tumble him and his iqyax, to break their bones. Ignoring his lungs, Cen thrust his paddle against those currents, and managed to keep himself straight most of the time. Just when he thought the water was brightening—as though the sky were reaching down to show him that he did not have much farther to travel—the wave slapped the bottom of his iqyax and thrust the point of the bow up into the breaking curl so quickly that Cen could not react.

It turned him end for end and hurled him down toward the bottom of the sea. He lost his paddle, so he clasped the edges of his coaming, drew up his knees until they touched the underside of the iqyax's deck, and in that way he held himself within the craft.

Pain knifed his ears, and he saw blood rise in curls around his face. The wave thrust him up again, and the pressure eased. His hands, clenched into tight fists, were bruised by the force of the water, but that pain was nothing compared to his lungs, now aching so badly that it seemed as if someone had reached inside his chest and shredded them.

Ghaden's face burned into his mind, then again he saw Daes, heard her voice as though she welcomed him into death.

"Daes," he whispered, and released his last small bubble of air. It rose past his eyes to join the froth of the breaking wave and was lost there.

He drew in a great mouthful of water, knew for an instant the relief of that drawing, and then he was choking, taking water into his lungs, his belly, coughing and breathing until his whole body shook with spasms.

Then, suddenly, all things were calm. His lungs, as though satisfied with the water that filled them, no longer tried to draw in more, and the iqyax steadied within the wave. Even his ears stopped throbbing, although thin trails of blood still curled before his eyes, red as fireweed blossoms.

The beauty of the water gripped him, and he was grateful for seeing the sea from inside, as if he had been granted the eyes of an otter in compensation for his death. And why not? His friend Chakliux, that man of otter foot and otter wisdom, had made Cen's iqyax.

Then, as though the iqyax knew itself as otter, it shuddered and thrust its bow up, nose toward the sun. It climbed within the water, finally breaking out into the dawn, sliding sideways down the back of the wave, like a river otter on ice. It landed on its side, then righted itself, bobbing in the wave's choppy wake.

All this Cen saw as though he were watching some other man caught in the sea. But then the water he had swallowed thrust itself out of his lungs and belly, up his throat and through his mouth and nose, burning like salt on raw flesh.

He gagged and choked and retched, his hands still clutching the coaming, his fingers so cold and stiff that it seemed that they had taken the grip of a dead man, and so would ever remain bound to the iqyax.

He brought up the contents of his stomach, fish and bile and more sea water, then was finally able to draw in a breath. He realized that even more than the cold and the water, his own fear had filled him, and now as it drained from his body, his fingers finally relaxed, and he began to shake.

For a long time, he could do nothing but sit and battle down his dread, try to lift himself above his pain. He was rock, then animal, and finally man, able to catch his thoughts, twist them together like one who makes a rope from many strands, and in that joining finds strength.

THIRTY

The Traders' Beach

Two days after the storm, hunters brought pieces of broken iqyan to the Traders' Beach, and a young man was sent to the Walrus Village to tell the families that Dog Feet and He-points-the-way had died in a storm. The sea had swallowed the bodies, as the sea often does, and though they had little hope of finding the remains, Dog Feet's brother and several older hunters from the Traders' village went out to search shores and inlets.

Though Daughter begged Ghaden to stay in the village, reminded him that none of the wreckage seemed to belong to Cen's iqyax, Ghaden went with the hunters. For all the days they were gone, the skies remained clear and the sea calm, as though all the summer's anger had been spent in one storm.

When the village's four days of mourning had ended, life continued as it always had, traders coming and going, women fishing and gathering and sewing, men hunting and repairing their iqyan.

The storm had brought some bounty to their inlet, and children helped the old ones gather kelp bulbs, which the women would stuff with meat and bake, or dry and grind for medicine to help bones heal. The young women collected driftwood to use for cooking fires and hunters' hats, iqyax frames, and ulax rafters.

Daughter did more than her share of work, starting her days too early and staying awake long into the nights. She walked the beaches, a pack of driftwood heavy on her back, waiting with hope and dread for Ghaden, afraid of what he would find, but needing him to return to her.

K'os seemed to observe her own strange kind of mourning, at first singing for Cen as if she were his wife, insulting Seal with her tears and even slashing her arms as a wife might do. But on the fourth day she had risen from her bed with clear eyes and new strength, so that when Daughter was near her, she could feel the humming of some power move the air like the quick beat of duck's wings.

That day, K'os joined Daughter on the beach, helped gather driftwood and kelp, but K'os kept her eyes on the inlet, pausing to watch whenever an iqyax came into view.

At first Daughter thought that some dream had come to K'os and told her Cen was still alive. Though Daughter waited mostly for Ghaden, she found herself straining to see if any incoming iqyax carried Cen's bright markings.

Finally, Daughter had asked K'os if she thought Cen was still alive. K'os had laughed, ridicule in her voice, and said, "How could any man survive a storm like that? It came too quickly. Did you hear what one trader said about the village near the place they found the remains of the iqyan, how many of the ulas were damaged?"

"But what if the men were on shore and the iqyan were merely swept out to sea?" It was a hope that Daughter had heard some of the younger women express.

K'os shook her head. "Even if they had time to get to shore, I heard the chief hunter say that where it hit the hardest, women found driftwood at the tops of the foothills. They might have lived, but there is little chance. When Ghaden returns, we should leave this place and go with him to the River villages. Cen's family needs to know what happened.

Perhaps they will find some comfort when they hear that Ghaden has taken you as wife. Perhaps Cen's wife will rejoice that she has a new daughter."

Thoughts of a journey to Cen's village seemed to pull K'os from her mourning, so Daughter did not mention her doubts about their welcome. Best let K'os find happiness where she could. But Ghaden had told Uutuk that Cen's wife Gheli had never even met him and seemed to have no desire to claim him as son. So why would she want Uutuk? Better for Daughter to put all her thoughts on Ghaden's safe return to the Traders' Beach.

Herendeen Bay, Alaska Peninsula
602 B.C.

A loud voice cut into Yikaas's words, and he began to regret that he was telling his story mostly to men. Women were more polite as listeners, and men were more quiet when their wives and mothers were with them.

"So Cen lived," one of the River traders called out to Yikaas.

"He lived," Yikaas said.

Several men started a hunters' chant, a song of victory sung in River celebrations, but they were interrupted by a rude shout that echoed down from the top of the climbing log. Yikaas recognized Sky Catcher's voice, but because the man spoke in the First Men's language, he had to wait for Qumalix to translate.

"He has questions," Qumalix said. " 'If Cen is alive, why do we have to hear about the women? Tell us about him. Where is he? Why has he not yet returned to the Traders' Beach?' " Qumalix smiled an apology and said, "Sky Catcher's words, not mine."

Yikaas stalked over to the log, shielded his eyes against the gray light coming from the hole in the roof of the ulax. "You have been listening, then?" he asked.

Sky Catcher's voice was still belligerent when he spoke,

and Qumalix leaned close to Yikaas to tell him, "He said that it has stopped raining and that he has better things to do than listen to stories about women."

Yikaas went back to the storytellers' place to continue his tale as though he had not been interrupted, then Qumalix met his eyes and said, "He's rude, but he's right. These men don't want to hear about K'os and Daughter. They want to know what happened to Cen. Tell them that story."

The men sitting close enough to hear Qumalix murmured their agreement, and so Yikaas lifted his voice to ask the others in the ulax what they wanted.

"Make the Daughter part quick," one man called out.

"Tell us what Ghaden found," said another.

"Where's Cen?"

Yikaas shrugged and lifted his hands. "What choice does a storyteller have but to please those who listen?"

He laughed, and the men laughed with him. Even Sky Catcher settled himself on one of the notches cut partway down the climbing log and perched there, hands on his knees, as if ready to listen.

"So concerning Daughter and K'os," Yikaas said, "it is enough for you to know that K'os is anxious to start her journey back to the River People she had left so many years before, and Daughter is a good wife, worried about her husband's return.

"But before I tell you about Cen, let me talk a little about Ghaden."

There was a murmur of agreement, although Sky Catcher grumbled out complaints. Qumalix scolded him, and the two began to argue. For once Yikaas was glad he did not understand much of the First Men language and so did not need to hear Sky Catcher's opinions about his stories.

He pressed his lips together and considered where to start. Finally he raised his voice above Sky Catcher's bickering and said, "Though Ghaden loved his father, he was also angry with him because Cen had never taken Ghaden to the Four Rivers Village and sometimes went years without seeing him. But as Ghaden searched for Cen, he forgot his anger and remembered only the good things . . ."

The Bering Sea
6435 B.C.

GHADEN'S STORY

The mist lay so wet and heavy that it slowed Ghaden's hands on the paddle and dimmed his eyes as if they were cauled by age. The men had kept their iqyan close to the shoreline, twice leaving the sea to poke among heaps of driftwood beached by the storm, but they found nothing. Ghaden's thoughts moved as slowly as his hands, and he saw his father's face again and again, in the waves, in the sky, even in the grasses as they moved in the wind.

His first full memory as a child was of Cen smiling at him during a serious discussion about some broken toy. A spear, yes, that was it, carved from a stick that Cen had sharpened and hardened by charring in the hearth fire. Ghaden had taken the spear outside. In the innocence that allows a child to think he is capable of all his father does, he had truly believed he would bring back a hare. But his first effort at throwing had ended with the spear sunk deeply into a tussock of tundra grass. To his horror, when he had attempted to pull the spear out, he had stumbled, fallen against his little weapon, and cracked the shaft.

Even now, as a man, Ghaden could feel the sorrow he had known at the loss of that spear. When he had taken it back to Cen, expecting to be scolded, Cen had merely grunted, then whittled Ghaden another. Ghaden had made his first kill with that spear, though by then Cen had left their village.

Months later, Cen had returned and stolen Ghaden and his older sister Aqamdax. He took them to the Cousin River village, a village that had eventually been destroyed in the battle between the Cousin River and Near River People.

Somehow during that battle Cen had disgraced himself. Ghaden had heard the people discuss how Cen had run even before the fighting began. Ghaden had always wanted to talk to him about that, but how does a son bring up his father's cowardice? Ghaden wanted denial, or at least an honorable reason for Cen's choice, but what if Cen had no reason other than his own fear?

When Ghaden's mother Daes had been killed, and Ghaden had been knifed and left for dead, Cen was blamed. At the time, the people of the village had nearly taken Cen's life in revenge, but Cen had stood before them all, asked if his son Ghaden still lived, and, grabbing a knife from one of the men who held him captive, had cut off his own finger as a sacrifice for Ghaden's recovery. How could a man who had the bravery to do that be afraid of battle?

Cen was no coward, and he would have faced the storm in strength. If anyone could have survived, Ghaden assured himself, it would have been his father.

A shout from one of the other men pulled Ghaden from his thoughts. The hunter used a paddle to point toward the beach, and Ghaden saw another heap of broken wood. The tide was low, but there were few rocks and the sea broke gently against the shore, an unlikely place for anything to wash up, but in a storm any beach could become treacherous.

One of the men was Dog Feet's oldest brother, a Walrus trader with perhaps eight handfuls of years. The others—three of them—Ghaden knew only as First Men hunters, and he was even unsure of their names, but they were so skilled with their iqyan that by watching them, Ghaden had added to his own abilities.

Dog Feet's brother had already turned his iqyax toward land, and Ghaden followed. When the sea was shallow he loosened the spray skirt that made a watertight seal around his coaming and jumped from his iqyax before it ran aground.

The sea was cold against his bare feet and ankles, but it felt good to stand after such a long time of paddling. He looked up into the sky, tried to make out the position of the sun, but the mist was too thick. The color of the light that squeezed down to them let Ghaden know that the day was near its end, and that they might be wise to consider staying on the beach for the night.

One of the hunters, now in shallow water, held up a stringer of fish, kelp greenlings he must have caught sometime during that day of traveling, but Ghaden did not remember seeing him trail a handline.

"I am hungry," the man called out. "Will you eat with me?"

Each of the others held up something, a pouch of dried fish, a net of sea urchins. Dog Feet's brother, standing atop a foothill that browed over the gravel tide flats, called, "There is iitikaalux here." He pointed to several tall, thick-stalked plants that towered above the grasses.

Uutuk had given Ghaden a belly of smoked fish and another of seal oil, and her mother had added a packet of dried fireweed leaves for tea. He pulled the storage packs from his iqyax, and Dog Feet's brother—striding down the hill with the iitikaalux bundled in a sheaf of grass—cried out his readiness to eat. But suddenly the man's voice broke, and he made a sound as though he were choking. He ran to the heap of driftwood and began digging through it, wailing as he worked.

The others, still out on the sea, dealing with the undertow of waves and the few rocks that studded the shallow water, did not seem to notice, but Ghaden heard the despair in the man's voice and felt his own heart clutch within his chest. He dropped his packs and hurried toward Dog Feet's brother.

When Ghaden saw the arm, he added his own groan of agony, and began throwing aside the driftwood. Days in the sea had bloated the body, turned the skin as white as the underbelly of a fish. When Ghaden saw the body's left hand, the smallest finger missing, he was sure it was his father. But then he realized that the finger and much of the hand had been eaten away. He looked at the chigdax, still mostly intact, and knew the man was not Cen. Dog Feet's brother turned and retched, and when he was heaving up nothing but his own sorrow, he managed to choke out, "It is my brother. I know his chigdax."

Ghaden squatted beside him, placed an arm over his shoulders, and helped him to his feet, drew him to where the wind blew away the stench of the dead.

When the others beached their iqyan, they lifted their voices together and sang the mourning songs as best they could without women to make the high ululations that reach beyond wind and sky to the dancing lights where Dog Feet would hear and know that he was honored.

They made a burial of stones. Dog Feet's brother laid one of his own harpoons over the body so Dog Feet would have weapons in the spirit world. Ghaden gave a sleeve knife; one of the other hunters offered a handline and hooks, another a hunter's lamp.

"He will be glad for your gifts," the brother said, forcing his words past a throat that sounded raw with pain.

Afterward, as Ghaden sorted through the rubble of driftwood at the water's edge, he found nothing that belonged to Cen, and so although he mourned Dog Feet he felt relief that he could still cling to some hope.

They made their camp far enough from the burial that they could not see the mound of stone, and so that any spirit lingering, called to the beach by Dog Feet's death, would not easily see them. They set out food but ate little, spoke little before rolling themselves into sleeping furs for the night.

Ghaden woke often, plagued by dreams of death and drowning. The next morning, Dog Feet's brother had traded sorrow for anger, and his loss had sharpened his tongue.

"Your father, too, is dead," he told Ghaden, "and so is He-points-the-way. No man was better in his iqyax than my brother. If he is dead, then all are dead."

Ghaden, his spirit still possessed by his dreams, was convinced by the man's words. So that day on the sea, Ghaden sang mourning songs, and in his thoughts laid stones, one by one, over Cen's body as they had over Dog Feet's, and when after three more days they found two paddles drifting, Ghaden was not surprised to see that both belonged to Cen.

He buried one on shore that night, made chants in hopes that the paddle would find its way to Cen in the spirit world, and he also buried a knife, a harpoon, a sax, and a pair of seal flipper boots he had brought in hopes of finding his father, new clothes to take away the bad luck of the old.

They found nothing of He-points-the-way, but how could that trader have lived when the others did not? And so the next night they made mourning and burial for him, offering more weapons and a belly of oil. Then they turned back toward the Traders' Beach, and when they arrived, the village again mourned the three men lost, made gifts of food and clothing and weapons, so Cen and Dog Feet and He-points-the-way would have what they needed to keep them strong in that other world where they now lived.

THIRTY-ONE

CEN'S STORY

The sea had stolen everything he needed to survive: both his paddles, all his harpoons. Somehow it had even ripped the hood from his chigdax and pulled his sleeve knife from its sheath. Cen's ribs were broken, both his own and those of his iqyax. Each breath Cen drew rattled, as though the wind were throwing gaming bones in his chest.

But far worse, somehow the sea had taken his hearing. Even yet, a whole day after the wave had passed, new blood still oozed into the crust that blocked his ears. He remembered elders whose inner ears had dried up with age. They complained of hearing nothing, but Cen's ears were filled with the roar of that wave, as though it had taken all the sounds of the earth and replaced them with its own voice.

The sea had battered his head so that his eyes were swollen shut and his nose was broken. He had lost two teeth, a dog tooth and the one behind it. That tooth was not entirely gone, but what was left ached more than his nose. Long ago, when the Near River People had accused Cen of killing Daes, they had beaten him and smashed his nose, splintering the bone. Somehow over the years the nose had sewn itself into a hump. Now it was flat again, but he had long ago learned to breathe through his mouth.

The pain he could live with. What trader does not learn to accept injury as a companion? But when a man has no paddle, when his iqyax is held together only by its seal hide covering and his chigdax can no longer hold out the sea, what does he do? He listens, and when he hears the birds, kittiwake, and gull, then he directs his iqyan with movements of his legs, by paddling with his hands, until, if he has good luck, he is caught in a current that brings him toward shore. If his luck is bad, he is thrust by breakers into cliffs, though at least there is a chance for him.

But a man without hearing, how does he even know which way to direct his iqyax? By watching. When he sees those gulls, he follows them, but a man who cannot see and cannot hear, what does he do?

Cen asked himself that question many times, and the answer that came to him was this: A man has two choices. He can quit and wait to die, or he can sing. For there was always the chance that some hunter or trader would hear his voice and come his way. Even if that did not happen, the songs might please the spirits so they themselves would direct his iqyax. And of course, if he lived long enough, his eyes would most likely open again, for when he pried at the lids, he could see light, and so had hope that the injury would heal.

The wave had taken much, but it had also left him a little, too. He still had dried fish and two bladders of water. His hands were cut and sore, but no fingers were broken, and his arms were strong, his legs also. The spray skirt of his coaming was still watertight, and he drew it as high as he could under his arms.

He lifted his voice and sang, but without his ears, he did not know whether he sang loudly or only in whispers, for his lungs screamed agony with each breath and his throat was rasped raw by the sea water he had swallowed. But still he sang, praises mostly to the earth and the sea and the One who created them, for Cen was not sure which spirits hovered close, if any, but none of them should be insulted by songs lifted to the Creator or to the earth or even the sea. So he sang and waited, trailing his hands in the water to catch any change in direction by his iqyax. And while he sang he raised prayers that a good current would push him to a safe beach where he might wait until his eyes could see again.

The Traders' Beach

DAUGHTER'S STORY

During the days Ghaden was gone, Daughter found many reasons to work near the beach. She needed to watch over her husband's trade goods and those of his father. She needed to collect sea urchins, and to fish with a handline from the shore, or to wade out and cut limpets from rocks at low tide, to dig for mussels. But even as she worked, her eyes were always on the bay, always searching the horizon, hoping to see her husband and his father in their iqyan.

The day Ghaden did return was full of fog, so that although she was on the beach, Daughter did not see him until he was already out of his iqyax and dragging it ashore. She had a moment to study his face, and so knew that Cen was dead. It was not until several women began wailing a mourning song that she managed to make her feet move toward her husband.

Even as she walked, she found herself pondering the pain that enveloped her. She had been wife only a short time, yet it seemed that a strong tether already bound her to him, her agony a reflection of Ghaden's own. Why else would she mourn a trader she hardly knew?

Then Ghaden saw her and pushed his way through the wailing women, past the men who called out questions, the children who danced and chanted, because they understood only the excitement and not the cause. Among the First Men, husbands, when they were with others, did not often show their affection for their wives with touching and holding, but

Daughter decided that River People must be different. For Ghaden grabbed her and pulled her into a rough embrace. He still wore his chigdax, and the garment was wet to her touch, cold, even through the feathers of her sax.

"Did you find anything?" Daughter asked.

Ghaden tried to speak, but his voice cracked and broke. He coughed and began again. "Only Dog Feet's body," he said. "Not He-points-the-way, but we found pieces of his iqyax, and we found my father's paddles."

She felt him shiver, his arms trembling even as he held her. "Ghaden, my husband, I am so sorry," Daughter whispered.

His arms tightened around her so that she could scarcely bring in a breath. "All this day, as we traveled, some spirit taunted me with the thought that I had lost you as well, that I would return to this beach and find you gone."

Daughter pulled away from him, looked into his eyes, saw the weariness there and the pain. Her throat tightened with tears, but she said, "You think that I would leave you so easily? I promised to be your wife. You think I would forget that promise?" She forced a smile. "I remember when my grandfather died how I was afraid of losing others, my friends and my mother."

Daughter felt someone stroke her head, and at first thought it was Ghaden, but then knew the hand belonged to K'os, the fingers stiff and knotted. She turned in her husband's arms to see her mother standing behind her.

"Come with me," she said to Ghaden and Daughter. "Seal will take care of your iqyax." Her eyes were hard and dry, and she asked no questions, as though she had known long before the men returned that Cen was dead.

Ghaden trudged behind her up the beach, an arm around Daughter's shoulders. He leaned on her so hard that Daughter was afraid the journey and his mourning had taken all his strength, but when they came to Qung's ulax, he was the first to climb up, and he reached down to help each of the women, pulling Daughter up so effortlessly that her feet barely touched the sod.

"Are you hungry, husband?" she asked.

Before Ghaden could answer, K'os said, "Of course he is hungry. Go down into the ulax and help Qung with the food. Seal will be here soon, and probably others."

Daughter wanted to stay close to Ghaden, but he said, "I am hungry, wife. We did not eat this morning."

She started down the climbing log, but even when Qung began to ask questions, she remained for a time standing just below the roof hole, listening to what K'os was saying. She asked about Cen, and Ghaden told her what he had said to Daughter about the paddles, about finding Dog Feet's body and pieces of broken iqyan.

Qung came to the bottom of the climbing log, started shouting her questions, as though Daughter had not answered because she could not hear. Daughter clasped Qung's arm and walked her to the oil lamp, told her what Ghaden had said.

"I thought I heard mourning cries." Qung twisted her hands together until Daughter heard the joints groan and pop.

"Ghaden is outside, and he needs to eat."

Qung's face cleared, and she gave a quick, short nod. "Then why do we stand here doing nothing?" she asked, and pointed a crooked finger at one of the food caches. "Bring me oil and fish, and be quick."

Daughter hurried to the floor cache, set aside the wood cover, and knelt to reach inside.

"Is Seal coming?" Qung asked.

"Seal and probably others as well."

Qung clicked her tongue. "It is sad that they cannot leave Ghaden alone to grieve. But no, everyone has questions. Everyone wants to know what happened. And then everyone wants to tell him how they were such good friends to the dead one." Qung flung her hands up in a gesture of helplessness. "All people are the same. They never change. There is no hope for it. He will have to listen and pretend that what everyone says is important to him."

"Perhaps it will be important," Daughter said. "When my

grandfather died, one of the old women in the village had just the right words for me."

Qung shrugged. "Some people do. Other people say all the wrong things." She sighed, then pointed with her chin at the food caches, and Daughter set out bellies of oil and fish, a packet of dried caribou meat.

Qung hobbled over to stand beside Daughter, then her old face crinkled in on itself, and she said in broken words, "He gave me that caribou meat. He did not need to do that. I was glad to offer my hospitality. Who could guess that I would be feeding it to those who mourn him?"

Still on her knees, Daughter pulled the old woman into her arms, patted the hard lumpy bones of her back.

"Aaa, we do not have time for this!" Qung said, and brushed at her eyes so fiercely that she raised welts on her cheeks. "Stop crying and get the food ready. You think you will help your husband with your tears?"

Daughter raised her fingertips to her eyes, found that she had been crying, the tears seeping, her face wet.

When K'os and Ghaden entered the ulax, Daughter glanced up from the food she was arranging on mats and wooden dishes. Ghaden's face was drawn and gray, his weariness even more pronounced. Had K'os said something to add to his sorrow? Or had Daughter's first joy in seeing him dimmed her eyes so that she had not fully realized how much his pain had marked him?

He came to her, stood close, as though to draw strength. She tucked an arm around his waist and ignored K'os's raised brows. What did it matter with only K'os and Qung to see? If her touch could help, then she would forget the normal ways of politeness. He raised a finger to stroke the thin braid that Daughter had tucked into the bun at the back of her head, and she wished that she had braided her hair like River women. Such a small thing to please a husband.

Then voices came to them, some loud, some lifted in mourning songs. Ghaden squatted on his haunches, and K'os moved to help with the food, pulling down water blad-

ders, hissing when she noticed how many needed to be re-
filled. She handed the empty bladders to Daughter, gestured
with her eyes to the ulax roof.

As wife of the one who had lost his father, it was not
Daughter's place to fill water bladders. K'os was playing the
wife's part. When the chief hunter and the elders came inside, K'os directed them toward Ghaden and even accepted
condolences from them, allowing herself to cry when their
wives hugged her.

Daughter glanced at Qung and saw the angry set of the
old woman's mouth, but Daughter merely closed her eyes in
embarrassment and hoped Ghaden would not be dishonored
by K'os's actions. She was used to K'os's need to center
people's attention on herself.

Daughter bent close to whisper into Ghaden's ear, told
him she needed to go for water. He stood and, taking some
of the bladders from her hands, went with her. Daughter saw
the wide eyes of those in the ulax, the surprise of the men
and women still on the roof.

"We need water," Ghaden said, and held up the flattened
bladders he had clenched in his hands.

Several women came forward, took the bladders, then
Ghaden climbed back into the ulax, waited at the bottom of
the log for Daughter, led her to that place where he had been
sitting.

"Sit beside me," he said, his voice low and soft.

"Qung needs help, husband," Daughter told him.

"There are other women here. She will have enough
help."

Then he called K'os. She came over, frowned for a moment at Daughter, mouthed, "Water?"

"Several of the village women are bringing water,"
Daughter said.

Ghaden pressed Daughter's hand so she knew he wanted
her to be quiet. "I need my wife with me," he said in a firm
voice. "But Qung is an old woman and she needs help."

K'os held out her hands as though to remind Ghaden that

her fingers were crippled, but he kept his eyes on her face. "You are not the wife," he said.

Daughter held her breath. K'os tipped her head and made a smile over clenched teeth. "You are right. Your wife should be here with you. I will help Qung."

Ghaden squeezed Daughter's hands, then turned to accept the sympathy of those who had come into the ulax. But Daughter's breath came with such difficulty that it seemed as though someone had laid rocks against her chest. Yes, K'os would help Qung, and she would work hard, but Ghaden would live to see her anger, and K'os would strike at a time when neither Daughter nor Ghaden expected it. That was her way.

You have lived through her vengeance before, Daughter reminded herself. Be concerned for your husband. There is nothing more important than that.

She set her teeth in fierceness and drew into her mind the remembrance of that long-ago time when she and the grandfather had been adrift on the sea. He had been too sick to help her, and though she was only a child she had been the one who told their boat which way to travel. She had pointed out the mountain that marked the First Men's island. She had been the strong one.

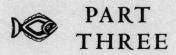

PART THREE

THIRTY-TWO

DAUGHTER'S STORY

The seal hide iqyax cover was too close over Daughter's face, and a storage pack pinched her feet, but since K'os lay in Seal's iqyax without complaint, could Daughter do less? Besides, she had been the one who had asked to travel in her husband's iqyax rather than with her father, and because Ghaden also wanted that, Seal had exchanged his larger boat for an iqyax of his own.

Uutuk had always been the one whose wishes were ignored, and what woman expects anything different? After all, she was only a daughter, not a son who would become a hunter. So now, when one softly spoken wish had caused so many changes, she would die before voicing a complaint.

They spent the first night on a wide, gray sand beach. It curled back so far into the foothills that it was nearly an inlet, a beautiful place with many birds and high drifts of wood brought in by the sea.

"Why does no one live here?" K'os had asked.

"Too far for water," Ghaden told her, and raised a hand toward the hills. "Half a day's walk. But it is a good first night's camp when a man still has full water bladders from the Traders' village. Sometimes, if you are lucky, you will even see a few caribou here."

Daughter began gathering enough driftwood to keep their fire strong throughout the night, for if there were caribou, there might also be wolves, or so it seemed in those stories K'os had told her. She had always been glad to be First Men rather than River, for the River People had so many animals they must worry about. Wolves and wolverines, lynx and foxes, moose and caribou, each able to do some kind of harm, large or small. And now, here she was wife to a River man and traveling with him to his village.

After Ghaden's return to the Traders' village, they stayed to keep the second mourning. Ghaden had considered continuing that mourning into forty days as First Men often do, but K'os had convinced him that it would be better to go to the Four Rivers village where Cen's wife lived, tell her what had happened, and stay with her for those forty days.

"Until then, mourn him in your heart, as we all do," K'os had said, and how could Ghaden disagree with wisdom like that?

Daughter had hoped to spend the whole forty days at the Traders' Beach. She had learned to love the old woman Qung and had wanted to hear more of her stories and enjoy Qung's wisdom. But K'os was right. The weather would soon turn toward fall, and then the seas were less predictable. If a summer storm could kill someone like Cen who had traveled for many years, what hope would Ghaden and Seal have, cursed with wives in their iqyan?

She dropped the last armful of driftwood near the blaze that Seal had started. He had a scowl on his face, and he was watching Ghaden and K'os. Suddenly Daughter realized that since they had beached the iqyan, they had been speaking the River language, which Seal did not understand.

"He explains why there is no village on this cove," Daughter said to Seal. "He uses the River language because it is easier for him than First Men, and also because he knows that you, being both hunter and trader, would need no explanation, that any man could see why there is no village, though the beach is good and driftwood is abundant, and even the trees that top the hills are straight and tall."

Seal puffed out his chest. "Yes, a man would see such a thing," he said. He pointed his chin toward the trees and laughed. "But you think those are tall? Wait until we get into the River People's country. Then you will see trees so tall that they block the sky. Is that not so, Ghaden?"

Ghaden squatted beside Seal and, speaking in the First Men language, said, "It is true, wife. Those trees are so tall, their shadows blanket the earth. Under their branches, it almost seems like night even during the brightest day."

Daughter shook her head in disbelief. "I know what you say is true, but it is difficult for me to imagine it."

K'os had knelt beside one of the iqyan, was struggling to pull a pack of dried fish from the stern. When she finally managed to free it, she turned and said, "There are treasures in those forests. A healer can find many things to help others. I will teach you, Uutuk, and then the River People will be glad that Ghaden brought you, even if you are First Men."

Daughter knew K'os's words were meant to encourage her, but they put a chill of fear into her bones, so that even her fingers and feet began to ache with dread. Later, after they had eaten and the darkness of night had cloaked their beach, she and Ghaden curled up together under their sleeping robes, and the touch of his hands soothed her, so she slept well with good dreams and no fear.

Herendeen Bay, Alaska Peninsula
602 B.C.

"Enough of these stories about women!"

Yikaas glanced up at the climbing log. He was not surprised to hear Sky Catcher's protest. Who else caused him so many problems?

"We already told you that we did not want to hear so much about Daughter. Almost everyone here is a trader or a hunter. Tell us a man's story. We have all made the journey from this village to the mainland."

"Yes," Yikaas said after Qumalix translated Sky Catcher's words, "but what if you were a woman, lying in an iqyax, unable to see the sky? That is something to think about."

Many of the men mumbled their agreement. One shouted out, "No wonder women do not like to travel. It would be difficult not to be afraid."

"Ha!" said another. "If she trusts her husband she should be glad just to lie there all day, doing nothing, not even paddling."

Sky Catcher moved down the climbing log, crouched on one of the notches that still allowed him to be above the other men in the ulax. "You sound like you wish you were a woman," he said to the hunter.

Several men laughed. "Who has the penis in your ulax?" one First Men trader called out. "Your wife?"

Qumalix leaned close to tell Yikaas what the trader had said, and Yikaas, angry at their foolishness, answered, "Man or woman, it is good to see life through another's eyes."

Some of the men shouted their agreement, but others began to call out more insults, even to question the possibility of curses when a man tried too hard to understand how a woman felt, how she saw the world.

"It is best to leave such things to storytellers," the chief hunter finally told them, then said to Sky Catcher, "you need to come down and sit with us." When Sky Catcher remained where he was, the chief hunter stood and stabbed the air with a finger, like a father scolding a child. "Now!"

Sky Catcher scrambled from his place on the climbing log and sat down at the back of the ulax, but he held his mouth in a scowl and mumbled out complaints until Yikaas said, "Cen's story."

Then the men shouted their approval, except for Sky Catcher, who crossed his arms over his chest and closed his eyes as though he planned to sleep rather than listen.

The Bering Sea
6435 B.C.

CEN'S STORY

For three days the sea controlled Cen's iqyax. There were moments when the roaring in his ears seemed to diminish, and he began to hope that some of his hearing would return. But though he listened carefully each time the sea's voice grew quiet, no other sounds came to him.

His eyes could tell night from day unless clouds hovered too close. During those times of grayness, he almost believed that he was dead and traveling toward the spirit world, for what did any man know about that journey? There were shamans who claimed to have gone to that place of spirits, but they did not describe their journeys. Besides, Cen was a man who had learned not to trust too much in what others claimed, especially if what they said would bring them gain.

He tried to keep track of the days that passed, to number them in his head, but without eyes and ears to set boundaries for his mind, his thoughts seemed to travel in devious paths and on foolish trails. He drank his water sparingly, limiting himself to three sips taken only after a long time of darkness, the end of a night. By that measure, it seemed that four or five days had passed, for he had nearly emptied one water bladder.

At first his belly had been unable to hold in anything he ate, but the last dried fish had stayed down. He had enough fish yet for many days, though somehow the pack had allowed water in, and although so far the fish were only softened by the damp, he feared they would mold.

He continued to sing to the Creator, the wind, and the sea, asking that the sea carry him to a good beach, but his throat was still raw, and the words scraped over his tongue like an adze. If the pain in his throat was any indication, his songs would not be pleasing to hear, and Cen wondered if it would be better to stay silent rather than give insult with his poor voice. But finally he decided that all things knew what he had gone through, and that the sea, hearing, might admire his courage and consent to guide him.

During what he thought was the fifth night, Cen was suddenly awakened by something bumping against one side of his iqyax. His first impulse was to curl himself as tightly as he could, make himself small, giving whatever it was less chance to grab him with teeth or claws.

The storm had not taken the long knife he wore strapped to his calf. He pulled it from the sheath, held it in his right hand, then fisted his left hand and slowly moved it out over the water. He held his breath, his heart thudding until the blood pounded in his veins. Nothing happened. He took a long breath and lowered his hand into the sea.

"It is night, and so you try to trick me into thinking you are not there. You think that I cannot see you in the darkness. You are wrong. I know where you are. Do you see my knife?" He raised his right hand, flexed his wrist so that any light from the moon, if there was a moon, would catch on the obsidian blade. "My knife is hungry for the taste of blood."

He said those words once and then again, but still nothing happened, and because he could not hear his own voice, he wondered if perhaps he was speaking only in a whisper. He filled his lungs with air, shouted the words.

Nothing.

Again he lowered his left hand into the water and waited for pain, but there was only the cold of the sea.

"What are you?" he demanded. "Fish? Otter? Seal?"

Something touched the stub of his smallest finger, and he jerked away his hand. Something slapped against his iqyax. Through the thin skin of the cover, he felt it move, but not like an animal moves. His heart leaped for a moment in hope. Seaweed? That would mean he was near shore.

No, he told himself. It was too solid for seaweed. Perhaps it was driftwood, carried by the same current that had claimed his boat.

Gathering his courage, Cen again thrust his hand into the

water, this time with fingers splayed, ready to clasp whatever had found him.

It came into his hand, wet and hard and slimy. A limb from some tree. He tried to wrestle it into his iqyax, but the limb was heavy and nearly pulled him into the sea. He slid his knife back into its sheath, used both hands, leaning right as he lifted. He finally got it into the iqyax and settled it across the coaming, moved it until it seemed centered. He extended his left hand as far as he could reach and did not feel the end of the limb, did the same with his right. It was longer than a tall man, but only as big around as his wrists, and it smelled like cedar, the best wood for paddles, light and strong.

A limb like that could be a good thing for a man to have if some wave were casting him against rocks, but it was too long. He would have to shorten it. Perhaps he could even use it as some kind of paddle, not a good paddle, but better than nothing.

Of course, not seeing, not hearing, how could he know which way to direct his iqyax? Cen thrust that thought from his mind. The sea had given him a gift. Why see it as less than that?

He had always made his paddles the measure of his arms outstretched, with the blade extending beyond. So he leaned forward, reached as far as he could with both hands, caught the place where his right fingertips touched. He used his thumbnail to gouge a mark in the sea-softened wood. The end of the limb widened out into branches like the bones of a hand, and suddenly in his mind he saw a new kind of paddle, the bellyskin that held his dried fish pulled taut over those fingered branches and tied in place to make a blade.

A blade like that would not hold up against rock or strong currents, but in calm seas, it might be useful—if he knew which way to paddle.

He moved his hands to the other end. The limb was twice the size of his wrist where it had broken away from the tree, that end still prickly with splinters. A good sign. Perhaps it had not been in the sea long enough to rot.

What should he do? Cut off the stout end where the strength lay, or cut off the branches that might be useful as a blade? He considered his choices, then decided to cut the branch in the middle. The paddle part would be short, but he could bend close to the sea to use it, and then he would still have enough length at the thick end to push himself away from rocks and shallows.

Twice he measured the stick in hand lengths, then used his knife to cut at the center. The sea had stripped off the bark, and the wood was punky under his blade, but after he had carved a deep notch, he came to the heartwood, still dry and strong, fighting his knife with each cut.

"Good, you are a warrior," Cen said to the branch. "I need that in you. We might be small against this giant sea, but we both have strong hearts."

He turned the branch and again cut past the punk to the heart, continued until he was nearly through, then broke the branch in half. He whittled the cut ends smooth and slid them down into the iqyax. He was tired and needed to sleep. When he woke, he would cover the branch end with the seal belly from his fish pack. Then he would have a paddle.

During that sleep Cen dreamed as a man who could see, and so when the sun woke him, prising his right eye open with strong light, he did not think it anything unusual to see that brightness, to shield his eye against it. Then he remembered where he was and what had happened to him. He opened his eye as wide as he was able, cried out against the pain of the light, then crowed in joy as he realized that he could see the brown and yellow hide of his iqyax.

He forgot the caution that any man should use in recovering from wounds, and he pried open his eyelid to gaze at the sea. The fog had lifted itself into white clouds that stood as high as mountains above the waves, so it seemed to Cen that his iqyax had found a valley at the center of the sea, with white mountain walls and the water cutting a valley floor.

His eye was still swollen enough that it did not stay open

by itself, so Cen held the lid up with one thumb and, using a hand and the movements of his body, turned his iqyax in a circle, but there was nothing except the sea and clouds.

He decided to finish his paddle, then set his course as soon as the fog lifted, for surely then he would be able to make out some dark edge of land, but if not, at least the stars would guide him, those few that might be strong enough to push their light through clouded night skies.

But by the time he had pulled the skin of dried fish from the bow of his iqyax, the light had drilled through his eye and into his brain, making his head ache so badly that he could do nothing but sit still and allow the iqyax to again choose its own path through the sea.

He slept, and when he woke, it was night. The pain in his head had subsided into a throb that beat at the base of his skull and just above his ears, but it was a pain a man could ignore. Again he pried open his eye and looked out at the night. Fog lay wet and thick, even masking the sea. He lifted his head to the skies and saw a rift in the clouds, the clearing full of stars. Then he knew with great despair that he was far from land, that somehow he had been drifting north and west rather than south and east.

"Well, then," he finally said, speaking aloud so the sea would know he had not given up, "I will finish my paddle tomorrow and will start toward land. It will not be forever before it rains, then I will stop and fill my drinking cup, and I have enough fish to live for a long time."

He let himself fall again into sleep, hid his fear so deeply that it did not color his dreams.

GHADEN'S STORY

It was more than a moon before Ghaden, Seal, K'os, and Daughter arrived at Chakliux's village. They had stopped to trade with the Walrus Hunters, though K'os had been concerned that she might again be claimed as slave. They had not recognized her, and Ghaden had seen the relief and anger that had warred within her when she realized that.

Still, she had been careful, collected no plants for medicines if any Walrus women were nearby, and kept her misshapen hands carefully hidden, for they had changed little since those years she had been a slave.

During their trading, she did not speak in the Walrus language, nor in River, only in the First Men tongue, and though she had kept her hair in braids once they left the Traders' Beach, she had reverted again to the bun worn by First Men wives.

It would not be so at Chakliux's village. Ghaden had no doubt that they would recognize her. After all, they had known her always, and she had been wife as well as slave. Besides, he had to tell Chakliux that Uutuk was daughter to K'os, and thus sister to Chakliux. Except for the relationship of mother to child, what was more important than uncle to a sister's son? If he and Uutuk had children, Chakliux would want to help Ghaden train the boys to hunt and fish.

Ghaden's memories of K'os from his childhood, when she owned his sister Aqamdax as slave, were memories of an evil woman who would betray anyone for her own gain. But how could he reconcile those memories with what he now knew of her? She was a very good mother to Uutuk, caring and concerned. Sometimes he saw a selfishness in her that most mothers did not possess, but she often gave Uutuk the best portions of food, and she treated her husband Seal with respect, though Seal was a weak man and did not always deserve K'os's deference. Were his early memories twisted by anger and fear during that time of war? Perhaps. What child ever understands all that is happening around him?

At least he owed K'os respect. She was Uutuk's mother and had taught her well. Though Uutuk was a new wife, her skill with needle and awl, in storytelling, and in preparing food rivaled that of old women. She gave herself eagerly when they were in bed, and she was careful to follow the taboos she had been taught as a First Men woman. Though she still had much to learn about River ways, Ghaden had no doubt that she would make him a fine wife, even if they chose to live among the River People.

But he also had no doubt that by claiming Uutuk, he would no longer find himself truly welcome in Chakliux's village.

He sighed, for a moment lifting the weight of sorrow that had invaded his chest since his father's death. He wished he could ask Cen for advice. He wanted to live in his own village with Aqamdax and Yaa and their families, but he had made his choice, and he would not give up Uutuk even for his sisters. Perhaps once K'os and Seal returned to the First Men, Chakliux would allow Ghaden and Uutuk to stay in his village, but if not, there were other villages. Perhaps Cen's wife, Gheli, would appreciate having Ghaden provide meat for her and her daughters now that she was a widow.

Ghaden looked up. Uutuk was watching him. She would not worry so much if she knew how much comfort she gave him. Ghaden smiled at her, and she returned his smile.

They would be happy no matter where they lived, but surely Chakliux would see that K'os was now no more than a harmless old woman, concerned only that her daughter have a good life.

THIRTY-THREE

They took their iqyan upriver toward Chakliux's village and stopped for the night less than a half-day's walk away. Ghaden wanted to go on, but he knew K'os was right when she cautioned that they should stop. It was a good place to camp, a clearing that both K'os and Ghaden knew, though K'os exclaimed at how much smaller it had become. In the years she had been gone, spruce and birch had crowded in on all sides.

They put up a spruce bough shelter and removed the iqyan covers, then raised the wood frames high in the trees in hopes of keeping them away from bears and wolverine that might chew at the sinew that bound the joints or the blood paste that held the ivory wear plates in place where wood met wood.

There would be damage, Ghaden had explained to Seal. Unlike the First Men's islands, there were many animals in River country, and the small hungry ones could easily climb trees. Seal grumbled about that, but Ghaden ignored him. The man had traded with River People before. Perhaps he had not come this far inland, but he knew about the trees and the animals.

"They give as much as they take, if not more," Ghaden

had said, then found Uutuk and went into the forest, where they sat watching, so Ghaden could point out the various birds and animals and explain their spirit powers.

After a time, K'os came looking for them and took Uutuk to find medicine plants. For a little while Ghaden walked with them, but K'os picked so many different plants, told so much about each, that soon everything was jumbled in his mind. He wondered if Uutuk was remembering what K'os told her or if her attention was only a politeness. But later in the evening as they sat roasting two hares that Ghaden had taken with a throwing stick, he heard his wife ask questions and repeat information so that K'os could correct her. He was glad, proud of her. A woman with a quick mind usually made a good mother, and if Uutuk could learn to be a healer perhaps that alone would be enough to merit them a place in Chakliux's village.

As the sun was setting, K'os sent Uutuk out to collect more wood to get them through the night.

"It is warm," Ghaden told her. "Why worry about a fire?"

"To keep away bears," she said.

He shrugged. There was always some worry about bears, but most of those that lived this near to Chakliux's village were black bears and not likely to come too close once they smelled the smoke of a fire, even one that burned out sometime in the night. He supposed that K'os was more nervous about such animals now that she had lived so many years on a First Men's island.

"Besides," she said to him, "I need to talk to you without Uutuk listening."

"What I know, my wife will know," he said.

K'os raised her eyebrows at him and smiled as if she were a fond mother considering a foolish child. "As you choose."

Ghaden wanted to walk away from her, but he told himself that he was stronger than her insults. So, as if she had been respectful, as a wife's mother should be, he squatted on his haunches, crossed his arms over the tops of his knees, and nodded so she would know that he was listening.

"I will not be welcome in my son's village," she said. "I think that I should wait for you and Seal here at this camp. When you are ready to go to the Four Rivers village, come back for Uutuk and me."

"Uutuk?" Ghaden said. "I will take her with me to my village. Chakliux may have told you to leave, but he has nothing against my wife."

"She's my daughter. That will be enough. They'll accept Seal as a trader, and he is a man able to take care of himself. Besides, what First Men trader is not welcome in Chakliux's village, married as Chakliux is to a First Men woman? But Uutuk is young, and I am afraid for her. Leave her here with me."

"You think I cannot take care of my own wife?"

"I think it would be wise to go first by yourself."

Ghaden considered K'os's words for a long time, and before he gave his answer, K'os added, "When I was young, I was a fool. I had good husbands, but I didn't appreciate them. I owned a slave, and I did not treat her well. I had a son who saw things differently than I did. Sometimes he was right, sometimes I was, but just because we did not see life in the same way was no reason for me to carry the anger I had against him.

"One good thing about growing old is that it gives you time to get wisdom. When I found Uutuk and her grandfather on the beach of my husband's island, I thought only of myself, that they might help me gain more respect from the people of that village. But Uutuk's grandfather was a very wise man. He taught me much, and for the first time I saw how selfish I was and how little I did for others. I've changed since my son last saw me. I don't expect him to believe that, but I hope you will."

In the falling darkness, the fire seemed to take on strength, and Ghaden saw it now, yellow and red, in K'os's eyes.

"I know that you've been a good mother to my wife," he said. "I see that you treat your husband with respect. If you think that it is best that Uutuk stays with you here, then I will leave her, but I would feel better if Seal also stayed to protect you."

"We'll be safe," K'os said. "But be wise in speaking to Chakliux. If you tell him that you've taken a wife, I think it best that you do not mention I am her mother. There are people I would like to see who live in that village—your sister Yaa, the boy Cries-loud." She let out a soft laugh and shook her head as though she were reliving old memories. "He must be a man by now. If you think you can trust him, you might bring him to see me. If Chakliux is pleased that you took a First Men wife, and you decide that you want to take Uutuk back to the village to meet your sisters, then you might bring Cries-loud with you when you come to get her. He had much sorrow in his life, losing his mother as he did, and I've always admired his strength in that loss."

"He's a strong hunter and provides well for my sister Yaa," Ghaden said.

K'os released another riff of laughter. "Yaa is his wife?" she asked.

"For many years now."

"I'm sure he has filled her with sons and daughters," said K'os, and narrowed her eyes at Ghaden when he did not reply.

Ghaden turned his head and saw Uutuk carrying a bundle of wood, a good excuse for him to end the conversation with K'os. She did not need to know that Yaa and Cries-loud had no children, that each baby Yaa carried came too early and died soon after birth. If he trusted K'os more he might ask if she had any medicine that would help, but if her claims in having changed were not true, she did not need to know more than necessary about Yaa or Cries-loud. After all, Cries-loud had been one of the young men who had taken her to the Walrus Hunters to be sold as slave. Perhaps K'os still resented him for that. Chakliux had always claimed that she was a woman who lived for revenge. What if he was right? What if she knew curses that would spoil any chance Yaa still might have to bear a healthy child?

Ghaden strode to his wife and took her armload of wood. Uutuk murmured a politeness and winked her eyes at him. He felt a warmth grow in his groin, thought of his wife's fingers, her soft and cunning touch.

"Daughter, you have worked hard," K'os said. She got up from the log where she was sitting and offered Uutuk her place. Then she stood behind the girl and began to comb out her braids.

Ghaden watched K'os in the firelight, untangling the strands, saw his wife close her eyes and relax, heard Seal's muffled snore coming from the spruce bough lean-to.

There were better men than Seal, and women who could be trusted more than K'os, but nothing Chakliux could say would convince him that he had not chosen wisely in taking Uutuk as wife.

The first to see Ghaden when he and Seal entered the village the next day was Yaa. Two long funneled gathering baskets full of fall cranberries, ripe and overflowing, were slung from her shoulders by wide bands of caribou hide, but she squealed and dropped the baskets, did not even turn her head to see whether or not the berries scattered when the baskets hit the ground.

She flung herself into his arms, and to Ghaden's amusement Seal asked, "You have another wife here in this village?"

He spoke in the First Men language, so as Ghaden laughed out his denial and introduced his sister, he began to translate the words for Yaa, but she had heard enough of the First Men language in her life to have an idea of what he said, and the three of them stood laughing together as the villagers gathered around.

When Chakliux pushed his way through the people, he grabbed Ghaden in a rough hug, then turned to look at Seal.

He took in his sax, labrets, and nose pin, then smiled and spoke a welcome in the First Men language, but Ghaden could see the questions in Chakliux's eyes, the beginning of worry there.

Chakliux stepped back and slapped a hand on Ghaden's shoulder. "Where's Cen?" he asked.

To his embarrassment, Ghaden felt his eyes fill with tears.

Chakliux sighed out several hard breaths, then began to shake his head and finally said in denial, "No, tell me Cen is well."

The words were like a blessing, and for the first time since Ghaden had found his father's paddles floating in the North Sea, a small shaft of hope lightened his sorrow, but then the reality of his own knowledge came to him, and he told Chakliux, "My father's iqyax was caught in a storm. He and the two traders he traveled with all drowned."

The words made the truth of his father's death hit him again, and his throat closed on his sorrow. Then, though Ghaden had not seen her approach, Aqamdax was with them, her youngest, a daughter born just before Ghaden had left in the spring, slung on her back. She pulled him into an embrace, laughing, joyous, until she leaned back and looked into his face.

"What's wrong?" she asked, her words a demand as though she were a mother asking a child the cause of his tears.

"Cen," Chakliux said softly, and Ghaden was grateful, because his sorrow over Cen's death and his joy at seeing his sister again had stolen his words.

Yaa pressed close, clasped Aqamdax's hand, and pulled her older sister away, repeating Ghaden's explanation as she did so. As though he were seeing the people of his village for the first time, Ghaden noticed that each man, each woman looked a little older, Chakliux with a few gray strands of hair over his ears, Aqamdax with worry lines etched a little more deeply between her eyes.

Sok came up behind him, planted a large hand on his shoulder, yet even Sok seemed smaller—still huge, but not quite as large as he once had been.

"I'm sorry," he said. "Dii and I will mourn him, even if you have already made a mourning."

"We honored all three men the four days it takes for a spirit to leave the earth," Ghaden said, "but a remembering here in this village would be a good thing. After that, I will go and tell his wife and my sisters in the Four Rivers village."

He had mumbled the last words, speaking more to himself and Chakliux than to anyone else, so he was surprised to hear a voice raised, a man volunteering to go with him. He turned and saw Cries-loud.

Yaa pushed between them. "Perhaps you would take me as well," she said.

"I think there are things here a wife should do while her husband is away," Cries-loud said to her.

Yaa's face pinched tight in hurt, and Ghaden knew that though they had lived together as husband and wife for a long time, the years had not bound them closer. They had taught one another well how to quarrel, how to wound.

"I will take my wife," Ghaden said, speaking before he thought, thinking only of how to ease the tension between the two. He had never liked to see his sister unhappy.

"You have decided to take a wife? Soon?" Chakliux asked, and Ghaden wished he could pull the words back into his mouth and swallow them down before anyone heard.

He had meant to speak first to Aqamdax, then to Chakliux, to tell them about Uutuk, rather than spill out what he had done before the entire village. There were mothers here hoping he would choose one of their daughters as his wife.

For some strange reason since the fighting so many years ago, more boy babies had been born than girl, but still, among people his age, there were too many women for the number of men. So Ghaden had many young women to choose from.

"Now that I mourn my father," Ghaden said, "I will not

take another wife at least for this year. Though if there is some woman who needs food, I will provide it."

He saw the understanding come into Chakliux's eyes.

"Where is she? Who is she?" he asked.

Ghaden stood on his toes to see over the crowd, and finally found Seal standing at the edge of the group. He had turned away to study the village. Several younger boys had ventured close to him and were eyeing his sax, discussing the harpoon slung over his shoulder. The weapon did not have much purpose in the woodlands of the River People, and Ghaden wondered why Seal had brought it. Perhaps to tempt some hunter into a trade.

"A First Men woman," Ghaden said, and heard the murmuring begin, saw angry looks cast at Seal.

"His daughter?" Sok asked and jerked his head toward Uutuk's father.

"Yes," Ghaden said quietly. "She is a wise woman, a healer who knows many plants . . ."

"What good will a First Men healer do in this village?" Sok asked, then before Ghaden could answer, he added, "I hope you've told her that you plan to choose a wife from your own village as well."

One of the women said, "What man would do that to a new wife?"

Ghaden turned his head at the voice and saw that it was Dii. In disgust, she gave her husband a shove, and several hunters in the group raised hands over mouths to hide their smiles. Dii was only half the size of Sok, and though no man in the village, save Chakliux himself, would dare voice disagreement with him, Dii was afraid of no one.

"A healer is a healer," she said. "We need one in this village, nae'? If she has learned the useful plants that grow near First Men villages, then she will learn our plants as well. Gull Beak will help her." She lifted her voice as she left her husband's side to shout her question into Gull Beak's ear.

The old woman opened her mouth in a smile. "Aaa, long ago I had a slave who taught me much," Gull Beak said, her voice too loud. "What use will my knowledge be if I die without passing it on? But there is much I do not know."

"It will be a beginning for her," Dii said to Ghaden. "But you will have to help your wife learn our language, and learn quickly."

"She speaks it."

"How so?"

Ghaden paused. He did not want to mention K'os, not even the fact that Uutuk's mother was River. There would be too many questions, but then he smiled and turned that smile on Chakliux as well. "She's a storyteller," he said, "and sometimes translates for the River and the First Men at the Traders' Beach so they can understand each other."

He saw a softening in Aqamdax's eyes. She arched her brows at her husband as though daring him to question Ghaden's choice.

"She comes to you, my sister, with a message from Qung," Ghaden said, and though he knew his words would bring Aqamdax joy, he was not prepared for the sudden tears, her choked voice as she asked, "Qung is alive? She is well?"

"She is well," Ghaden answered, "and has taught my wife several new stories for you."

Then Aqamdax, as though she had never left the First Men, covered her face with her hands, forgetting that she was a River wife and should hold in her tears until she was alone in her lodge.

Though Sok was still glowering at Ghaden over Dii's head, Chakliux said, "Your wife is welcome. Did you leave her alone somewhere? Most First Men women would be frightened in our forests."

"She's with her mother," Ghaden said. "I'll go and bring her to the village tomorrow."

Chakliux lifted his chin toward Seal. "Let him stay if he wishes. Is he hunter or trader?"

"Trader."

"Tell him that once his daughter is here, we'll have a day

of mourning to remember your father, but then we'll be glad to make trades. Will he and his wife spend the winter with us?"

"Perhaps here or at the Four Rivers village," Ghaden said. "He plans to return to his own people in the spring."

"Then he has a long time to trade. Ask him to join us for food in our lodge. He'll be happier, I think, with people who speak his language."

Chakliux turned and said something to Aqamdax, who hurried away. Those who had gathered also left, except for a few of the older women who stood together with hands cupped around the edges of their mouths, whispering, no doubt, about the wife Ghaden had married. Most of the old ones would not be kind to her. He remembered how he and Yaa and Aqamdax were treated when they first came from the Near River village to live among the Cousin People. But the old women had gradually become used to seeing them, to hearing their voices, and finally had accepted them. It would be the same for Uutuk if he could keep K'os a secret.

Thoughts of K'os brought her request to his mind, and he hissed out his apprehension. Things were no better between Yaa and Cries-loud.

He and Cries-loud often hunted together, but not as partners. Ghaden did not trust the man enough for that. Cries-loud was strange. He often disappeared into the woods for long days and nights, hunting, he said, though there were times when he came back with nothing at all, even in the fall when the forests and tundra were blessed with summer-fat game.

Yaa, gifted at all things a woman should do well save having children, could not always pull Cries-loud from his dark moods. Surely it did not help that every baby she gave her husband had died, the last just before Ghaden left for the Traders' Beach.

It was difficult to know a man who seldom joined in the jokes and laughter that hunters and warriors share, who did not often speak out his ideas or thoughts. Ghaden wished

K'os had asked for someone else, but maybe she understood Cries-loud, for it seemed to Ghaden that K'os herself was also given to dark moods. Perhaps for that reason she believed that Cries-loud would not betray her to a village of people who would rejoice more in her death than in her life.

"Are you coming?"

The question pulled Ghaden from his thoughts, and he looked up into Chakliux's face, saw the softness in the man's eyes, and knew that Chakliux, too, mourned Cen. "I lost my father when I was just a little younger than you," he said. "The pain will lift, but slowly. The best mourning is to live a good life."

Ghaden called Seal to join them, and they walked to Chakliux's lodge, where Aqamdax waited for them. Aqamdax had three strong sons and three daughters. The youngest daughter was asleep in a carrying board hung on one of the lodge poles; the oldest son, Angax, a boy who looked much like Chakliux, worked on a spear shaft settled on his crossed legs.

The lodge was filled with the smell of meat cooking, and Aqamdax and Chakliux soon had Seal telling stories about his life as trader among the First Men.

Ghaden sat with a niece on his lap and discussed hunting with Angax. Tomorrow he would bring Uutuk to this good place. He could imagine no greater happiness, save if his father were alive and here with them as well.

Cries-loud thrust out his lower jaw and said, "Your brother was never lauded for his wisdom."

Yaa ducked her head and did not answer, though Cries-loud knew that she had been gifted with as sharp a tongue as ever lived in a woman's mouth. The only good was that she seldom used her words against him, and this time was no exception. But after all, how could she answer?

Ghaden's foolishness was legend in this village. He had managed to get himself nearly killed by a brown bear; he had kept a dog in his lodge as though it were a child. Even before he was to the age of remembering, he had drawn evil down on himself and his mother.

"Why bring a wife into a village that has too many women already?" Cries-loud said. "He could have had a good River wife, without even paying a large brideprice. I expect that First Men fathers get much in trade goods for their daughters."

Yaa lifted her hands as though to concede, and Cries-loud was suddenly ashamed. Why blame Yaa? A sister did not have the power to change the choices her brother made. But more words of derision jumped from Cries-loud's mouth, as though there were some spirit in his throat that spoke for him.

"He's a fool. He talks about visiting the Four Rivers village, perhaps spending the winter. He should stay here, he and his new wife. At least he could help feed our people."

Yaa turned her back, busied herself with caribou packs. He could tell by her stiff, jerky movements that she was upset, and he waited, hoping she would say something. He carried a heaviness in his chest that seemed to lift only when he exhausted himself hunting, or when he became mad enough to set his heart racing. He was close to that degree of anger now, but he needed Yaa to fight against him, otherwise his anger merely dissolved into disgust.

Yaa said nothing.

Cries-loud watched her for a moment, then asked, "What are you doing?"

"Are you hungry?" she asked.

"I just ate. You know that."

He strode over and stood behind her. When they were young, he and Yaa had been nearly the same size. It gave him pleasure now to look down on her, to see how small she was compared to him. Her neck suddenly seemed so fragile, a pale V of skin between her dark braids. He stroked a finger down the part at the back of her head. She jerked, suddenly still and alert, like an animal, frightened and wary.

Her reaction angered him. He had never hurt her, had never set his hand against her, even when they fought.

"What are you doing?" he asked again.

"Counting," she said. "You made me lose my place."

"Counting?"

"We're to have a mourning for Ghaden's father. You heard Chakliux say that, nae'? I want to give a share toward the feast that will follow."

Cries-loud grunted. There were better ways to use their meat, but how could he refuse to give for a feast that Chakliux would most likely host?

"Go talk to Dii, see what she plans to give. Be sure not to give more. I don't want to shame my own father."

He saw Yaa's face turn dark. He had insulted her. Every wife knew not to outgive her husband's father, unless the man was old and unable to hunt; then the son's gift was also considered to include the father's.

She set the food pack down and left the lodge, did not look back or speak any politeness in leaving. For a moment, Cries-loud thought about going after her, forcing her back into the lodge until she acted as a respectful wife should, but then he sighed and sat down. She was more trouble than she was worth.

He pulled several arrow shafts from a sheath. He had tied them together so that as they dried they would keep one another from warping. He loosened the bands and studied each shaft, holding it horizontally to sight along the length. Each was straight, so he found a bit of sandstone to smooth the remaining rough spots.

He heard someone in the entrance tunnel, set aside his work, and stood, sure it would be Yaa. But it was his father's wife, Dii. Like all tunnels into winter lodges, his was slanted down, then up to make a small valley. That way cold air would settle into the lowest section and not get to the heated lodge. Some tunnels were tall enough for a man to stand in a crouch, but he and Yaa were young and did not mind crawling, so when Dii came into the lodge, she was still on hands and knees.

She jumped quickly to her feet, brushed her palms against her hips, and set her mouth into a grimace. She had good teeth, small and even, scarcely worn from the chewing of hides all women must do. With her pointed chin and large eyes, she reminded Cries-loud of a fox ready to attack, and it was all he could do not to lift a hand to the sheathed knife he wore hung at his neck.

"You're not very kind to your wife," she said to him.

"Is she whining to you?" he asked.

He liked Dii, though she seemed more sister than stepmother. When she had first come to them as Fox Barking's widow, he had seen the strength in her, and that strength had only grown since she had married his father. It could not have been easy being wife to a coward like Fox Barking, but Dii had always presented herself on her own merits. She was a good wife to Sok, though not as talented with needle and awl as Cries-loud's mother had been. But what husband would complain about that when his wife had been given the gift of caribou dreams? To his knowledge Dii had never been wrong when she told the hunters where to find caribou.

But she was also a woman who almost always took Yaa's side in any argument. Cries-loud wished she were more like Aqamdax, who turned her head at harsh words, as though they had not been said. He thought of Ghaden's new wife. She was First Men like Aqamdax, and so perhaps was more quiet. How could Cries-loud fault the man for wanting a woman like that? He would trade Yaa any day for a soft-spoken wife, had even considered throwing her away and taking several of the oldest women in their village as wives, hoping that in their gratitude, they would live without complaining. But then how would he get children? Old women were no good for breeding. Of course, in all the years they had been married, Yaa had had no luck in making healthy babies. They had lost three sons and a daughter. Some curse was in her.

"You know your wife does not whine," Dii told him, and he had to think for a moment to remember what he had said to her to get that response.

"What then?"

"She's sad. That is all, and worried about what to give for the feast that will follow the mourning."

"I told her to see what you would give."

Dii's laugh was as harsh as a dog's bark. "You insulted her. She knows what to do about a mourning feast. Why do you treat Yaa like that? She tries her best to be a good wife."

"She seems more mother than wife."

Dii sucked her bottom lip into her mouth, and Cries-loud knew that she could not disagree with him.

He waited, said nothing more, hoping that his silence would make her decide to leave.

Dii looked into his face. "You act like a spoiled child," she said. "Perhaps that's why Yaa finds it so difficult to be wife rather than mother."

She turned then and left, but her words lingered like a slap burning red on Cries-loud's face.

THIRTY-FOUR

Cries-loud pulled several throwing spears from his weapons cache, hung a pack of dried fish from his belt, and left the lodge. He did not want to be there when Yaa returned, her mouth full of advice and caution. He walked through the village with his head down, ignoring any greetings given to him. For a quick moment the remembrance of someone long dead came to him, a hunter named Night Man.

Night Man had been husband to Aqamdax before she belonged to Chakliux. There had been some good in him. After all, he had bought Aqamdax from K'os, made her wife rather than slave. But he had suffered long from a wound in his shoulder, and the poison finally seemed to affect his mind, so that he had even killed his own son, drowned the infant shortly after it was born, though Aqamdax had claimed the baby was strong and whole.

Cries-loud remembered Night Man walking through the village, grunting insults in payment for cheerful words. Had he become like Night Man? The thought made Cries-loud call out a greeting to an old woman at the edge of the village. She was on hands and knees, scraping a hide she had staked out on high, sandy ground. She looked up at him in surprise and stammered a blessing for hunters. Her words lifted his heart, and he told himself that his only problem was Yaa.

Suddenly he turned back, called to the old woman. "Grandmother, would you tell my wife that I have gone hunting, that I might not be back until tomorrow?"

"Do not forget the mourning," she said.

"I will be here for that," Cries-loud replied, but he shook his head in wonder. Were all women only mothers?

The familiar lodge, the good smell of his sister's cooking, Chakliux's voice all soothed Ghaden's spirit, and though he was trying to prepare himself for a day of mourning, some of his sorrow lifted as though it were no more than smoke. His arms tightened around Chakliux's daughter, the little girl snuggled on his lap.

"Tomorrow," he said to Chakliux, "I'll get Uutuk and bring her here." He nodded at Seal. "Her father will go also and stay with his wife until she gathers the courage to visit us in this village."

"Tell the woman that I am First Men," Aqamdax said. "Tell her that I have found the River People to be good and generous." She smiled at her husband.

"What name has your wife chosen for herself?" Chakliux asked Seal. He framed his words carefully, in politeness, so Seal would know he did not expect to be given the woman's true and sacred name—a name that would too easily carry curses back to its owner.

"Old Woman," Seal said, giving the name as the First Men word *Uyqiix*.

"Tell Uyqiix she is welcome in our lodge."

Seal grinned, a wide smile that showed the gap where he had lost a dog tooth when as a young man his iqyax had slammed into a rocky shore. Uutuk had told Ghaden the story, made it into something funny, and the thought sent a stab of pain into Ghaden's chest. He missed his wife.

Chakliux's little daughter looked up at him, pressed a

small finger at the top of his nose, as though trying to smooth out a wrinkle. "Smile," she said. She looked much like Aqamdax with her round face and full lips, but her eyes were those of her father, and, most surprising, she had been born with an otter foot, the only one of their children to carry that sacred mark. Now with two summers, she was able to stand if someone set her on her feet, but she could walk only a few steps before falling.

As always, Aqamdax seemed to know what Ghaden was thinking. She crouched close and clasped the small turned foot. "She will have some difficulties in life, but that is the way of all gifts. If gifts were easily owned, we would not work hard enough to find the best way to use them."

Ghaden nodded and made his sister's wisdom his own by telling himself that her words also applied to his life with Uutuk. Would he appreciate her as much if he had no worries about her mother or father?

The doorflap was thrust aside, and Yaa came into the lodge. She hung a boiling bag from a lodge pole, dipped her head in greeting. Ghaden closed his eyes at the good smell of fresh caribou meat, then complimented her on the food she had brought, but the smile she gave him in return was forced and stiff.

"My husband is a good hunter," she said. Then her mouth tightened in embarrassment, and she added, "He decided to spend the night hunting. I'm sure he'll be back tomorrow." Her voice took on the timbre of a child's. "I hate to see him go alone." She looked at Ghaden, and he felt the urgency in her eyes.

"I could go . . ." he told her, but Chakliux interrupted.

"How would you find him?" he asked. "And even if you did, what would you tell him? That after a summer away from your village, on your first day back, you suddenly decided to leave your family again and go hunting? He would know that Yaa sent you." Chakliux lifted his head and let his eyes rest for a long time on Yaa's face. "Young men sometimes see their wives as ropes which bind. A wise wife will see that there are no knots in that rope."

Yaa turned her back on them and pretended to fuss with the meat she had brought, but Ghaden could see by the rigid way she held her shoulders that she was angry.

"Aaa," he said, "I return to my village as hunter, and before half a day passes, I am merely a knot."

Even the children laughed, and Yaa's shoulders sagged, as though her anger had left so suddenly that there was nothing else to hold her straight.

"I worry, that's all," she said, the words so soft that Ghaden could hardly hear them.

"I understand your worry, sister," said Ghaden, and set Chakliux's daughter from his lap so he could stand up. "But as a hunter I can tell you that though a man is flattered by a little worry, he is insulted by too much. If a wife doesn't believe he can take care of himself when he hunts, then she must also think that he's not a very good hunter."

Yaa whirled, a stirring stick in one hand, gravy from the meat dripping to the floor mats. "You know I sing the praise songs as loudly as any woman when my husband brings meat back to our village."

"So does a mother praise a son," said Ghaden.

She gritted her teeth, and Ghaden caught her wrist, lowered the stirring stick back into the boiling bag. "Be a wife, Yaa," he said. "Just be a wife."

Cries-loud walked until dusk, walked without stealth, paid little heed to the path he followed. He brought the faces of every unmarried woman he knew into his mind, considered who would make a suitable second wife. He could not throw Yaa away without bringing the anger of Chakliux and Aqamdax down on himself, but if he took a second wife and provided another lodge for her, he could live at that lodge, with that woman. How could anyone protest?

This time he would choose carefully, and not allow himself to be lured by a woman's face or body. He wanted someone who saw his strength and wisdom as greater than her own.

Since the Cousin and Near River Peoples now lived as one, Cries-loud seldom thought about enemies, and so continued to walk without caution, breaking branches that were in his path, making no effort to step on soft ground to muffle his passing. He did not even smell the smoke of a hearth fire until he stopped to build his lean-to shelter for the night. Then he suddenly realized his foolishness. He licked his fingers, wet the insides of his nostrils, and sniffed until he was sure that the fire was small and burned just to the west of his campsite.

He walked carefully then, crouched as though he were stalking an animal, his hunting knife in one hand. He heard one of the voices before he saw the glimmer of the flames, bright in the darkening forest. Women's voices. That was always a good sign. Men intent on raiding villages did not usually bring wives with them.

Cries-loud lay flat on his belly, slid closer until he could see that the camp had only one small lean-to, and that there were two women, no men. Suddenly he realized that they were Ghaden's women, his wife and her mother. They spoke the First Men language, words he did not understand, but there was a familiarity about one of the voices.

They sound like Aqamdax, he told himself. The accent she still gives to the River language, the depth of her voice, the music in the rhythm of her words.

No, it was more than that. One of the women, the older, not only sounded familiar, but looked familiar, the way she held her shoulders, the way she used her hands. Then he knew. K'os! The mother was K'os!

In his surprise, he stood, and both women started. Each grabbed a knife, and Ghaden's wife also leaned forward to clasp a fist-sized rock from the edge of the hearth circle.

"I am Cries-loud," he called, "brother-by-marriage to Ghaden of the River People."

K'os sighed her relief and slipped her knife into a sleeve

sheath. She leaned close to the younger woman, said something Cries-loud could not hear. The woman dropped the rock, but kept the knife in her hand.

"Tigangiyaanen!" K'os said. "Welcome. Are you alone? Did Ghaden send you?"

"I am alone, hunting. Ghaden is well. He plans to come for his wife tomorrow."

He waited, thinking K'os would translate the words to the young woman. After all, Ghaden had said she was First Men, and it had seemed that the father, Seal, had not understood the River language, despite his claim to be a trader. But the young woman also called to him, and her words were in River.

He stepped out from the brush, and she asked K'os something in the First Men language. He did not remember K'os speaking First Men, and wondered how she had gotten this daughter. She had left their village years ago, long enough, he supposed, to have a daughter. But Cries-loud knew she had been barren, had no children, save Chakliux, whom she had found, not birthed.

During his trading visits to the Walrus Hunter village, he had noticed that she no longer lived with them, but he had supposed they had traded her to someone or that she had died. A slave's life was not easy, and in a hard winter, slaves were the first to go without food. Somehow, by trade or by escape, she had gotten to the First Men.

"You wonder how I managed to return," K'os said. "Don't look so surprised. Your face has always reflected your thoughts." She lifted her chin toward the young woman. "My daughter Uutuk, Ghaden's wife. I see he didn't tell you that I'm her mother."

"No, he did not," Cries-loud said, "and I see that you made no haste to come to our village."

"Uutuk will go, but I'll stay here. I've had my share of nights in the forest alone. I'm not afraid. Since you are surprised to see me, I will guess that Ghaden didn't give you my message."

"No, he didn't."

"I told him that I wanted to speak to you."

"Me? Why?" He crossed his arms over his chest, lay his right hand casually on the sheath of his sleeve knife. Who could say what a woman like K'os would have in her mind? After all, he had been one of the men who sold her to the Walrus Hunters.

She pursed her lips to point at his knife. "You have no need of that. I've changed much since I left this village, and in truth have more reason to thank you than to resent you, but I'm not fool enough to think that Chakliux will believe that. I hope that when he gets to know my daughter, he will see how good she is and know that I've changed."

"So what will you do?" Cries-loud asked. "Stay here until Chakliux decides you are welcome? A woman alone or even with her husband will have a difficult time living outside a village in winter. Besides, your husband is a First Men hunter. How will he get enough meat to feed you? There are no seals in this land, except the few that come upriver in the summer, but beyond that nothing."

Uutuk was crouching by the fire, patiently feeding sticks into the flames. She raised her head and said to Cries-loud, "Ghaden plans to winter in a village named Four Rivers."

Unlike most new wives, she spoke boldly and did not keep her eyes lowered, but studied his face, as though to set it in her memory. She stood and wiped her hands on her sleeves. Though K'os wore River clothing—a lightweight ground squirrel parka and caribou hide leggings—Uutuk wore a feathered sax. Cries-loud could see her calves when she stood, and so knew she wore no leggings, though she had wrapped strips of hide around her feet, secured at her ankles and over her instep with lengths of babiche.

"A good place to go," Cries-loud said.

K'os turned her head, smiled at her daughter. "I taught Uutuk our River language, and also our customs. She will have no trouble living in a River village, and I have no doubt that Ghaden is hunter enough to provide for all of us."

She lifted a hand toward the fire, invited Cries-loud to join them. "We've eaten," she said, "but there's food left for you, if you do not mind dried fish dipped in seal oil."

Aqamdax always had a belly of seal oil in her lodge, and Cries-loud had learned to like the taste of it. He crouched by the fire on his haunches, imitating K'os rather than sitting cross-legged like most River men. He lifted his chin toward her and said, "I see you are First Men now."

"In many ways," she told him.

"How did you get yourself this daughter?"

Her jaw jutted as though she had been insulted, and she said, "How does anyone get a daughter?"

He kept his other questions hidden under his tongue. Why risk the anger of a woman like K'os when Ghaden could tell him what he wanted to know? He watched Uutuk as she brought him a wooden bowl of seal oil, a handful of fish, and a water bladder. She was a beautiful woman, round-faced and small-boned, with eyes even more narrow than Aqamdax's. Except for her thick dark hair, there was no resemblance between her and K'os.

He turned his mind toward the man Seal, decided that the girl was his and somehow K'os had earned herself a place as his wife. Most likely the girl's true mother was dead. Cries-loud wondered if K'os had killed her.

"So why did you want to see me?" he asked after he had begun eating. The fish was good, dried and smoked, rich with the seal oil.

"I thought perhaps you would like to travel with us to the Four Rivers village. Ghaden wants to tell his father's wife that she is a widow."

Cries-loud was suddenly very still. He was wise enough to know that K'os was wolf as well as woman, rejoiced in the stalk nearly as much as the kill. He gave his attention to the food, drank long from the water bladder, then asked Uutuk several questions about their journey.

Finally, K'os interrupted to say, "So I thought you might like to come with us and see if your sister is still living in that village. Or perhaps you have visited her already in these years since I've been gone."

"Once I went, in summer," Cries-loud said, "but the people were all scattered into fish camps and I never did find her."

He had not told the Four Rivers People that he was her brother. Why give his sister problems that she did not need? There were sure to be questions about the mother they shared, dead though she was. He himself thought about Red Leaf too often, and Yaa never tired of reminding him that he did so. Because he preferred to hunt alone, she accused him of searching for her. Yaa was wrong, of course. What man would waste time foolishly looking for someone who no longer walked the earth? But still, there was something that called him into the forests. Perhaps her spirit.

Red Leaf might have killed others, but he had never doubted her love for him. He was not afraid of her, not even her spirit. So why, then, did he avoid the Four Rivers village? Did he not want to know his sister, or take a brother's responsibility for her children?

Those children would be young—a good time to visit them, so they would learn to recognize his face, and in future years when he returned, they would know him as uncle. But what of Yaa? Each year that passed, each baby that died, made her cling more tightly to him. Would a sister with children hurt or help?

He shook his head. Who could say? Yaa was not a woman easily understood. He looked up to see K'os watching him.

"You don't want to go, then?" she asked him.

He looked at her, puzzled, then realized that she had misunderstood the reason he was shaking his head.

"I haven't decided," he said, and was glad she did not know that he had already told Ghaden he wanted to accompany them. To escape K'os's questions, he turned toward Uutuk and said, "I'm sorry I cannot speak to you in your own language."

"That is no problem, since I speak yours. My mother taught me well."

"A wise thing to do," said Cries-loud, "especially now that you are a River wife. Of course, she could not have known that would happen."

He caught the sudden darkening of K'os's eyes as she leaned forward to thrust a few sticks into the fire.

Aaa, but she had known, Cries-loud thought, or at least had hoped for such a thing. He was suddenly cold and moved closer to the flames. Why believe K'os had changed just because she had a good daughter?

"You should come with us to the Four Rivers village," K'os said, and Uutuk added, "My husband has missed all of the people in his village very much. He'd be glad for you to come."

"I was thinking of my wife," Cries-loud said. "She has recently mourned the death of another baby, and I think it would be good for her to leave the village for a while. The child's ghost seems to linger."

"Yes, bring her," Uutuk said. "She can tell me about the village, and how I can be a good wife to a River man." A smile lighted her face, and she clapped her hands like a child, but K'os's voice cut into the darkness, rose above the snapping of the fire.

"Uutuk, I should have told you that this man is married to your husband's sister, Yaa."

"I know," Uutuk said. "Ghaden told me all the people in his family."

"You see how quickly my daughter learns, Tigangiyaa-nen," K'os said, boasting as any mother might, but Cries-loud heard more than boasting in her words. Her pride was eclipsed by some darkness. Jealousy, and something else as well. Fear?

Most likely she did not want Yaa to come with them. Yaa might be able to tell Uutuk more than K'os wanted her to know, for unlike Ghaden, Yaa, being older, was more likely to remember some of the evil that K'os had done when she lived in their village and owned Aqamdax as slave.

"Perhaps you will want your wife to go with you, or perhaps you will not," K'os said quietly.

Uutuk began to protest, and Cries-loud was surprised that the girl should do so. Perhaps K'os had softened, raised this child differently than she had raised Chakliux.

"Be still, Uutuk!" K'os said sharply, and lifted one hand, palm out, as though to stop her daughter's words. "There are things here you do not understand and don't need to know. Go get wood. The fire is eating more than its share, and the night gives warning that winter isn't far away."

Uutuk's face puckered into worry, but she left them. Cries-loud felt his heart walk with her, into the evening shadows of the trees. A First Men woman would fear the forests, yet K'os seemed to give no thought to her terror.

"You shouldn't send her out there alone," Cries-loud said. "She'll be afraid."

"My daughter knows how to live above her fear," K'os told him. "Besides, what I have to say will not take long; then you can go with her if you wish." She looked into the fire and said, "A question first. You mentioned that Yaa lost a child. How many children do you have?"

"Four in the spirit world, and now she spends most of her time treating me like a child."

The words were out before he could stop them, the complaint as nasty and whining as anything he could have said. He closed his eyes in regret. How stupid to give K'os such a weapon against him and against Yaa.

"I fear I did the same to my husbands in my longing for a child. It's difficult for men to understand, but every woman does. You have another wife?"

He expected the question. Anyone who heard that Yaa had no living children was surprised that Cries-loud had not taken himself another woman. He gave K'os the answer he had given others.

"When Yaa has ended her mourning, I plan to take a second wife." He did not tell her that Yaa never ended her mourning, that with each birth and death, she wrapped herself more tightly into her sorrow.

"Perhaps you'll find someone at the Four Rivers village."

"There are still more than enough young women in our village for any hunter," Cries-loud said.

K'os lifted her brows in acknowledgment. "Wars are foolishness." She shook her head as though she had had no part in the hatred that had pushed the Near and Cousin River villages into battle.

"You need to go with us to the Four Rivers village," she said. "Without Yaa. Not for your sister, but for yourself."

He began to offer reasons Yaa should go, excuses, but she cut him off. "Listen to what I have to tell you, then make your decision, about yourself and about your wife.

"Cen died in a storm. I suppose Ghaden told you that."

"They'll have a mourning for him tomorrow night," Cries-loud said and was embarrassed at the sullenness in his voice. His wife had made him too bitter with her condescending ways, and now it seemed he had begun to act like a child.

But K'os continued as though she gave no consideration to his words. "Before he left the Traders' Beach, I had time to speak to him of his life in the Four Rivers village. Once, years ago, I nearly took Cen as my own husband. We did not forget that friendship."

"I didn't know," Cries-loud said.

"You were too young to know," K'os told him. "Besides, that was when I lived in the Cousin village and you were with your mother and father in the Near River village. But that doesn't matter. You remember when Chakliux forced me to leave his hunting camp?"

"I remember."

"I went to live in the Four Rivers village."

"You told me that. Long ago, you told me that."

"Yes, when you sold me to the Walrus Hunters."

"You said that my mother had survived even after she left my father, but that she had died in childbirth."

"I thought she had."

Cries-loud narrowed his eyes. In the light of the fire, K'os's face had shadowed so it seemed as though she wore a dancer's mask. Her mouth moved with her words, but otherwise she was very still, as though someone else were speaking, someone who stood behind her, hidden by the mask of her face. She sounded as though she told him the truth, but who could trust her? Perhaps she had lied before just to give him pain.

"You're telling me that she's alive?" he asked.

"I'm telling you that somehow she lived through that terrible birth and the illness that followed and when Cen left the Four Rivers village in early summer to trade, she was still alive."

"No longer ill?"

"Strong enough that she had just given him another healthy daughter."

Cries-loud had many questions, but he could not pull them from his throat. They crowded there choking him until he began to cough, finally gasping for breath.

He heard K'os's low chuckle, and his anger burned against her. She did not tell him this to bring joy, but to see what he would do, to watch as though he were a dancer, to listen as though he were a storyteller.

"Decide then if you want to go with us, and if you want your wife to know about Red Leaf." She paused for a moment, lifted her voice to call Uutuk back to the fire, then leaned close to say, "I suppose your father Sok is still alive. I suppose you don't want him to know about your mother."

"What does it matter?" he asked. "Ghaden is going. He still bears the scars of my mother's knife. You think he will let her live?"

"Ghaden was only a child when Red Leaf tried to kill him. You think he will recognize her?" She shook her head. "Of course not. She has taken the name Gheli—I told you that, nae'? Ghaden won't remember her, and I will not tell him. The choice is yours. Will you come?"

"Do you know when you will leave?"

She shrugged. "Most likely after the mourning. Should I tell my husband that you'll travel with us?"

Uutuk walked into the light of their fire, set an armful of branches near the lean-to. K'os threw the branches over the coals until she had coaxed the flames into a leaping roar, forcing Cries-loud to move back from the heat.

"No, I will not go with you," he said.

K'os smiled. "No," she said, "of course not. If Ghaden comes to get Uutuk for the mourning, what should I tell him?"

"Tell him that I'm hunting. Tell him that I mourn his father in my own way and carry his sorrow in my heart."

"Should I tell him that you carry his sorrow to the Four Rivers village?" K'os asked, but Cries-loud did not answer.

THIRTY-FIVE

Herendeen Bay, Alaska Peninsula
602 B.C.

Sky Catcher spoke out in the River language, and his voice
was like a knife cutting into the story. Men shook their heads
to bring themselves back to the day they were living.

"He says your tale has become foolish, Yikaas," Qumalix
translated. "He asks why Cries-loud would trust K'os.
Surely through the years the storytellers would remind the
people about the enmity that rose between the two villages
and about K'os's part in it."

"Sky Catcher is wrong," said one of the First Men traders.
"Cries-loud is unhappy with his wife, and taken with this
new woman, Uutuk. She is a beauty, right? He is thinking
about *her*. Not K'os. I know more than one man who has
gotten himself into trouble like that."

The hunter next to him began to laugh. "Just because you
are a fool, do not think all of us are," he said.

The trader twisted his fingers into an insult, thrusting
them toward the hunter, and the men's attention was drawn
from Yikaas and Sky Catcher to the two First Men, who had
risen from their haunches as though ready to fight.

"Aa, men! A bunch of children, all of you. What are you fighting about now?"

It was Kuy'aa. Sometime during the stories she had slipped into a curtained sleeping place, and now she thrust her head out to scold them. She had spoken in the First Men's language, but Yikaas had caught enough of the words to understand what she meant.

"They're fighting over my story, Aunt," Yikaas said to her.

"And what story did you tell them that brought out this foolishness?"

"A good story. About Cries-loud and his decision to go to the Four Rivers village. You remember."

She wagged her head at him, and he saw a smile lurking at the sides of her mouth. "A good story," she said, "but not worth fighting about. I would guess those two have something more than that bothering them."

She hobbled to the storyteller's circle to stand beside Yikaas and Qumalix. She raised her voice, shouted out several First Men words that Yikaas did not know, and suddenly there was quiet. "You men," she said, alternating between the River and First Men languages, "take your argument somewhere else. The rest of you be quiet! You men have had this storytelling ulax for far too long. It's the women's turn now."

There were groans and protests, but most were good-natured. A few men left, pushing their way past Kuy'aa, slapping hands on Yikaas's shoulders, expressing their opinions of his stories. Kuy'aa whispered something to Qumalix and she left also. A short time later, the women began to come, and Yikaas was surprised to find that he was disappointed that Qumalix was not among them.

As if he had asked about her, Kuy'aa said, "She's hungry. I expect she'll come back in a little while. Meanwhile, continue your story. I'll do my best to translate for you."

"My story is done," he said. "Cries-loud has decided to go to the Four Rivers village. He wants to find his mother, and he's tired of listening to his wife Yaa complain all the time."

"Aa, Yaa, poor child," Kuy'aa said, as though Yaa were

some niece or granddaughter whom she had known all her life. "She truly has very few complaints against her husband. Her complaints are with herself and her own life."

Yikaas nodded as though he, too, knew Yaa, then he set his hand against his throat, rubbed his neck, and said, "Aunt, I have had enough of telling stories. My throat is sore from too many words. Would you tell one of yours?"

There was a murmur of agreement from those nearest them, and Kuy'aa smiled so widely that Yikaas was glad he had asked her. She was the best storyteller among them, but it seemed that even the best sometimes needed to know that others appreciated their tales.

"Yes, Aunt," Yikaas said softly, "please," as though he were again the boy who listened in her lodge.

"A little different story, then," she said. "Daes's story, a strange woman, that one."

And a difficult story to tell, Yikaas thought. He fixed his eyes on Kuy'aa, saw the frown of concentration on her face. She usually told the story only to other storytellers because it was so easy for listeners to misunderstand. Why, then, try to tell it to this group, half of them rough men who wanted stories full of killing and hunting, of battles and anger? Even now, as they waited, a few of them had begun to grumble.

Kuy'aa raised her head and looked hard at them, then said, "There are things you need to know before I begin this story." In politeness she spoke in the First Men's language, then again, after, in the River tongue.

"Some of you have heard our tales of Chakliux and Aqamdax, those storytellers, husband and wife, River and First Men, who unite our peoples."

Heads nodded, and there was a mumble of agreement. "Some of you have heard about Sok, Chakliux's older brother, the chief hunter of Chakliux's village. When he was young, before he was chief hunter, he had a wife called Red Leaf. That wife wanted him to be given the place and honor of chief hunter. She thought that his grandfather, the old man Tsaani, was keeping him from having that honor. So she dressed herself up as a man, went to Tsaani's lodge in the night, and killed him. Sadly, another woman saw her, the woman Daes, who had an old husband, but had taken the trader Cen as her lover.

"Red Leaf killed Daes and also tried to kill Daes's little son Ghaden." As she spoke, Kuy'aa had closed her eyes, as though to keep her thoughts from drifting to what she might see in the ulax, but now she opened them and looked at the people gathered around her. "You all have heard of Ghaden, brother to Aqamdax and to Yaa."

Again, they murmured their acknowledgment.

"Ghaden, of course, lived. At first the people did not know who had killed Tsaani and Daes, but eventually they discovered that it was Red Leaf. Her husband Sok decided to kill her, but she was pregnant with Sok's child, and so he let her live until the baby was born. It was a girl, and after the birth, Sok and Red Leaf's son Cries-loud helped Red Leaf escape. She went out into the wilderness with the baby and was trapped in the first hard snowstorm of the winter. Everyone thought she had died, but she managed to get to the Four Rivers village where the trader Cen was living. She changed her name to Gheli and eventually became Cen's wife.

"Cen, who did not know Gheli was Red Leaf, took the baby daughter as his own and named her Daes after the woman he had loved, the mother of his son Ghaden. Many years passed and this second Daes grew up."

"There are too many names here to remember," one of the women complained.

"You are right," Kuy'aa said. She shrugged her shoulders. "But this is the story I have decided to tell. Leave if you want. Not every story is for everyone."

The woman stood and worked her way through the crowd to the climbing log.

"The rest of you, go if you wish," Kuy'aa told those who remained. "It is a difficult tale to understand, and some of you have been listening nearly all night."

She waited quietly, helped herself to a water bladder while others left the lodge. When there were only a few left,

Yikaas thought she would begin, but still she waited, humming a song under her breath. When another man left and an old woman followed him, then Kuy'aa lifted her voice to sing the song out loud.

"According to storytellers," she said, "this is something Daes often sang."

Kuy'aa sang it twice, in both languages, a child's song about trees living their summer lives, then sleeping through the winter. She sang until even Yikaas was losing his patience waiting for the story. Finally, he heard someone at the top of the ulax, saw a woman's feet on the climbing log. It was Qumalix. He turned his head away, pretended not to notice her, but still his heart was glad, and when she sat down he could not help but glance at her.

"I am about to tell the story of Daes," Kuy'aa said to her, and Qumalix nodded as though she had come to hear that very tale.

"I had hoped you would tell her story," Qumalix said, her voice polite and soft.

"I had hoped to have opportunity to tell it to you," Kuy'aa replied, and Yikaas realized that the old woman had been waiting for her, thus her long explanation, her song, her water drinking.

Then Kuy'aa's words rang out in the River tradition of storytelling: "Once in times long ago, a woman named Daes lived in a River village with her mother and father and baby sister. She was a large woman, wide of shoulder and as tall as a man, and she was also strong like a man, able to use a bow to kill animals and yet also gifted with needle and awl."

So Kuy'aa began.

Fish Camp, Yellow Creek
6435 B.C.

DAES'S STORY

Daes threw the head of another fish into a caribou hide bag to boil for stew. She pulled her knife lengthwise over the fish's belly from tail to gills and tossed the egg sack into another bag for drying. She emptied the guts into a bark container to be saved for the dogs, cut out the backbone, then tossed the fish to her mother. The two meaty halves were joined only at the tail, and Gheli laid it skin side down, flat against the slab of wood she used as a cutting board. She deftly slashed the pink flesh into diagonal slices, careful not to cut through the skin. Then she pushed it aside to be hung on drying racks.

Daes was angry at her mother, and with each slice of her knife, that anger grew. Summer had ended. They needed to leave their fish camp and return to the winter village. There were so few fish spawning, it was hardly worth staying, and besides, she and her mother had dried and smoked enough fish to last through two winters.

She thought of the people who would now be in the winter village, repairing summer damage to the lodges before leaving on the fall caribou hunts. She loved the hunts—the long days of walking, the hope of seeing the herds with every crest of a rise, the tang of cold in the air, the smell of summer-weary grasses and seeded flower heads. She was one of the strongest women in the village, and her strength was much needed when the people built brush fences to direct the caribou to the hunters. And each year she lived in hope that her father would allow her to join the men with her bow and take caribou herself.

Women seldom hunted, usually stood with the children as part of the fence, waving lengths of red-dyed caribou hide to frighten the animals into the surround, where hunters waited with spears and bows. But storytellers told of women who had been gifted with weapons. Those women had hunted caribou. Daes's father seemed as proud of her hunting abilities as if she were a son. Perhaps someday he would let her hunt caribou, too.

Of course, if she and her mother stayed too long in this fish camp, they would miss the hunts. And there was always the possibility that if they did not soon arrive at the village, the people would believe they had chosen to spend the winter elsewhere. Then someone might claim the circle of sod and rock that was the base of their lodge. Her father had dug nearly an arm's length into the ground before lining the dirt wall with stone. Like a First Men's lodge, he had explained, better to stand against the wind, better to keep away the cold, using the earth like a blanket.

The village site was high, built on a rise of sand and gravel, so they could dig into the ground without worry of flooding themselves in spring when the tundra changed from the hard crust of winter to the soggy wet of summer. Still, no one else in the village had built a lodge like Cen's, but Daes had little doubt that one family or another would be willing to live there, snug and warm against winter winds.

She looked at the racks of fish, felt despair wash through her, cold as river water. At least three or four days for those fish to dry, most likely longer. And what if her mother decided to smoke them after that? Worse, they still had a weir set in the river and were still catching fish.

Did Gheli think they could live on fish all winter without the fat of caribou? Did she think Cen would not worry when he returned from his trading trip to find that they were not yet in the village?

Of course, it wouldn't be the first time that had happened. Whenever Cen left to trade, Daes's mother changed, as though her husband took all her common sense with her. Almost always, they left the village, found some new place for a fish camp, far from other camps, and many days' walk from the Four Rivers village. Gheli nearly always went upriver, where the fishing was not as good, for most salmon did not run that far or were caught in the weirs set downriver.

A sudden wail told them that the new baby was awake. She no longer made the short, breathless cries of a newborn, but was still very little. At least she was old enough to smile at them and so seemed a little more like a person. Daes had been glad when she was born, but had also felt a little sadness at how happy her father had been, even though the baby was a girl. He had the man Ghaden, that brother Daes did not even know, and now this new daughter, whom her mother had nicknamed Duckling.

He also had Daes, but she knew that she had another father, one her mother would not talk about. A lazy man, worthless, Daes had heard the old women of the village say, cupping their hands around their mouths as though they were ashamed even to mention him.

At least Duckling was a girl. What chance would Daes have had to keep a place in Cen's heart if the baby had been a boy?

"I'll finish the fish, Mother," Daes said. "Go feed her."

Gheli nodded and went to the baby, reached up to take the carrying board from the branch where it hung. Daes watched her mother settle herself back against the tree, untie the baby from the carrying board, and slip her under the soft summer parka to nurse.

Her mother closed her eyes, wrapped her arms around the child, now only a bulge over Gheli's stomach. Again Daes felt a sudden thrust into her heart, a rise of senseless anger against the baby.

She was a pretty child, would most likely grow to be one of those delicate women that all men seemed to favor. What good did it do them, a woman like that? She would never be able to hunt, might not even be strong enough to survive the birth of children. Look what had happened to Bird Hand's wife. Of course he should have known better than to take himself a tiny woman, big as he was. Who could doubt that he would put a large baby into her, one that she could never push out? She had lived four days trying to birth that child before both she and the baby died.

Bird Hand and Daes had always been good friends, had hunted and spent nights together in a hunter's lean-to. The year after Daes's first moon blood, he had claimed her as a man claims a woman, and Daes had been sure that he would take her as his wife, but when he offered a brideprice, it was for the pretty-faced Lake Woman.

Daes had tried to forget that day, but the images often returned to her, thudding into her head like the blows of an ax against a tree: Bird Hand's walk through the village, the bundle of caribou hide he was carrying, the ground squirrel pelts in his little brother's arms as the boy followed. She remembered that as the two neared her father's lodge, how her heart grew so large it seemed near to bursting within her chest. Then the terrible weight of her disappointment as Bird Hand called out a jaunty greeting, but passed by.

She had been sitting outside the lodge, sewing a parka she had intended to give him. She had watched, unable to move, so light-headed that she was sure she would fall if she stood. She could hear the joy in his voice as he spoke to Lake Woman's father, and she saw his politeness as he presented the first portion of Lake Woman's brideprice. He had made three trips that day from his father's lodge, and each time his arms and the arms of his brother had been full of gifts. With each trip, Daes had felt the darkness grow inside her, until it was so large it had pushed her heart up into her mouth so that she could not speak, could scarcely breathe.

And what did he have to show now for all that giving? A dead wife and a dead son, cut from Lake Woman's belly to lie beside her in death.

Daes did not like to admit to the hope that had taken root during the long summer she and her mother had spent alone in this fish camp, but now, as the caribou hunts neared, she knew that Bird Hand must be considering a new wife. What man did not want a woman to accompany him on the hunts, to butcher the animals he killed? Of course, his mother and his oldest sister, nearly a woman, would go, so perhaps he would still live in his sorrow and take no wife to his bed. But few young men were like that, and Bird Hand might decide that he wanted a large, strong woman, one who could not only butcher his animals, but help him hunt as well.

But how could she be his wife when he did not even know where she was?

Her frustration made her knife work all the faster, and she sped through the gleaming heap of fish so quickly that her mother finally called out and cautioned her to be careful, clean the fish well, or they would rot in storage.

"I've done this all summer, Mother," Daes answered. "You think I've suddenly forgotten how?"

She seldom spoke to her mother in anger, and when she did, she usually dropped her head, lowered her eyes. But this time her mind was so filled with fear of loss that she looked directly at Gheli, though she knew that was more of an insult than her words.

Daes watched with lifted chin as Gheli set her teeth into her bottom lip and seemed to struggle over what to say. She finally began to fuss with the baby, giving no answer at all.

Some small part of Daes was ashamed, but mostly she was angry. She began to work even more quickly, so that the curved stone blade of her knife was nearly a blur to her eyes.

When she finished splitting the pile of fish, she saw that her mother had fallen asleep where she sat, and Daes's anger burned even stronger against the woman. She thought about packing her own things and leaving alone, but instead moved to where her mother had been working and began slicing each fish to the skin, stopping when she had a heap, to hang them from the drying racks.

When she had completed that job, she cleaned her knife at the edge of the river, then stood silently for a moment looking out at the tops of the willow stake weir. She and her mother had slanted the weir across the river, so it would funnel the fish toward the bank, where they were easily caught with gar or basket net.

For a moment, Daes considered catching those few that had swum into the shallows since morning when she and her mother had taken the night's catch. But then she looked back at their lean-to, at the stacks of caribou packs already filled with dried fish, and she realized they had so many that even with their three dogs and she and her mother carrying, they would have a difficult trip back to the village.

Daes took a long breath, fixed Bird Hand's face in her mind, then removed her caribou hide leggings and tied her parka up around her waist. She waded into the river, crossed over, battling the current. Once on the other side, she began to pull the willow stakes up from the river bottom, allowing the current to take them and the woven branches that formed a web between the stakes.

The cold water made her bones ache as though knives were scraping away her flesh, but her anger still burned hot enough to keep her fingers warm. She had most of the stakes pulled when she heard her mother shouting.

"Daes! What are you doing!"

"We have enough fish, Mother," Daes called.

She pulled another stake.

"We will go when I say so!" Gheli shouted, but Daes acted as though she did not hear. Her mother scurried away from the riverbank, and Daes smiled when she realized that Gheli was still holding the baby, could not come after her until she had put the child in a safe place.

By the time Gheli had laced Duckling into her carrying board, Daes had only three stakes left, those closest to shore. She stepped up on the bank, ripped up handfuls of grass, and used it to rub the feeling back into her legs. Her parka was wet to the shoulders, and she sluiced water from the sleeves.

"Build another weir," Gheli said, her voice calm but strong.

"Why?" Daes spread her hands toward the trees. "Look, the leaves have turned. Summer is over."

"We need more fish."

"We have more than we can carry," Daes said. "Do you plan to make two trips to the village and miss the caribou hunts?"

"Your father will bring enough meat for winter from his trading trip. We don't need to join the hunts."

"What if something happened, and he cannot bring meat?"

Gheli sucked in her breath and raised her hand as though to strike Daes.

"You think my words are strong enough to curse him?" Daes asked. "He's stronger than both of us. My words are like a mosquito against him."

"Fool! You're only a girl. You think you understand the ways of evil? You think you know what has power and what does not? Shut your mouth!" She bent to retrieve a willow stake that had escaped the river's current and bobbled its way to the bank. She gave it to Daes. "Here. One less you have to cut."

"I will not make another weir," Daes told her. "I'm not staying more than the few days it will take to dry those fish. You stay if you want, but I'm going back."

"Go, then, but don't expect me to give you one of the dogs," Gheli said. "You'll have to find your own way. You think you can?"

"I can," Daes said, though as she spoke the words, doubt had already begun to cloud her mind. She was used to following the steps of the one before her, and often paid little heed to the way they went. But she knew that their fish camp creek fed into the river that flowed near their village. She would walk downstream until she came to familiar places. She could do that without a dog.

She spun away from her mother, went back to the caribou lean-to, and began to gather her things. Since her mother would not go with her, why wait until those fish dried? She looked up at the sky. It was midday, and without Gheli and the baby, she could walk fast, even with a pack on her back. She might make it to the winter village with only two nights on the trail.

She rolled her bedding and gathered her personal things—a frayed willow stick to clean her teeth, several women's knives, dried fireweed leaves to make tea when she stopped to rest, a spare pair of leggings, extra boots, a packet of club grass fluff to catch her blood during her moon time or to help start a campfire.

She found a wooden bowl that she could suspend from her belt. She would fill it with a little damp moss and a smoldering knot from their fire. She also had a fire bow, but after a long day of walking it was always good to be able to have fire quickly rather than have to make it herself.

She filled several water bladders from the river, tied them so they would hang over her shoulders, then selected the packs of dried fish she would take. She tried to choose the heaviest, to spare her mother, but when Gheli saw what her daughter was doing, she began to scream out insults.

"You can take them yourself if you want, Mother," Daes told her, "but I'm strong and can carry a good load."

Gheli closed her mouth and considered the packs. Finally she said, "You would leave me here with Duckling? What if wolves come? How will I protect her?" She lifted a hand to where the baby hung, and Daes looked long at her little sister.

"Four days until those fish are dry?" Daes asked.

Her mother looked up at the sky, pointed as though to show Daes that no rain threatened.

"I'll stay that long," Daes said. "But if you're not ready to go by then, I'll go alone."

THIRTY-SIX

Near the Four Rivers Village

Daes shifted the packs on her back to release the pressure on the tumpline across her forehead. The dog at her side had begun to whine. He was the oldest of the three she and her mother had brought with them to fish camp and a son to Tracker, her father's favorite dog, now long dead. He had been a gift from Cen, and Daes had named him Jump.

"Almost there," she said as much to herself as to the dog. She reached into a bag at her waist and pulled out a dried fish, gave half to Jump, and ate the other half.

Since that morning she had known the comfort of recognizing trees and landmarks. She had run a winter trapline not far from where they stood. But she also had begun to feel anxious, realizing that when she returned to the village, everyone there would ask about her mother and the baby. How could Daes admit that she had left them?

She reminded herself that she was justified in doing so, that her mother had twice convinced her to stay, even after the last fish was dried. Of course she could not tell them that Gheli would rather stay alone in a lean-to than live in her husband's warm winter lodge. Who would ever understand that?

Soon the old women would begin their whispers: Gheli was not quite human. Hadn't she come to them in a storm? Hadn't Cen dug her out of the snow like a ptarmigan in winter? Maybe she was tired of her human husband and wanted to go back to being bird.

Daes had heard those stories whispered before, and she could give no better answer to her mother's strangeness, but she knew that Gheli was not bird. Surely a daughter would see things through the years, feathers in the soup, a hint of claw or beak. But there was nothing, and if Gheli wanted to be rid of her husband, why was she so happy when he was in the village?

When Cen was home, Gheli was full of singing, always smiling, and even made small jokes, but when he was gone, especially on trading trips, she grew gaunt, her mouth sucked in as though she were drying up from the inside.

Daes continued to walk, making soothing sounds to keep Jump with her, for he had begun to stop for any reason, a ground squirrel, a branch across the path, even the sound of a bird. Daes decided to lighten his pack, adding a roll of bedding to her load, but finally she saw the village, the trail of lodges strung out along the river, another group making a V to the first as though the lodges were geese ready to wing south for winter. She held her breath, wondering if someone had already claimed their lodge, but it was there, the gaping hole of it on the river side of the village. A log cache sat high on legs next to it. Her mother kept the lodge cover in the cache over the summer, away from greedy animals and the rot of rain. Even most of the lodge's domed roof poles were still in place, though one was split and would have to be repaired.

Jump ran ahead of her, his tale wagging. He ignored the challenges of other dogs tied beside other lodges and ran inside the circle of stones, the base of the lodge. In spite of

Daes's demands that he come out, he sat down as though he belonged there. What dog was allowed into a lodge, even one without its lodge cover? Finally in exasperation she went in after him, untied the bundles on her back and those on Jump's, then dragged him outside. As she tethered him, he lifted his howls into a dog song of celebration and set other dogs to yipping.

Children were the first to gather, hands over ears at the dog noise, and they were the first to ask about Gheli.

"She decided to stay a little longer to fish, but didn't want my father to worry about us. If she isn't here in a few days, I'll go back for her myself."

Daes had not thought ahead to what she would say when asked about her mother, so she found herself glad at her answer. How could her mother object? Would she want everyone in the village to know that they had argued?

"Has my father returned yet from his trading trip?" she asked one of the older boys.

"Not yet," he said. "Maybe he'll be gone for the winter."

"Maybe," said Daes, but she did not like to consider the possibility. She and her mother would not have enough to eat, unless Daes was claimed as wife; then it would not be a terrible winter, even for Gheli.

Daes studied the village, noticed that things seemed quiet. "The men, have they left yet to hunt?" she asked, and in her anxiety, the words rushed too quickly from her mouth.

"What? What did you say?" the children shouted, but the boy nearest her said, "A few went to hunt bear."

Daes sighed her relief. Women did not go with men on bear hunts. There was too great a chance of a curse. She wanted to ask about Bird Hand, but thought she should not. Better to keep her mouth closed and listen at the village hearths. The women would soon tell her everything, one way or another.

Their lodge was tall, and though the cover needed little repair, it took Daes the rest of the day to secure it in place over the lodge poles. Once or twice several of the older boys stopped their play to help her, but if her mother had been there, they would have been able to do the task in half the time.

When she had finished with the cover, the sky was still light enough for her to gather firewood, fallen branches in the nearby forest. She brought back enough to get her through the night, adjusted the smoke hole flaps, and started the fire. When it was burning well, she took all her water bladders, those she had brought from their fish camp and others that she found in the cache, and went to the river to fill them.

It was the time of evening when trees and lodges are dark, but the sky still holds some light. She was crouched on her toes at the edge of the water, on a bit of sand that sloped gently into the river, when she heard two voices, that of a man and a woman, both teasing.

In the darkness at the river's edge, Daes knew she was well hidden, so she filled the bladders quietly, smiling as she listened. The two were laughing softly, whispering, but Daes was unable to hear well enough to tell who they were. Surely not husband and wife.

They were suddenly quiet, and Daes thought perhaps they had moved downriver, away from the village. She filled another bladder, then heard an explosion of laughter. She knew that laugh. It was Crane, a great hulk of a girl, too long of leg and arm. Even her neck stretched out like a crane's neck. She was a good lesson to all mothers for caution in naming. Daes's thoughts went to her baby sister, and with some satisfaction, she pictured the child growing short and squat, waddling and murmuring like a duck.

Aaa, it was good for a woman like Crane to find a man, even if just for a night of play. Perhaps that would be enough to fill her heart for all her life, or even to give her a child. Then most likely someone would take her as wife. After all, Crane was gifted with common sense, and not terrible with her needle.

The man began to laugh, a deep laugh that made Daes hold her breath in glee. It was Bird Hand's father, she was sure. Chief hunter of the village and already with three wives! Surely he did not want another. Was Crane so foolish to think that he would take her? Was she so desperate that she would be satisfied to have a man use her and then pretend nothing had ever happened between them? What about the chief hunter's second wife? She was a jealous woman, unable to do anything about the first wife, and satisfied to have her sister be third wife, but what if the chief hunter brought Crane into their lodge? The thought made Daes's throat swell with laughter.

Crane and the chief hunter were very quiet now, without doubt into the serious work of mating. Daes would not hear any more from them until they were done, and the wind was too cold, blowing down the river, and her belly was too empty to stay longer. She filled her last water bladder, gathered the bladders into two bundles connected with a short braid of babiche, and slung them over her left shoulder. She smiled in the darkness. She had enough to keep her mind busy for the evening. She might as well return to the lodge.

In the morning, she would go to the village hearths and see what the women had to say about the caribou hunts. If the men planned to leave soon, then she would go, too, and let her mother worry about getting herself back to the winter village, but if it would be a while, then perhaps after a day or two of rest she would go back and help her mother carry the remaining packs of dried fish to the village.

Satisfied with her plans, Daes pushed her way along the river's edge, past willow brakes and brush, until she came to a little clearing. As always, when she filled the water bladders, her own bladder seemed to fill itself as well. In the darkness, she jerked down her caribou leggings and pulled up the edges of her parka, began to release her water. She was squatted on her haunches when she heard Crane's voice again. Daes made a face. She did not need them to stumble upon her. Crane was the kind of woman who would make a joke for the whole village out of such a thing.

They stopped short of where she was crouched, and Daes was able to pull up her leggings and adjust her parka without letting them know she was there.

The chief hunter was saying something to Crane, words of endearment, clear enough for Daes to hear. She covered her mouth with both hands to hold in the sound of her breathing.

"Aaa, two fine, fat pups, they are," he said, and Daes knew his hands were on Crane's breasts, "and here the mother."

The words were a blow that knocked away Daes's wind. Yes, of course, his hands were on Crane's breasts, then on her belly, but how did Daes know that? Would a father make love with exactly the same words used by his son? The voice was not the chief hunter's, but Bird Hand's, deepened by his lust.

Daes moaned, did not realize she had made a sound until she heard Bird Hand say, "Listen, I heard something."

In quietness she held her breath, and even the blinking of her eyes seemed to make noise, but finally Crane said, "I don't think it's anything, just the river."

Daes heard them walk away, and she crouched again on her haunches, pressed her fingers into the corners of her eyes until she had pushed her tears so far down her throat that her lungs shuddered with each breath.

Daes did not sleep well that night. Her dreams were woven with images of Crane and Bird Hand finding her by the river. For some reason she had no clothes, and stood before them naked while they laughed. When she woke in the morning, she lay exhausted on her sleeping mats, playing what had happened over and over again in her mind. Finally she convinced herself that Bird Hand had used Crane only for a night of pleasure, that he would never want her as wife.

If Crane's father were someone important, that would be

different, but he was not. He limped badly from a leg broken years before, and seldom hunted but relied on others to provide for him. Crane's brother was still a boy, and her sister, beautiful to look at, as Crane was not, had yet to have her first moon blood time. Perhaps Bird Hand thought it worthwhile to take Crane just to have the best chance of claiming the sister once she was a woman, but that could be several years yet.

No, Daes told herself, she had nothing to worry about. But she took special care that morning, combing out and braiding her hair, carefully brushing the dirt and grease from her summer parka and leggings. When she went to the hearths, she did not go as most girls would, empty-handed, but brought a packet of dried blueberries and made a show of offering it to the chief hunter's third wife, Wing—Bird Hand's mother—for the cooking bag she was stirring.

Wing looked surprised at the gift, hesitant to take it. Such berries were usually saved for feasts.

"It will add flavor to the stew," Daes told her, and the woman nodded as though still unsure of what to say. She dumped the berries into the broth, and Daes hurried away, brought back several armloads of wood, stacked them near the fires.

"Where is your mother?" Wing asked, waving a hand before her face as a gust of wind changed the direction of the smoke and set several women to coughing.

"Still at fish camp," Daes told her.

"You returned alone?"

"With one of our dogs."

"You left your mother with the baby and all her fish to carry?" another woman asked.

It was Crane's mother. Daes wondered if she knew who Crane had been with the night before, and if she worried that Daes would take Bird Hand from her daughter. She should worry, Daes thought.

"I brought most of the fish back with me," she said. "My mother was concerned that someone might claim our lodge if my father had not yet returned from his trading trip." She held her hands out, palms up, and added, "You see she was right. He hasn't yet returned."

"A trader was here several days ago," one of the women said. "He had heard that Cen was at Chakliux's village."

That was good news. Daes did not want to face a winter without her father in the lodge. She remembered a year he had spent away trading. That hungry winter, her mother had slept both day and night, so Daes had done all the work and felt as if she lived alone like some old woman.

"How many days does it take a man to walk from Chakliux's village to ours?" she asked.

"A strong man like your father, paddling upriver?" said the chief hunter's first wife, an older woman, but still with some of the beauty of her youth. "Four days with portages, maybe five." Then she asked Daes, "Long enough for you to go get your mother?"

The question made Daes uncomfortable. "Perhaps," she finally said, "but who knows when my father started out? It would not be a good thing for him to come tomorrow and find me gone. Who would welcome him? I can reach my mother in two, three days walking, but with the baby it will take us much longer to return."

Several women nodded, but Bird Hand's mother said, "A good daughter would go now. We will watch after your father. You've already set up the lodge and brought fish, nae'? Then he has food to eat, and he can always get more from the hearths."

Daes turned her head as though she were looking back at her lodge, at the job she had done in tying the cover in place, in stacking firewood, but she was really turning so Wing would not see the anger in her eyes. What right did she have to tell Daes what to do? Did she know where her son had been last night? What if Crane got with child, would Wing want Crane for a daughter?

But Daes willed her anger away, and by the time she spoke, her eyes were soft. "I think I'll take the day to gather wood, and in the morning, if my mother has not yet returned, I'll go back for her. Though she was the one who told me to come, she'll most likely be glad for my help. And I'm already lonesome for them, my mother and my sister."

Then the women at the hearth urged her to eat and eat well, for the journey ahead would be a difficult one, and the journey back even more so, a heavy load of fish on Daes's back.

So for that day, Daes gathered wood, made large stacks at the sides of the lodge, but stopped often, looked upriver and down, hoping to see her mother coming, so she would not have to go after her; hoping to see her father, his iqyax laden with treasures from the First Men and Walrus Hunters, gifts for a good daughter.

The morning broke cold and dark, the belly of the sky so heavy that Daes knew it would rain. She thought about staying another day, but then saw herself returning with her mother, Daes laden with most of their fish. What man would not want a woman like that, who would do so much for a mother who foolishly stayed too long at fish camp? Why wait because of a little rain?

She was ready by midmorning and left thinking that the day would grow warmer as the sun climbed in the sky, but even by the time she reached the last lodges in the village, the rain had gathered strength and changed to ice, dancing around her feet as she walked.

Jump was by her side, the dog joyous at promised adventure and a light pack. She held him back, slowed her steps, hoping that she might see Bird Hand before she left and have opportunity to tell him what she was doing. But everyone was inside, save a woman here or there, sent out to feed dogs or get wood. These she hailed and told where she was going, in the hope some word of her unselfishness would get back to Bird Hand.

Then she was out of the village, ducking under low-branched spruce to follow a trail that led through the woods.

Many women would not consider taking such a journey alone. And though Daes reminded herself that she had just made this same trip safely a few days before, thoughts of wolves and wolverine filled her mind.

She comforted herself with quiet words, saying that surely her mother had left fish camp and that they would meet this day or the next on the trail. At each turn of the path, she expected to see her, at the top of each hill, at the far side of each tundra clearing. But though Daes walked through that whole day and well into the evening, she saw nothing but her own dog and a few hares, one already mottled white, preparing for winter.

Her feet ached, and her shoulders, and even her eyes, for watching so hard. She began to walk in anger, stomping the soles of her caribou hide boots into the orange needles that lay over the path. Next year, she vowed, she would be Bird Hand's wife. She might even have a belly full of his child. Then it would not matter how foolish her mother was, Daes could leave fish camp when she wanted.

She had brought dried fish with her, so during that day of walking, she had not bothered to hunt, but when Daes finally stopped for the night and built herself a fire, she began to wish for fresh hare. She filled her belly with fish, then pulled grass to make a bed, rolled out a caribou hide to sleep on, but the ground was wet, and her stomach rolled and complained for want of roasted meat. Jump lay close beside her, the smell of his damp fur filling her nose. She dreamed of dogs, of nursing puppies at her breasts, as women must sometimes do to save a dog or two in starving moons of late winter. She awoke hungry, and the next day, as she walked, she watched for hares. Finally she killed one, caught it in the head with a good throw of her walking stick. It was a fine, fat buck, long of ear and still in his brown summer coat.

That night, she and Jump feasted, and Daes slept without dreams.

THIRTY-SEVEN

On the middle of the third day, when Daes came to her mother's fish camp, it looked as it had when she left. Fish still hung on drying racks, the lean-to tent was in place, and her mother sat beneath a tree with Duckling on her lap. The baby cooed and reached out a hand when she saw Daes, but Daes could only stare. Finally she ripped the pack from her back and called her mother all the vile names that came into her head. When she had screamed out all her anger, she bent, chest heaving, and tried to remove Jump's dog packs. But he backed away until she stomped her feet in frustration.

Gheli rose, careful to keep a firm hold on Duckling. "I decided to stay a little longer," she said.

Daes stretched her mouth into a firm line and closed her eyes against the sight of her mother and the fish camp.

"I thought you might need help carrying the rest of the fish," she said slowly, as though she were speaking to a child who was not quite old enough to understand. "We need to leave soon. I don't want to travel in snow."

"Has your father returned?" Gheli asked.

"People say that he is at Chakliux's village. Or he was a few days ago. By now he may already be home."

"Was he traveling alone?"

Daes opened her eyes and flung back her head, clenched her hands at the stupidity of her mother's question. "How should I know?"

"I thought, well, I thought they might have . . ."

Daes sighed. Her mother's gentle response made her suddenly ashamed of herself. She took one of Gheli's hands in her own, smoothed her fingers over the roughened skin. She felt her throat close a little. Her mother's hands were dry and lined like an old woman's.

"We will leave tomorrow morning," Daes told her. "Help me pack everything."

They worked together that afternoon. Daes took the last of the fish from the drying racks, put them into caribou hide packs, and made heaps of all the goods, one for each of the three dogs, another for herself, and one for her mother. Last of all, in the morning, she would take down the lean-to, add its caribou hides to her pack. Then there would be only the drying racks to show where they had spent the summer.

But when morning came, a bright day, full of the sun, Gheli was again sitting outside the lean-to, Duckling in her lap. "I think I need to stay one more day," she told Daes, and because Daes was ashamed of the curses she had shouted at her mother the day before, she agreed to wait.

She followed animal trails into the forest, killed three hares with her throwing stick, then took them back to the fish camp, where she spitted them to roast over hearth coals. During the afternoon she went out to search for mouse caches—the little tunnels in the tundra sod where mice store seeds and bulbs for winter. She dug up several small caches and one that was large, filled a waistpack with what she found. She parched the seeds on a flat stone heated in the fire, ate more than her share that night, and said little to her mother.

She did not sleep well, as though she knew through her dreams that her mother would do the same thing the next morning. So when Daes found Gheli again sitting outside, she only pursed her lips and spent another morning hunting.

She came back with nothing, and that afternoon lay on the bedding in the lean-to. She fell asleep, slept hard, and woke to a meal of fresh fish that her mother had cooked.

Daes ate, but that night when Gheli was asleep Daes sneaked from the tent, took the dogs to the edge of the woods, and strapped on their packs. Then she returned to the lean-to where Duckling was asleep in her cradleboard. Daes strapped the board to her belly, hefted her pack to her back, then quietly slipped away.

She kept a lead line on each dog, but they carried so much weight that she had little trouble with them. Mostly they seemed glad to leave the fish camp, and when one sat on his haunches and turned back, as though to wait for Gheli, Daes, said, "She will come. You think she'd let me take this daughter of hers, knowing I have no milk to feed her?"

But though Daes walked slowly all that day, sure that her mother would catch up with them, by night they were still alone, the baby wailing for want of food, the dogs whining under the loads they carried.

Daes considered returning to the fish camp. How long could a child live without its mother's milk? But Duckling sucked water from Daes's fingers, and later the baby managed to choke down broth from a bowl, snorting it out her nose, coughing it from her throat, but swallowing at least half of what Daes gave her.

Then Daes decided to continue the journey, decided to set a faster pace. Better to get back to the village before bad weather set in, before the men left on the fall caribou hunts, before the baby grew weak from lack of milk.

After two and a half more days, Daes came to the Four Rivers village. She unloaded her packs and those of the dogs, then left everything at the entrance of the lodge to take her sister to a woman who had a baby of her own. By the time Duckling was sucking at the woman's breast, several women—including Wing, Bird Hand's mother—had gathered at the lodge.

Daes, in the hardship of walking, had not thought ahead to

what she would say. Should she tell them Gheli had foolishly refused to leave the fish camp? Would that justify Daes
taking Duckling? Surely any woman could see that the
baby's eyes were sunken, her little belly swollen with
hunger.

"Has someone died?" one of the older women asked, and
Daes knew she was afraid to say Gheli's name, afraid of
bringing her ghost to them.

Daes squeezed her eyes shut so tightly that tears beaded in
the corners. Then she looked at the old woman, addressed
her politely, saying, "Grandmother, no one knows what has
happened, but I waited as long as I could, went out looking
for her, called for her, found only my sister and our dogs and
packs there, and finally decided to bring back as much as I
could carry. I hope that my father has returned, and that he
and I might go out and look for her."

Then all eyes were downcast, and Daes felt a sudden
catch of fear. She pulled in a long breath and said, "Something has happened."

"Get him," said several of the women. Two left, and Bird
Hand's mother bent over Daes. With tears close under her
words, she whispered, "We had to stop our celebration . . ."

"She probably doesn't know about the celebration," one
of the others said.

"Aaa," agreed Bird Hand's mother. She brushed at a tangle of hair that had come loose from her braids and said,
"My son's marriage to Crane. You knew about that, nae'?"

For a moment Daes sat without speaking, then she realized that her mouth was hanging open like the mouth of
some old woman who has spoken all her words before using
up her life. "I knew," she said, and closed her mouth with a
snap.

"See," said Bird Hand's mother. She drew her brows into
a frown and told Daes, "A man came from Chakliux's village. He told us he was looking for your mother. He said that
her husband had drowned in a storm somewhere."

"Aaaaeeee," Daes murmured, a soft mourning cry, but

also a denial. "Aaaaeeee." How could her father be dead? He was a strong man. He had traveled the North Sea nearly to the ice edge of the world. Once he had even walked over the mountains to the South Sea. She looked into Wing's eyes, suddenly remembered that Bird Hand had taken Crane as wife. Anger wove itself through her sorrow, and she spat out words as sharp as bird darts.

"You are wrong," she said. "My father is alive."

Wing did not try to convince her.

"If he is dead," Daes said softly, "what will I tell my mother?"

The oldest woman in the group leaned close. "You said you couldn't find her." She stared into Daes's face, blinking rheumy eyes.

"I did not say she wouldn't come back," said Daes.

"Perhaps you did not look hard enough," the old woman told her.

Daes held her breath, waiting for questions from the others, but though they glanced at her from the corners of their eyes, they said nothing, and when the women returned with the man from Chakliux's village, all but Wing and the eldest of them left. That old one closed her eyes, began a soft chant, something to protect the village.

Daes played the part of politeness, her eyes downcast as the young man spoke.

"I am named Cries-loud," he told her.

His voice was low, as though he spoke from sorrow.

"You've come to tell me that my father drowned in a storm," Daes said, and met his eyes as though her boldness would be strong enough to make him deny the death.

He lifted a hand, brushed it nervously against his cheek, and Daes found herself staring at him, saw that Wing also stared. What was there about this man that seemed so familiar?

"Yes," he said. "I need to find your mother and tell her."

Wing poked her head between Daes and Cries-loud. "She is also dead," Wing said.

The grandmother stopped her chant and hissed at her. "We do not know that!" she said. She clasped an amulet, dark with age, as protection against Wing's words.

"You said . . ." Wing began.

"I said I couldn't find her," Daes shouted. "Only that. Not that she's dead!"

Cries-loud lifted a hand as though to calm the women, and it seemed as though Daes were looking into still water at her own face. She shook her head, noticed that Wing was doing the same.

She looked at Cries-loud. "I have wood for a fire and food in my lodge," she said. "Come and tell me about my father and the storm that took him."

They left the grandmother and Wing behind, left the mourning chant that the old woman had wound around them, and somehow Daes knew without seeing that Cries-loud followed her, so it was not until she reached the lodge that she looked back, and then only to hold the doorflap open for him to go inside.

CRIES-LOUD'S STORY

Cries-loud followed his sister to a fine, large lodge. At least it seemed that Cen had treated his mother well, that in taking her as wife, he had given her a good life. And this sister of his, she was strong and healthy, a large woman, with wide hips, good for babies. He had been careful with his questions since he came to the village, had asked cautiously—only as messenger—about his mother, and always called her by the name Gheli. He had said nothing about his sisters, and it was nearly a day before someone mentioned Daes by name. Even then he sensed some hesitation, as though there might be something wrong with her, so he was relieved to see that she looked normal and seemed to do all things as a woman should, quickly starting a fire, offering him water, and dragging in the packs that were set in the entrance tunnel.

"They say you just returned from fish camp," Cries-loud said. "It's late in the year for that."

Daes shrugged. "My mother wanted to stay. She doesn't like to come back to the village too soon. She says we miss too many fish doing that."

He nodded, then asked, "Where is your sister?"

"They told you about my sister?"

"I've been waiting for you and your mother three days. A man can learn much in three days."

Daes hung a boiling bag from the lodge poles, poured in several bladders of water, and added dried fish.

"Did you see the baby in that lodge where we were?" she asked. "That's my sister. I brought her back from fish camp. I couldn't find my mother. She was gone a long time. She went to pick berries or gather plants." Daes stopped, passed a hand over her face.

There was something wrong about what she was telling him. Berries? Plants?

"You looked for her?" he asked.

"I spent a whole day looking for her, my sister crying in hunger," Daes said. She began stirring the fish in the boiling bag, then with no explanation hurried into the entrance tunnel.

Cries-loud sat there thinking she had left the lodge, and wondered whether he should leave as well or wait for her return.

She came back with a handful of lovage, thrust it toward him as though it were something important. "She was looking for lovage. We dry it for winter to add flavor to our boiling bag."

She shredded the leaves and dropped them into the boiling bag, stirred again.

"So she went for lovage, not berries."

"Probably," Daes said. "But if she found berries she would bring them as well. Highbush cranberries are good this time of year, after the first frost."

Her words made sense, Cries-loud told himself, so why did he feel as though she were lying? And why hadn't she asked about Cen?

During the days walking to the village, he had tried to decide how to tell his mother and sister about Cen's death. He had not even considered that they wouldn't be in the village. Who stayed in fish camps when caribou hunts were about to begin?

Your mother, some small voice told him, when she's worried her husband will bring Ghaden to the village. Ghaden, who might recognize her as Red Leaf.

Cries-loud watched his sister and wondered what it had been like for her, named after the dead Daes. Had the ghost followed her name to this new Daes? Had his mother—Red Leaf, Gheli—feared the power of that name? Surely she lived in dread lest someone come to the village who would recognize her. There were always men—hunters, traders—going back and forth between villages. How better to hide herself than to spend the summers in some remote fish camp?

She also must have learned to sew differently, for, according to Yaa, a woman can recognize other women's work, especially sewing as gifted as Red Leaf's. And Cen would surely want to trade his wife's fine parkas. Had she somehow changed her stitches so they no longer spoke her name?

Suddenly he realized that Daes was holding a bowl of food before him. He wrapped his hands around the bowl, inhaled the steam, smelled the smoky fires that had dried the fish. The smell pulled him away from the lodge, from his sister whom he had known only as a baby. He stayed for a moment in that safe place, then opened his eyes and came back.

"Thank you," he told Daes.

He lifted the bowl to his lips, used his fingers to push a little of the meat into his mouth. He chewed and swallowed, then lowered the bowl to his lap, and motioned for her to sit down beside him. "Do you want me to tell you what I know?"

She squatted on her haunches, as though to be ready to refill his bowl.

"Sit," he said, "unless you want to get yourself something to eat."

"No."

"Your father was a good man," he began, and thought how strange it was to be telling this sister about Cen, to be telling her that her father was dead, when all along she belonged to Sok, a father who was alive and strong.

During the whole telling, she did not cry, and when he had finished, she stood, brushed her hands together, and pulled off the soft ground squirrel parka she had been wearing inside the lodge. Cries-loud expected her to begin a mourning cry, but she only stirred the boiling bag. Finally she calmly picked up a woman's knife that lay on a hearthstone and drew the blade across her left arm, once, twice. She lifted her hand and leaned over the fire so the blood ran down her arm into the coals.

She showed no sign of pain, as though she had only cut a fish for drying, but she said to him, "Thank you for coming to tell us."

He hoped she would add something about her mother, at least how to get to their fish camp. If Red Leaf were still alive, she needed to know about Cen, and she also needed to know that K'os was coming, she and her daughter Uutuk and Ghaden.

But when Daes spoke she said, "The man Ghaden, do you know him?"

"I know him. He lives in my village." Almost he told her that he was married to Ghaden's sister Yaa, but then for some reason did not.

"No one else from your village is coming, nae'?" she asked.

"There's a woman from our village who knew your mother. Perhaps you recognize her name. K'os."

"No," Daes said.

"She's coming to share your mother's mourning, and she plans to travel with her husband Seal, a First Men trader, as well as a daughter and that daughter's husband, Ghaden."

For a moment—so quickly that Cries-loud almost missed it—Daes's eyes widened, but she went to one of her packs and rummaged through it until she came up with a strip of caribou hide. "Let me help," he said, and she held her arm out toward him.

He wrapped the strip tightly, then bent to look into her eyes, clasped her chin when she tried to turn away. "You know Ghaden," he said.

"My mother speaks about him sometimes."

"And me?" he asked. "Does she speak about me?"

Daes looked at him, puzzled. "No," she said slowly. "Why should she?"

She glanced down when Cries-loud tucked the end of the hide strip into place near her elbow. For a moment, he thought she was studying the wrap, but then she raised her hand to his, held it there. His hand was larger, but otherwise they looked the same, even to the pattern of their veins.

She lifted her eyes to his face and asked, "Who are you?"

THIRTY-EIGHT

Herendeen Bay, Alaska Peninsula
602 B.C.

There were murmurs of protest when Kuy'aa stopped her
story. One of the bolder women said, "We want to know what
he tells her. We want to know if he decides he can trust her."

"Do you think he can?" Kuy'aa asked.

"No!" most of the men called out.

"Of course," said one of the chief hunter's wives. "Once
she knows she is his sister, she will not do anything to harm
him."

Another woman said, "You cannot trust her. Look how often she lies, and she just took her baby sister and left her
mother."

"Her mother deserved to be left. Who could live in a fish
camp all winter? The baby would have died!"

The arguing continued, the voices rising. Yikaas glanced
at Kuy'aa and saw that she was smiling. Qumalix moved to
sit beside her, and Sky Catcher did the same.

"It must be a difficult story to tell," said Qumalix, "because it is a difficult story to hear. You don't know whether
Daes is good or bad. You don't know how to feel about her."

"There are many ways to tell this story," Kuy'aa said. The old woman licked her lips, and Yikaas saw that they were dry and cracked. He asked if anyone had a water bladder, and soon one was thrust into his hands. He gave it to her, waited as she drank, and then said, "So then, Aunt, why did you tell it this way?"

"It needed to be short," she said. "There are too many people in this ulax, and they distract one another from the telling. If I were to tell it only to you, I would also have let you know what Gheli was thinking and perhaps even how the baby felt. That way you would have other people to think about, and you wouldn't be so frustrated with Daes."

"You want her to be good," Qumalix broke in to say. "And gradually you realize that she's not as good as she should be."

"But she's not as bad as K'os," Yikaas said. "She does think about others. She was worried about her sister." He saw that Sky Catcher was trying to listen, and so asked with a gesture of his eyes for Qumalix to translate what he had said into First Men words.

Then Sky Catcher said, "Not worried enough to take her back to Gheli after that first day on the trail."

"Well," said Yikaas, "think about this. Daes turned out better than she could have. Look how selfish her mother, Gheli, is. She won't go back to the winter village because she thinks Ghaden might be there. She puts her own daughters' lives at risk . . ."

"Ha! That is foolish," said Sky Catcher. "Better to be a little cold in a fish camp tent than dead because someone remembers that you killed his mother."

Qumalix interrupted in a soft voice. "What about her name?" she asked. "What do you think of when I say the word *daes*?"

"It is a River word. What does it mean?" Sky Catcher asked.

"A shallow bit of water, not much good to anyone."

"The right name for her," said Yikaas.

"But what chance does it give her?" asked Sky Catcher. "The name itself is a curse, and it would always remind Gheli of what she did to that first Daes."

"If you remember the stories of the first Daes," Yikaas said, "you know that she was a selfish woman. Not wicked, but selfish. She left her daughter Aqamdax to run away with Cen. She married an old man she did not care about just because he would take her son Ghaden as his own. It really wasn't until she was dying, Red Leaf's knife slicing away her life, that she reached beyond herself and thought of someone else."

"Who?" asked Sky Catcher.

"Remember, she lay over Ghaden so he would not freeze to death."

"But Ghaden was just a little boy. Any mother would do the same."

Qumalix translated what Sky Catcher had said, then raised her hands to press them against the sides of her head. "You two need to learn each other's languages," she told Sky Catcher and Yikaas. "My head aches from carrying your words back and forth."

Sky Catcher laughed and thrust a hand toward the top of the ulax. He said something and started up the climbing log, but Qumalix shook her head at him. Yikaas realized he had been holding his breath, waiting for her answer, afraid she would do as Sky Catcher asked. Instead, she looked at Yikaas, lifted her mouth in a half-smile.

"He complains for lack of sleep," Qumalix said, but avoided Yikaas's eyes.

Sky Catcher said something else, yelled it down rudely from the top of the ulax before he went outside. Qumalix's face turned red, and to cover her embarrassment, Yikaas asked, "So, do you think the name *Daes* passed on that first Daes's selfishness?"

Qumalix shook her head. "How could anyone know?" she said.

Kuy'aa had settled down on her haunches, and Yikaas

squatted beside her, asked her the same question. She tipped her head to look at him and said, "Perhaps. Perhaps not. The important thing to remember is that she was selfish, and she lied without shame."

Yikaas noticed that the old woman was lifting her voice higher and higher to be heard above the arguments of those around them. Finally she began to laugh and said, "Yikaas, you are the loudest of us all. Tell them to be quiet. I think they need another story."

So Yikaas whistled and clapped his hands until the people in the ulax had stopped their arguing.

"My aunt is ready to continue her story," he told them, but Kuy'aa tugged at his hand, shook her head.

She placed her fingers against her throat and said, "You take a turn."

"I don't know Daes's story."

"They've heard enough about Daes. Tell them about K'os and Daughter. Talk to them about Ghaden. A storyteller has to realize that people don't want to think about someone like Daes for very long. We are often too much like her, not quite evil and not quite good. Tell us about K'os. She is so evil, we feel good about ourselves. Or tell us about Ghaden and Daughter. We want to be like them, so it is easy to fall into their story."

"But they want to know what Cries-loud tells Daes."

"You can't think of some way to put that in a story about K'os or Ghaden?"

Yikaas smiled at his aunt's wisdom and lifted his voice to begin.

Near the Four Rivers Village
6435 B.C.

K'OS'S STORY

K'os woke from her dream smiling. They were less than a day away from the Four Rivers village. The path was familiar now to her feet. Aa, she had been young when she lived here, wife to the boy River Ice Dancer. She laughed under her breath. He had cost her much, that one. The fool! Who could believe he would steal her brideprice from his father's caches? And worse, that his father would take K'os as slave after River Ice Dancer died?

She owed Cen for that death. Who else would have killed the boy but him, though she had never decided why he did it. Perhaps only so she would take the blame, and the Four Rivers People would drive her out of their village.

Cen was dead, but surely his spirit would know what she did to Ghaden, the son receiving the revenge she had intended for his father. And the people of the Four Rivers village, they, too, would know her vengeance. It would not take long. She had found a wonderful poison on her First Men's island, a plant that also grew here in the River People's country, but was not well known and was difficult to find.

The First Men placed it on the points of their whale harpoons, a secret K'os had learned while bedding a hunter. It had taken her some time to learn how to use the plant, dry it down to increase its strength. She had tried it on birds—baby gulls children kept as pets—watched in delight as the birds staggered and gasped and died within a day, the poison so strong that none of them escaped.

K'os always buried the birds after the poison had stopped their hearts. After all, what would a mother do with a dead bird her child brought her other than strip the feathers and add the flesh to her boiling bag? And who knew when someone might in generosity give you a bowl of that soup?

Age had changed K'os much, but she did not doubt that some of the Four Rivers People would recognize her. She would have to play the part of a First Men wife and play it well, satisfy them that they had been wrong in driving her away. How strange that with all the people she had killed, the one she did not—River Ice Dancer—had been responsible for her slavery. Gheli, Red Leaf, would be an enemy, but with Cries-loud sent ahead to warn his mother of Ghaden's arrival, they would probably not see the woman at all.

"We are close?" Uutuk asked.

"I have set traplines near this trail," K'os told her. "It is less than a day's walk to the village. You think it is better to travel like the First Men, with iqyan and paddles?"

Daughter rolled her eyes toward the sky. "Much better," she said.

"You will like the village. It is not as large as Chakliux's. At least it was not when I lived there, but the people are good and generous. I stayed for a time with an old man and woman. They are surely dead by now. But they were like a mother and father to me, even helped me celebrate my marriage with a give-away. It was a good time, but when my husband died, some of the people in the village thought that it was my fault. They made me leave, but I hold no anger against them."

K'os had never told Uutuk about River Ice Dancer's death, and the girl looked at her now through frightened eyes.

"They blamed you?"

"He was killed as he slept, most likely by a young hunter who had something against him, but I was a new wife and not of their village. It was easier to blame me than to think that one of them did it."

"How can you not be angry?"

"Think of this," K'os said. "If I had stayed, I would never have found you and your grandfather."

K'os cut her eyes away quickly when she saw the tears on Uutuk's cheeks. The path narrowed, and Uutuk dropped back to walk behind her. By the time they could walk side by side again, the girl's tears were gone, but K'os clicked her tongue in satisfaction when she saw the worry in Uutuk's eyes.

"You think they still blame you, Mother?" Uutuk asked.

"No, it happened too long ago, and to a young man who was not of their village. They will have forgotten, most of them. And those who remember will see that I could not have been guilty. If I had killed my husband, his spirit would have never allowed me to survive those days of wandering alone in the forest and tundra."

"Yes, Mother," Uutuk said, but though she smiled, her forehead was still creased with concern.

Good, K'os thought. Worry, Uutuk, and take none of them into your heart.

Ghaden began a traders' song as soon as he saw the smoke from the village hearths lying in a thin haze above the trees. Even before they came to the village, a hunter met them on the trail, he and two of his grown sons. Ghaden glanced at K'os, and she called out a greeting. "Blue Lance! We come to trade."

The man squinted at her for a moment, then Ghaden saw the dismissal in his face. He didn't recognize her, but she was only an old woman. Why worry? What harm could she do?

"Your song says that you're a trader," Blue Lance said, the words rising like a question.

"My wife's father, Seal, is the trader," Ghaden told him. "He's First Men and doesn't speak the River language, so I sang the song for him."

Ghaden did not intend to introduce K'os. What man would? But Blue Lance had begun to stare at her again, even as he told Ghaden that he was the village's chief hunter and introduced his sons, Moon Slayer and Bird Hand. Blue Lance said that soon the Four Rivers men would leave to follow caribou, but that the traders were welcome to stay until then.

"It will be good for the young men of the village to have something to think about besides hunting," he told Ghaden with laughter in his voice. "We have too many fights, too many loud words."

It was the same in every village, Ghaden thought. Older hunters had learned to keep their excitement within, spend their energy to make and repair weapons, then pray for the strength and purity to have a good hunt. The young men were like dogs too long tethered, barking and snapping at one another, at their wives and even their children. Yes, traders would be a good diversion.

"We accept your hospitality," Ghaden told him, "and thank you for it." Then, turning to Seal, he explained what Blue Lance had said.

Seal's dark face split into a grin. "Just like our young men, anxious to hunt."

Ghaden translated, and Blue Lance began to laugh, slapped a hand on Seal's shoulder, a good sign for any trader. Then Blue Lance lifted his chin toward K'os, asked, "She is wife? Mother?"

"Perhaps you remember her," Ghaden said. "A long time ago she lived in your village. She is here now as wife to Seal and mother of my wife." Ghaden glanced at Uutuk, huddled at the back of the group.

"Aaa! Too bad that one is already wife. You could get much in trade for her."

"She's a good wife," Ghaden said carefully, so not to give offense. "I don't want to trade her."

The chief hunter did not seem to hear what he said, and Ghaden realized that the man's eyes were again on K'os.

"Yes," he said softly. "I remember her. She is called K'os . . ." He grimaced. "Her husband was a boy from the Near River village. When he died, some people thought that she . . ." He paused.

Ghaden had discussed the problem with K'os the evening before and was ready with an answer. "K'os has told me that she thinks the people of this village did the right thing. How could they know who killed the man? But as you can see, she did not. Otherwise, surely his spirit would have taken revenge on her when she left the village. Instead it guided her to the First Men, where she became wife to Seal."

Blue Lance was a small man, short but powerful in his arms and shoulders. Unlike most River hunters he let his hair go free, without braid or ornament. A scar, wide and white, crossed the top of his nose, and at some time in his life he had had tattoos sewn into the skin on either side of the scar. He wore necklaces, many different kinds, but his parka was plain, though well made. His sons were much like him, but taller and not so quick to smile.

Blue Lance escorted Ghaden and Seal and their wives into the village. His sons, scowls on their faces, ran ahead to tell others that traders were coming. It was a small village, smaller than Ghaden had anticipated for all K'os's fine words about it, and he turned to see if there was surprise or disappointment on her face, but she was smiling, and he heard her say to Uutuk, "Little has changed since I was here. Aaa, but look! Three new lodges near the river!"

Ghaden followed her gaze to the lodges, saw by the growth of grasses and plants near them that they were not new at all, but had been in place for some time. But of course, K'os meant since she had lived in the village, and that had been what? Ten years ago? Even more.

Children crowded around them, shouting out questions, tumbling and arguing and jumping as all children do. Women asked for this thing and that, making offers even before goods were displayed. Then several grandmothers came, each carrying bowls of stew. They offered them to Seal and Ghaden and even to K'os and Uutuk.

Ghaden accepted the food gladly, ate where he stood, scooping the hot meat from the bowl into his mouth. The food warmed his belly, let him relax a little, but he had not forgotten the main reason for their stay, and as he ate, he peered over the rim of his bowl at the various women, tried to decide which one was his father's widow.

One of the grandmothers came close, peered into his face, and said, "He looks like that one who just died."

There was a sudden murmur of surprise, then agreement, and even Blue Lance drew close, squinted at him, and said, "Yes." Then in explanation he added, "That man was a trader also."

Ghaden lowered his bowl. How had they found out about

Cen's death? He pressed his lips together, licked at the grease that had coated them. "I'm his son, Ghaden," he said.

There were more murmurs of amazement, then one old grandmother spoke out. "He told us about you. He said that one day you would come to our village. I hope you can stay until your sister Daes returns. She had to go back to her mother's fish camp and tell her what had happened."

"My father's wife is still at fish camp?" Ghaden asked.

"Yes, but your other sister, the baby, is here in the village. Don't worry about Daes. She didn't go alone. Someone came from Chakliux's village to tell us, and he went with her. You must know him. Cries-loud."

"Cries-loud?" Ghaden said. "I thought he left to hunt, at least K'os . . ."

He realized that he was speaking his thoughts aloud and closed his mouth, flushed in embarrassment.

Then K'os stepped forward and said, "I'm only an old woman, but some of you will remember me."

Blue Lance held up a hand, gestured for her to be quiet. "Let me tell them," he said, and explained who she was and what had happened to her.

Some of the people turned away, making signs of protection against spirits, but several old women came forward, one to apologize for what had happened to K'os years ago, the others only to stare.

"We've come to share your mourning," K'os said.

Then there was a whispering in the crowd, a movement of women's hands, and Ghaden heard the cry of a baby. A young woman stepped forward and Blue Lance said, "This is Long Wolf's wife. The baby is your sister. They call her Duckling."

The woman thrust Duckling into Ghaden's arms so quickly that he did not have time to protest. The baby was heavy, round and fat, and he could not help but notice that she looked very much like Cries-loud, but how could that be? Cries-loud was not related in any way to Cen.

Duckling smiled at him, poked a baby finger at his face, and he was suddenly full of sorrow for a little girl who would never know her father. He swallowed hard to open his throat, then noticed that Uutuk had come to stand beside him.

"May I hold her?" she asked, and Ghaden, balancing the baby on the flats of his hands, was glad to give her up. Uutuk looked into the child's face, made a little song, and said, "She looks like her brother."

"Her brother?" Ghaden asked, still thinking of Cries-loud.

"Like you, her brother," said Uutuk, then Ghaden saw the shine of tears in his wife's eyes. "Perhaps someday she will have sons that you can teach," she said.

She handed the baby back to Long Wolf's wife. Duckling pressed her head into the woman's chest and began to squawk. The woman tucked her under her parka, and the baby was suddenly quiet.

"She was hungry," Long Wolf's wife said to no one in particular, as if they did not already know.

Then Blue Lance lifted his hands, and the people parted, allowed him and Ghaden to walk through. Ghaden turned to gesture toward Uutuk, but the crowd had already closed around her, and he saw that she and K'os and Seal were digging into packs to lay out trade goods. Perhaps not a wise idea when the people were still mourning Cen, but he would have to discuss it with them later.

Blue Lance's lodge was made in the same way as those in Chakliux's village, with a down-slanted entrance tunnel of sod to trap cold air, and several storage areas dug out at the sides of the tunnel. Inside, the caribou hide lodge cover tinted all things gold.

Two women were at the back of the lodge, and Blue Lance barked something to them, set them scurrying to bring water. Gratefully, Ghaden drank. Walking always made him thirsty, but when they offered food he realized that his stomach was unsettled and he did not really want to eat.

"I mourn," he said, to soften his refusal.

Then Blue Lance's face crumpled. He closed his eyes and sat very still for a long time.

Finally he said, "Your father was my hunting partner when he was not trading." He opened his eyes, but tented his fingers over his face. "We need to make a mourning," he said, "and we need to get his wife and daughter back into the village."

He suddenly jumped to his feet as though he were the one who must do all these things. He began to pace, and his wives looked at one another, worry evident in their eyes. They were sisters, without doubt, faces nearly identical.

"Do you think this man Cries-loud will also want to share the mourning?"

"He might. I wonder if I should go after them. It might comfort my sister to know I'm here."

Blue Lance shook his head. "There is no need to go," he said. "Surely Cries-loud will return with them in the next few days. But it might be best to tell Seal that we should wait to trade until after the mourning. What if your father's ghost comes to visit us and sees that instead of making a mourning for him, we celebrate his death with trading?"

Ghaden almost smiled. "I don't think he would be insulted," he said.

K'os watched the people, her eyes narrowed to slits. It was not difficult to tell that they had loved Cen. For some reason the thought made her angry, and once again she wished that she had been the one allowed to take his life, rather than the sea. But, she told herself, at least his spirit could not take revenge on her.

In spite of the chief hunter's request that Ghaden and his family stay with him in his lodge, Seal was pouting. Even now, as they joined the elders in that lodge, Seal spat out complaints about people who would make a man wait through a mourning to trade his goods. He told K'os to translate, but as they took their places near the hearth fire, she made up compliments rather than passing on his insults. When he realized what she was doing, he closed his lips and refused to speak at all.

Then she simply said, "My husband, too, mourns for Ghaden's father, and among the First Men, respect is shown by a man's silence."

Then the people stopped directing questions to him, whispered among themselves, and nodded, watching Seal from the corners of their eyes.

"What did you tell them?" Seal finally demanded.

"Only that you mourn as we all do," K'os said.

He grunted at her and she added, "You have earned their respect. Can you not see that?"

Then Seal lifted his head, began to hum a mourning song under his breath, and K'os saw him stiffen with pride each time he noticed one of the elders watching him.

K'os got up and, over the protests of the women, began to help serve the men. Few were eating, but she kept busy, arranged fish on mats, handed out water bladders. She even managed to slip away and bring in an armload of wood for the fire, and finally she was able to get one of the wives alone, to ask softly, "How long ago was the man Cries-loud here? When did he leave to find the dead one's wife?"

"Yesterday . . . no, the day before," the woman said.

"And how far to her fish camp?"

She shrugged her shoulders. "I've never been there," she said, "but I think her daughter Daes said three or four days' walking. But that would be with heavy loads, dogs, and a baby."

K'os nodded and gathered a handful of bladders. "Let me fill these," she said. "You know that I used to live in this village. You were only a girl then, but I think you remember me. In those days they called you Wing."

The woman looked at her with caution in her eyes, a carefulness that told K'os she was right in thinking the wife remembered her.

"I know where to fill these, the place on the river where the bank dips."

But Wing shook her head. "No," she said, "the river has changed. That part of the bank was swept away one year during spring breakup. Sit down with your husband. I'll send one of the children for water."

K'os sat down behind Seal, closed her eyes, and thought of Cries-loud. Surely his fear for Red Leaf's life would have made him walk quickly. Perhaps even by tomorrow he would reach her to warn that Ghaden was coming to the village. Then they would be on their way north or east, where no one could find them. K'os held a smile under her tongue. All the better, she thought. She didn't want Red Leaf in the village when the poison began to work. The woman knew too much about K'os's gifts and might figure out what was happening, blame it on K'os.

Cries-loud, be a good son to your mother, K'os thought, take her far from this village and don't bring her back until I've had my revenge. Then, if you wish, bring her. Since she so cunningly saved herself from my poison, I would like to see if she can save herself from Ghaden as well. If she can, then perhaps she would agree to work with me to seek her own revenge on Chakliux's village, on Sok, that husband who tried to kill her, on Chakliux, who did nothing to save her. Then K'os's thoughts were so sweet that it seemed as if her mouth were filled with the rich taste of new fat.

THIRTY-NINE

CRIES-LOUD'S STORY

Cries-loud tried to slow his steps, to give heed to his sister's begging.

"You walk too fast, Brother," she said, panting out the words. "Look, it's almost night. We need to make camp."

"How much farther?" he asked. He stopped and waited for her.

"A long way," she said, but she did not look up at him, and so he decided that she was lying.

He had known her only three days, but already he understood her quite well. She was strong for a woman, and could make a good campsite quickly, but she told untruths about the smallest things. At first he thought she did so only to protect herself. When she brought in a small armload of wood, she would say there were few branches on the ground, or when the meat burned she would babble about some spirit that had distracted her. He had heard many women do the same.

But other times, Daes would tell a story that he knew could not be true, some great feat she had done, saving Cen's life when he overturned his iqyax in the river, making medicine for the chief hunter whose cut arm healed in one day. They were foolish stories, but the strangest thing was that she seemed to believe them. At first he had been amused, but then when some of her stories were about people who had died, he began to fear their ghosts, and so he told her that his sorrow over her father's death had risen from his heart to plug his ears, and he could not hear her.

Then she was quiet, and when she finally rolled herself into her sleeping robes, Cries-loud made soft chants of protection, waved an amulet into the smoke of the fire, even burned a few pieces of dried caribou meat in hopes of protecting himself from whatever spirits she might have angered.

So now he had little doubt that she was lying again, that the camp was close. He was also tired, but it would be much better to get to his mother's fish camp this night, to talk out their plans before they slept, then in the morning be ready to go. He had little idea where he would take her, and he supposed that Daes would have to come with them. He also knew he would have to tell his mother that Cen was dead. He wondered if she had truly loved the man or had become his wife only to get his protection. Surely she could have chosen a better husband. Cen had been a good man, but Red Leaf must have lived in fear that he would find out she had killed that first Daes.

Why not take a husband who was only a hunter, who never left the Four Rivers village to trade, who owed no revenge for the death of a woman or for the stabbing of his son?

But then, Red Leaf had never been one to plan wisely.

"You lie," he said to Daes, and his words were hard, loud.

Daes took a step back, then another. "No," she said, and made tears come into her voice. "I do not lie. It's a long way yet, and I'm weary with my mourning. I need to stop and sleep and sing prayers for my father's spirit."

"Stop if you wish, but I'll go on as long as I have light enough to see."

She crouched down on the path, the pack on her back nearly as large as she was. He had told her to bring extra clothing and food, and unlike most men who traveled with women, he, too, had a pack. She had asked to bring a dog, but he did not want the worry of feeding it, keeping it quiet. He flicked his fingers at her in irritation and strode away.

He wished he had not brought her. If he had known that once they were little more than half a day from the village it would be only a matter of following a river until they came to the camp, he would have sent her back. But he had not known, had not even thought to ask, and she had not told him. He felt another spurt of anger flood his chest, and then he heard her coming behind him. Almost, he turned, almost, he told her to stay, that she should go back to the village alone. But those other times she had made the journey, she had at least had a dog to protect her. What if wolves got her? Did he want to add the loss of a daughter to his mother's sorrow? It was enough that she had lost her husband.

So he only quickened his pace, went on as though she did not follow, and he didn't even look back to see if she kept up with him.

That day, at midafternoon, the wind had turned cold, cutting down from the north, and when the sun tucked itself into the trees that stood dark at the horizon, snow began to fall. It was not a snow that would stay. It was mixed with rain, and even that which gathered on the north side of grass tussocks and at the base of willow brakes was soon eaten away, but it chilled Cries-loud to the bone, and he began to wonder if Daes had been telling the truth about the fish camp.

He saw that the river forked, so he stopped to look for high ground, a place where they could make camp. But Daes came up beside him and said, "Take the left fork. We're nearly there. It's only a short walk now."

He hunched his shoulders against the weight of his pack, heard his bones creak under the straps. He reminded himself that his sister carried a heavier load than he did. Then he began to walk again, head lowered against the wind.

* * *

Gheli pressed the milk from her breast, felt the relief from its aching fullness. The thin stream spurted out toward the fire. Each day she told herself that she must return to the village and reclaim her baby, but then in her mind she would see the child Ghaden, think of him as a man, grown and powerful, standing over her. But worse than that, she could see Cen beside him, screaming his fury when he realized that he had protected the woman who had killed Daes, that one he still called to from his dreams.

It was dark when she heard the voices. She retreated to her tent, but kept her head near the entrance, even stopped breathing to listen. Daes and at least one man. Cen? Her heart thudded in hope, and thoughts crowded her mind—reasons she would give to explain why she had stayed at the fish camp, had allowed Daes to take Duckling back to the village without her.

Her worry suddenly turned into anger. She hadn't allowed Daes to make that trip without her. Daes had taken the baby without permission, had left although Gheli had told her to stay.

As the voices came closer, Gheli realized that she was not hearing Cen. No, it was someone else, not even a voice that she recognized. She pulled the few weapons she had from their places against the tent wall, grabbed a handful of dried fish, and crept away in the darkness. What if Daes had brought Ghaden?

Gheli slipped into the thick brush of alder that stood behind the lean-to and waited there, still and quiet, until she saw Daes come into the clearing. The girl lifted her voice and called, looked behind at her companion and said something that Gheli could not hear. The young man strode into the camp, and as his face was lighted by her fire, Gheli's heart lurched against her ribs. Not Ghaden, Cries-loud! Her eyes suddenly burned with tears. He looked much like Sok, tall with a hawk-beak nose. But his face was square like hers, and he also had her eyes. Her son. Her son!

She took a deep breath and pushed through the brush back to the campsite.

"Daes!" she exclaimed and held her arms out as if she were glad to see this daughter who caused her so much trouble.

She slowly lifted her eyes to Cries-loud, made herself squint like she was trying to understand some riddle. Then, as though she had just recognized him, she said in a soft voice, "Cries-loud?"

He stood, staring at her, so that at first she thought she might be mistaken. She shook her head to clear her vision and walked up to him, looked into his face.

"My son," she said, without doubt.

He was a man, but he had not changed so much that she did not know him. Had he grown to hate her during all the years they had been apart? Had Sok and others in Chakliux's village told the story of what she had done so many times that Cries-loud had decided he no longer wanted to claim her as mother?

But then he opened his arms, and she stepped close, lay her head against his shoulder. He enclosed her in a tight embrace. She was crying, could not stop. She felt her son's chest convulse, and knew that he, too, wept.

"I thought you were dead, you and this sister," Cries-loud finally said.

Gheli pushed herself away, but held tightly to Cries-loud's wrist, as though he might suddenly disappear like some trickster spirit if she did not keep a hand on him. He smiled, a half-smile so much like Sok's that Gheli's throat thickened and she could scarcely breathe. She looked at her daughter, thinking to see that the girl shared her joy, but Daes's mouth was caught in a frown.

"You understand that he is your brother?" Gheli asked, and reached out toward her, but Daes backed away.

"I understand much," she said quietly. "He told me everything."

There was fear in Daes's eyes, and accusation. It was a bad time for her to be told all that Gheli had done, a time when Daes was not happy with herself, when she looked with longing eyes toward men who chose other women for wives. Gheli understood such pain, often remembered her first years of being a woman, when no man in the village seemed interested in her. Then Sok was there, and all things changed.

Her life had been filled with joy and light. It no longer mattered that her face was plain, that she walked with heavy steps on the earth, more like a man than a woman. She had worked with her needle and awl until her fingers bled, had learned to sew beautiful parkas, and had finally won Sok's heart. At least until Snow-in-her-hair threatened to take him from her.

I understand, Daughter, Gheli thought, but she also knew that Daes would reject her pity. So Gheli put a hard smile on her face and said, "Then you understand why I needed to wait at this fish camp. You know that your father plans to bring Ghaden back with him."

"And you would keep me and my sister here, to try to live through a winter in this place, without a good lodge, without enough food!"

Daes screamed the words, and Cries-loud lifted his hands to her shoulders to calm her. She pushed him away and stepped close to Gheli so that she was yelling into her mother's face. "You would let us die because of something you did. You deserve to die, not us!"

"Why do you think I didn't come after you?" Gheli asked.

"Because you were afraid Ghaden was already at the village!"

"I was getting ready to leave, to take us all to another village. I know of one only a few days' walk from here."

"You lie! You had no plan."

Gheli lifted her chin in defiance. "You think I fear only for my life?" she asked. "What if Cen in his anger decided not only to kill me, but to kill my daughter? Remember, you are full sister to Cries-loud, not Cen's daughter as I have always told you."

Gheli thought Cries-loud would have already told Daes this, but she could see by the surprise in her daughter's face that he had not, that Daes assumed Cries-loud was half-brother, that they shared only a mother.

"He would not," she breathed. "My father . . ." She paused. "Cen would never hurt me."

"I don't think he would," Gheli answered truthfully, "but the chance that his anger would carry him into doing something terrible kept me here. Your life is more precious to me than mine."

Then Daes's eyes filled, and she dropped to her haunches, crouched there hugging her knees. "I need to understand," she said softly. "My brother and I have walked a long way, and we are tired. After we eat, you can tell me why you did what you did. There is something also that we must tell you."

Gheli's heart jumped.

"Duckling?" she breathed.

"Duckling is fine and strong, living in Long Wolf's lodge, being fed by his wife."

"What then?"

Daes looked up at Cries-loud, covered her eyes. Gheli pressed a hand to her mouth, turned her back on her daughter and Cries-loud.

"Cen," Gheli said, and began to weep.

FORTY

K'OS'S STORY

The people of the Four Rivers village waited nine days for Gheli's return. Finally the shaman decided that the ceremonies would take place without her. Perhaps the mourning the First Men gave Cen was enough to start him toward the spirit world, but if it was not, by now he would have surely found his way back to this village, and it was not a good thing to allow a spirit to linger. Even the spirit of a good man might become envious of those who still lived with their children, slept with their wives, and ate well. Besides, the men had to leave soon for the caribou hunts. Perhaps they had already waited too long.

And so the mourning began, four days of drum songs and chants and prayers. At the end of that time, Ghaden came to K'os, told her that he wanted to take Uutuk back to Chakliux's village.

K'os was sitting beside the hearth fire in the chief hunter's lodge. She sat idly, with nothing in her hands, no basket, no sewing. She smiled at him, but Ghaden did not return her smile. His stance, with shoulders thrown back, chin lifted, reminded her of those days when he was only a small child and she had owned his sister Aqamdax.

K'os was not surprised that he wanted to leave. She had watched him during the mourning, saw the depth of his sorrow. The Four Rivers village would always remind him of Cen's death. But K'os knew how to use questions to get her own way.

"You would leave us?" she asked, and kept her voice as thin and quiet as a child's. "Now that the mourning is ended, my husband has begun trading. How can he do that without your help? You know he doesn't speak the River language. How will we live through the winter if he cannot get meat through trade? You know he's never hunted caribou."

"You're good with words, K'os," Ghaden said, one eyebrow raised as though he were amused by what she said. "I'll stay a few days to help Seal with his trading, to translate for him, but after that, I and my wife will leave. That way, I may get back in time to join Chakliux in his caribou hunt. Then, if you and Seal choose to stay in this village, I will bring half the meat to you."

K'os's anger made her voice shrill. "If we choose to stay in this village?" she said. "What choice do we have? You know I can't go to Chakliux's village. At best he would make me spend the winter by myself in the forest. At worst, he will kill me. You think Uutuk will stay with a man who cares so little about her family?"

"You're safe here," Ghaden said. "The people won't let you starve. In the spring, my wife and I will come back and share your fish camp before you and your husband return to the First Men's islands. If Seal wants to stay another year and visit other River villages in the summer, I will go with him to speak for him."

K'os's thoughts tangled together, and she could not decide what to say. Ghaden was right. The Four Rivers People would not let them starve, and if Ghaden brought meat, how could she and Seal protest that he was not taking care of them? She lifted a hand to rub her forehead as if trying to push her thoughts into straight lines. The older she got, the more slowly ideas came to her, as though her mind, like her hands, had become stiff and misshapen. She was an old woman, and her helplessness made her angry.

She grasped for an idea that teased from the edges of her thoughts. Finally it came to her, whole and shining. "Didn't you say that you wanted to wait for Gheli? You told me that you planned to promise her your help now that she must raise your sisters alone."

The words caught him. K'os knew he had spent much time in Long Wolf's lodge with his baby sister. He would be a good father to Uutuk's children, and she had been surprised to find herself glad for that. Now, even though Uutuk had a husband, K'os seldom thought about grandchildren, but babies grew into useful children, and more useful adults. Someday her grandchildren might have to take care of her, and she would be glad they had a father who taught them to live respectful lives.

"You're right," Ghaden said. "I want to find Gheli, but I can't wait too long. I need to get back to Chakliux's village in time to take Uutuk on a caribou hunt."

"Go with the Four Rivers People," said K'os.

He shook his head. "I'd get a smaller share here, and I need enough to feed all of us, perhaps even Gheli and Daes."

K'os knew he was right. He needed to hunt with Chakliux. It would be an easier winter for her if Ghaden brought a good share of caribou meat. Of course, with her medicines, she could get herself and even Seal through the year. People were always willing to make trades for something that eased pain or healed sickness.

"Then let me help my husband with the trading," she said. "You need to find Gheli. Then you will feel free to go to Chakliux's village and see if he will include you in his hunt."

She stood and pretended to have a stiffness in her knees, reached out as if to balance herself, placing a hand on his back. She knew where to put pressure to make him wince. Red Leaf's knife wound still held pain within the scar. She pressed and he flinched.

She put a look of concern on her face, then hissed, drew in breath over her teeth. "The wound from the knife?" she asked.

"Yes," he said, his voice tight. "As you well know, K'os."

She dropped her hand and caught at his sleeve. "What do you remember about that time?" she asked. "I've always wondered."

She did not think he would answer her, but her purpose was to bring into his mind a remembrance of Red Leaf's attack, however dim that memory might be.

To her surprise, he turned and looked into her eyes, said, "I remember everything, and I remember it well. My mother lying over me, the pain of the wound, the caribou hoof rattlers on the killer's boots."

"Do you remember the woman Red Leaf?" K'os asked, and glanced away as Ghaden made the sign for protection at the mention of her name.

"I remember her," he said. He flexed his shoulder, and he seemed to be looking at something far beyond the lodge walls. He left without saying anything else. A puff of cold air blew in from the entrance tunnel when he closed the inner doorflap.

"Good," K'os said to herself, holding the word under her tongue. "Remember well, Ghaden. Remember well."

Later in the day, Uutuk came to K'os, her eyes full of tears. "My husband is leaving the village with one of the chief hunter's sons. They go to tell Cen's wife of her husband's death. They also go to look for Cries-loud. Ghaden is worried that something has happened to him."

K'os spoke in a soft voice, as though she were trying to comfort her daughter. "Why do I see tears?" she asked.

Uutuk sank to her knees, covered her face with her hands, and began to sob.

"Cries-loud went and has not returned. What if the same thing happens to my husband?"

"I have known both men since they were children," K'os

told her. "Ghaden is strong and wise, but Cries-loud is full of complaining. Even the smallest task is large for him. Ghaden will be safe. Cries-loud is probably safe as well. Most likely he just stayed with Gheli to help her through the mourning. Remember what Ghaden said about his sister Yaa? She has not given Cries-loud any children. Perhaps he likes Gheli's daughter and wants to spend time with her, even ask for her as second wife. He could probably get her without much of a brideprice now that her father is dead."

As she spoke, K'os pretended to be busy with the needle and caribou hide she had in her hands, but she glanced often at Uutuk, and when the girl stopped crying, K'os said, "If I were you, I wouldn't want to go with him. Any husband who takes a wife on a journey like this only wants someone to carry their packs and prepare their food."

The next morning, K'os and Uutuk walked with Ghaden and the chief's son, Bird Hand, to the edge of the village. They watched until the brush that lined the trail hid the men from their sight, then they went back to Seal, helped him with the trading. But as the people came, K'os planned, and by the end of the day, she had chosen the man who would first taste her poison.

His name was Ptarmigan, and he was old, with a cough that wheezed from his lungs at nearly every breath. K'os had already overheard two women in the village complain about providing him food.

"Why waste what we have?" one had said. "He cannot even fish anymore. His coughing scares everything away. Surely he will die this next winter, and all the meat he has eaten this past year might as well be thrown into the river."

"He's not even wise or able to tell good stories," the other had said. "If he could do that, he'd be worth his food."

"The chief hunter should have given him to the wind last winter. There are too many soft hearts in this village."

K'os had smiled at their words. Two women who thought as she did, and a man no one would miss.

When Seal decided to take a nap in the afternoon, a rest from trading, K'os brought him water and food, and when he lay down, she rubbed his head until he was snoring. Then she took out her otter skin medicine bag and found the red sack, full of the good whale hunters' poison that seldom purged the bowel or the belly, but stopped the breathing, slowed the heart. She dipped a long stick into the sack and pushed out enough powder to fill a small wooden cup. She poured the contents of the cup into a full water bladder, then strapped the bladder under her parka with her medicine bag.

Ptarmigan lived with a daughter, but she was a woman of busy mouth and meddling eyes, her nose stuck into other people's lodges most of the day. K'os did not have to wait long until she saw the woman leave Ptarmigan's lodge. K'os walked easily, rubbing her eyes, as though she were outside only to escape the smoke of the lodge fire. She circled the village, her eyes always on Ptarmigan's lodge. Twice she walked past it, but the third time she reached up and scratched against the lodge cover. When no one answered, she went inside.

She clasped the medicine bag in her hand, had ground fireweed ready for tea in case someone other than Ptarmigan was inside, but she was lucky. The old man sat alone, rocking and coughing, his back to the door, his hands stretched out to catch the warmth that came from the hearth coals.

He did not hear her until she was nearly upon him, though she called his name as she entered. When he saw her, he jumped, then laughed at his foolishness, but the laughing made him cough, and soon he was gagging in his need for breath. K'os knelt beside him, turned him so his back was to the fire and the smoke would not enter his mouth and nose so easily.

When he stopped coughing, she took a bladder from a lodge pole, held it as he drank so he would not spill the water with the shaking of his hands.

"I am K'os," she said.

He nodded, and when he was able to speak, he said, "I remember you and your young husband."

He laid a hand against his neck, and K'os knew he was also remembering the knife wound that had killed River Ice Dancer.

"I did not kill him," she said.

"You would have been a fool to kill him," said Ptarmigan, then began another bout of coughing.

She rubbed his back until she felt him relax. The coughing stopped.

"Your daughter asked that I bring you medicine," she told him, and hid a smile at the surprise, then joy that filled his eyes.

"My daughter?"

K'os held up one hand to stop him from speaking. "Yes," she said, and pulled out her water bladder. "I need a cup."

He pointed to a jumble of bowls and stirring sticks not far from the hearth. She shook the bladder, chose a bowl, and filled it. He took it from her hands with pathetic eagerness, but she did not relinquish her hold. He would spill it before he got it to his lips.

"It will make you tired," she said, "so drink and then I will help you to your bed."

He turned his head toward a pile of sleeping mats that lay unfolded on the floor. He opened his mouth to say something, but K'os put a finger against his lips and pressed the cup to his teeth. He drank.

"More?" he asked when he finished, though by his face she thought the drink must be bitter.

"Perhaps tomorrow I will bring you more," she said. "First we need to see if it helps you."

She hauled him to his feet, and he leaned on her as they shuffled to his bed. He sat on the sleeping mats and coughed for a long time, but finally he was quiet. K'os helped him lay down, then she pulled a cover over him. He closed his eyes. Then she backed away, taking in the lodge, where she had sat, where she had walked, to be sure she had left nothing behind. Though she wanted to watch, to see if she had given him enough poison to bring on death, she crawled into the entrance tunnel. She opened the outer doorflap and peeked outside, waited until no one was passing, then slipped away.

She walked to a nearby thicket and cut some willow, though the thin autumn bark was not much good for anything. Seal was still asleep when she got to the chief hunter's lodge, the bouquet of yellow-gray branches in her right hand, the bladder of poison in the left. She hid the bladder under a pile of her belongings, then went outside to sit in the chill autumn sun. She pulled her parka hood snug and chopped up the useless willow, made a show of saving it in small sealskin packets. Those who passed watched and smiled, and K'os saw the satisfaction in their faces. It was always good to have someone in the village who understood plant medicine.

FORTY-ONE

GHELI'S STORY

Gheli made a long mourning, eight days in all, twice as many as she needed, though as wife, her private mourning would last at least another moon. She could not ask for longer. One of them—she or Daes—would have to get a husband, both of them if possible. She did not want Cries-loud to worry about them. He needed to return to his wife.

Of course, Gheli's tears were not only for Cen but also for Duckling, whom Daes had so foolishly taken back to the village, thinking that Gheli would follow. Now Daes understood why Gheli could not follow, and somehow that understanding had softened the girl's anger.

You should have explained everything long ago, Gheli told herself. Daes knew you were hiding something. Why do you think she learned to be such a good liar, even about small, foolish things?

Gheli sighed and helped Daes tie the knots on another caribou hide pack. Because they had no dogs, Cries-loud was making a long, narrow travois that she and Daes could take turns pulling. Cen had once told her that the next village was a twelve-day walk from the Four Rivers village. She did not know anyone except Cen who had been there, but he said they were a good people, generous and full of laughter. They lived so far from other villages that they did not raise their young men to fight, only to hunt. It would be a good place to live, and according to what Cen had told her, she could get there by following rivers.

Each night during her mourning, she promised herself that the next day she would ask Cries-loud to return to the village and tell the people that she and Daes were dead, killed by wolves. She would give him some of their clothing, shredded and bloodied. But what were the chances that she would ever see him again once he left her?

She had not realized how much she had missed him. In many ways he reminded her of Sok, and also a little of her father, dead now so many years, but he was quieter than either of them, given to sitting without speaking, some bit of wood in his hands that he would whittle away into nothing.

He seldom talked about Yaa. Who could have guessed that Yaa—so good with children even when she was a child herself—would be unable to have babies of her own? As a girl, Yaa had been forced to grow up much too fast, working hard for her mother's sister-wife, a woman who lived with anger wrapped around her tongue. At least Yaa had gotten herself a good husband, but Gheli wondered if she was wise enough to keep him. When Cries-loud did speak of her, it was with sadness, as if he were never able to please her.

Gheli knotted another braid of babiche. Other than fish, they had little to take with them. She wished she could sneak back into the Four Rivers village and get what she needed from their cache and lodge.

She was kneeling outside the lean-to when she realized that her son was standing behind her. He squatted down beside her, knees apart, leaned forward to look into her face.

"I've been thinking about something," he said. "You know if I don't soon return to the Four Rivers village, Ghaden may come looking for me. Today is a good day to travel."

Gheli felt her heart drop within her chest, and she blurted out, "Perhaps some summer before I die, you will visit this new village. Your sister will have a husband by then, and their children will need to know their uncle. Perhaps even Duckling would be willing to come with you. She would be old enough to help you by then. Maybe cook your food and carry your packs."

She saw the pity in his eyes, the sadness there. He smiled at her. "Yes, watch for me. One summer I will come, and perhaps I will bring Duckling."

Her tears surprised her. Long ago she had left this son, thinking she would never see him again. Once Cen had spoken about him, telling a story of a good hunt he and Cries-loud and Ghaden had made when Cen was at their village. After the story, Gheli had left the lodge, making the excuse that she needed to bring in wood, but she had needed only to hide her tears. At least she had found out Cries-loud had survived to become a man. Now she would lose him again, and since she knew the depth of that sorrow, the loss would be all the harder the second time.

Her throat closed, and she could not talk, but Cries-loud seemed to understand. He reached to clasp her hand and said, "I think we should tell the people that you are dead. We can ask Daes if she wants to go back or if she would rather go on with you to this new village."

Gheli nodded and finally found her voice. "You can say it was a wolf kill. We can shred some of our clothing. The women of the village will recognize my work and know that you carry one of my parkas."

He stood, and she said, "I will get you food." Then her voice broke.

"Mother, why do you cry?" he asked. He lifted her to her feet and used a fingertip to wipe her tears. "How long does it take a man to go to the Four Rivers village? Two days, that's all. I'll be there a day and then come back. Five days, and I'll return."

"You will . . ."

He laughed at her surprise. "You think I'd let you go alone to this other village? Yaa can wait for me a little

longer, and my father will share his caribou meat. I'll ask
Ghaden to tell them that I have decided to hunt by myself
and will return before winter. Go get Daes and ask her what
she wants to do."

"She'll go with me," Gheli said.

"She's a woman grown. She will do what she wants to do."

"I'll go with her," said Daes, and Gheli looked back to see
that the girl stood behind them. "But what about my baby
sister?"

"You can't take her," Cries-loud said. "How could I convince the people that you're dead if I take your daughter
when I leave to mourn?"

"Let Long Wolf's wife keep her," Gheli said. "She's a
good mother to her boys. She needs a daughter to help her
do all the work sons make for a woman."

Her words were firm, but her eyes burned with tears. Forever, she was giving up children, all for the sake of a husband who had long ago thrown her away. What a fool she
had been when she was a young woman, killing to get what
she wanted. She had lost almost everything. And what hope
would she have as an old woman with the spirit world close?
Surely, Tsaani and that first Daes were waiting for her, and
River Ice Dancer, also. Someday even Sok and Ghaden and
K'os would be in that world of the dead, and all of them
would want revenge. Even Cen.

She sighed, hoping to lift her heart back into its place.
What good would it do to fret about the dead? she asked herself. She could not change what she had done. She would
live as best she could and try to find joy in small things.
What other choice did she have?

GHADEN'S STORY

Ghaden stopped and lifted the straps of his pack to flex his
shoulders. He had walked hard for two and a half days, following Bird Hand. The man seemed to know where he was
going, but twice they had backtracked. Finally they were at
the place where the river divided.

Bird Hand motioned toward the left branch, then turned and started back toward the Four Rivers village. Ghaden watched in disbelief, his mouth open in surprise.

"Your sister Daes hates me," Bird Hand called over his shoulder, simply those words, nothing more, as if that would explain everything. "You're almost there. Maybe a half-day. Maybe a day." Then he was gone, swallowed by the willow that grew dense near the river.

Ghaden considered running after him, then in his mind he saw Yaa's face. What would he tell his sister? That he had grown weary of walking and decided to quit searching for her husband?

He trudged on, picking his way through the brush along the overgrown animal trail, cursing Bird Hand and Cries-loud and all the small branches that caught at his pack and his parka. His feet ached, and his back, and finally he promised himself that when he came to the next clearing, any bit of high ground, he would camp for the night.

The willow thinned into tattered birch, and the tussocks of grass crowded into a mat that made his walking a little easier. The river split around a small swampy island, and just past that, he could make out a wide, flat clearing. He unbuckled the chest strap on his pack, swung it off his back and up over one shoulder. A man never knew. Animals might come to such a clearing, to drink from the river. Ghaden needed to be ready to drop his pack and pull out a knife or lance.

He smelled smoke, stopped to be sure. Listened for a moment and heard voices. Cries-loud!

Ghaden called out a greeting, laughing as he strode into the clearing. Cries-loud was there, just hefting a pack to his back, as though he were about to leave.

"Brother!" Ghaden called.

But Cries-loud gave no welcome, merely set his pack on the ground and stood where he was. Then Ghaden saw the women with him. One was young, no doubt his sister Daes.

He had pictured her differently, as someone small and lovely, but she was a big woman, wide of shoulder and hip, with a hard face. She scowled at him, and for a moment he was puzzled. She looked familiar, as if he had seen her before. He glanced at Cries-loud. They were so much alike that they could be brother and sister, with eyes and mouths and noses nearly the same.

An older woman, without doubt his father's wife, crowded behind Cries-loud, as if she were trying to hide.

Standing awkwardly, waiting for Cries-loud to speak, Ghaden finally said, "You're leaving?"

Cries-loud looked down at his pack as though he were surprised to see it sitting beside him, then he forced a smile and gestured toward the girl with an open palm.

"Your sister Daes," he said to Ghaden. "I'm sure your father told you about her."

"Yes," Ghaden answered. Her eyes were red, and he knew that she had been crying. "You share my mourning," he said to her.

She raised a hand to cover her face as if she did not want to see him.

"I brought gifts for you and for your mother," he said.

The woman behind Cries-loud lifted her head, and for the first time Ghaden saw her face. The air slammed out of his lungs as though someone had set a fist into his gut. He gasped and reached for his knife.

"My father took this woman as his wife?" he shouted. The words felt as though they ripped through the flesh of his throat, and bled the strength from his body. "And this daughter, is that the baby Red Leaf took with her? Sok's daughter?"

"She is," Cries-loud said softly. "And so, my sister."

"But how could my father . . ." Ghaden's voice cracked. "How could he name her for my mother?"

"He didn't know," Cries-loud said. He spoke slowly, as if he were talking to someone very young or very old. "My mother changed her name when she came to the Four Rivers village. How would a trader remember one woman from all the villages he had visited? He didn't know she was Red

Leaf, the one who had killed Daes. Only K'os knew, and she didn't tell me until after your father died."

"K'os knew." Ghaden's words were bitter.

"For a short time, K'os lived in the Four Rivers village. That was after Chakliux threw her out of our caribou camp. You remember."

"Yes, I remember."

"That was when she tried to kill me," Red Leaf said.

Her voice surprised Ghaden. It was soft, and she spoke in fear, trembling. Then her words rushed out as though she had been saving them for Ghaden during all the years she had lived with Cen. "K'os tried to poison me. She wanted Cen for herself, and he would not take her as wife, even as second wife. She said that if I didn't agree to swallow her poison, she would tell Cen the truth. Then he would kill me and my little daughter as well."

"My father was not that kind of man," Ghaden said. "K'os knew that. I do not say that he would have spared you, but he would never kill a child."

His words seemed to give Red Leaf courage, and she stepped out from behind Cries-loud. "And are you like your father?" she asked. "You owe revenge for your mother's death, but will your revenge include my daughters?"

Cries-loud took his own knife from the sheath at his neck. Daes sank to her knees and began a loud mourning cry.

"Your daughters are safe," Ghaden said, shouting to be heard above Daes's song. He pointed at Daes with the tip of his blade. "This one carries my mother's name, and thus some part of her spirit. How could I kill her? The baby is my sister by blood. I would not insult my father by harming her."

"If you kill my mother," Cries-loud said, "what stops me from seeking revenge for her death? Then what about Yaa? If you die, will she seek revenge on me, her own husband? If I die, will she seek revenge on you?

"Remember this, for what she did to my mother, I owe K'os revenge." He met Ghaden's eyes. "Perhaps for the sake of your wife, you will decide to leave things as they are. No killing.

"Put away the knife and we will leave now—my mother, Daes, and I. I'll take them to another village, and you can tell K'os that they're dead, killed by wolves.

"When I return from taking them to that new village, I will say the same thing. Agreed?"

"Not for the sake of Red Leaf," Ghaden said. He paused, then added in a soft voice, "but I would for Uutuk. And for my sisters Daes and Duckling and Yaa."

He set down his pack, then, matching Cries-loud move for move, he slipped his knife into its sheath.

FORTY-TWO

Herendeen Bay, Alaska Peninsula
602 B.C.

Yikaas often spoke with his eyes closed, but this time he watched the people, and he noticed they were shifting and sighing, moving to stretch arms or legs.

The storytelling had lasted long enough. It was time to do other things. He ended his story and waited for Qumalix to make the final translation.

There was a murmur from the people, a polite thanking in soft, tired words. Yikaas lingered as everyone left, men first, then the women with their children. He helped Kuy'aa to her feet. She looped an arm through his, and he walked her to the sleeping place she had claimed as her own.

"An old woman cannot tell as many stories as she used to without wearing out her tongue," she said, and wrinkled her nose as though she were a child who did not like what she was tasting.

"And some storytellers are lucky," he told her. "They never, ever get old, no matter how many years they live."

She laughed at that and batted his arm as though he had told a joke, then he pulled aside the grass curtain and helped her into her bed, unrolled a furred sealskin over her. She closed her eyes and within only a short time was breathing like one asleep. He allowed the curtain to fall, then heard her say, "Be ready for tomorrow night. I want you to tell the story of Cen."

"I'll be ready, Aunt," he said, and turned to find Qumalix waiting for him.

"She's asleep?" Qumalix asked.

"Almost."

"Are you very tired?"

"I could sleep."

"Do you have time to talk for a little while? There's something I want to ask you."

"Ask," he said.

She shook her head and gestured toward the climbing log. "Outside, where we can see the sky."

"It's raining."

"No."

He followed her outside and was surprised to see that she was right. The rain had stopped, and stars had begun to find their way through the clouds. She squatted at the top of the ulax, and he did the same, trying to sit in the manner of the First Men so he did not get his rump wet, but even though he rested his haunches on the backs of his heels, he felt the damp cold of the sod roof seep through his caribou hide leggings.

"Ask," he said again.

His tiredness made him feel irritated. The First Men did not know a lot about comfort, he thought, and he wondered how they could crouch on their heels for so long. His ankles already ached.

Qumalix did not look at him as she spoke, but sent her words out over the village, speaking so softly that he had to lean toward her to hear.

"Sky Catcher says you have a wife back at your own village. A River woman. He also says that you've asked for those two sisters . . ."

"No!" he said, so loudly that he felt her jump. He placed a hand on her arm and repeated, "No, I have no wife, and I don't want those sisters." He thought she might say something else, but she did not. Finally he added, "Sometimes men are foolish. We take what we don't want because we think we can't have what we do want."

She was very still then, and when she spoke it was in a whisper. "A man like that might be difficult to have as husband."

Her words made him ashamed, and then angry. "A man like that would be a good husband. He's already made his mistakes."

She stood up and he stood also, staggering a little as his calves cramped.

"How do you sit like that?" he asked.

She laughed but had no answer. Instead she said, "So what has happened to Cen while Ghaden and Cries-loud have been solving their problems?"

"You don't know?"

"Everyone tells the story a little differently. I'd like to hear your way. Will you tell more stories tomorrow?"

"So Kuy'aa says."

"About Cen?"

"If you want."

"I want," she said.

Then she went down into the ulax, but Yikaas stayed for a time on the roof. He knelt on the wet sod and looked up at the clearing sky. He wondered what exactly she had meant in speaking about husbands and the taking of wives. Aaa! Some man would have his hands full when he married that woman. Yikaas laughed and tried to picture Sky Catcher and Qumalix as mates, Qumalix's voice raised high and shrill as she yelled at him for one thing or another. But for some reason as he thought of that, he became angry, and so instead he began to whisper his story of Cen to the stars, a good way to practice what he would say when all the village had gathered to listen.

As he spoke it seemed that the stars grew larger, came closer, as though they, too, wanted to hear the story. The familiar words made him bold. He tipped his face toward the sky and raised his voice. He did not see Qumalix as she squatted at the top of the climbing log, her chin cupped in one hand, her eyes also lifted to the stars as she listened to Cen's story.

The Bering Sea
6435 B.C.

CEN'S STORY

Each day the swelling around Cen's eyes lessened, and he was able to see a little more. Finally, even the roaring in his ears began to dim, so he could hear himself shout, and once thought he heard gulls crying.

At first he had been afraid. Each wave that rocked his boat, each swell that lifted it, brought his breath in gasps from his throat, and lifted his belly in nausea. What else did he have that the sea could want? His iqyax, his sax, his water bladders? His rotting fish? Perhaps it coveted those lashings that had once held paddles and harpoons. There was still a small bundle of trade goods in the bow, sodden and battling for space with his legs. If the sea wanted those things, he would gladly give all. If it chose to pluck him from the iqyax, he only asked that it be quick about it, play no games. He had heard too many storytellers speak of hunters who lived for days in the cold depths without wind to breathe or sax to warm.

His prayer had become the prayer of an old man:

"Let it come quickly. Let it come quickly."

But as his vision returned, so did his courage. His right eye saw light, then shapes. He had heard elders speak of seeing in such a way, as though somehow fog had dimmed their sight. And to Cen, it seemed that even the sun had aged, cauled white like an old man's eye. But each day his vision became clearer, and finally even his left eye began to see, though through a thin haze of brown-red light, some-thing that gathered and flowed like a strange sea within the eye itself.

His eyeballs ached; pain pierced from brow to neck. But what was pain when each day brought him closer to seeing? He tried not to think that each day also meant he had less water, less food.

He could paddle for only a short time before he had to stop in his desperate need to breathe. His strokes were weak, his cedar branch paddle cumbersome. His helplessness made him angry.

Sometimes he sang death songs to honor his life, but he sang them defiantly like a warrior who prepares himself for battle. Most days, the sea remained calm, so Cen had no one to fight except himself. And how does a man battle such an enemy? Does he raise his knife against his own flesh?

He often brought Gheli into his thoughts, their daughters, and his son Ghaden. Then he would remind himself that he was a trader, and who more than a trader better knew the sea? It was not some bowl of water that sloshed side to side within its basin, but rather rivers and lakes all thrown together, currents acting and reacting. Surely, in his paddling he would find a sea-river that led him to land, a current that pulled him to a shore where he could find fresh water.

At first he had counted the days, but as he used up his water, he stopped keeping track. There was too much discouragement in knowing that soon he would have nothing to drink. Where was the rain? He had never seen the sky go so long without weeping. Did it rejoice with dry eyes over his agony?

The evening he used the last of his water, he fell into a light sleep. He dreamed of a feast, and of his wife holding a water bladder where he couldn't quite reach it. He became angry. Why didn't she come closer?

Then the iqyax lurched, and he was awake. He saw that it was night, the stars hidden by a cover of clouds. At first he did not know what had taken him from his dreams, but then he felt it again, a sudden movement as if someone were pushing his iqyax from behind, shoving it through the water.

He dipped a hand into the sea, even stopped his breathing, so he would feel nothing but the water. Yes, it was a current, running in a direction different than he had been traveling. Was the current running toward land, or should he paddle his way out of it? Had his iqyax turned while he was asleep? He needed the stars!

Best to stay with the current, he decided. He would have more difficulty finding it again than getting away from it. He sat awake through the night, impatient for the darkness to pass.

Dawn light came gray, with fog and clouds so heavy he could not see beyond the bow of his iqyax. He groaned in frustration, shouted curses with raw throat and angry words.

In spite of his disrespect, by midday the clouds had begun to lift. Then he noticed that his left eye was much clearer than it had been, the brown-red now covering only half his vision, as though someone had drawn a curtain back from the inside corner of the eye.

In all directions he saw nothing except the sea, but by the placement of the sun he could tell that the current flowed toward the northeast. Though his throat was parched for need of water, his tongue swollen so that he could not even sing, hope slaked his thirst.

By night he thought he saw a darkness in the east, something more than the line of the horizon dividing the sea from the sky. He slept fitfully, waking often in his need for morning. At daybreak, clouds again lay over the sea, but the sun had pushed in close to the earth, and its warmth burned off the haze until Cen was able to see clear sky, as warm as midsummer, blue from horizon to horizon.

He squinted, shielded his eyes, and watched until he knew that he was seeing land. When he shouted out his joy, he broke open the dry skin of his throat, tasted his own blood.

The sea-river he had come upon was lazy, and all that day he paddled beyond his strength. By night, the only way he could tell the land was any closer was by the shallow cuts he had made on the side of his thumb as he held it up to measure the height of that bit of land against the far edge of the sky.

He continued to paddle, even in the night, but the effort made him light-headed. Finally, he decided that he would have to eat, even if just a little. He still had a few dried fish, but they were softened by the sea and beginning to stink. He choked one down, its soft flesh slimy and rank. It made his stomach ache, but his head felt better. He started to paddle again, and his belly began to churn.

He fastened his paddle to the deck and lay back against the coaming, but his stomach only grew worse, until finally he vomited up all that he had eaten, gagging and choking until he was bringing up yellow bile. When the spasms finally stopped, he slid down as far as he could in his iqyax and lay very still. The water rocked him, and he was able to sleep.

It was still night when he awoke, the sky darkest in the east, the water black. Once again, he had dreamed of being caught in the wave. It had slammed him against the iqyax coaming, shattered his ribs, ripped open his stomach. The dream was so real that Cen had to shake it out of his head, but the pain in his belly did not subside. Instead, the spasms moved into his bowels.

He moaned. The fish had poisoned him. He unlashed his waterproof dripskirt and jerked his sax and chigdax up around his waist so that he was naked from hips to boots. He untied one of the empty water bladders, cut off the top, and raised himself up to crouch on his haunches. He opened the bladder and set it under his rump, then allowed the release from his bowels. The pain clenched him from waist to anus, twisted, pulled, as if dogs fought over the poor scraps of his gut. Well into morning his body continued to empty itself, until he felt hollow except for the air he breathed. But the pain had become a bearable ache.

When he was sure the spasms had stopped, he cleaned himself with sea water, threw out the bladder, and readjusted his clothing. His thirst was no longer something only of his mouth or throat. It had spread even to the ends of his fingers, the edges of his feet, so that he felt thin and brittle, as if a touch would crumble him. But finally he was able to sleep, and his dreams were of freshwater lakes, clear foaming streams.

FORTY-THREE

Cen woke to rain, steady and cold. He opened his mouth to the sky, let the water wet his tongue, fill his throat. Then he took off his chigdax, knotted the sleeves at the wrists, and held them open to catch the rain. The sleeves were nearly a quarter full before the rain turned into the spit of drizzle. He clenched one of the sleeves above the tie, undid the knot, and folded the wristband into the narrow neck of his water bladder. He lifted the chigdax, and the water flowed into the bladder. Then he did the same with the other sleeve.

He stoppered the bladder, then wrung the water from his hair into the palms of his hands, drank what he managed to claim, sucked the wet from the feathers of his sax. He scooped a handful of water from the bottom of the boat and drank it. But it tasted of salt, spoiled fish, and his own waste. Afraid it would make him sick again, he bailed it from the iqyax.

He was still weak from the vomiting and diarrhea, but his cleverness at catching the rain made him happy with himself. His sax was wet, the wind cold, so that his shivering became trembling. Suddenly he was afraid again. Cold could kill him more quickly than thirst. He slipped the chigdax on over the sax, felt some relief as it cut the wind and allowed the poor heat of his body to warm the sax, wet as it was. He pulled his arms in from the sleeves and crossed them over his chest, wincing at the pain in his ribs. He looked up at the sky, hoping to see a break in the clouds, and sent up a song asking for heat from the sun.

The rain had moved north, the edge of the clouds revealing clear skies south and west, but it was nearly night, so he knew the clearing would not bring him the heat of the sun, but the cold of the stars. He glanced toward the east and realized that he was seeing more than just the normal darkness at the end of a day. Even with his poor eyes, he could make out the jagged tops of mountains some distance from the shore. He lowered a strand of babiche into the sea, watched as it floated out behind him. The current was much swifter, more than just a river within the sea, but now also the force of waves driving themselves toward land.

For a moment another spasm grasped him, and he tensed against it, but he then realized it was only nervousness, a man considering an unknown shore without a strong paddle, with injuries and weak vision. What chance was there that the waves would bring him to a gentle cove? He had found a river within the sea, but it would approach land with the strength that any river holds. More than likely, he would make landfall at night, blinded by darkness. Low tide or high?

With a stronger paddle, he could have moved himself parallel to the shore until morning, but with what he had, and with most of his strength gone, he knew he could not escape the sea-river's current and the power of the breakers that would drive him ashore. He moaned, and a voice came into his head, something old from long ago.

"So you are complaining again?"

His father's voice? No, stronger than that.

"I need a good paddle," Cen answered, speaking aloud.

"You're worried about your paddle?"

"Of course. Look at it. It's just a branch, a piece of driftwood."

"Worry is just another form of complaint. Look at all the good things you have. You needed water, and it rained. You needed to see, and your eyes have cleared."

"But my ears . . ."

"You needed to hear, and you can hear me."

Cen grew angry, began to shout. "You speak to my spirit. That's not hearing! If I could hear, I would know how the currents run against the beach, how the waves break."

He shouted until his throat grew so raw that his words were no more than the movement of his lips. Then he no longer heard the voice. The clouds covered the eastern sky throughout the night, darkened land and sea into blackness. Cen sat, eyes and ears straining, ready any moment for the crush of waves breaking.

When morning first grayed the edges of the sky, he realized that somehow the current had slowed. He could see sea birds wheeling and turning, but there was still some distance to the shore.

He made a prayer of gratitude, one he had learned as a child. Though the simple words did not seem enough for a man, he could think of nothing else.

The sea grew choppy, and the iqyax bounced on the water. Cen untied his paddle and used it to keep the bow into the waves. As he neared the shore, he floated over a bed of kelp, and found that he could direct himself by grabbing the stipes of the plants, pulling until he could grab another. In that way, he moved past a cliff that dropped sheer into the water.

His hands and fingers grew numb, and he could hardly make them grab the kelp, could scarcely let go when it was time for another handhold. He had seen men drown this close to land. He had been little more than a boy when he went out with a group of hunters after harbor seals. A current had pulled them all into rocks, and several of the iqyan covers were sliced open. One of the men managed to crawl across the bow of his hunting partner's iqyax, but the others, three in all, had held to their own crafts, which had sunk as water filled the hulls. The sea had been so cold that soon their muscles cramped, arms and legs clenched so they could no longer flail to keep themselves afloat.

In trying to save the man closest to him, Cen had driven his iqyax into the rocks and sliced its cover as well, but the worst of the cut had been above the waterline. He had not been able to reach the hunter before the man drowned, and by the time Cen managed to get ashore, his iqyax was full of water, the craft riding so low that even the smallest waves broke over the deck.

Now he forced his hands to grasp the shaft of his cedar branch paddle. Pain pierced each of his fingers, sent sharp messages up his arms.

"Be grateful," he heard the voice say, and in anger Cen ground his teeth.

He lifted tortured hands, plunged the paddle into the sea, and willed the kelp to ignore the wide and awkward blade, but it wrapped itself over the paddle, bound it tight.

Cen pulled, but the waves worked with the kelp, jerked his iqyax toward an outcropping of rocks. Cen pulled harder, and his ribs seemed to rip from his spine. He screamed and lifted the paddle, twisted it, heard the snap of the wood, not with his ears but with the bones of his hands. Then the kelp swallowed the blade and half the shaft.

"Be grateful," the voice whispered.

Cen's scream needed no words, and he began to jab the stick into the sea. Again and again he plunged the broken end into the water, screaming until a layer of the skin in his throat peeled away, until he could no longer draw breath through the blood that filled his mouth.

Then he was still, exhausted, cradling the remains of the paddle in his arms, spitting up blood, crying.

But finally, when his throat had stopped bleeding and he was again able to draw air, he whispered, "I am grateful."

He bound the remains of his paddle to the deck. With fumbling hands, fingers like stone, he managed to pull the stout end of the cedar branch from where he had stored it inside the iqyax. He tied it to the deck with a harpoon line, so that if the waves pulled it from his grasp, he would be able to bring it back to himself.

Then he lifted his hands toward the sky and shouted, "I am grateful!"

Without the stick, he could never have brought his iqyax safely to shore. Rocks lurked under the surface, hidden until Cen was nearly upon them. Then he would push off, shove himself away before the rock could tear through the thin iqyax cover. Once he cracked the keelson hard on the seaward edge of a reef, but the iqyax was well made, and though the keelson stove in for a moment, it popped back out when Cen pushed away.

He followed the edge of the reef until it opened. The split was narrow, hardly the width of his iqyax, and the current was strong, a river flowing between the two sides of the gravel reef, but he managed to aim the boat well, and the current carried him through. Once past the reef, he was in a deep pool of calm water. Cen laid the stick over the bow and studied the shore.

He was close enough now that there was little danger. Even if he destroyed his iqyax on rocks, most likely he could escape. The cliffs had given way to a rolling beach, duned with large hills of gray and golden sand, striated as though fingers had pulled the colors together, drawing them into one another. But the land came up quickly from the water in a rise that was as tall as a man—not an easy place to bring in an iqyax, especially for someone as battered and weak as Cen.

He poled himself along the beach until it widened, the dunes receded, and the land grew flat. He had not realized how afraid he had been until his fear seeped away, leaving him empty, tired. Perhaps fear was the only thing that kept him trying. Now he just wanted to sleep. But he forced himself to consider the land, to set his mind on the problems that would face him there, dangers different from what he had faced on the sea.

He had few weapons, the knives the storm had left him, and his stout cedar stick, but little else. What good would those things do against wolves or bear? He had nothing left that anyone would take in trade save a bundle of shell necklaces and his iqyax. The iqyax needed a new cover, but the frame still seemed strong.

He glanced at the beach he was passing, saw the mouth of a small river, and grimaced. Most likely the outflow of the river would have carved itself a path through the reef, and he did not want to get caught in a current that might carry him back out to sea. It was time to put his iqyax ashore.

Dread caught at him, pushed fingers into his throat and crept down to squeeze his heart.

Fool, he told himself. You have wanted nothing more than this since the wave took you. Here you are on a good beach, in a place where it will be easy to land, and you are suddenly afraid!

He shifted his knees and legs, dug his pole in at the seaward side of the iqyax, and turned it toward the beach. Waves took him, sped him toward shore, and he wished he could backpaddle to slow himself.

"This is nothing," he said aloud to the iqyax, hoping to lend it courage.

He was right; the land rose gradually under the water, so that when the waves finally drove him ashore, there was no more than a small jolt, a scraping of gravel against the hull.

Cen lifted his voice in a cry of thanksgiving. "Be grateful," he shouted. "Be grateful!"

He thrust the stick under the paddle bindings that crossed the top of the iqyax, then braced his hands on either side of the coaming. Usually he jumped out with legs spread, one on either side of the iqyax, but this time, when he landed his legs did not hold him, and he found himself sitting awkwardly in the coaming, a leg on each side. He started to laugh, rolled himself off the iqyax and onto the wet sand. A wave dashed in and slapped over his chest, up into his mouth. He pushed himself up with his arms and again tried to stand, but his legs were weak, and all he could do was crawl. He thrust a hand into the paddle ties of the iqyax and managed to drag it with him up the rise of the beach and finally out of the reach of waves. Then he collapsed. He lay there breathing hard, and the ground moved in undulations as though the sea still held him.

FORTY-FOUR

Cen drank his fill from the river, and he managed to catch a few fish by constructing a makeshift weir with driftwood and scrub willow. He wasn't sure where the sea had left him, but during low tide the sand and silt flats that extended past the shore reminded him of land near the Walrus Hunters' village.

For three days, he rested. He repaired his weapons and clothing the best he could with what the sea had left him. Then he decided he was strong enough, his hearing and vision improved enough, to set out for the Walrus Hunters' village. He walked the shore at the mark of high tide, his iqyax on his back, the curl of the bow high over his head. He had considered stripping the craft of its covering, rotted and leaking as it was, but then decided that it gave him some shelter in the night from wind and rain, and so he put up with the extra weight, took more rests, stopped earlier in the day.

Two days' walking brought him to a large river, and he chortled when he saw it. He was less than a day away from the Walrus village. Thoughts of warm lodges and fresh meat, of hearthfires and fur sleeping mats, warmed him even in the gray mist.

The third day, he came to the village, heard the dogs barking, saw the light haze of hearthfire smoke rising into the darkening sky.

"I am grateful," he murmured under his breath, and set his feet more firmly against the earth, tightened his grip on the iqyax.

He thought children would come to meet him. Unlike the River People, the Walrus did not go after caribou, but should at this time of year be in their winter villages. If the caribou came to them, as they did some years—walking the beaches as though they sought some way to cross the North Sea— then the Walrus hunted them, but did so in foolish ways, driving the animals into the sea, taking them with harpoons as if the caribou were seal or sea lion.

When no children came out, in spite of the dogs' barking, then Cen himself raised his voice, shouted greetings. When he came to the first lodge, he set down his iqyax, well away from any tethered dogs, and scratched at the hide doorflap.

Walrus lodges seemed to be a mix of the First Men ulax and River lodges. The men dug them partly into the earth, then built stone and sod walls. The women covered the roof poles with split walrus hide or sea lion skins and, like the River, made tunnels as entryways. But inside, except for the light that came in through the hide roof, their lodges seemed more First Men, with stone oil lamps for cooking and heating, and the walls and floors covered with woven grass mats.

Finally a woman flung open the doorflap. By watching her lips and listening hard to hear over the roar in his ears, Cen realized that she was scolding him, asking why he had waited for someone to come and let him in. Didn't he know that everyone was welcome in her lodge? Why force her to leave a warm place beside the oil lamp?

When she finally looked at his face, she clamped a hand over her mouth and began a high-pitched wail. Then another woman came into the entrance tunnel. She made signs of protection and waved her hands as though to push him away.

"I am Cen," he said, and her wailing grew louder.

Suddenly he understood. Someone, perhaps Ghaden himself, or a visitor from Chakliux's village, had told these Walrus people that he had drowned. Now here he was, clothes rotting on his body, his face marked by the battering he had taken. Worse, his tattered iqyax lay behind him on the ground.

"No," he said, speaking in the Walrus tongue. "I am not dead. You heard I was dead, but I am not."

The two began a chant, something to appease spirits, and Cen shook his head at their foolishness. The women jerked down the doorflap, held it in place when Cen gently tried to pull it from their hands. He let go, stepped back in frustration. His belly churned, and he realized that he could smell meat cooking, seal meat, rich and fat.

For a moment his head seemed so light that he was dizzy, but he closed his eyes to steady himself, then picked up his iqyax and walked to Yehl's lodge at the center of the village.

He had known Yehl for a long time, since the man's father had been the village shaman. Yehl was not as wise or as gifted as his father had been, but he knew how to make people afraid of his powers, of his chants, and so he was the leader of the village. Gradually some of the Walrus Hunters had left, two families one year, another the next, each year more until the village itself was only half the size it had been when Yehl's father was alive, but the people who remained were a good people, generous with what they had. It was a fine place to trade.

Cen set his iqyax at Yehl's door, and this time did not scratch for entrance, but boldly went into the tunnel and scrapped his fingernails against the inner doorflap. "I have come to trade and to share the warmth of your lodge," he said. Then gently he pulled aside the doorflap, saw Yehl's surprised face.

Yehl wore only a pair of fur seal pants, his bare chest shining with oil and weighted down by many necklaces. His wife, a new one, very young, wore her hair hanging free over her shoulders, parted at the top of her head, the white line of the part painted red to show her husband's approval. She, too, wore only fur seal pants, and her breasts were so small that she looked more like a boy than a woman, but her face was beautiful, round and smooth, marked across the cheeks with charcoaled tattoos in lines and circles.

"Welcome!" the girl said and she smiled, showing strong, white teeth. She gestured toward a floor mat beside her husband. "We have food."

But Yehl was still staring at Cen, his mouth open. Finally he scrabbled in the floor mats until he came up with a thin-bladed knife, something a woman might use to do the delicate work of scraping hides near tears or eye holes.

He looked foolish, holding that knife, but Cen kept himself from smiling and said, "You have most likely heard that I drowned in a storm on the North Sea. You understand now that I am alive." He held out his hands as though to prove he was not spirit.

The wife hid behind Yehl and pressed her face against her husband's back.

Cen sighed. "I am not spirit. I am alive," he said, stressing each word. "My iqyax was strong enough to withstand the power of the storm and the wave that took me, but I lost paddles and harpoons, and for a time my sight and hearing. Even now it is difficult to know what you are saying, for the voice of the sea has stayed in my ears."

Yehl began a spirit chant, dropped the knife to touch the amulets that hung at his neck, at his waist, on bands bound to his arms.

"I am not spirit!" Cen shouted, and did not realize how loud his voice was until both Yehl and his wife covered their ears with their hands.

"Look!" Cen said. He pulled out his sleeve knife, held up his hand, and drew the blade across his palm.

Yehl looked at him with wide eyes. He leaned forward and thrust a fingertip into the blood that ran from the cut. He rubbed his finger and thumb together, then brought them to his mouth. At that moment, two young men burst into the lodge, both with hands full of amulets.

They stopped, both breathing heavily as though they had been running.

"How many are you?" Yehl asked.

"Many," one said. "The whole village. All the warriors and behind us, the elders."

"Good," Yehl said, and pointed with his blood-tipped finger. "Have you ever known a spirit to bleed?"

The young men had no answer, and Yehl smiled at Cen, a sly smile, as though they were conspirators.

"Ask the elders," Yehl told them. "See what they think."

The men passed the question back to those behind, and soon the answer came: "Spirits do not bleed."

"Then," said Yehl, "it is time to welcome my friend Cen, who has returned to us. Tell the women we will have a celebration tomorrow. All day there will be feasting. All night we will eat and dance and be glad."

Cen put his knife back into its wrist sheath and clenched his fist to stop the bleeding. He sighed. He would rather not have a celebration, but how can a man refuse hospitality? He knew Yehl from years of trading, knew him well. During the feast, Yehl would give Cen new clothes, amulets, weapons, everything he needed, but how could any man accept such gifts without giving in return? He had nothing but his iqyax, his torn and tattered chigdax, necklaces, a few weapons, a few water bladders.

Aaa, he would have to give up his iqyax. The thought was a weight in his chest, but he kept his sadness within and set a smile on his face, listened to Yehl plan the celebration, listened and pretended to be glad.

The feasting lasted three days, and when it was done, Yehl had Cen's iqyax and Cen had new clothing, new weapons, and enough food to get him to Chakliux's village. He left the next morning, paused for a moment to stroke the iqyax and thank it again for its strength. Even as he walked the beach, he began to pick up good dry pieces of driftwood, strapped them to his back with thoughts of keelsons and iqyax ribs. He had the winter to build himself another, and though it would most likely not have the same spirit as the iqyax Chakliux had made him, it would be a brother and he would treat it well, hoping for its favor as he traveled to hunt or trade.

Though Cen was still not as strong as he had been, he made good time, and arrived at Chakliux's village six days after leaving the Walrus.

The children ran to meet him, recognized him and began to call out his name in joy, though some asked questions about his lack of trade packs, disappointment strong in their voices.

So perhaps somehow the people of Chakliux's village had not heard that he was dead. He puzzled over that until the first women came out, gathered their children to themselves, and held amulets over their eyes, huddling back into the entrance tunnels of their caribou hide lodges.

"You heard I was dead," he called to them as he made his way through the village to Chakliux's lodge. "I am not. The storm sent me far into the North Sea, but I lived, and I have come back."

He called the words over and over like a song, like a chant, but still the women kept their children away from him, as though he carried a curse. When he came to Chakliux's lodge, he stood outside and bellowed the man's name.

"Chakliux, my friend, come out to meet me. I have come a long way to spend time with you and your wife."

He waited, but there was no response, and the women's voices behind him had begun to rise in a high ululation of fear. He might have to cut his hand again. He hated the thought of that. The cut was healing nicely, thanks to Yehl's young wife and the medicine she had given him. It was scabbed over and had begun to itch furiously, especially at night. He did not want to start again with a fresh cut, but better that than death at the hands of men who thought he had come as a spirit to curse them. A spirit could take abuse that a man could not.

"Chakliux!" he called again. "Aqamdax!"

"Cen?" The voice was so quiet that he barely heard it, and he turned to see Aqamdax standing behind him. "Cen?" she said again. "Are you spirit or man?"

"Man," he said. Then, lifting his chin toward the women who stood at the entrances of their lodges, he added, "Though you would not know by listening to them."

"They're afraid, and I am, too. Ghaden told us you were dead. He was here only a few days ago, he and his wife and her father, on their way to the Four Rivers village to tell . . ." She stopped and clamped a hand over her mouth.

"To tell my wife and daughters that I'm dead," he finished for her.

"And you're not."

He almost laughed. "No, I'm not."

She was wearing a caribou hide parka, the hood flung back to reveal the dark head of a baby on her back. She also carried a little girl, straddling her hip. Cen smiled at the child. "They have grown much," he said.

"Especially this one," Aqamdax replied, and set her daughter down. The girl stuck a finger into her mouth and slid behind her mother, clasping the furred edge of Aqamdax's parka.

Cen noticed that she was otter-footed like her father, and somewhat unsteady on her feet. He crouched to his haunches and reached in under his parka for a necklace of fish bone beads, held it out toward the girl on the tips of his fingers. "And your oldest, your son Angax?"

"Is with his father. They're hunting birds and should be back soon."

"Little one, this is for you," Cen said to Aqamdax's daughter. He moved his hand to set the necklace swinging.

The girl sidled out from behind her mother and took a tentative step.

"You remember Cen?" Aqamdax asked her. "He is father to Ghaden."

"Uncle?" the little girl asked in a small voice.

Aqamdax cocked her head at Cen.

"Yes, Uncle," he said.

At the confirmation, the child darted forward and grabbed the necklace, then retreated behind her mother.

Aqamdax and Cen began to laugh, and soon the women of the village had joined their laughter, coming out from their lodges to crowd around Cen as he told the story of his survival.

When Chakliux and Angax arrived home, the boy proudly carrying a brace of ptarmigan, Cen was sitting beside the hearthfire, leaning against a woven willow backrest, his belly full and his feet warm.

Chakliux came bursting into the lodge, his mouth full of laughter.

"We wanted to surprise you," Aqamdax told him as she stood on tiptoe to stir the soup that was hanging over the hearthfire.

"Even before we got to the village, the children ran out to tell us," Chakliux said.

Chakliux had eight, perhaps nine handfuls of summers, yet he still looked like a young man, little gray in his hair, his belly firm and flat. Aqamdax, too, still looked young, though she had the fuller breasts and wider hips of a woman who has birthed and suckled children. They were happy with one another, and their joy together made him long for Gheli.

As Aqamdax plucked and cleaned Angax's birds, Cen retold his story. Chakliux listened carefully, sometimes asking questions, things a storyteller would want to know, and so Cen understood that Chakliux wanted to add this tale to those he already told.

When his story was finished, Chakliux asked the question

that Cen had expected. "This is a good story," he said, "one that the people should hear often. Do you think that someday you might give it to a storyteller so it will not be forgotten?"

Cen smiled at him. "Today, it is given," he said. "It's my story, and I will tell it again, but both of you may also tell it whenever you wish. I know you'll tell it well.

"I can't stay but just this night," he added, wanting to avoid any celebration. "My son thinks I'm dead, and now most likely my wife and daughters do also. I need to go to them."

Chakliux rubbed his hands together and held them out toward the fire. "I'll travel with you," he said. "You don't want the Four Rivers People to think you're a spirit and try to send you back to the spirit world." He began to laugh, but Cen opened his hand and showed Chakliux his wound, explained how he had convinced the Walrus Hunters that he was alive.

Then he said, "You told me my son came here and his wife and her father."

"The three of them," said Chakliux.

"Four," Aqamdax said, and knelt beside her husband, handed him the baby who had begun to fuss. "Hold her while I put the birds into the boiling bag," she said. "The wife's mother came, too, but would not stay at the village. She's First Men and afraid of us."

Cen blew out his breath in sudden anger. "When I left to go on this trading trip, my son had no wife. This woman, her name was Uutuk?"

"Yes, Uutuk," said Chakliux.

"A good woman," Aqamdax said, "a good wife to your son. You'll be glad to have her as daughter."

"No," said Cen. "They lied to you. Even Ghaden lied." His words were bitter. "His wife I can forgive. I know that she doesn't realize what she has done by bringing her family with her, but Ghaden knows."

"Cen, you're tired," Chakliux said. "You're worried about things that aren't important. Her father Seal is a boastful man, but he treated both Ghaden and Uutuk well."

"Her mother is K'os."

Cen's words were like knives, and it seemed as if they slashed the caribou hide walls, gave entrance to a fierce wind. The fire flickered and sputtered, and the baby began to cry in hard, breathless sobs.

Cen saw the questions in Chakliux's eyes, the disappointment, and he braced himself for the man's anger, but when Chakliux finally spoke, he said, "It's good that I've decided to go with you to the Four Rivers village."

FORTY-FIVE

CHAKLIUX'S STORY

Chakliux and Cen took seven days traveling to the Four
Rivers village. As they walked, Chakliux tried not to think
about the caribou hunts that he was missing. The men had
planned to leave any morning that the sky promised several
days without rain. Of course, Sok would provide for him,
but a man preferred to feed his own family. How else could
he share with those who were old or sick? How else could he
truly join in the celebrations once the hunts had ended?

When his regrets became too great, Chakliux reminded
himself that his own loss in missing the hunt was nothing
compared to what Cen had suffered.

Cen's eyes still bothered him, tearing so much at times
that he could not see well enough to continue walking. If
Chakliux spoke while ahead on the trail, Cen did not even
realize that he had said anything, and if Chakliux were walking behind, Cen had to turn and watch his mouth to make out
the words.

The sea had taken much from the man, and Ghaden in his
foolishness had only made Cen's life worse, and not only
Cen's but perhaps the lives of all the River People. K'os had
many reasons for revenge.

With Uutuk as his wife, Ghaden would never be rid of K'os, and what River village would welcome them? He would have to live with his wife's people, at least until K'os died, and she was a woman who never seemed to grow old, as though the evil within kept the years from marking her.

As the days of travel passed, Chakliux's anger at Ghaden grew, so that at the end of an afternoon walking, his otter foot aching, he could scarcely keep sharp words from flying out of his mouth, though Cen did nothing to offend.

Finally, on the last day, Chakliux began to fill his head with stories, thinking most often about Cen's tale of survival, humming the story under his breath as he walked, giving the sea its due, but also praising Cen for his ingenuity as he fought for his life.

The story seemed to pull away Chakliux's anger. When he and Cen stopped that night to rest and eat, Chakliux could smile without fear that bitter words would slip out in foolish whining.

"If we get an early start, we'll be in the Four Rivers village by midmorning," Cen said. He folded a bit of caribou hide into a square and softened it on the edge of his sleeve knife, then pressed it against his right eye. "It's worse in bright sun," he told Chakliux.

"My wife makes an eyewash of the mouse ears plant," Chakliux said softly. "Perhaps some woman in the Four Rivers village will have some."

Cen pulled the pad away from his right eye, switched it to his left. Neither man said K'os's name, but Chakliux knew they were both thinking about her, a woman who knew medicine, but could not be trusted.

"There's an old grandmother named Two-heeled Fish," Cen said. "She knows something about plant medicine. Even if she doesn't have any mouse ears, perhaps she can tell us where it grows."

Chakliux was building a fire, and he grunted his agreement. When the kindling caught and the flames began to lick at the larger branches, he pulled dried meat from his pack, set a basket of fat and dried berries between them. He ate enough to pull away some of his tiredness, then cut spruce boughs to make a lean-to shelter and a mat for them to sleep on, then gathered firewood for the night.

They slept, Chakliux waking now and again to keep the fire burning, and in the morning they ate again, then started out. Chakliux thought ahead to what he would say to Ghaden, but Ghaden was no longer a child who could be scolded for foolish decisions, or for holding the truth away from his family. So when Chakliux reconsidered his words, they seemed futile.

Could he change what Ghaden had done? And even if he could, would it be for the best, now that K'os was already among them? Perhaps Ghaden should stay with his wife and her family just to be sure that K'os did as little harm as possible. The best thing might simply be to remind Ghaden what kind of woman K'os was. Did Ghaden know that K'os had killed Chakliux's first wife and baby? Most likely not. And if not, then Ghaden's decision to marry K'os's daughter was partly Chakliux's fault. But what man wants to speak of things so painful or bring that remembrance into the happiness of his new family?

Cen was leading the way, but when the trail widened, Chakliux took several hurried steps to walk beside him.

Cen gave him a tight smile and said, "We're nearly there."

For a time Chakliux didn't say anything, but finally he asked, "How much did you tell Ghaden about K'os? You once lived in her lodge, nae'? Was she your wife?"

Cen sighed. "In my heart, at that time, she was my wife," he said, "but I didn't pay a brideprice for her, and one day I found her with another hunter. Then I knew that she would never be content as one man's wife."

"Did you tell Ghaden?"

Cen shrugged. "I think I did. At least I warned him about her when we were at the Traders' Beach and I saw that he was interested in Uutuk."

"Did you ever tell him how K'os helped start the fighting between the Near River and Cousin River villages?"

"No, but he lived through those times. He should remember. He knew Aqamdax was her slave. He saw how she was treated."

"But he was a boy. Who knows what children understand?"

Then Cen lifted his arm toward the sky, and Chakliux saw gray plumes of smoke above the trees.

A sound came to Chakliux's ears, a thin keening. "Listen," he said to Cen.

Cen cocked his head, and with a bitter look said, "I hear nothing."

"Most likely it's only dogs," Chakliux told him, leaning close and speaking loudly enough for Cen to hear. "They're wailing as if they're about to be fed."

The path widened, and the trees thinned, all their lower branches taken by women for their hearthfires. The keening grew louder, as did Chakliux's discomfort. Not dogs, no. Not dogs. The ululations came from each lodge, and he needed no one to tell him that they were mourning cries. Finally even Cen heard it.

He looked at Chakliux, shook his head. "Those aren't dogs," he said, and he broke into a run, holding his side as if the jolting gave him pain.

Chakliux followed as quickly as he could, limping, hindered by his otter foot. Cen did not stop until he came to a large lodge at the river side of the village. He threw back the outer doorflap and made his way inside. Chakliux followed.

K'os was hunkered at the back of the lodge next to a body covered in caribou hide and tied in a fetal position.

"Why are you here?" Cen demanded. "Where is my wife?" He thrust a finger toward the body. "Who is that?" he asked, and his voice was terrible. "Where are my daughters?"

Chakliux easily recognized his mother, though she had

cut huge jagged hanks from her hair and scratched her cheeks until blood oozed. She looked old, and that surprised him. Her hair was graying, and her face was lined, her neck roped with slack flesh. She opened her mouth, and he saw that she had lost a few teeth. Strangely, her face was still beautiful, the bones defined, the eyes large and clear.

She stared at Cen, then let out a long hollow wail and crossed her arms over her chest.

Finally she screamed, "You are dead!"

"Where are my children? Where is my son?" Cen demanded.

Chakliux realized that they would get no answers until he could reassure K'os that Cen was not a spirit who had come for revenge.

"Cen is not dead," Chakliux said.

K'os looked at him, first in surprise, and then he saw the hatred slide into her eyes.

"You!" she said.

"He's not dead," Chakliux repeated. "Who is this one that you mourn?"

She tore her eyes away from Cen and glanced at the bound corpse. "My husband Seal," she told him, lifting her chin. But then her eyes were again on Cen. "How did you live?" she asked.

"I'll tell you later. Where is my wife? Where is Ghaden? Where are my daughters?"

K'os pushed the hair back from her face and stood. "You see that we all mourn here," she said. "Some illness has come to this village as a curse. The people say that we have brought it, but if we brought it, then why is my own husband dead?"

Chakliux felt a draught of air at the back of his neck, and he turned to see that the woman Uutuk had entered the lodge. She sidled past him, her eyes on her mother, her hands full of bulging water bladders. But when she saw Cen, she dropped to her knees, her mouth open.

Chakliux thought she would begin to wail, but she only stared, and finally she told Cen, "My husband needs to know that you're alive."

"Where is he?" Cen asked.

"He went to find your wife and your daughter Daes."

Cen let out his breath. "They're alive?"

"I think so," she answered, "but who can say with this whole village dying? Gheli and Daes were still at their fish camp, and Ghaden went to find them. Your other daughter, the baby, is with Long Wolf's wife. They are well. I just came from their lodge."

"The baby's not with Gheli?" he asked. "Why?"

"Daes brought her back to the village. I don't know why."

"You gave Long Wolf's wife my medicine for protection?" K'os asked.

Her words chilled Chakliux, but before he could say anything, Cen strode over to K'os and grabbed her, one hand grasping her shoulder, the other twisted into her hair. "You will stay away from that lodge," he told her. "If you do not, you will be dead."

He released her so quickly that she stumbled and fell to her knees. Uutuk hurried to her, and Cen, his lips curled in anger, held a fist in Uutuk's face and said, "I have nothing against you except your mother, but what I said to her, I say to you. Leave my baby daughter alone. I don't want you in Long Wolf's lodge."

Cen strode toward the entrance tunnel, paused only to tell Chakliux, "Watch them!"

Chakliux unstrapped the pack from his back and let it fall to the floor mats. His foot ached, and he needed to rest.

"Your water is safe, Uutuk?" he asked in a gentle voice.

"It's safe," she told him.

He held out a hand, and she gave him a bladder, but then she clasped his wrist, pulled out the stopper, and drank.

"It's safe," she said again.

He drank, and she busied herself with women's tasks,

hanging the bladders and adding wood to the fire, a handful of dried meat to the cooking bag. K'os fixed her eyes on Chakliux and raised her voice in a mourning cry.

Chakliux ignored her and instead said to Uutuk, "Has she told you that I am more than brother by marriage to you?"

Uutuk frowned and turned away from the cooking bag, wiped her hands on her leggings, then squatted beside him.

"Did K'os give birth to you?" Chakliux asked.

"Ghaden didn't tell you? I wanted him to tell you. I'm not . . ." She stopped and seemed to search for words. "Before I was First Men, I was from another place and another people. My grandfather and I came in a boat to escape the Bear-god warriors. The sea brought us to the First Men, and there K'os became my mother."

Chakliux considered her words. He was Dzuuggi, storyteller, and knew all the wisdom of his people. He had never heard of the Bear-god warriors, and surely if they existed he would have known about them. He knew stories about the fierce warriors who had come long ago, killing the First Men. Perhaps they were Bear-god and the First Men gave them a name different from Uutuk's people.

"Who are your people?" he asked.

"We are the Boat People," she said in the First Men language, and then said something in another tongue, a strange language that Chakliux had never heard. That more than anything convinced him that she was telling the truth.

"Like you, I was found," he said to her.

K'os had stopped her mourning cries and crept a little closer.

"He lies, Uutuk," she said. "I should know."

"Yes, you should know," Chakliux said to her. "Since you are my mother."

Uutuk gasped, then began to cough, as though the knowledge were choking her.

"Ghaden said nothing about that to me," she said.

"Don't blame Ghaden," K'os told her. "My life began

over with the First Men, and I no longer call this man my son. He has betrayed me many times. He even sent me away as a slave from his village. I've told you that story."

Uutuk covered her mouth with both hands. "You are the one?" she asked.

"See why I didn't tell you?" K'os said. "It was better that you thought of Chakliux as brother, for although he treated me poorly, he has been kind in most ways to Ghaden."

K'os's words were like strong arms squeezing his chest, and Chakliux drew a deep breath in order to break their hold. "You told her also how you treated my wife, Gguzaakk?"

K'os's eyes narrowed, and she spat out, "Don't believe him, Uutuk. He lies."

"Let her make her own choice about that," Chakliux said, then he told her how Gguzaakk and his son died of poison.

When Cen returned to the lodge, Uutuk was weeping, and K'os was hovering over her dead husband, her back to her daughter.

Cen began speaking even before he was through the inner doorflap. "Friend," he said to Chakliux, "I need you to stay and watch over my little daughter. The woman who nurses her is pregnant, and her milk is getting thin. But Duckling is old enough to eat soft food, broths and such. Will you be sure her food is safe?" He lifted his chin to point at K'os. "This one has somehow poisoned most of the people in the village."

"I did nothing to these people!" K'os said, her voice full of weeping. "Do you think I would kill my own husband?"

But Chakliux said to Uutuk, "She uses poison well. Be careful."

Uutuk began to tremble, and she clasped her arms across her chest as though she were cold.

"Many people think she killed all her husbands," Chakliux said. "I know what she did to my first wife and our little son. Don't trust her."

Then he looked at Cen, the man pacing from one side of

the lodge to the other. "You can't go now," Chakliux told him. "Rest and eat first."

Uutuk stood and scooped a ladle into the boiling bag, held it to K'os's lips until she ate. Then Uutuk filled bowls for both men.

FORTY-SIX

CEN'S STORY

Cen left the next morning. The day of rest at his own lodge, though marred by K'os's presence, had seemed to renew his strength, and he walked quickly, following the path that one of the women in the village pointed out. There were two handfuls dead and another two handfuls sick, three or four near death, others who looked as though they might recover. Each death was a wound in his heart. He had lived in this village for many years, and though he was related to none of the people by blood, save his baby daughter, they had become his family. If K'os had wanted revenge on him, she had chosen wisely.

By the third day walking, Cen was once again exhausted. His nights were torn by dreams of the sea; his days were filled with anger against K'os and Ghaden and even Ghaden's new wife, Uutuk.

He had no warning that he was coming upon the fish camp, no smoke from a fire, no smell of drying fish, no sound of dogs. He simply walked out of the scrub that grew on either side of the trail into a clearing that had a lean-to of spruce boughs and the old ashes of a dead fire. At first he thought the camp was abandoned, and he wondered why he had not met Gheli and Daes and Ghaden on the trail. Of course, people often made fish camps close to one another. Perhaps Gheli's was beyond this, but then he heard a distant bark, and suddenly a strong hand flung a pack from the lean-to, and Ghaden crawled out.

"Ghaden!" Cen shouted.

The anger that had been building in Cen's mind made him forget that Ghaden still believed he was dead.

The young man jumped quickly to his feet, began to back away, chanting as he clasped an amulet that hung at his waist.

"I'm not dead," Cen said, and sighed with the frustration of having to prove again that he had not been taken by the sea.

"I'm not," he said. "Look." He thrust the point of a knife into the fleshy pad at the palm of his hand, squeezed until blood dripped to the ground. "The sea did not take me, though it has stolen some of my hearing and dimmed my sight."

Ghaden approached slowly. Cen held out his hand, and Ghaden reached forward, caught a drop of blood with his fingers. Then suddenly he was crying in huge, hard gasps, and he grabbed Cen, pressed him to his chest, pounded his hands against Cen's back until Cen broke away laughing, his anger suddenly gone.

"We have to catch Gheli," Ghaden said, then stopped, shut his mouth as though he wished he had said nothing at all.

"She's all right?" Cen asked.

"Yes."

He studied his son's face, frowned at what he saw there. "Daes?" he asked with a catch in his voice.

"They're both fine. They're together with Cries-loud. You remember him? He's from Chakliux's village, son of Sok . . ."

"I remember," Cen said. "Why is he with them? Where are they going? Why haven't they returned to the village?"

Ghaden tipped his head to look up at the sky. Finally he said, "There are things you need to know."

"I can't hear you unless you speak to my face," said Cen.

Ghaden grimaced. "I'm sorry for what the sea did to you."

Cen shrugged. "It didn't take my life. Tell me again what you said."

"I said, 'Are you hungry? Let's sit down and eat. There're things I need to tell you.'"

The Four Rivers Village

UUTUK'S STORY

"She didn't kill him, I know," Two-heeled Fish said to Uutuk.

Two-heeled Fish was so ancient that she scarcely had the strength to sit up. Her granddaughter knelt behind her, so Two-heeled Fish could lean back against the granddaughter's legs. The old woman raised a bony finger and pointed it at Uutuk's face, a rudeness that made the granddaughter reach forward, lay a hand on her wrist, and pull the arm down.

"Most of these people in this winter village are so young that they were only children when she lived among us. My granddaughter says that Cen has returned. He knows K'os. He hates her. He was the one who made K'os leave." Her voice was scratchy, and she spoke barely above a whisper. She turned her head to look at her granddaughter. "I told them last winter to let me die. But this one has a soft heart and a husband who is a good hunter." She raised a hand to stroke the young woman's face.

"Do you remember when K'os lived with us?" she asked her granddaughter.

"I remember," she said. "Many people remember, and some want her to leave again, but others say she did no harm to anyone. They were only frightened because her husband died so horribly, and they are frightened again because of the sickness in this village. We're fortunate that my sons and husband have already left on a caribou hunt. I spend much of my time with my grandmother, so I don't eat out of the village hearths. The ones who ate from the hearth cooking bags are the ones who got sick."

The granddaughter wore her hair twisted into a tight knot at the crown of her head. She had threaded thin slices of bone through holes in her earlobes. Her lodge was well made, nearly as large as Cen's, and it seemed unusually empty with the men's weapons and bedding gone.

"My mother lost a husband in this village?" Uutuk asked.

"A young man," Two-heeled Fish said. "Very young, almost a boy. K'os could have been his mother." She chuckled. "But he did not act like a son."

Again the granddaughter's face darkened in embarrassment, and she fussed with her grandmother's thin white hair, brushing it away from the old woman's face until Two-heeled Fish slapped at her hands.

"It's true. He was always touching her," Two-heeled Fish said. "I remember that they had a feast in the middle of winter and gave everyone gifts. I still have the shell comb she gave me, and a necklace of fish bone beads. I still have them both."

Two-heeled Fish was without most of her teeth, and when she paused in her speaking, she moved her jaws as though she were chewing. Spittle gathered at the corners of her mouth, flecked white on her lips.

"She helped me, too, taught me about medicines. Why do you think I have lived so long? She told me how to make teas to heal diseases. Has she taught you?"

"Yes, she has taught me," Uutuk said. "But there's much I don't know, especially about the plants that grow in this place. Everything is so different from the island where I lived."

"You lived on an island? I did wonder about your name. Uutuk. It's not River, nae'?"

"First Men." Then, before Two-heeled Fish could ask another question, Uutuk said, "Tell me what happened to this husband."

Two-heeled Fish pursed her lips into a tiny circle, shook her head, and said, "It was terrible, something that shouldn't be talked about, but since she's your mother, you need to know. He was killed with a knife."

"Not poison?"

"No," Two-heeled Fish said, "and that's why I know your mother didn't kill him. She knew too much about plants. If you want to kill a young husband like River Ice Dancer and you know about plants, it is easier to kill him with poison."

"Enough!" the granddaughter yelled. "Enough, Grandmother. You'll bring curses on us. Be quiet." She looked across her grandmother's head at Uutuk and lifted her chin toward the door of the lodge. "Go now. Surely your mother will tell you if you need to know anything else."

Then Uutuk thanked them and leaned forward to press a yellow puffin feather into the old woman's hand. "A good protection for you, Grandmother," she said, and left the lodge.

Uutuk could still hear Two-heeled Fish chuckling as she walked back to Cen's lodge. River Ice Dancer. Yes, K'os had told her about him. And there was an old man who had been her first husband, she had overheard her talking to Seal about the good gifts he used to give her. Then there was that chief hunter who had died in a fire. K'os had outlived them all.

Uutuk went back to Cen's lodge. Chakliux was working on the thin, fine blades that River men used to make points for the tiny spears they shot from their fire bow weapons. She had seen those weapons for the first time at the Traders' Beach, but they were not worth much. None of the First Men wanted them.

K'os was still sitting beside her dead husband, moaning and rocking. There would be a burial ceremony that evening. It would be good to get Seal's body out of the lodge. It had begun to stink.

The River People put their dead on scaffolds, Ghaden had once told her, or they burned them if there was some curse involved. Most likely Seal would be burned. She worried about his spirit, if it could survive the flames, and she had made prayers for his safe passage to the world of the dead.

She went to K'os, laid a hand on her shoulder, leaned close to whisper, "Mother, tell me again about your young Four Rivers husband."

Her mother looked up at her, and though K'os had been crying, there was no puffiness in her eyes, no redness. "Why, Uutuk, did someone in the village speak to you about him?"

"The old woman Two-heeled Fish," Uutuk said quietly.

"Aaa, well, as I told you, he died. Someone in this village stabbed him. I think it was Cen, but I was blamed."

Uutuk began to shake, and she clamped her teeth together to keep them from chattering. "Why would Cen do that?" she asked.

K'os smiled. "He wanted me for himself. But the people of this village thought that since my husband died in such a terrible way, I might curse them all. They made me leave. In the middle of winter, they made me leave."

Her eyes darkened. "They thought I would die, but I didn't." Her words were a whisper.

Uutuk wrapped a fur seal pelt around her shoulders and sat down with a partially completed boot upper in her hands. She tried to sew, but her fingers trembled so much that all she could do was lift prayers for the dead.

The Wilderness Northwest of the Fish Camp

GHELI'S STORY

It did not take them long to catch up to Gheli and Daes and Cries-loud.

Gheli screamed when she saw Cen, and Daes dropped as though she had been taken by a spear, but Cries-loud stood where he was and said, "Is he alive, or are we all in the spirit world?"

"Alive," Ghaden answered.

Then Gheli dashed away her tears and ran to Cen, flung her arms around him. He did not move to hold her, and finally she pulled away, looked into his face, and said, "Ghaden told you."

She stepped back. "I will die for what I did to your woman and your son. I deserve that, but please don't take revenge on my daughters."

Daes stepped between the two. The girl was as tall as her mother and nearly as wide. She carried a large pack on her back, the tumpline cutting across her forehead, pulling her head back toward the pack. She curled her lips away from her teeth, spoke with words harsh and loud.

"So you did not know who she was."

"I did not," Cen told her.

"Will you kill me for what she did?"

"What blame do you hold? None of this was your fault."

"Do you still claim me as daughter?"

Cen's eyes grew soft. "Always, you will be my daughter."

"A woman may throw away a husband and a man may throw away a wife. Can a daughter throw away a mother?"

"But then who would be your mother?"

"Perhaps that first Daes, who rides so uneasily within my body, sharing her name with me."

"Perhaps that one," Cen said quietly.

"I'll return with you to our village."

Gheli began to cry soundlessly, tears dripping from her jaw to the fur of her parka.

"Wait," Cen told Daes.

"You won't take me with you?"

"You need to know something. You all need to know something." He looked at Gheli. "Ghaden has married a First Men woman. She and her family came with him to the Four Rivers village. She's called Uutuk. Her father, Seal, is a trader, but he has died. Ghaden needs to return to the village for the mourning."

"They know, everything except Seal's death," Ghaden said. "And they know that Uutuk's mother is K'os."

Gheli choked out a strangled sound. "Don't trust her," she said to Cen. "The last time she was in our village, she wanted you as husband."

The hardness in Cen's eyes faded, and he wrinkled his brow, studied Gheli's face. "I remember," he said.

"She threatened to tell you who I was." Gheli held her hands out as though to beg for understanding. "I was afraid for my daughter. I thought if you knew who I was, you might kill Daes in revenge."

"You know me better than that," said Cen, sadness in his voice.

"I knew how much you loved that woman I killed. I knew how much you cared about your son Ghaden. K'os said she would kill our Daes if I didn't convince you to take her as wife, and when I could not, she said that I must choose between my own life and Daes's. She had poison to give me, and I pretended to take it. I pretended to get sick."

"But by then K'os had River Ice Dancer as husband," said Cen.

"What problem is that for a woman who kills as easily as K'os? If she could have you, River Ice Dancer would die. If not, he was young and a hunter, good enough to keep her fed through the winter."

"But she did kill him."

Gheli shook her head. "I needed to get K'os out of the village. To save my own daughter's life." She glanced at Daes, and the girl closed her eyes, hunched her shoulders against her pack.

"You killed him, too?" Cen asked.

"I knew they would blame K'os. How could anyone think I did it? I was sick, nearly dead."

"I stayed with you that night," Cen said, as though speaking to himself. "I was awake . . ."

"You slept. Long enough."

Daes began to moan, a long cry, as though she were in pain. Cen pulled the tumpline from her forehead, unstrapped her pack, and set it on the ground. She backed up to sit on the pack, and he put an arm around her shoulders, placed a hand under her chin to lift her face toward him. "Whatever your mother did, still she has loved many, including you. Including me. The woman K'os has never loved anyone but herself. Listen to me, Daes. There are terrible things happening in our village. Seal is not the only one who died.

"You heard what your mother said. K'os once tried to poison her. Why not poison the people who blamed her for a murder she did not commit?"

"What about Bird Hand?" Daes asked. She spoke slowly, as if she had been afraid to ask the question.

"He's alive, but his new wife died."

Daes rubbed her forehead with the heel of her hand, then stood and hefted the pack to her back. "I need to go to him," she said.

"Wait, we'll all go," Cen told her.

"What about her?" Daes asked, pointing at Gheli.

Cen was silent for a long time, and when he raised his eyes, he looked at Ghaden. "She was a good wife and gave me two daughters to make up for a woman I lost, but I can't stop you if you want to kill her. Your mother died, and you will always carry the scars from Red Leaf's knife."

"I've spent five days now with her and Cries-loud and Daes," said Ghaden. "We've talked through our anger and our grief. How can I kill a woman who is mother to my sisters, wife to my father? But I don't think she should return to the Four Rivers village. K'os will tell others about her." He looked into Cen's eyes. "Cries-loud had planned to take her and Daes to the next village. He can still do that."

"Yes, take her," Cen told Cries-loud. "Perhaps she'll be safe there."

Gheli opened her mouth in joy, began to babble out her gratefulness. Cen raised a hand. "You've cost us more than you can ever repay. You have supplies and a son willing to take you to another village. I throw you away. Find another husband. My daughter Daes stays with me."

Gheli began to cry, but silently, her eyes open, her mouth firm. She watched as Daes and Cen walked away from her, then turned to follow Cries-loud.

FORTY-SEVEN

GHELI'S STORY

They slept that night on the trail, Cries-loud and Red Leaf, the two speaking of days long ago, of good times and caribou hunts, feasts and celebrations. She asked about Sok and his new wife, his children, and she also asked about Cries-loud's wife.

Cries-loud tried to tell his mother good things about Yaa, but could think of nothing but that she worked hard, that she always kept his clothing clean and repaired.

"You need another wife," Red Leaf told him. "It's good for a man to be loyal to his first wife, but you need sons and daughters to take care of you when you're old. What would I do if I had no one?" And she dared to lay a hand on his arm.

"I plan to get another wife. Soon," he said.

He did not try to explain how each time, when he had a woman chosen, that somehow he waited too long to ask her, so another man claimed her before he had a chance. He told himself that it was because he didn't need another woman playing mother to him, telling him what to do. Planning his life. He didn't tell her about those nights when he lay awake, still holding Yaa after their lovemaking, his heart so filled with her that he doubted he had enough room for another woman. Or how after he returned from a hunting trip, all he wanted was to see Yaa, to talk to her, to take her to his bed. How could he explain those things to his mother when he did not understand them himself?

"Yes," he finally said. "This time, when I return to Chakliux's village, I'll find a young woman to be my wife. You're right. I need a son or daughter to take care of me when I'm old."

Then, though the sky still held a little edge of the day's light, he wrapped himself in his bedding furs and escaped into sleep.

Each day as they walked, Red Leaf talked about Cries-loud's childhood and all the joys she could remember from that time. Each night as they sat near their small fire, she studied his face as though to help herself remember him.

The walking took longer than they had thought, nearly three handfuls of days, but finally they saw the smoke from the village, rising above the tag alders that bordered the trail they followed.

Then Red Leaf told him, "I had a dream in the night, and it said that I should go into the village alone, that a woman will be welcomed with less suspicion than a man and woman together."

He began to protest, but she laid a hand across his mouth. "This is what I want."

Her stubbornness reminded Cries-loud of Yaa, so he knew there was little chance she would change her mind.

"Let me stay here at least for the day," he said. "Then if they won't take you in, you can come back to me, and we'll go somewhere else, to another village, until we find a place for you."

She considered what he said, finally agreed. "That's good. Do that. If I'm not back by tomorrow morning, then return without me to the Four Rivers village, and be sure that Cen has told the people I'm dead." She clasped her hands into fists, clenched and unclenched her fingers.

"They will mourn you," Cries-loud said, "and I will join that mourning." He looked away when Red Leaf's eyes filled with tears.

"Someday, bring Duckling and Daes to see me."

Cries-loud thought of the many days walking, too much of a summer lost in traveling, but he said, "I'll bring them. Watch for us."

Then Red Leaf smiled, looked into his eyes one last time, and left him.

UUTUK'S STORY

By the time Cen, Daes, and Ghaden returned to the village, three more people had died, but no one else had become sick. The rest had recovered and were weak, but it seemed that they would live. Ghaden found his wife in Two-heeled Fish's lodge, grinding boneset root for medicine.

"Did you find Cen's wife?" she asked.

"It's not good what we found," Ghaden told her, then, noticing that Two-heeled Fish was listening, he said, "Cen's wife is dead."

"From the sickness?" Uutuk asked.

"No, wolves," Ghaden told her.

The old woman began to croon something that he assumed was a death song. He pulled Uutuk to her feet and made excuses to Two-heeled Fish, led Uutuk from the lodge.

"You know the scars I carry on my back," he said to her, his voice low so anyone passing could not hear what he said.

"I know."

She ran quick fingers over his shoulder, and the heat of her hand made him realize how much he needed her. But first he wanted to tell her what had happened. They found a place near the river, in the lee of trees that cut the wind. There he told her about Red Leaf. As he spoke, she covered her mouth with both hands and made small cries of sadness.

"Uutuk," Ghaden said quietly, "you know that Chakliux stayed here because he thinks your mother did this to the village. Red Leaf also told us that K'os tried to poison her."

"Do you believe my mother would do that?"

"Did she say anything to you about eating the food here in this village?"

Uutuk's eyes grew wide.

"She told me that the taboos of the Four Rivers village were very different. That women here eat things that might make my children sick or cursed. We've eaten only from our own boiling bag since we came."

Ghaden moved to kneel in front of her. "Don't you see, Uutuk?"

Then Uutuk leaned forward to put her arms around his neck, and she wept.

"I have this question, Brother," Uutuk said. She and Chakliux were just outside Cen's lodge, the two of them. K'os was inside, where she had stayed since Chakliux had come to the village. He did not even allow her to go to the women's place to relieve herself. Instead she used a watertight salmon skin basket, and complained of Chakliux's foolishness.

"Ask," Chakliux told Uutuk.

"Why is she still alive? If she has done all the things you say, or even some of them, why have you not killed her?"

"I owed her a life," he said.

"You paid that when she killed your son." Uutuk's words were loud, but she spoke in the First Men language, which they both understood, though the people of the Four Rivers village did not.

He shook his head. "Each time I decided that she should die, something happened to change my decision."

"You are afraid of her," Uutuk told him. "She is a woman who curses everyone she knows. If she has this much power in life, think what she would be able to do in death, especially to the family of the one who kills her. But we could cut her bones apart, like men do when they take a powerful animal. That will keep her from coming after us."

Her words shocked Chakliux, and he had no answer for her.

"Do the River People not also believe that the cutting of joints protects the killer?"

"Sometimes we do that, but the best protection comes through prayers and chants and amulets."

"Then we will do both."

"You hate her so much?"

Her eyes overflowed, and she turned away from him. "She has always treated me well," she said in a small voice. "But when so many people tell me what she has done, how can I trust her not to hurt my husband or the children we might have?"

"Uutuk, we have no spirit powers, and the shaman of this village is old and weak. Even with our prayers and chants and the cutting of the body, how can we be sure we do not bring her anger again to us and to our families? Ghaden has told you how much she hates my wife, Aqamdax."

"I will take the chance, Brother," Uutuk said. "And now is the time to do it, when your wife is not here in the village, so if K'os's spirit has a moment between death and my cutting, at least she will not be able to reach Aqamdax or your children."

Chakliux crouched on his haunches, his back to the lodge. "We have to wait until her forty days of mourning have ended," he said. "Even if she does not truly grieve over Seal, I would not want to bring the curse of a widow's taboos on either of us."

"We are stronger than you think, my brother," Uutuk said. She sat on the ground, crossed her legs like the River People do, and unlaced her caribou hide boots. "I have heard the stories of your otter foot, and the power in it." She smiled. "Has no one told you the stories about my feet?"

"You have otter feet, too?" he asked, the doubt clear on his face.

"Not otter," she said. "Look."

She pulled off her boots and flickered the grass that lined them from her feet, then pointed to the place where her small toes should be.

"What happened?"

"This toe I cut off in mourning for my grandfather," she said, lifting her right foot. "The other toe my grandfather cut off when I was very small. They say a child does not remember when they have only three summers, but I remember."

"It is good that the man is dead," Chakliux said.

"Oh no, Chakliux. Let me tell you what happened. I told you how my grandfather and I took a boat from our island to the islands of the First Men."

"Yes."

"It was not an easy journey, and we did not do it willingly, but a storm had taken our paddle, so we could not return to our own people. We were caught in a current that carried us north. During that time we ate all our food. My grandfather cut off his own toes to use as bait for fish, but he caught nothing. We were starving, so I asked him to use my toe, and finally he did." She smiled at Chakliux, showing her white and even teeth. "Then he caught many fish, and so we had food enough to live until K'os found us."

"So that toe saved your life and your grandfather's life."

"Yes."

"A strange family we have, you and I, that both of us have our power in our feet!"

They laughed together, then Chakliux said, "It is not much, that kind of power."

"So far, it's been enough, nae'?" she said to him in the River tongue, then switched again to the First Men language. She pulled on her boots, straightened, and said, "I told you my story so you would understand that as a little child, I was willing to give much to protect my grandfather. I am willing to do even more for my husband and any children we might have."

She lay a hand over her belly, and Chakliux, having seen his own wife do the same, asked, "Already?"

Her answer was shy. "I think so," she said, "though my husband does not yet know. Please do not tell him until we decide what to do with K'os."

"We will give her nothing beyond her mourning," Chakliux said. "We cannot allow her to take more lives."

The Wilderness Northwest of the Fish Camp

CRIES-LOUD'S STORY

Cries-loud spent the day hunting, and brought two fat hares and a brace of ptarmigan back to his campfire. He cleaned them and cooked them on spits, ate as much as he wanted, and wrapped the remainder in grass to save for the next day.

As the night darkened, he heard the noise of someone walking. He jumped to his feet, had knife and lance in hand before he even thought, but then his mother called out, and he ran to her. She was smiling.

Before he could ask questions, she said, "I couldn't let you leave without seeing you one more time."

Though she still smiled, he could see that tears brightened her eyes. "They didn't have a place for you?" he asked.

"They do. They know Cen and somehow had heard that he's dead. I didn't tell them any differently. There's an old man who will take me as wife."

"If he's old, how will he feed you?"

"He's not too old to hunt, and he has three sons who live in the village. We won't starve, and when we finally hear the truth about Cen, I'll tell him that even though Cen is alive, I want to stay with him, that I'm weary of being a trader's wife. By that time, my parkas and my trapping will have made him happy, and maybe I can even give him a son or daughter."

Cries-loud beckoned her toward the fire, invited her to eat.

"Just a little," she told him. "I must return, and I don't want to get lost in the dark. I just wanted you to know . . ."

"I'm glad you've found a place, Mother."

"Perhaps you can visit me someday," she said, "you and your wives and those children you will get."

She was eating quickly, as though she had had nothing all day, but he told himself that she was not that hungry, just that she wanted to leave and return to the old man.

She ate a ptarmigan and then wiped her fingers on her pants and stood. For a moment, Cries-loud once more became a little boy, and tucked himself into her arms. She was the first to break away, and she turned quickly and said in a voice heavy with tears, "Watch over my daughters."

Then she was gone, and Cries-loud heaped branches on his campfire until the flames leaped, making light to fill some of the emptiness.

The Four Rivers Village

K'OS'S STORY

K'os leaned close to the side of the lodge, tried to hear what her children were saying, but the double caribou hide cover and the rocks and sod of the walls swallowed their words. Somehow Chakliux had managed to turn Uutuk against her, and all this had happened because of the woman Red Leaf. If Cen and Ghaden had not gone after Red Leaf, then Chakliux would not have had so much time alone to talk Uutuk into hating her.

Still, the girl should know better! Had K'os been anything but a good mother to her? Aaa! What made children so selfish? Chakliux kept her in this lodge, did not allow her to see the sun. How could she store up heat in her bones against the coming winter?

"Don't allow your anger to eat your own flesh," she told herself. "How will you fight if you are weak?"

She settled her mind on the people of the Four Rivers village. How many had died? Three tens, she thought. Six handfuls! Yes, but many of the hunters had already left for the caribou hunts, so those she had killed were mostly children and old ones, a few of the wives who had stayed behind. Then, too, the young, strong ones had grown sick from her poison, but it hadn't killed them. She had not only used the purple-flowered plant from the First Men, but also baneberry. The First Men's poison was better. When she used it on the first few who died—all elders—it had caused no great alarm. They seemed to have died in their sleep, though one had stumbled from her daughter's lodge, clutching her throat and gasping for each breath.

Then K'os had decided to kill great numbers all at once by poisoning the hearth boiling bags. But Seal, greedy for more than her own cooking, had eaten from those bags. Stupid man! She had fed him more than enough here in Cen's lodge.

No one had suspected her of using poison. Why would she want to kill her own husband? But then Chakliux came, and Cen with him. Who could believe that Cen was alive? Who could believe that Chakliux would come to this village and accuse her of killing the people? And now he had turned Uutuk against her. K'os would have to make her plans much more carefully now that she did not have Uutuk or Seal to help her.

She heard voices in the entrance tunnel, Uutuk, yes, and perhaps Chakliux. She pulled a thumbnail against the whites of her eyes and turned to face them with tears on her cheeks.

The hardness on Uutuk's face melted away, and she held a hand out toward K'os, but then quickly drew it back. K'os said nothing, but she saw the furtive glance Uutuk gave Chakliux. His mouth was set, his eyes cold. He leaned over and whispered to Uutuk. Uutuk frowned, and, though she also whispered, it seemed that she was arguing with him. Finally he shrugged and spoke to K'os.

"My sister thinks that you should be allowed to attend the mourning ceremonies."

Each day the people made more ceremonies, trying to appease the dead. For more nights than K'os could count, the death drums had broken into her sleep.

She wiped her nose against the sleeve of her parka and said, "What, and have the villagers kill me? Surely by now you two have told them that I caused these deaths. Surely by now you've laid the blame for this curse on me, even though my own husband is among the dead."

Uutuk began shaking her head in denial, and K'os had to close her lips tightly over a smile. Chakliux had not taken Uutuk as far from her as K'os had feared.

"You think we're fools?" Chakliux asked. "If they believe you did this, then what chance do we have for safety, your daughter and her husband and I?"

K'os kept herself from blinking, and so was able to bring more tears from her eyes. "What will I do without a husband, now that I'm old?" she asked.

Uutuk went to K'os, pulled her into an embrace. K'os looked through her eyelashes at Chakliux, allowed herself a tiny smile.

"Uutuk . . ." Chakliux began, then shook his head and turned on his heel. Just before he left the lodge he said, "Sister, don't let her fool you with those tears. I'll come for you both when it's time for the ceremonies." He pointed at K'os. "Don't let her leave."

He slipped into the entrance tunnel, and K'os clung hard to Uutuk. "Oh, my daughter, what a fool I was to allow your husband to bring us to this village. I had many friends here, but now most of them have died with this sickness, and my memories are tainted by Chakliux's hatred."

K'os took a long breath and let it out in a shudder. "What will happen to my poor husband when his bones are left here among a people he did not know? How much better that he be buried on our own island, with your grandfather's wise spirit to watch over him."

She continued to speak about Uutuk's grandfather until she could feel Uutuk trembling and knew that the girl, too, wept. Then she said, "You are a good daughter, Uutuk, better than I deserve. You are all I ever wanted in a child. Though I was cursed with Chakliux, surely I have been blessed with you."

She waited, hoping to hear some words of kindness from

Uutuk, but Uutuk said nothing, and finally she loosed her hold on K'os, and went for a bladder of water, dumped some out on a rag of caribou hide and washed her face, then offered the rag to K'os.

"I am a widow," K'os said. "Let them see my grief."

FORTY-EIGHT

GHELI'S STORY
After leaving Cries-loud's camp, Gheli waited until it was
truly dark. Then she set out toward the Four Rivers village,
walking under the moonlight. She walked quickly so that
Cries-loud would not catch up with her during the next day.

The following night and all the long nights after, she allowed herself only a little sleep. When she finally came to
the Four Rivers village, she came from the direction that few
people would follow, near the death scaffolds. She held her
breath at the stink, but could not hold in her tears at the number of new bodies, small and large, stacked there.

Her heart pulsed in fear as she thought of her daughters.
Had they, too, died? Surely at least Daes would know to be
wary of anything K'os gave her. When she saw that the village hearthfires were dead, she breathed out her relief. The
women must have realized that anyone who ate from those
boiling bags had become sick. Or there were so few women
left in the village, there was no one to tend the fires.

Most likely that, Gheli thought when she crouched to
study the coals. They had not even been banked. No woman
healthy and strong would leave a fire to burn itself out. That
was too foolish. She stirred the coals with her walking stick

to be sure there was no hidden fire that the wind might pick up and dash against lodge covers. But there was not even an edge of heat.

So now she must see whether K'os was still alive or if Cen or Chakliux had killed her. If K'os was dead, then Gheli would leave as quietly as she had come. Why not go back to that village beyond her fish camp? There was always the chance that one of the men would take her as wife. Besides, someday Cries-loud might bring Daes and Duckling to see her.

Of course, there was good reason to believe that K'os was still alive. Her mourning for her First Men husband would not yet be finished. Why add unnecessary curses by killing K'os before her husband's spirit was completely settled in the land of the dead?

If K'os was alive, where would she stay? Surely Ghaden and his wife would be living in Cen's lodge. Which might mean that Uutuk's mother, K'os, would also be there. But would Cen allow K'os to live within the same walls as his daughters? Gheli heard a voice coming from Cen's lodge. She ducked down so quickly that she set the nearest pack of dogs barking.

Someone came outside. It was Chakliux. How could she miss his limp? She thought she heard the soft sounds of a chant, a spirit song, but she could not be sure. He lifted his head, looked up at the sky. He was praying.

She felt a moment of hope. Perhaps by now he had already killed K'os, then she could sneak away in the night. No one would ever know she had been there.

After a long time, Chakliux went back inside, and Gheli crept forward on feet and hands to the rear of Cen's lodge. She stood as close as she could to the caribou hide cover, but heard nothing. No voices. That was good. No mourning. No healing chants. Perhaps K'os was still alive, and Chakliux merely prayed for wisdom to know what to do.

Ah, Chakliux, sleep. Tomorrow you will have no worries. What is one more death? Just another mourning.

Gheli squeezed the pouch that hung from her left wrist, loosened the drawstring, and stroked the long-bladed knife she had borrowed from Cen's weapon cache before she left for fish camp. It was obsidian, and Cen claimed it had once belonged to a man who lived so long ago that even the story-tellers had forgotten about him.

The moon was just past full, one edge of it rubbed away, raw and ragged, bleeding out its light. She waited through the night, the pouch clasped in her fist, until the moon set and there was only darkness. Even the dogs stayed in tight circles beside the lodges, kept their faces covered with their tails. She moved to the entrance tunnel, placed a hand on the caribou hide doorflap. It was rough and hard against her fingers. Her stomach twisted and she gagged, then fought down the fear that choked her. She gripped the haft of the knife to give herself courage, moved her fingers over the pouch so she could feel the finely ground powder hidden within.

She waited in the tunnel until the air settled and warmed a little. An edge of the doorflap was pulled away from the opening, and Gheli leaned in close. Her eyes had adjusted to the darkness, so the few remaining hearth coals gave enough light for her to see. She scanned the lodge. There were three, no, four, on the men's side. She recognized Chakliux and Ghaden. The one so close to Ghaden was too small for a man. She had to be K'os's daughter, Ghaden's wife.

The other was Cen. Her eyes softened. She knew well the way he slept—on his side, his legs drawn up, an arm flung out over the fox fur cover. He snorted, mumbled in his sleep, and she froze until he was quiet again. On the women's side there was Daes. And K'os. Again Gheli felt the need to retch. She cupped a hand over her mouth until the nausea passed.

Daes slept as far from the woman as she could, her back pressed into the matting that covered the stone and sod of the lower wall.

The years had most likely changed K'os's face into some-thing much different from what Gheli remembered, but the hand that lay over the sleeping robe marked her. She studied K'os, grimaced. This would not be as easy as she had hoped. The woman was wrapped tightly in her furred sleeping robe. Would the obsidian blade cut through it? She could go for K'os's neck, but what if she missed, connected with jaw or shoulder bone?

Gheli lifted a prayer to whatever spirits might be willing to help her, then crept to the pile of sleeping robes stacked on the women's side. She pulled one over herself and lay down between Daes and K'os. Daes moaned and pressed even closer to the wall, but K'os did not stir, so when the voice came, it startled Gheli into jumping to her feet.

"You have returned." The words were whispered, and they came from K'os. "Cen told us wolves killed you. You seem to be good at cheating death. Perhaps I need to know your secret."

K'os sat up and pushed the robe down around her waist. She had changed much, was finally an old woman.

"You've come to kill me," she said.

"Yes, so Cen or Chakliux will not have to."

"My mourning has not ended. You will risk that curse?"

"Yes, to protect my daughters."

From the corners of her eyes, Gheli saw Daes scoot toward the hearth. The girl began to hiss, and called out to her father. Finally Cen awoke, Ghaden and Uutuk also, then Chakliux. Ghaden thrust his wife behind him while he groped for the weapons that he had laid near his bedding mats.

He lifted a short lance, and Gheli called to him, "Let me kill her. What is one more curse for someone like me who has earned so many?"

Ghaden looked at Cen and said, "Wait."

"They let me keep nothing except this small crooked knife," said K'os, and raised herself to her knees, swept away the sleeping robe. She lifted the knife. The blade was no longer than the last joint of a finger, and it had been set into the side of a caribou rib, the curve of the rib good for a woman who needed to use that knife for her sewing.

It could take out an eye, Gheli supposed, or make a slash in the flesh, but she wore a parka, and the small blade would not easily cut through the hide. She had only to watch her face and her hands. Nothing more.

K'os had grown thin in her old age, and she seemed much smaller than Gheli had remembered. Perhaps she had also grown weak. Gheli allowed herself to hope that she would live through the attack.

"Cen," she said, "if I kill her, will you let me go?"

"You'll leave the village?" he asked.

Gheli opened her mouth to answer, but Daes began to wail, a high-pitched keening.

"Be quiet!" Cen shouted at the girl, and Daes covered her face with her hands, muffled her sobs.

"I will leave," Gheli promised.

"You'll be dead," K'os said, then she called out to her daughter, "Uutuk, you'll let her do this to me? You won't ask your husband to help me?" K'os's voice was suddenly soft and pleading.

Uutuk was crying, but she turned her face away.

K'os looked at Chakliux, smirked. "Why did I ever think I should raise children?" she asked. There was hatred in her words, anger and also, Gheli thought, some fear.

"Be careful, Mother," Daes said in a small voice.

Gheli turned her head toward Daes, and at that moment, K'os lunged, laid Gheli's cheek open with the blade of the crooked knife.

Gheli thrust out with her knife. K'os was not wearing a parka, but only a loose caribou hide shirt. Gheli's knife went easily into K'os's belly. K'os screamed, slashed again with her crooked knife, this time catching Gheli's forehead, then the top of her hand. Gheli ignored the pain, ignored Cen and Chakliux. She thought they might pull her away, but they did not. And she jerked down hard on the haft of her knife, pulled with all her strength, leaving a long wound in K'os's abdomen. The stink of slashed bowels filled the lodge. Uutuk buried her head in her husband's shoulder and cried out her anguish.

K'os was screaming, her hands at the edges of her gaping wound. Gheli threw the knife, and it landed in the hearth coals where the rawhide that bound the blade to the haft began to sizzle and smoke. She opened the pouch and shook the contents over K'os's face and belly.

"You wanted to poison the people of this village," Gheli shouted at her, "well, now you are poisoned. Now you are dead. Tell your spirit to do to me as you wish. I've been cursed by many, so you will have to fight for your turn to destroy me."

She spun to face Ghaden and held her hands out, palms up. "I have no more weapons," she said. "Ask your wife if she wants me dead. I won't fight you."

Then, in a horrible voice, K'os cried out, "Ghaden, you have no need. She's already dead." Then her words were only curses, against Gheli, against Cen, against her children.

Uutuk covered her ears, and Ghaden, his arm around her, walked Uutuk to the entrance tunnel. They left the lodge, and Daes crept out after them.

"And you," K'os screamed at Chakliux. She lay back on the floor, and the pain took her voice. "You," she whispered. "You will . . . stay to watch . . . me die?"

He did not answer, but took down a water bladder and carried it to her. He lifted her head so she could drink. She took a mouthful but spat it in his face. He left her and went to stand beside Cen.

"I'm sorry this happened in your lodge," Chakliux said.

"I'll burn it," Cen told him.

Gheli, still on her knees, looked up at him. "You know I'm already cursed," she said. "Let me take what I need. What will it hurt, if you're going to burn it anyway?"

"Take what you want," Cen told her.

K'os's moans turned into laughter. "You need nothing," she told Gheli, "except to prepare for the spirit world." She lifted a bent finger to point at the cuts on Gheli's face. "I told you, you're already dead," she said again.

"I've had worse than this," Gheli told her. "What's a little blood?"

But Chakliux took a step toward his mother and asked, "What did you do?"

"Poison," she gasped. She lifted the amulet pouch that hung at her neck, opened it, and sifted the powder into the wound at her belly. "Now it will take me also," she said. "More quickly than Red Leaf's poison. I learned . . . from the First Men. It stops . . . the breath . . . Once in the blood . . . it works quickly." The last words hissed from her throat, and she looked up at Gheli, saw the horror on the woman's face.

"The knife blade?" Gheli asked, the question only a whisper.

K'os took one last breath and began to choke, and in Gheli's ears, the choking sounded like laughter.

FORTY-NINE

DUCKLING'S STORY
They burned Cen's lodge and all that was in it, weapons,
food and clothing, floor mats and boiling bags, baskets of
spruce root and bark. Not only those things burned but also
the bodies of K'os and Gheli, and when all that was left was
ashes and bones, the shaman of the village made chants to
protect them against the curses of those two women. Then
he took the bones and made a long journey to leave the
packet that held the charred remains far from any village of
the River People.

Cries-loud returned the day after the deaths, and joined
his sister and Cen in mourning Gheli. But no one mourned
K'os. When Chakliux, Cries-loud, Ghaden, and Uutuk left
the Four Rivers People to return to Chakliux's village, Cen
and Daes went also, and they took Duckling with them.

The night before they arrived at Chakliux's village, Cen
came to Cries-loud, crouched on his haunches beside him.
Cen held his baby daughter in his arms, perched her on his
knee.

"I've decided to go with Ghaden and his wife to the
Traders' Beach once this winter has passed," he said. "Perhaps I will go even beyond that to Uutuk's island. I have so

little left to me that I must begin once more as a trader, as if I were a young man. How better to make that beginning than to visit those people who still hunt the whale? My daughter Daes wants to join me, and even Chakliux might come as far as the Traders' Beach. But I have this good daughter who needs a father and mother—or perhaps a brother—to raise her." He looked into Cries-loud's eyes. "She will be strong like her mother, and perhaps with the right family, she'll also grow wise."

When Cries-loud held out his arms, Cen gave him the child quickly and walked away. He was gone a long time before he returned to the warmth of the campfire.

The last day they traveled, Cries-loud refused to carry Duckling on his back, as most children are carried. Instead he held her cradleboard in his arms the whole way, talked to her about everything they saw, listened in delight as she babbled back to him.

When they arrived at Chakliux's village, he didn't stop to talk to the elders, their mouths filled with questions. Instead, he carried Duckling into the entrance tunnel of his lodge, set her down carefully, and waited to see if she would cry. She did not. She was well wrapped in a soft woven hare blanket, and so he knew she would not get cold. He left her and crawled into the lodge. Yaa looked up at him, then leaped to her feet, gladness in her eyes.

He told her quickly about K'os and his mother, and she stood with her mouth open as though trying to decide whether or not to make a mourning song. He lifted a finger in the sign for quietness and said, "I have something I need to tell you."

Fear, then sadness crossed her face. She nodded her head as though she knew what he was going to say.

"I brought someone with me," he began. Yaa took a long breath, and he added, "To help you with your work."

"That is good," she said, but her voice was thin, fragile. "She's welcome, my husband. Here in this lodge . . ." Her words broke. She cleared her throat, then continued, "Until you are able to build her a lodge of her own."

"No," Cries-loud said.

"I'll be a good sister-wife to her," said Yaa, and she began to speak of all the things the two wives would do together.

"No," Cries-loud said again, but knew there was only one way to quiet Yaa once she started talking to hide her pain, and so he went back into the entrance tunnel and picked up Duckling. The girl had fallen asleep, but she opened her eyes and, seeing his face, smiled. He pressed his cheek against her forehead, and crept into the lodge. He expected to hear Yaa cry out, but she was quiet. He stood up and saw that her eyes were closed, her face drawn tight.

"Yaa?" he said.

Her eyes flew open, and she stretched her mouth into a wide smile of welcome. When she saw the baby, she clasped her hands to her chest and stood with her mouth open, as though she had forgotten how to speak.

"You don't want your daughter?" he asked.

"My daughter?"

"Yes."

She took the child, began to laugh. Suddenly she stopped and said, "She belongs to your new wife?"

"You are my only wife, Yaa," he told her. "She belongs to you, to both of us."

Then Yaa started to cry, silent sobs that shook her so hard she had to give the baby back to Cries-loud. He stood there holding them both, his wife and his daughter, and he reminded himself that hunters do not cry over such little things as babies, hunters do not cry for happiness. But then he thought, Perhaps sometimes they do.

Herendeen Bay, Alaska Peninsula
602 B.C.

The next evening, when a group of men had returned from six, seven days hunting sea lions, and the women had de-

488 / SUE HARRISON

cided to take a rest from fishing, Yikaas again told his story about K'os's death. Qumalix was there to translate for him, and other storytellers, including Kuy'aa and Sky Catcher, also listened.

When Yikaas had finished his tale, Sky Catcher called out, "Wait. You claim that is how K'os died?"

"So it is said," Yikaas answered, using the words familiar to all storytellers.

"I have heard a different story."

Sky Catcher spoke belligerently, and Yikaas saw him for what he was—a child whose body had grown into manhood, but whose mind stayed small.

"Tell it," Yikaas said graciously, and stepped back to make room for him.

Qumalix gave Yikaas a bleak look, and so he understood that she did not like to translate for the man, but Sky Catcher stretched his mouth into a broad smile and began, even forgetting the polite words most storytellers use to let their listeners know a new tale is being told.

"K'os was an evil woman," he said, "and she wanted to kill the Four Rivers People for throwing her out of their village many years before. She also wanted to kill Chakliux." He paused for a moment as if searching for what to say about Chakliux, and finally he added, "She hated Chakliux for many reasons, mostly because he was so wise and good."

The people in the ulax murmured at that, and a few threw out suggestions as to why K'os wanted to kill her own son, but Sky Catcher ignored them and went on with his story. It was not a good story, and Yikaas soon grew impatient. Sky Catcher spoke too long about the conversations between Cen and Ghaden and the agreement they made to kill K'os.

The two carried out their plan, and K'os died in the night, with both men's blades in her chest. But even in describing the death, Sky Catcher's words were flat, and Yikaas tried not to rejoice in the people's complaints.

When Sky Catcher finished, most of the listeners were polite, but one man, a First Men hunter, said, "Keep the story as Yikaas told it."

Sky Catcher began to shout insults at the man, but Qumalix laid a hand on his arm and said, "I have also heard a different story about K'os's death. Perhaps you would like to hear that one."

Sky Catcher curled his lip at her, but at least he sat down to listen.

Qumalix's story started much like Yikaas's had, but when Gheli left Cries-loud, she stayed to live in that far River village as wife to an old man there. Yikaas listened patiently, thinking he would find fault with her story as he had with Sky Catcher's, but then, as with all Qumalix's tales, he was caught into her words, and somehow he was again a boy, learning stories that he would someday tell himself.

FIFTY

The Four Rivers Village
6435 B.C.

QUMALIX'S STORY OF K'OS'S DEATH
Chakliux sat alone, staring into the hearth coals. He had
been given a place in the lodge next to Cen's. The man who
owned the lodge had lost his wife and children, and after his
mourning had decided to go hunt caribou. The empty lodge
seemed full of the dead ones' ghosts. They haunted Chakliux's dreams and pushed him into a decision to kill K'os.
How else could she be stopped?

Chakliux banked the hearthfire and pulled on his parka.
He walked through the village. Though it was a sunny day,
there were few people outside. Many were still sick, and
others kept mourning vigils in their lodges.

He saw an old woman scurrying toward the river. She was
carrying empty water bladders, and when he caught up to
her, he offered to fill them. She raised her eyebrows at him
and for a moment hugged the bladders to her chest, as
though she were afraid, but then she smiled, showing a
mouth empty of teeth, her lips collapsed in over the gums.

But her eyes were bright, peeking out at him from the wrinkles of her face.

She waited at the top of the bank while he slid down the incline to the pool where the women got water. He filled each bladder, tied their strings together, and slung them over his shoulder. When he climbed back up toward her, she held out a hand, as though she were strong enough to help him up the last few steps to level ground.

"You're the otter foot," she said to him, and her voice was surprisingly clear and loud, a young woman's voice coming from an old mouth.

"Yes," he said, "and you, Aunt, what do you call yourself?"

She looked at him warily as though trying to decide whether to trust him with her name. Finally she said, "Aunt is good," and Chakliux hid his smile. Who could blame her? With all that had happened in this village, why trust anyone?

"Did you lose people, Aunt? Do you mourn?"

"A grandson," she said softly, and her eyes filled.

"I hope there is some way to lift the curse that has come to your village."

She looked down at his foot. "Some say you have power," she said, "others that you brought the curse."

"What do you think?" Chakliux asked her.

"I think it is the woman, but who listens to me? I am old. But they forget that I remember the first time she came."

"You remember when K'os was here before?"

The old one hissed and lifted a hand, tapped his mouth with her fingers. "Don't say her name. It might give her the power to leave the lodge."

"Cen is with her. He won't let her leave."

"She can do all kinds of things. She's like a shaman. She can sit there and be with Cen while her spirit is out here doing evil. She is like that. I saw it in her the first time she came to us. She lived with my friend and her husband. They were old then, and died long ago, but they didn't see what she was. We should have sent her away the first day she came." She nodded and began to mumble as though arguing with herself, and finally she spoke out to say, "Of course, she still might have come back. She's one of those who forgets nothing." She gave him a sly look, arched her sparse brows. "They say you are her son, and the girl, the young wife Uutuk, she's the daughter. Is that true?"

"She raised us both. There was a time when I called her mother."

"So perhaps you helped her in the cursing," the old woman said.

"No, we did not."

She laughed. "What else would you say? That you helped her? We still have enough men left in this village to kill you both."

Her words were a boast and also, Chakliux recognized, a way to comfort herself.

"You're lucky you have Cen," she continued. "He's the only one who stands between you and death. And look what has happened to him. Your mother's curse has even taken his wife.

"I know what it is to mourn, but this curse is more terrible than most. I sat beside my grandson for two days watching him die." Again her eyes were wet, and she did not bother to blink away the tears. They pooled in the pouches above her cheekbones. "Everything he had ever eaten came up," she said, gesturing toward her mouth, "and his bowels . . ." She shook her head. "I wanted to take his pain. Why did this happen to him when he was young, and here I am old and nearly worthless?" She held out her hands to show him that they were shaking. "I should be the one dead," she said. "I should be."

"Aunt, there's always need for your wisdom," Chakliux said gently. He gave her the water bladders, and before she went into her lodge, she said, "Sometimes people call me Near Mouse."

* * *

He knew the poison. It was from the baneberry plant. Years ago, K'os had tricked the woman Dii into poisoning her own husband with it. The death had been no loss. Fox Barking was a man who caused all those around him problems, but at that time he had been leader of a village, and Dii was fortunate to avoid the punishment of death.

The man's death had been a blessing for Chakliux's family. His brother Sok had taken Dii as wife, and their marriage was a good one. She had given Sok healthy children, and not only that, she had the gift of dreaming caribou. Their village had not been hungry since Dii came to them, for she could almost always tell the hunters where the herds were traveling. What a fool Fox Barking had been to see her gift as a threat to his own power.

Chakliux sighed. K'os's death would cost him much. Perhaps his own life. Uutuk had offered to help him, but how could he allow her to be involved? She was too young, and still loved K'os as mother.

Chakliux was not a vengeful man, and though Cen thought it was only just for K'os to die a slow and painful death, Chakliux did not want to see her suffer. Besides, a lingering death would give her time to curse those who caused it. He went back to the lodge and chose two throwing spears, each with a long stone point, then went to the village hearths. The four fires had been started again, but there were no women tending boiling pots. The fires burned only so that anyone careless enough to allow their own hearth to go out could come and get coals.

Chakliux squatted beside one of the fires and held his spears in the smoke. For a long time he prayed for strength, for wisdom, for safety. He took his hunting knife from its sheath and prayed over it as well, and when he felt he had gathered enough power, he left the hearths and walked to Cen's lodge.

K'os was waiting for him. She stood slowly, her eyes

burning. "You will kill me yourself," she said, then held a hand out toward Uutuk. "In front of my daughter?" she asked.

"Leave, Uutuk," Chakliux said. "You don't have to be here. Why see this? Remember the good things this mother did for you, and think of nothing else."

Uutuk scrambled to her feet. She had begun to cry.

"Where is your husband?" Chakliux asked her, but he did not take his eyes from K'os.

"He and Cen went hunting ptarmigan." Her crying made the words difficult for Chakliux to understand.

"And Daes?"

"She doesn't want to stay with me in this lodge any more than she must," K'os answered, and Chakliux could not help but marvel at the calmness of her voice. She was wearing only caribou hide pants and a few necklaces, her chest bare in the custom of the First Men. If he could not have seen her hands or face, he would have thought she was young. She held her shoulders so straight, and her breasts were still plump, unlike those of most old women. Her eyes, too, were bright, but hard and cold, as they had always been. She was holding the upper of a caribou hide boot, furred, and cut to fit to a sealskin sole that lay on the floor at her feet. Uutuk had a similar boot in her hand, this one with the sole partially attached, dangling at the heel, gaping like an open mouth.

"You think you can kill me?" K'os said. "Why now, when you have never been able to do it before?"

"Go, Uutuk!" Chakliux told the girl, but Uutuk hesitated, looking first at him, then at her mother. "Now, Uutuk!"

"Do it quickly," Uutuk said to him and suddenly gagged. She caught her breath and straightened, moved a hand to her belly. K'os's eyes went wide.

"No!" Uutuk said, and she covered her stomach with both hands.

K'os threw back her head and began to laugh. "No wonder you are both so anxious to kill me. Even you, Uutuk. You think I will curse that babe you carry?" She dropped the boot from her hand and spread her arms wide, took a step toward Uutuk, and suddenly Chakliux realized that she had a knife in her hand, a small-bladed crooked knife. One a woman would use for sewing. She clapped a hand on Uutuk's shoulder and the girl flinched, but K'os's grasp was strong. She pressed the knife close to Uutuk's neck.

"Such a small blade," K'os said. "What damage could it do?" She laughed. "There is poison you probably don't know, Chakliux."

Uutuk groaned.

"You were foolish, Chakliux, not to get her out of here one way or another before you came in with your spears. But how good for me that you did not. For now I know that I have a grandchild. I think I might like to take him with me to the spirit world. It's a long journey and better made with a companion, nae'? Think what a favor I did all these Four Rivers People who once tried to kill me. I let them go together. Now they'll have a village there. And you think I have no compassion. Remember, they made me go alone, in winter." She moved the knife. "Aaa, I was telling you about the poison. It's used by whale hunters on the tips of their harpoons. It stops the breathing; it stills the heart. Uutuk, a small scratch might allow you to live and only take the babe, but I'm not sure. I've much to learn about this poison. Perhaps it will take you, too. Then the three of us can go together, you and me and our baby."

Then, suddenly, someone in the entrance tunnel called to Chakliux. The old woman Near Mouse came in carrying a bag that smelled of cooked meat. She stopped just inside the door. Her mouth fell open, and she let out a scream. In that moment, Uutuk dropped to the floor, and K'os lost her grip on the girl's shoulder. Then Chakliux threw a spear, took K'os high in the center of her chest, threw another that caught her in the throat. The weight of the spears and the thrust of Chakliux's throws took K'os backward to the floor.

Blood pooled around her head and neck, and when she no longer twitched, Chakliux went close enough to kick the crooked knife from her hand. Uutuk came into his arms, and they held one another. He thought she was crying, but when she finally pulled away, he saw that her eyes were dry.

"I cannot mourn her," she said softly.

"Leave now," he said, and asked Near Mouse to take Uutuk back to her lodge. When they were gone, he knelt beside K'os's body and carefully cut her apart at each joint.

Herendeen Bay, Alaska Peninsula
602 B.C.

"Your story is better," one of the River men told Qumalix.

"No," said another. "Yikaas's story is the way it happened."

An old woman spoke up and said, "I heard that Ghaden killed her, to protect his wife, and when K'os was dead, her throat looked like a wolf had torn it out, so everyone knew that the dog Biter had come back to protect Ghaden."

Several others murmured that they had heard the same story. Another said that Uutuk had killed K'os, and another that Cen had done it. One old man told them that he heard Cries-loud had killed K'os to protect his mother.

"Which one should we believe?" a little boy asked. "How do we know what is true?"

Then Kuy'aa stood up. "Perhaps the truth is that K'os died many times in many ways. Did she deserve any less than that?"

Yikaas and Qumalix sat together in the storyteller's ulax. By the time everyone had left and old Kuy'aa was snoring in one of the curtained sleeping places, Yikaas himself had been ready to sleep. But now that he and Qumalix were alone, his mind was suddenly clear. Even his eyes no longer burned from the smoke of the seal oil lamp.

"Your story about K'os's death was good," Yikaas said. He turned so he could watch Qumalix's face as he spoke to her. The walls of his heart suddenly seemed too thin, so that with each pulse of his blood, they trembled, but he held his voice steady, and spoke with a boldness he did not feel. "I still think my story is right, but that doesn't mean that yours isn't good."

He expected an angry retort. Qumalix always said what she thought, and he had grown to like that. She looked at him with brows raised.

"Why do you say that?" she asked.

"Because it *is* good," he told her.

"No, not about my story, about your own. Why do you say yours is right?"

"The storytellers in my village have been telling the right story since it happened."

"And mine haven't?"

He shrugged, turned his head to stare at the seal oil lamp. He missed the good hearthfires of his own people. The poor flickering lamp gave so little flame. How was a man supposed to have his thoughts strengthened by that?

"Look," he finally said, and slipped his caribou hide boot from his right foot. He expected her to be surprised, and she was, so surprised that she spoke in her own language, then, apologizing, said, "Otter foot," in the River tongue.

"I understood the first time," he told her. He had not lived in a First Men village most of the summer without picking up some of their words. "This is why my story is right and yours is wrong. My foot proves that Chakliux's spirit, some small part of it, lives in me."

Yikaas cupped the foot in his hand and spread his toes. They were webbed. "See?"

He allowed himself a little smile, but said nothing more, waiting for her to agree with him. What else could she do but agree?

"I'll be back," she said, and left to go into one of the curtained sleeping places. She returned carrying two small seal-skin bags.

"I have these," she said. "You know the stories of Chagak and Kiin?"

"I know them."

"Do you remember the carving Chagak owned, the one of man, wife, and child?"

He was not happy about the way this was going. He shifted so that his otter foot was more visible to her. She opened one of the bags. It had a drawstring top, and she dumped out a little lump of dark yellowed ivory.

"See, look," she said.

He picked up the ivory, turned it in his hand. It might have been a carving of three people, but it was so old and cracked, worn smooth by handling, that the faces were no longer truly faces and the bodies were merely suggestions of what they once had been.

"Who can tell by this?" he asked. "It could be something the sea itself tumbled into being."

She leaned close to him and turned the carving upside down. "You can see that there was a little hole here where the carver Shuganan hid a knife blade."

There was a hole, but Yikaas shrugged his shoulders and shook his head. Qumalix blew out her breath in irritation and opened the other sealskin bag. "You cannot deny that this is a whale's tooth carved to look like a shell."

He picked it up. "Yes, but why should I believe that it was the whale tooth shell that Kiin made? Anyone could have done this."

She snatched it out of his hand and dropped it back into the bag. "But anyone didn't."

He smiled at her. "Even if it is Kiin's, what does that prove? She wasn't a storyteller."

"One of her children was."

He shrugged his shoulders and opened his mouth wide in a smile. "You just don't want to admit that my story is true, and that the otter foot is the best proof."

She bowed her head, and for a moment, he felt a twinge of sadness for her.

"I said your story was good," he told her.

She nodded. "But you are right," she said. "The otter foot is the best proof."

Then she slowly unlaced her left boot, sat down on her rump and pulled it off, extended her leg until her foot was in his lap. She spread her webbed toes and began to laugh.

EPILOGUE

Herendeen Bay, Alaska Peninsula
590 B.C.

The child wiggled in anticipation and looked up into his mother's face. He never tired of the storytelling, though he had heard the stories so often. His mother leaned down to rub his foot. It ached a little after the long day playing with his new friends here. This was the first time his parents had brought him to the Traders' Beach. When they visited the First Men, they usually left him with an old aunt at his father's River village. But he knew the First Men language because his mother spoke it.

"One last story," his father was saying, and the people groaned that the storytelling was almost over for that day. "A tale of an old woman's joy," he said. "You remember the storyteller Qung who long ago lived in this very village?"

There was a murmur of acknowledgment.

"She finally grew so old and so bent that she stayed in her ulax all the time and depended on others to come to her. Her hearing had grown dim, and she lived mostly in the stories she held in her mind. But one day even her old ears could hear the excitement in the voices outside her ulax . . ."

The Traders' Beach
6427 B.C.

QUNG'S STORY

Qung's heart trembled within her chest. She remembered stories about villages attacked, of women raped and men killed. Her people had lived in peace a long time, but still, who could say when strange warriors might decide to come upon them? She pushed herself up on thin, gnarled legs and hobbled to her sleeping place. At the back of that small niche, under the grass mats that lined the walls, was the entrance to a hidden tunnel that led out of the ulax.

The tunnel rose gradually, and Qung followed it on hands and feet, her knuckles scraping the bare earth of the floor, her fingers grasping at any handhold as she climbed the slope. When she reached the end of the tunnel, she thrust her head and upper body outside, trusted that the long grasses that grew over the sod of the tunnel roof would hide her from her enemies.

The day was warm, even for summer, and a haze shimmered in the sky, blurring the sun and dimming the horizon. In spite of her age, her eyes were good, and she could make out men and women milling between the ulas.

No one seemed afraid. No one seemed angry. She pulled herself up with stringy arms to sit on the edge of the opening, lifted her head as best she could to see through grasses that shifted in the wind.

Aa, yes, there was Beach Cutter—the old fool—and his new young wife. But who was that beside them? He wore a chigdax, so she knew he had just come from his iqyax. There was a boy with him, nearly as tall as he was. Several more children. A woman.

Qung gasped, and without even feeling the pain of old joints, she was on her feet, lifting herself as straight as she could possibly stand. And then she was calling, shouting to be heard above the voices of the grass.

The woman lifted her head, cried out, then ran up the hill.

She scooped Qung into her arms as if the old woman was just a child.

"Aunt!" she said. "You waited. I thought . . . I was afraid . . ."

"I told you I would wait," Qung said in a querulous voice. "You thought I would be dead? Ha!" Then her bravado was lost to tears.

She lifted a veined hand and smoothed back a tangle of hair that had come loose from the braids Aqamdax wore at the sides of her head. Qung clicked her tongue. "You need to learn how to fix your hair," she said, and jerked on one of the braids. "Someone might think you are a River woman."

"Aunt, can you walk down to meet my family?" Aqamdax asked. "Chakliux and I brought them all, our son and his wife, two more sons, three daughters not yet married, and our youngest, another son."

Qung leaned on Aqamdax, turned her head to study the woman's face as they walked to the beach. Small lines spread from the corners of Aqamdax's eyes, as though her face was often crinkled in laughter. A swath of white, bright in the darkness of her hair, fell from the crown of her head to be caught into one of her braids. Her hands were splotched and red, most likely from the days traveling in the iqyax.

Chakliux came to Qung, gathered her in his arms, squeezed until her bones creaked.

"Enough!" she said and batted at him with her hands. He introduced their children, fine and strong with the look of Chakliux in the eyes, but with Aqamdax's nose and round face.

"Angax has come to hunt, and his wife wants to learn to make birdskin garments, but this daughter . . ." Chakliux pushed the girl forward. "We want you to teach her your stories."

Qung looked at the girl in surprise. She appeared to have eight, nine summers, and she was shy. She met Qung's eyes only for a moment, gave her a quick smile, then looked down at the ground, stood balanced on one foot. Qung was not surprised to see that her raised foot was otter.

"How long will you stay?" Qung asked. Though the question seemed rude, she needed to know. If she was to have only a few days, or only a moon, she would teach this girl differently than if she had a whole winter.

"As long as you have stories, we will stay," Chakliux said.

"As long as I have stories?" said Qung. Her surprise lifted those words so they sounded like a question. She cleared her throat and repeated herself: "As long as I have stories," she said in a firm voice. "As long as I have stories."

Suddenly she raised her head and laughed.

"As long as I have stories!" she shouted. "How wonderful. You will be here forever!"

AUTHOR'S NOTES

I believe without doubt that my path as a novelist was surveyed and cleared when I was still a tiny child. My parents love books and are each gifted storytellers. During any long car trip my father kept us enthralled with a continuing comic saga of the "Goody-Goody Family," who faced incredible dangers, but always survived against the odds. Each week, as she ironed clothes, my mother delighted us by telling the traditional well-loved fairy tales. Each night as I lay in my bed, I became the heroine of my own adventures until dreams claimed the story rights.

Even now, as an adult, when I walk into a bookstore or hold a book in my hands, I sense the magic. It dances in my head, lifts my heart, and slips the silver shoes on my feet!

I'm sure my readers have come to realize that *The Storyteller Trilogy* is a series of stories within a story, and in that way, very much an imitation of life. Each of us lives our own story, but at the same time we play parts in the stories of others. Circles intersect circles and at the best of times, in the best of worlds, create a marvelous mosaic of color and realization. In the worst of times, of course, the creation is one of chaos, which is, as all readers and writers know, the stuff of which novels are made—the incredible, fertile soil from which spring the alluring and beckoning words that draw storytellers and listeners alike. What if . . . What if . . . What if . . .

The first "what if" that planted the seeds for *Call Down the Stars* came from our friend Mike Livingston. My husband, Neil, and I were having a conversation with Mike and his wife, Rayna, about Mike's Aleut heritage. He happened to mention that he believed there was some link between the Japanese and Aleut cultures and peoples. It was an intriguing thought, but at the time I didn't follow it up. Several years later, when Neil and I were in Japan on a book tour for my Japanese publisher, Shobun-sha, Mike's words came back to me.

A scheduled interview with Hashida Yoshinori, a writer for *Kyodo News*, opened a whole new world of possibilities when he began to talk about the Jomon era of ancient Japan. He gave me books and introduced me to the Jomon Era Information Transmitting Association. I found the similarities between the ancient Aleut and the Jomon People to be fascinating.

A little research in the Aleutian Islands turned up various written and word-of-mouth tales about ancient people from strange lands who came to the islands via storms and shipwrecks. Some oceanic sleuthing led to information about the Kuroshio Current, which pulses north from the eastern side of Japan to the southern Aleutian Islands. What more does an author need than such fascinating weft and warp to weave a tale of possibilities?

As with all my novels, in *Call Down the Stars*, legends play a large part in determining my storyline. Readers familiar with the mythology of northern peoples will recognize Daughter's story as a gentler version of the widespread and well-known Sedna legends. In the original, the daughter loses more than a toe, and for less pressing reasons than starvation.

A few other comments, mostly for clarification: I am aware that the tundra and northern boreal forests are not as plentiful in game as more temperate regions in North America, but when Chakliux's people comment on the blessings of their game-filled land, the reader must realize that those ancient hunter-gatherers had not experienced life in other areas, where a greater number and variety of plants and animals abound.

Anthropologists and population experts have noticed that after a devastating war, a disproportionate number of male babies are born in the ensuing years. Not being an expert in this area, I'll take their word for it, and rather than try to explain it, include the phenomenon as fact in my novels.

It was my pleasure in the late 1980s and early 1990s to teach creative and advanced creative writing at Lake Superior State University, a small school on the eastern shore of Michigan's northern peninsula. I'm sure my students taught me more about writing than I was able to teach them, and in this novel much of what I learned is revealed through the conversations, successes, and failures experienced by the young storyteller Yikaas. For example, in Chapter Thirty, Yikaas unwisely continues his tale beyond its natural conclusion, and thus dilutes the power of the denouement. I purposely include this and various other storytelling weaknesses or errors to highlight the growth process that every storyteller experiences. It is a continual struggle. Perfection is impossible. What joy! What frustration!

Among Athabascan peoples, and indeed, within all Native American cultures I have studied, names are considered sacred and carry spiritual significance. Thus, when Red Leaf agrees to name her daughter Daes, she has committed an immense betrayal that will place her daughter in spiritual danger.

One last note, and this is for those readers, so close to my heart, who celebrate the etymology of words. In Chapter Twelve, when K'os tries to get Cries-loud to take the name *Tigangiyaanen* (expert hunter or warrior), she is tempting him to step beyond his rights as a young hunter to boast of a prowess he does not yet possess. She also seeks to control him by elevating herself to the position of name-giver. The root of this Ahtna Athabascan word is *yaa*, which has multiple meanings, but in this context refers to growing into maturity. Within the word *tigangiyaanen*, the root *yaa* most likely originated from another root, *yae*, in which growth means the healing of a wound. If Cries-loud assumes the name, then he is also recognizing K'os's worth as a healer. Thus, in tempting Cries-loud with the name *Tigangiyaanen*, K'os is seeking to increase her own power and status by compromising Cries-loud's integrity.

GLOSSARY OF NATIVE AMERICAN WORDS

AA, AAA (Aleut, Athabascan) Interjection used to express surprise: "Oh!" (The double or triple *a* carries a long *a* sound.)

ANGAX (Aleut) Power. *Anga* is the root used in the Aleut word for *elder brother*. (The *a*'s are short; because it falls before the letter *n*, the first *a* takes on more of a short *e* sound. The Aleut *n* is quite nasal; the *g* is a voiced velar fricative, quite guttural; and the final *x* is a voiceless velar fricative.)

AQAMDAX (Aleut) Cloudberry, *Rubus chamaemorus*. (See Pharmacognosia.) (The *a*'s are short. The Aleut *q* is like a harsh English *k*, the *m* like an English *m*, and *d* much like the English *th*. The Aleut *x* is a voiceless velar fricative.)

BABICHE (English—probably anglicized from the Cree word *assababish*, a diminutive of *assabab*, "thread.") Lacing made from rawhide.

CEN (Ahtna Athabascan) Tundra. (*Ken*—The c sounds like an English *k*. The *e* carries a short sound like the *e* in the English word *set*. The Ahtna *n* sounds like the English *n*.)

CET'AENI (Ahtna Athabascan) Creatures of ancient Ahtna legend. They are tailed and live in trees and caves. (The *c* sounds like an English *k*. The *e* carries a short sound like the *e* in the English word *set*. The *t'* is much like an English *t* followed by a glottal release. The diphthong *ae* is pronounced like the *a* in the English word *cat*. The *n* is much like the English *n*, and the final *i* has a short *i* sound as in the English word *sit*. The *t'aen* is accented.)

CHAGAK (Aleut) Obsidian, red cedar. (The Aleut *ch* is much like the English *ch*, the *g* is like a guttural English *g*, and the *k* is a voiced fricative. The *a*'s are short like the *aw* in the English word *paw*. The accent falls on the last syllable.)

CHAKLIUX (Ahtna Athabascan, as recorded by Pinart in 1872) Sea otter. (The word is pronounced as it would be in English, with the *a* taking on the sound of the *u* in the English word *mutt*, the *i* assuming a short sound as in the English word *sit*, and the *u* the sound of the *oo* in the English word *brook*. The final *x* is a voiceless velar fricative.)

CHIGDAX (Aleut) A waterproof, watertight parka made of sea lion or bear intestines, esophagus of seal or sea lion, or the tongue skin of a whale. The hood had a drawstring, and the sleeves were tied at the wrists during sea travel. These knee-length garments were often decorated with feathers and bits of colored esophagus. (The Aleut *ch* is much like the English *ch*, the *g* like a guttural English *g*, and the *d* carries almost a *th* sound. The vowels are short. The *x* should be properly written as a careted *x*, and is a voiceless uvular fricative.)

CHISUM NAGA (Aleut) Vagina. (The Aleut *ch* is much like the English *ch*, and the vowels are short. The Aleut *s* is like the English *sh,* the *m* like the English *m*, the *n* quite nasal, and the *g* is a voiced velar fricative, quite guttural.)

CIXUDANGIX (Aleut) Sea gull flower—white anemone, *anemone narcissiflora*. (See Pharmacognosia.) (The *c* is pronounced like the English *k*; the vowels are short; the *x*'s are voiceless velar fricatives. The Aleut *d* carries almost a *th* sound, and the *n* is quite nasal. The *g* is like a guttural English *g*.)

DAES (Ahtna Athabascan) Shallow, a shallow portion of a lake or stream. (The *d* is pronounced with tongue tip touching the backs of the top front teeth. It carries almost a *t* sound. The diphthong *ae* has a sound similar to that in the English word *hat*. The final *s* carries almost a *sh* sound.)

DII (Ahtna Athabascan) One alone, on one's own. (*Dee*—The *d* is pronounced with the tongue tip touching the backs of the top front teeth. It carries almost a *t* sound. The double *i* carries a long *e* sound as in the English word *free*.)

DZUUGGI (Ahtna Athabascan) A favored child who receives special training, especially in oral traditions, from infancy. (The *dz* takes the sound of the final *ds* in the English word *leads*. The *uu* sounds like the *ui* in the English word *fruit*. The Ahtna *gg* has no English equivalent. It is very guttural and pronounced with the back of the tongue held against the soft palate. The *i* has a short *i* sound as in the English word *sit*. The accent is on the first syllable.)

GGUZAAKK (Koyukon Athabascan) A thrush, *Hylocichla minima*, *H. ustulata*, and *H. guttata*. These birds sing an intricately beautiful song that the Koyukon people traditionally believe to indicate the presence of an unknown person or spirit. (The *gg* has no English equivalent. It is very guttural and pronounced with the back of the tongue held against the soft palate. The *u* sounds similar to the *oo* in the English word *book*. The *z* is similar in sound to *zh*, or the *s* in *treasure*. The *aa* carries an *aw* sound. The *kk* is a very hard *c* sound.)

GHADEN (Ahtna Athabascan) Another person. (The Ahtna *gh* has no English equivalent. It closely resembles the French *r*. The *a* sounds like the English vowel *u* in the word *but*. The Ahtna *d* is pronounced with the tongue tip touching the backs of the top front teeth. It carries almost a *t* sound. The *e* carries a short sound like the *e* in the English word *set*. The Ahtna *n* sounds like the English *n*.)

GHELI (Ahtna Athabascan) True, good. (The Ahtna *gh* has no English equivalent. It closely resembles the French *r*. The *e* carries a short sound like the *e* in the English word *set*. The Ahtna *l* sounds like the *l*'s in the English word *call*. The *i* is like the *i* in the English word *sit*.)

HAYH (Ahtna Athabascan) Expression of disgust. (The Ahtna *h* is a voiceless glottal fricative and rarely used before a vowel. In *hayh* the first *h* takes on a more voiced sound like the *h* in the English word *house*, while the second *h* combines with *y* to give a rare sound in the Athabascan languages. It is pronounced as a voiceless front velar fricative. The *a* is pronounced like the *u* in the English word *mutt*.)

IITIKAALUX (Atkan Aleut) Cow parsnip, wild celery, *Heracleum lanatum*. (See Pharmacognosia.) The *ii* is pronounced like a long *e*. The *t* and *l* are much like their English equivalents. The single *i* and *u* are short, and the *aa* carries a long *a* sound. The *k* is a guttural English *k*. The *x* should be properly written as a careted *x*, and is a voiceless uvular fricative. The accent is on the penultimate syllable.)

IORI (Japanese) Hut.

IQYAX, pl. IQYAN (Aleut) A skin-covered, wooden-framed boat, a kayak. (The two vowels are short. The *q* is like a harsh English *k*, the *y* much like an English *y*, and the final *x* is a voiceless velar fricative. The Aleut *n* is quite nasal. Accent the first syllable.)

KIIN (Aleut) Who. (The *k* is a guttural English *k*. The *ii* carries a long *e* sound. The Aleut *n* is quite nasal.)

K'OS (Ahtna Athabascan) Cloud. (The Ahtna *k* has no English equivalent. It is similar to the Aleut *x* and is pronounced in the back of the throat with a very harsh, guttural sound. The apostrophe denotes a glottal stop. The *o* carries a short sound similar to the *o* in the English word *for*. The Ahtna *s* is pronounced like an English *sh*.)

KUY'AA (Ahtna Athabascan) A highly respected woman, female chief. (The Ahtna *k* has no English equivalent. It is similar to the Aleut *x* and is pronounced in the back of the throat with a very harsh, guttural sound. The *u* sounds similar to the *oo* in the English word *book*. The *y* is a voiced frontal velar fricative similar to the *y* in the English word *yes*. The apostrophe denotes a glottal stop. The *aa* sounds like the *aw* in the English word *paw*. Accent the last syllable.)

LIGIGE' (Ahtna Athabascan) The soapberry or dogberry, *Shepherdia canadensis*. (See Pharmacognosia.) (The *l* is voiceless and has no corresponding sound in English. The tip of the tongue is held on the palate just behind the front teeth and breath released so as to push air off both sides of the tongue. The *i* has a short *i* sound like in the English word *sit*. The single *g* corresponds most closely to the English *k* and is pronounced in the back of the throat. The final *e* is pronounced like the *e* in *set*. The apostrophe denotes a glottal stop. Accent the final syllable.)

NAE' (Ahtna Athabascan) Yes. (The Ahtna *n* sounds like an English *n*. The *ae* acts like a diphthong and takes on the *a* sound in the English word *fad*. The apostrophe represents a glottal stop.)

NUHU'AHN (Koyukon Athabascan) The word refers to a creature of legend somewhat like the Windigo of the Cree people, but less violent. The Aleut refer to this creature—generally considered to be a man—as an "outside man," someone who no longer lives within a village, but for some reason has been forcibly exiled. Literally, *nuhu'ahn* means "It sneaks around." (The *n*'s sound like the English *n*. The *u*'s carry the sound of the *oo* in the English word *cook*. The *h*'s are similar to the *h* in the English word *help*. The apostrophe denotes a glottal stop. The *a* sounds like the English vowel *u* in the word *but*.)

QUMALIX (Aleut) To be light, bright, shiny. (The initial *q* is like a harsh English *k*. The vowels are short. The Aleut *m* is pronounced like an English *m*; the Aleut *l* is a voiced dental lateral. The *x* is a voiceless velar fricative.)

QUNG (Aleut) Hump, humpback. (The initial *q* is like a harsh English *k*. The *u* is short, and the digraph *ng* is a nasal, pronounced much like the *ng* in the English word *gong*.)

SAMIQ (Ancient Aleut) Stone dagger or knife. (The Aleut *s* is like the English *sh*, the vowels are short, and the Aleut *m* is pronounced like the English *m*. The final *q* takes on a harsh English *k* sound.)

SAX (Aleut) A long, hoodless parka made of feathered bird-skins. (The *s* is pronounced like the English *sh*; the *a* is short. The *x* is a voiceless velar fricative.)

SHUGANAN (Ancient word of uncertain origin) Exact meaning unsure, refers to an ancient people. (Pronounced *shoe-ga-nen*, accent on the second syllable.)

SOK (Ahtna Athabascan) Raven call. (The Ahtna *s* is almost like the English *sh*. The Ahtna *o* is like the *o* in the English word *for*. The *k* is a guttural English *k*.)

TAADZI (Ahtna Athabascan) Large deadfall trap. (The initial *t* is much like an English *t*. The *aa* sounds like the *aw* in the

English word *paw*. The *z* is pronounced like *zh* or the *s* in the English word *treasure*. The *i* sounds like the *i* in the English word *sit*. Accent the first syllable.)

TIGANGIYAANEN (Ahtna Athabascan) Warrior, great warrior. (The initial *t* is much like an English *t*. The *i*'s sound like the *i* in the English word *sit*. The single *g*'s correspond most closely to the English *k* and are pronounced in the back of the throat. The Ahtna *a* is like the *u* in the English word *mutt*. The *n*'s sound like English *n*'s. The *y* is a voiced frontal velar fricative similar to the *y* in the English word *yes*. The *aa* sounds like the *aw* in the English word *paw*. The Ahtna *e* is pronounced like the *e* in the English word *set*. Accent the penultimate syllable.)

TSAANI (Ahtna Athabascan) Grizzly bear, *Ursus arctos*. (The *ts* takes a sound similar to the *ts* in *sets*. The *aa* carries an *aw* sound. The *n* is pronounced like the English *n*, and the *i* has a short sound like the *i* in the English word *sit*. The first syllable is accented.)

ULAX, pl. ULAS or ULAM (Aleut) A semi-subterranean dwelling raftered with driftwood and covered with thatching and sod. (Pronounced *oo-lax*, with the accent on the first syllable. The *a* carries a short vowel sound, and the final *x* is a voiceless velar fricative.)

UUTUK (Aleut) Sea urchin. (The *uu* takes on a long *u* sound. The Aleut *t* is much like a blunted English *t*—almost a *d* sound. The *k* is a voiced fricative.)

UYGIIX (Aleut) Old woman. (The single *u* takes a short vowel sound. The *y* sounds much like an English *y*. The *g* is a voiced velar fricative, more guttural than the English *g*. The *ii* carries a long *i* sound. The *x* is properly written as a careted *x*, and is a voiceless uvular fricative.)

YAA (Ahtna Athabascan) Sky. (The *y* is a voiced frontal velar fricative similar to the *y* in the English word *yes*. The *aa* sounds like the *aw* in the English word *paw*.)

YEHL (Tlingit) Raven. (A similar pronunciation to the English word *yell*.)

YIKAAS (Ahtna Athabascan) Light. (The *i* is pronounced like the *i* in the English word *sit*. The Ahtna *k* has no English equivalent. It is similar to the Aleut *x* and is pronounced in the back of the throat with a very harsh, guttural sound. The *aa* sounds like the *aw* in the English word *paw*. The Ahtna *s* is pronounced like an English *sh*.)

The words in the glossary are defined and listed according to their use in *Call Down the Stars*. Most spellings, pronunciations, and words in the Aleut language are used as per their standardization in the *Aleut Dictionary, Unangam Tunudgusii*, compiled by Knut Bergsland. Spellings, pronunciations, and words in the Ahtna Athabascan language are used as per their standardization in the *Ahtna Athabascan Dictionary*, compiled and edited by James Kari. Both dictionaries are published by the Alaska Native Language Center, University of Alaska, Fairbanks.

PHARMACOGNOSIA

Plants listed in this Pharmacognosia are *not* cited in recommendation for use, but only as a supplement to the novel. Many poisonous plants resemble helpful plants, and even some of the most benign can be harmful if used in excess. The wisest way to harvest and prepare wild vegetation for medicine, food, or dye is in the company of an expert. Plants are listed in alphabetical order according to the names used in *Call Down the Stars*.

ACONITE (Monkshood), *Aconitum delphinifolium*: Growing up to three feet in height, this purple-blossomed plant has deeply serrated, elongated palmate leaves. The flowers grow at the end of the stem and are purple (occasionally white). The top petal has a hoodlike shape. Caution: All parts of this plant are extremely poisonous and kill by paralyzing the central nervous system. The Aleut people used to dip the tips of their whale harpoons in a decoction of aconite.

ALDER *Alnus crispa*: A small tree with grayish bark. Medium green leaves have toothed edges, rounded bases, and pointed tips. Flower clusters resemble miniature pinecones. The cambium or inner layer of bark is dried (fresh bark will irritate the stomach) and used to make tea said to reduce high fever. It is also used as an astringent and a gargle for sore throats. The bark renders a brown dye. Caution: Leaves are said to be very poisonous.

BANEBERRY *Actaea rubra*: The baneberry is a vigorous plant that grows in southeastern and coastal Alaska north to the Yukon River area. It attains heights of up to four feet, though two to three feet is normal. Leaves are elongate, dentate, and compound; delicate white flowers grow in balllike clusters at the tips of the stems. Berries are red or white with a characteristic black dot. Caution: All portions of the baneberry are poisonous and ingestion will cause pain and bloody diarrhea. Death may result due to paralysis of the respiratory system and/or cardiac arrest. Do not even touch these plants with bare hands!

BITTER ROOT (chocolate lily, Kamchatka lily or Kamchatka fritillary, wild rice, rice root), *Fritillaria camschatcensis*: An erect stem bears a dark brown flower with six lanceolate petals. Leaves grow in whorls of six on the upper part of the stem. The flower's odor is quite unpleasant. The bulbs form edible ricelike corms and should be harvested in late summer. Eaten raw, they are quite bitter, but when boiled and mixed with oil they are very palatable.

BLUEBELLS (chiming bells, lungwort), *Mertensia paniculata*: Two- to three-foot plants sport hairy, elongated ovate leaves that grow opposite one another on the stem. Small groups of delicate, purplish, belllike flowers cluster at the ends of short, drooping stems. Flowers and leaves are said to be good added to teas. Leaves are better picked before the plants flower. The plant has been said to relieve asthma and other types of lung congestion.

BONESET (purple boneset), *Eupatorium purpureum*: A tall (five to six feet) perennial, its clustered purple flower heads appear in September. Coarse leaves grow in groups of three or five. The root, crushed in a water solution, is said to be a diuretic and tonic as well as a relaxant.

CARIBOU LEAVES (wormwood, silverleaf), *Artemisia tilessii*: This perennial plant attains a height of two to three feet on a single stem. The hairy, lobed leaves are silver underneath and a darker green on top. A spike of small clustered flowers grows at the top of the stem in late summer. Fresh leaves are used to make a tea that is said to purify the blood and stop internal bleeding, and to wash cuts and sore eyes. The leaves are heated and layered over arthritic joints to ease pain. Caution: Caribou leaves may be toxic in large doses.

CIXUDANGIX (seagull flower, narcissus-flowered anemone), *Anemone narcissiflora*: A hairy-stemmed plant that grows up to two feet in height. The flower clusters have five rounded white petals. The hairy, palmate leaves are deeply serrated and grow just below the flower clusters and also at the base of the stem. The Aleut people boiled the roots to extract the juices and used the resulting serum to stop hemorrhage. Caution: *Anemone* are considered poisonous.

CLOUDBERRY (salmonberry), *Rubus chamaemorus*: Not to be confused with the larger shrub-like salmonberry, *Rubus spectabilis*, this small plants grows to about six inches in height and bears a single white flower. The salmon-colored berry looks like a raspberry and is edible, but not as flavorful as a raspberry. Berries are high in vitamin C. The green leaves are serrated and have five main lobes. The juice from the berries is said to be a remedy for hives.

DULCE (water leaf), *Palmaria mollis*: A rubbery, reddish-brown algae with "leaf" blades up to a foot in length. It can be harvested on the beach and eaten raw (with a rinsing to get rid of stray seashells). High in calcium and vitamins A and B, dulce is said to be healthful for menstruating women. May be dried and used as a seasoning.

FIREWEED (wild asparagus), *Epilobium angustifolium*: Fireweed grows throughout Alaska and northern North America. Plants grow upright to a height of three to five feet and end in a spikelike flower cluster. Each flower has four petals which bloom from the bottom of the stalk up during mid- to late summer. Colors vary from a deep and brilliant red-pink to nearly white. Leaves are willowlike: long and narrow, and medium green in color. Early spring shoots (high in vitamins A and C) may be harvested prior to development of the leaves without harm to the plant. (Harvesting the white stem below the soil level actually promotes plant growth.) The tip of the stem should be discarded due to the disagreeable taste; the remainder can be steamed and eaten like asparagus. Leaves should be harvested before flowers bloom to add to soups as seasoning. Flowers are often used in salads and also make good jelly. Fireweed leaves steeped for tea are said to settle stomachaches. Salves made from roots are said to draw out infection.

HIGHBUSH CRANBERRY (crampbark, mooseberry), *Viburnum edule*: This erect but scraggly bush grows throughout Alaska from the Alaska Peninsula to the Brooks Range. Its lobed leaves are shaped somewhat like maple leaves, grow opposite one another on the branches and are coarsely toothed. The average height of the highbush cranberry is four to six feet, though they sometimes reach ten feet. Five-petaled white flowers grow in flat clusters and mature into flavorful but bitter red berries in August and September. (A frost sweetens the berries considerably.) Berries are high in Vitamin C and make tasty jelly. The inner bark, boiled into tea, is used as a gargle for sore throats and colds. Highbush cranberry bark contains glucoside viburnine, a muscle relaxant. Bark made into tea decoctions is used to relieve menstrual and stomach cramps, and is said to be effective on infected skin abrasions.

IITIKAALUX (cow parsnip, wild celery), *Hercleum lanatum*: A thick-stemmed hearty plant that grows to nine feet in height. The coarse, dark leaves have three main lobes with serrated edges. It is also known by the Russian name poochki or putchki. Stems and leaf stalks taste like a spicy celery but must be peeled before eating because the outer layer is a skin irritant. White flowers grow in inverted bowl-shaped clusters at the tops of the plants. Roots are also edible, and leaves are dried to flavor soups and stews. The root was chewed raw to ease sore throats and was heated and a section pushed into a painful tooth to deaden root pain. Caution: Gloves should be worn when harvesting. Iitikaalux is similar in appearance to poisonous water hemlock.

KELP (bull kelp), *Nereocystis luetkeana*: These long brown algae can grow to a length of 200 feet. Blades can be dried and used as seasoning. Stipes should be peeled as soon as harvested and can be eaten raw or pickled. The air bladders or floats that lie at the top of the water and keep the plant extended from sea bottom to surface can be stuffed with meat and vegetables and baked. Kelp is said to help heal bone fractures.

LIGIGE' (soapberry or dog berry), *Shepherdia canadensis*: A shrub that grows to six feet in height with smooth, round-tipped, dark green leaves. The orange-colored berries ripen in July and are edible but bitter. They foam like soap when beaten.

LOVAGE (beach lovage, petrushki), *Ligusticum scoticum*: The stems of this plant separate into three branches, each of which bears a lobed, serrated leaf. Though its growth is ground-hugging, stems may attain a length of two feet. Tiny coral-colored flowers grow in umbels. The leaves, dried or fresh, make good flavoring for stews and are best harvested prior to the plant's flowering. Lovage relieves stomach upset and is high in vitamins C and A. Caution: Use care in identification. Lovage is related to poison hemlock.

LUPINE (Nootka lupine), *Lupinus nootkatensis*: Tall, spikelike plants bear flowers in a spear-shaped cluster at the tip of the stem. Each flower has up to seven petals. Colors vary from white to pink or blue. The leaves grow in an alternate pattern up the stalk, each borne on a short stem and dividing into a whorl of blunted, fingerlike leaflets. Caution: Although the Aleut people used a concoction made from the taproot for drying scabs or cuts and as a gargle, lupine is considered poisonous and should be appreciated for its beauty rather than medicinal qualities.

MOUSE EARS (chickweed, winter weed), *Stellaria*: This widespread, brittle-stemmed plant grows low along the ground. The leaves are ovate and small, growing opposite each other in pairs on the stem. The five white petals of each flower are split giving a delicate appearance to the blossoms. It is said to be useful as an eyewash, expectorant, and a poultice for inflammations.

NORI (laver), *Porphyra rhodophyta*: This sea plant attaches itself to rocks with a very small holdfast. It has a reddish cast, and when floating in water looks like transparent pliable plastic. At low tide, it appears dark and may resemble an oily slick on the rocks. Gather during low tide, but leave the holdfast. Nori is high in iron and protein and a good source of vitamins A, B, and C. It may be eaten raw. Users claim that it helps heal goiters. It is also valuable for treating scurvy. Caution: Ingesting large amounts of nori may cause bloating and stomach distress.

PURPLE-FLOWERED POISON See Aconite.

RIBBON KELP (wing kelp), *Alaria marginata*: The main blades of this sea plant grow up to nine feet in length and are brownish green in color. The wavy outer edge of the main blade gives a ribbonlike appearance. The blade's midrib is flat. Between the main blade and the holdfast, small wing-like sporophylls grow in an alternate pattern along the midrib. Ribbon kelp is high in mineral content. It is good eaten raw, but the blades may be dried and stored for use throughout the year.

RYE GRASS (basket grass, beach grass), *Elymus arenarius mollis*: The inner blades of this tall, coarse grass are dried and split, then used by Aleut weavers to fashion exquisite baskets and mats.

WILLOW *Salix*: This narrow-leafed shrub or small tree has smooth, gray, or brownish-yellow bark. There are presently more than thirty species of willow in Alaska. The leaves are a very good source of vitamin C, though in some varieties they taste quite bitter. The leaves and inner bark contain salicin, which acts like aspirin to deaden pain. Bark can be chipped and boiled to render a pain-relieving tea. Leaves can also be boiled for tea. Leaves are chewed and placed over insect bites to relieve itching. Traditionally, roots and branches have been used to make baskets and woven fish weirs.

YARROW (milfoil), *Achillea borealis*: This hardy plant grows with feathery alternate leaves along one- to three-foot upright stems. The white or light purple flowerets grow on a flat, multistemmed head at the top of the plant. Yarrow has been used as a laxative, a cold remedy, and to combat asthma. It is said to help stop lung hemorrhaging, and also is used as a hair rinse to prevent baldness.

YELLOW CINQUEFOIL (five-leaves grass), *Potentilla tormentilla*: This plant has five-fingered palmate leaves, and it roots at the joints. Cinquefoil branches out from the root with yellow flowers at the end of eighteen- to twenty-inch stems. The root is boiled and used as a poultice for skin eruptions and shingles. It is said to be useful as a tonic for the lungs, for fevers, and as a gargle for gum and mouth sores.

YELLOW ROOT (gold thread), *Coptis trifolia*: The leaves of this creeping, fibrous perennial root grow in threes on foot-high stalks separate from the flower stalks. Tea made from boiling the root is said to be an invigorating tonic and also a gargle for sore throats and mouth lesions.